caffé americano

Sherre Cook

PRESS

Enjoy!

These look

Chapters

Chapter 1

Anchor's Aweigh

Andrew Gallagher reached under the hood toward the battery. He squeezed apart the red and black clamps, placed the cables on the workbench alongside the charger and then slid behind the steering wheel. Turning the ignition key, he pressed down on the accelerator. The Mustang's engine fired with a thrust of power, awakened at last from her two-year sleep—an isolated prisoner no longer incarcerated.

As though frozen in time, the window handle refused to budge—until Andrew put a little muscle into it. He cranked the glass pane completely open and settled into the familiar contours of the worn bucket seat. A sprung coil along the front edge poked against the back of his thigh before he remembered to shift his leg away from it. He leaned back and tried to relax, but couldn't. Pungent smoke and fumes began escaping from the tailpipe and wafting through the open garage, stirring up memories of what he'd left behind.

He gently pushed the accelerator again. A sense of gratitude and humility caused a smile to form on his set lips. She was responding to him the same as before, reminding him just how much he'd missed her.

Their separation, though unfortunate, had been necessary. For one thing, Andrew had wanted to serve his country. He'd also needed time to get his head (or was it his heart?) straightened out. However, the decision to join the Navy had not been about his head or his heart; it had been about duty. And yet while he served, he *was* served as well. Getting away from East Valley had given Andrew the opportunity to escape the frustration and dejection he could no longer handle. But now he was back, having promised himself that this time things would be different.

Andrew put the car in first gear and eased off the clutch. The engine revved in aggravation as the gearshift slipped into neutral.

Not a good sign.

She hadn't done that since high school. It was an issue he thought had been resolved, one he'd hoped was in the past—along with everything else that kept him feeling stuck. He caressed the gear-shift's polished wood knob, trying to finesse her into cooperating, and shifted back into first. His gentleness worked. This time the car rolled forward, along with Andrew's prayer that the next few days would work out the same way, as if nothing had ever been amiss.

With a crisp mid-October breeze flowing through the light blue classic car, Andrew cruised down Sycamore Street and through his old neighborhood. He made a left turn onto Hillcrest Boulevard, a main thoroughfare that would take him to Mo'Joes coffeehouse, his first destination.

Traffic was heavier than he would have expected for a Saturday morning; but then, metropolitan Los Angeles hadn't stopped growing just because Andrew was away. He passed by several landmarks he'd visited throughout his twenty-seven year life, with the exception of the last four years, of course. There was Buena Vista Park with its Olympic size pool, now drained until next spring. It had been a great place for Andrew, as East Valley High's varsity swim team captain, to practice his enviable butterfly stroke. A mile further down Hillcrest, Andrew saw The Supply Sergeant, an Army surplus store where over the years, the Gallagher family had purchased provisions and other essentials for their numerous summer camping trips.

And while various familiar places remained, Andrew realized that the area was, in many ways, different. In just a few short years— or long ones, depending on the circumstances—his hometown had gone through drastic changes. Like so many other cities across the nation, East Valley had seen many of its long-standing businesses close due to the stagnant economy. For rent, for lease, or for sale signs placed in the windows of vacant buildings told silent tales of tough financial times for the community of 75,000.

Still, even though the sights had changed, the smells and sounds were the same. At a red light, Andrew closed his eyes and inhaled exhaust mixed with the scent of fried food. He listened to revving engines and occasional horn honks and woofers on steroids blasting out hip hop music. For a moment, it felt like East Valley had gotten stuck in a time loop. At a louder horn blast, Andrew opened his eyes, waved an apology at the driver behind him, and aimed the Mustang toward the coffeehouse on the northwest corner of Hillcrest and Haven. The freestanding building, which had been a weather-beaten beige the last time he saw it, now came to life with a bold new paint job. Two bowl-shaped white mugs filled with steaming java and set against a tropical rain forest background created a colorful mural that was all but impossible to miss. Adding even more pizzazz to the visual effect was a larger, screaming-yellow sign placed high above the sidewalk. A clever artist had used smiling whole coffee beans to write out the name "MO'JOES." Andrew eased the Mustang through the driveway and into the first available parking spot.

Inside the building, rich and spicy coffeehouse scents flooded his head. In just one inhale he smelled hazelnut, caramel, vanilla and chocolate, along with the overriding powerhouse of espresso. He looked around, taking in all the unfamiliar details. As mellow, jazzy music calmed the mood, patrons gazed at cell phone screens, read newspapers or just relaxed. The new seating arrangement in the L-shaped room included several oak tables and chairs and a few wooden booths toward the rear. Four armchairs in bold and bright prints were placed near the front.

An Asian gal with short and spiky, licorice black hair greeted Andrew as he stepped up to a distressed dark oak counter. "Good morning." She pushed up oval, electric-blue-framed glasses. "What can I get you?"

"Hmm, let's see . . ." Andrew scanned the menu board, rubbing his chin with a thumb and index finger. He smiled at the clean-shaven skin. His buddies had always given him a bad time for shaving regularly when he was on liberty. Most of his friends skipped shaving when they could, but Andrew wasn't neat because the Navy required it. He was neat because he liked to be. "Which of these drinks is made with espresso and water?"

"Caffé Americano." The woman reached for a black marking pen and smiled. "We just say *Americano*."

Andrew nodded, keeping his attention on the board. "Yeah. That's the one."

"Would you like it hot or iced?"

"Good question," he said, glancing down at her friendly, round face and huge almond-shaped eyes. "I think I'd better get one of each."

* * *

After Allie finished her run through Wildflower Canyon Park, she jogged down Haven and trotted through the crosswalk at Foothill. Wiping the moisture from her forehead, she readjusted her visor and began removing the elastic band securing her long ponytail.

The motion drew the cord of her earphones upward and her ipod slipped out of her navy blue shorts pocket. It hit the sidewalk with a clatter.

Oh, great, I hope it's not broken. She bent forward and reached down just as a small blue car exited the driveway ahead of her. Turning left onto Hillcrest, the driver gunned the engine. Exhaust shot from the tailpipe and sent a hazy trail of gray smoke slithering past Allie's vision. It brought back to life a bad dream from the previous night, which wasn't just a nightmare, but a memory of what had taken place a long time ago, one dreadful afternoon in early May—a memory Allie could never erase, no matter how hard she tried . . .

Ten or so of Allie's friends surround her as she sits at the head of a cherry wood dining table. For the special occasion she wears a purple cotton dress—the one with the small white polka dots on the patch pockets and collar. Two braids fall down from either side of her head, secured by rubber bands and thin purple ribbons tied in bows. A homemade chocolate marble cake with choco-late frosting, aglow from the light of eleven burning candles is set before her. She closes her eyes tight, makes her wish and blows on the candles.

One stays lit.

She's been told that for the wish to come true she needs to blow out every single candle, so she tries again, and again. She keeps trying, but it's no use. Her eyes stay fixed on the one flame as it turns her wish into a puddle of melted wax, pooling on the cake's smooth surface.

Allie takes in one last breath, holding it until her head begins to spin. But then, in an instant, the flame disappears, leaving behind a wispy trail of smoke and a fading orange ember. When she looks up, all the children are gone, and in the next room she hears her mother crying.

Still a bit dazed, Allie stared down Hillcrest Boulevard. The taillights of the blue car glowed bright red as the driver, now two blocks away, made an abrupt stop in the middle of the street. A slight woman with a cane came into view. Using small and hurried steps she shuffled in front of the car, gingerly lifting herself onto the opposing sidewalk. Once the car began moving again, Allie crossed the driveway and pushed open the glass-front door.

Inside the coffeehouse, twenty-five-year-old co-manager, Phoebe Nagata was multitasking at a furious pace. The pretty and spirited Japanese girl and her family had moved to the U.S. fifteen years earlier. Having met for the first time the year before, Allie and Phoebe got along well and soon discovered a shared love of classic American films and television shows.

Allie stepped up to the front counter. "Large Americano—with room, of course."

"How would you like that?" Phoebe waited for a response before choosing the cup.

"Hot. No, cold." Allie ran a hand across her eyes and shook her head. "I mean *iced.*" She laughed. "I guess my mind was someplace else."

Phoebe nodded in understanding. "Don't worry about it. The guy who was just here couldn't even make up his mind. He ordered one of each."

"That's a lot of espresso for one person."

"I got the feeling they weren't both for him; but even if they were, I'm sure he could handle them."

"No lightweight, huh?"

Phoebe flashed her usual rascally crooked smile. "Not only that but he easily put the tall, the dark *and* the handsome in tall, dark and handsome." Her words had a Mae West cadence. Or was it Groucho Marx?

"Does he come in here often?"

"Nope, I've never seen him before."

Allie swiped her debit card then asked for some ice water. She took the cup over to her favorite stuffed armchair, drawing on the straw for several seconds and allowing the water to rehydrate and cool her off. She ran the same three-mile route inside Wildflower Canyon Park as many as five days a week. The park, located between Ridgeview and Haven Streets, was less than a mile from her townhouse. It consisted of rolling grassy knolls, both flat and steep hiking trails, and a fully exposed running path. Allie would drive down Ridgeview, leave her black company SUV inside the park and end up here at the coffeehouse. Most days, the run was an easy task, but today, for some unknown reason, it had been more of a strain.

* * *

Bright light glinted in Andrew's eyes as the midmorning sun's rays poured over the top of the Verdugo Mountains. Situated at the north end of East Hills, the picturesque mountain range was home to a municipal golf course, beautiful hillside houses, two public parks, and all manner of wildlife, including deer, coyotes, bobcats, and raccoons. Andrew continued making his way up Ridgeview with the two Americanos and a focused resolve. He and his Mustang were enjoying mutual rediscovery. The car, having gotten over her false start, hummed with something that sounded suspiciously like pride—and who could blame her? She was still as eye-catching as when Andrew first started driving the classic at age seventeen.

Even so, he knew the time had come for the two of them to part. Would the car hold it against him? Stephen King's novel, *Christine,* popped into his mind. He laughed and shook his head.

Andrew had already decided that once he got home he would sell the Mustang and look into buying a medium-size truck. It would be a more appropriate vehicle to drive, especially if he received a job offer from an aerospace company outside Los Angeles County; but a practical reason such as a commute didn't make his decision to sell the car any easier. She might soon be in another owner's hands, but all the youthful and idealistic memories attached to her would be his forever.

A moment later, Andrew reached the top of Ridgeview. He tried to envision how Allie would react when she saw him. Maybe the way she always did, with what Andrew perceived as mixed signals. Her emotions were as variable as the moon in the night sky. She could go from warmth to cool distance, from friendly attention to impersonal aloofness, from vulnerable tenderness to independent tenacity—all in a matter of minutes. It really didn't matter, though, how she reacted. He would *finally* be able to see her again—and that was all that mattered.

He had kept the one letter he'd received since she'd moved a year ago. He'd hung onto the envelope as well because it had her new address on it. It was now slightly dog-eared with a brownish red smudge on the flap, proof that in haste he'd used his index finger to open the letter—a letter that had become the only connection he'd had with her for far too long. She hadn't mentioned anything about buying her own place, until that letter. But they hadn't been keeping in touch on a regular basis.

She hadn't been anyway.

Andrew turned left at an engraved wooden sign welcoming him to the Valley Villas townhouse complex. The small neighborhood lay tucked up in the North Valley, hidden away from the area's countless jam-packed freeways and shopping malls. The last of the season's Crepe Myrtle blossoms, ranging from dark red to light pink, dotted the trees lining the private streets within. Tudor-style homes with well-tended lawns, a variety of trees, and colorful gardens filled with bright roses and flowers he couldn't identify made a noteworthy first impression.

After double-checking the address, Andrew spotted a parking area reserved for guests. It was a few units down from Allie's, and he dutifully headed toward it, pulling in next to a bright red Firebird. An older woman with fluffy white hair, wearing red lipstick the same color as her headband and jogging suit, emerged from the sporty vehicle just as Andrew turned off his engine. She was tall for her age, five-foot-eight or so, and she looked trim and fit.

"She's a beauty." The woman eyed the Mustang with approval then ran her hand along the edge of the open passenger's window. She leaned down to look at Andrew. "I drove one like this up in Frisco during my more rebellious days." She grinned and the skin around her observant blue eyes crinkled. "Mine was red, though. I like red."

Andrew angled his head. "Is that right?"

Glancing away, she smiled, a vacant look on her face.

After carefully removing the two Americanos from the Mustang, Andrew tapped the door closed with his knee, waking the woman from her reverie. She shook herself and turned toward her car. Tilting the driver's seat forward, she pulled out a paper grocery sack, all the while crackling a wad of chewing gum between her back teeth. "You new around here?"

"No. I'm a, um, . . ." What was he, exactly? "I'm a visitor."

"Oh, that's a relief. I thought you might be part of the roving Home Owner Association police force. The word is they're about to bust me for parking here. This section is apparently reserved for guests, but the spots are always vacant. And just because I own one of these babies," she waved a free hand toward the townhouse across from Allie's, "they expect me to park in front of my own unit." She snorted. "No way, José. My car leaks oil."

One of the cups in Andrew's hand felt extremely hot, while the other had begun forming condensation on the clear plastic above and below the cardboard sleeve. "Uh, I should get going." He started to turn away then looked back at the woman. "You might want to have that engine looked at. If it's leaking oil, there's a problem."

"Will do, Sport." A huge but mildly coffee-stained grin spread across her face. Andrew could see that she had probably been quite a handful, and rather attractive, in her "more rebellious days." She resumed making popping noises with her gum as she walked toward the steps to her unit.

After Andrew heard her front door close, he paused to take in the view. A giant canopy of pine trees loomed over him. Their dense green needles and fresh, clean scent was a reminder of a place that held bittersweet memories for him. He inhaled deeply. The abundance of greenery inside the complex created a woodsy atmosphere not found in the flatter parts of the Valley. Andrew felt himself going back in time, which was not where he needed to be. Shaking his head, he strode toward Allie's unit and stepped up onto her front porch.

A black security screen hung open, leaving the shiny brown front door exposed. His hands too full of coffee to knock, Andrew used an elbow to press the doorbell. He waited.

Nothing. Maybe the bell was broken.

Unlikely, he thought, since the unit appeared new. He set one of the cups on top of a slatted wooden bench and rapped on the door. It sprung open with a quick jerk. A short woman with light blond hair and a strangely familiar face stood before him. Her bright green eyes widened, and her pert nose pulled inward on the sides. She examined Andrew with such careful scrutiny that he felt like a museum exhibit.

Finally, she said, "Hi there."

"Hello." This woman wasn't Allie. Did he have the wrong unit? He looked at the number on the door then back at her. "I'm Andrew Gallagher . . ."

"Hi, Andrew Gallagher. I'm Gretchen." She shifted her hips sideways and leaned against the door jamb.

Like a fighter pilot's buzz over an air tower, the name jolted Andrew's memory. "Of course!" He chuckled. "I'm Allie's friend. I believe you and I met once before—at Allie's graduation party. You're her cousin, Gretchen."

"I am." She studied him with a careful eye for several more awkward seconds. "I don't remember Allie having a friend who looks like *you.*" Her gaze moved up and down, and now Andrew felt as though he was being scanned with a metal detecting wand. "Tall, built, gorgeous brown eyes." She ticked the words off on her fingers. "*And that haircut!* You're a military man, aren't you?" Her eyes flared, looking like two rocket blasts. *"I just love a man in a uniform."*

He smiled without answering her question. "Do you live here?"

"No." She puffed a little air through her chalk-white teeth at what appeared to be a ridiculous concept. "I've never been here before in my life. I just came by to pick up a few things. I didn't know what time I'd get here, so Allie put a key under the mat in case she was out. I worked the red eye last night, rented a car at LAX and drove right over. A thirty-five minute drive, which isn't bad, but I'm tired. I'm a flight attendant by the way, just transferred out of Dallas to L.A. I'm replacing someone on the L.A. to Hawaii route who *finally* retired." Gretchen rolled her eyes upward.

"Uh, congratulations."

"Thanks, but the problem is that I took the job before I found a place out here to live. My best friend, Bobbie Brennan, rents an apartment over in the West Valley. That's where I'll be staying—for a while anyway. Too bad her place is the size of a box of Kleenex.

Eight hundred square feet of pressed wood furniture, unmatched dishware, and the indoor lighting of an airplane lavatory." She shuddered. "Hideous."

Andrew could think of worse conditions to live in but, in the name of good sportsmanship, instead offered a conciliatory, "That's regrettable."

Gretchen tilted her head and tucked a few shiny strands of her long hair behind an ear. "You can say that again. I'd already planned to put most of my stuff in storage, but then I talked to Allie last week and mentioned the transfer. She said she'd hook me up with a unit in the storage place she uses, and for a better rate than I'd get near Bobbie's.

"But now, after seeing what this area has to offer," Gretchen gave Andrew a wicked smile and a nod, "I might have to see if Allie will rent me her spare bedroom for a few months." She glanced down the front of her fitted white shirt, toying with the top button. "Pity the fact we have almost nothing in common, aside from my dad and her mom being siblings, but it couldn't hurt to ask. And besides, time's running out."

Andrew waited for her to take a breath. "Any idea what time Allie might be home?"

"Later on, I imagine. She may have gone for a run. Can't say for sure."

"Okay, well, I just got back in town. I've been away for awhile and Allie doesn't know I'm back yet. I thought I'd surprise her."

Gretchen's bright expression dimmed a bit. She tapped a sandal-clad, tanned foot.

"There's going to be a get-together at my folks' house a week from today," Andrew rushed on. "I wanted to invite Allie." He stretched his neck forward and peered into a tastefully decorated entryway. Eyeing a wooden table with a rectangular glass top, which hugged a pale yellow wall, he asked, "Do you think there's a pen and paper nearby?"

"I suppose that's possible, but I wouldn't know where to look." Gretchen eased the door closed a couple inches. "You don't have a cell phone?"

"No. Not yet. I'll get one after I leave here."

"Well, I suppose I could give her a message for you."

"That would be great. Please let her know it's a barbecue, next Saturday at one o'clock. She can reach me at my parents' house."

Gretchen did her finger-ticking move again. "Next Saturday. One o'clock. At your parents' house. Call you there. Got it." She gazed up at him with the look of an abandoned calf caught in a hailstorm. Had he insulted her somehow?

15

Andrew grabbed the second cup of espresso from the bench and held them both up for inspection. "Hey, would you like a coffee drink? They're Americanos. I have one hot and one iced."

"Sure," she giggled. Her eyes twinkled. "How about the iced?"

"It's yours." Realizing he'd just indulged in his propensity to rescue maidens in distress, or anything remotely resembling distress, Andrew placed the cup in her hand. "Thanks for your help." Before turning away and hurrying down the steps, he added, "Maybe I'll run into you again."

Though he very much hoped that he wouldn't.

* * *

From inside the storage facility, Allie carried two boxes of pharmaceutical samples up the concrete steps and over to her black Ford Escape. She set them in the back of the SUV. Before she could return to her unit for a second load, her cell phone rang. Brushing away a drop of sweat that rolled into her eye, she answered the call.

"Hi there, Sunshine," Gretchen sang out. "I'm so sorry I missed you."

Allie smiled. Only Gretchen could be happy *and* sorry at the same time. "I just finished a run. I'm at my storage unit now."

"Well, I'm at my hotel. I picked up the padlock, keys, and paperwork from your place—it's super cute, by the way—and I got to thinking about a proposition I'd like to offer you."

"What's that?" Allie tensed, just a little. Her cousin was well known for making dubious propositions.

Gretchen launched into a spiel on how she'd planned to stay with Bobbie only until Bobbie's lease ran out in three months. After which time, the two would get a larger apartment or a small house, something big enough to accommodate two early-thirtyish women on the prowl for available attractive men. But now Gretchen was thinking she could rent a room from Allie instead. It would only be for a short time, she said in a reassuring tone, and maybe Allie could use the extra cash. Once Gretchen had finished the sales pitch, Allie tried to come up with a reason to say no, but nothing occurred to her.

"Sure, Gretchen. The answer is . . . yes."

"Hurray! Oh, you made my day, girl. Now this is the story with the move." Gretchen explained that the movers would load up her things in Dallas the next morning. She was flying back there tonight, and she'd return tomorrow, arriving at LAX late in the afternoon. And by the way, she'd need to be picked up from the airport, if possible. The movers would show up at the townhouse early Tuesday, so if Allie could take the day off, that would be a big help.

16

Allie shook her head at the way Gretchen was organizing her life. But then she thought, *Why not?* She still had five days of personal time to use before the end of the year. At least it would be spent doing something different for a change. "I guess this way you and Bobbie could use that three months to look around for a nice place to live."

"Yeah, I suppose we could. But I'm hoping by then I'll be married to a pilot. Or a fireman. Or a millionaire. Then I could just retire."

Allie sighed. Already thirty-one, Gretchen wanted more than anything to find a great guy and settle down. She'd said so countless times already. Whereas twenty-six-year-old Allie didn't feel even close to thinking about getting married.

"I guess it didn't work out with the accountant. Or was the last guy you dated the owner of the dry cleaning store?" Allie watched a red truck pull into the storage facility's driveway.

"No, it didn't. So, hey, Allie, thanks again for helping me out here." Gretchen just about ran the words together in her haste to get them out.

"Glad to do it. What are your plans for the rest of the day?"

"My flight back to Dallas is at 6:45 tonight, so Bobbie and I will grab a quick dinner at a restaurant near the airport. I need to give her a call when we hang up."

"Tell her hello for me, okay?"

"Will do." Gretchen exhaled a giddy sigh then snickered. "That woman is gonna be so happy I found someplace else to live."

* * *

Allie disconnected the call and sat down next to the boxes she'd just placed in her SUV. She felt certain she'd made the right decision about Gretchen moving in but wanted to take a minute to think about what it would mean for them both.

With regard to Allie's work-related goals, she supposed it was possible Gretchen could be an obstacle. Though it did seem as though Gretchen was as focused on her career as Allie was on her own, which meant they'd both be so busy they wouldn't see each other much. That was good. Allie had less than three months to accomplish a significant goal, and she couldn't risk having her attention diverted away from that objective.

She'd ended the previous year in thirteenth place at Horizon Pharmaceuticals, but this year she'd set her sights on becoming the number one sales rep in the country. With less than one quarter to go, she felt certain all the recent new sales she'd generated had improved her chances for success.

Two young children, a boy, about five, and a girl, seven or eight, in the midst of a boisterous game of tag, ran past Allie. A man and a woman, presumably their parents, were unloading items from the scratched and dented truck Allie had watched arrive.

"Get over here, you two," said the woman, "and stop horsin' around." Her impatience was emphasized by a staunchly Bostonian accent.

"Watch me, Daddy," the little girl called out.

Allie watched the girl do a cartwheel and skip past the SUV and over to her father's side. She wrapped her arms around his waist, like a tiny sailboat seeking safe harbor. When he gave her light brown ponytail a gentle tug she gazed up at him, grinning in adoration.

Allie could almost feel her heart expand. The scene reminded her of her own childhood, and of the relationship she'd had with her father. She envisioned a time in life when her dreams flowed without restraint, if only because the ground beneath her feet had felt so stable and secure. Life for Allie and her younger twin sister and brother had been consistent and predictable, steady and reliable. Similar to the little girl she watched, Allie had been free to do cartwheels or to dance or just be silly, and she'd received hugs whenever she wanted them.

Until a midspring tragedy changed everything she knew and trusted. Everything.

Dreams took a back seat to just getting by during the periods of pain and grief that haunted Allie for several years afterward. Fortunately, though, Kevin Rafferty, the Los Angeles district manager for Horizon Pharmaceuticals, had hired Allie as a rookie sales rep right out of college. This new career in outside sales helped her cultivate a real sense of independence, and also gave her the means to establish more order and structure in her life—a contrast to the turmoil and lack of security she'd experienced as a teenager.

Allie could remember when she had wanted to own her own company. When other little girls were having pretend tea parties, Allie was having imaginary board meetings. She didn't play house, she played corporation. She wanted to be the "boss lady," she used to tell her dad. He told her they called the heads of companies "CEOS," and she loved the sound of that. When she learned to write cursive, she used to scribble, Allison E. Hendrickson, CEO, on every surface she could find.

Allie sighed. Why had she never found her way back to her big dream? Because it was unrealistic, she supposed. After working for years in corporate America, Allie had nearly lost the desire to one day be in charge of a large company—nearly, but not completely. That old dream was still the driving force behind her yearning to be number one in sales. At least she'd feel like she was . . . what was that expression? *Master of her own destiny?* Earning national recognition might also be a springboard to a better position at Horizon. And that's why it mattered so much. It wasn't just the goal itself that was important but how achieving it would make her feel as though she'd accomplished something extraordinary—regarding her work *and* on a personal level.

Receiving a large bonus check would come with the honor of placing in a top spot, and Allie had already decided she'd use that money to help her brother and sister realize a dream of their own. The truth was, she felt that in a way she'd failed her seventeen-year old twin siblings, and she wanted (or maybe *needed*) the chance to make it up to them. Erin, a friendly, easygoing girl with their mother's dark hair and their father's cool blue eyes, loved people, nature, music, writing poetry, and volunteering at the local animal shelter. Edward, Erin's baby brother by fifteen minutes, had the same dark hair, though his eyes, like their mother's, were light green. He was a bright, courageous, witty, and caring young man, with a self-sufficient and enterprising spirit. Allie believed that, given the chance, he'd make his mark in the world through accomplishment and leadership.

Allie realized that her brother and sister looked up to her, though she often felt she didn't deserve such admiration. However, she was determined to prove herself worthy of their esteem by using her bonus money to help pay for their college-related expenses. After graduation from East Valley High the following spring, the twins were both set to begin their freshman year at Cal Poly Pomona. Of course Allie's mom, Elaine, the office manager of a small flooring business, would help to defray the costs for tuition, textbooks, lab fees, school supplies, and parking permits, which all added up for two university students. Allie had always assumed she'd be in a position to offer the twins assistance. Unfortunately, though, buying the townhouse last year, in an effort to assert her independence, left her little extra money to share. Instead of giving up on yet another dream, though, Allie chose to view her financial situation as an incentive to succeed. And succeed she would. She wasn't going to let anything get in her way.

When the pony-tailed little girl squealed with delight, Allie smiled and returned her thoughts to Gretchen. It was true that her older cousin sometimes annoyed Allie, but she had always admired Gretchen's verve and passion for life . . . something Allie had lost a long time ago.

After drawing in a breath, Allie closed her eyes, wondering if this situation with Gretchen was somehow meant to happen.

19

Might a little time spent together expose Allie to new opportunities for growth? Would Gretchen's passionate and bubbly personality inspire Allie to become more free-spirited and adventurous? More uninhibited and spontaneous? It seemed that something unusual or even profound was about to happen.

Allie could feel it.

Chapter 2

The Stranger

T he baggage claim area at LAX began loading up with passengers from several different flights. While frustrated parents corralled their restless children, confused foreign visitors sought out assistance using commendable broken English. And weary business travelers, awaiting the arrival of their luggage, stood by with such eager expressions you could almost imagine the feet-up, eyes-closed *ahhh* that awaited them in their hotel rooms.

Trying not to inhale too much of a heavy-set woman's jasmine-scented perfume, Allie stayed close to the carousel designated for Gretchen's flight, scanning the crowd for her fair-haired cousin.

"Hey there, Sunshine!" Gretchen's chirpy voice broke through the distorted din of travelers.

Whereas her stature kept her hidden, her voice and personality stood out. Allie followed the sound and spotted an energetic Gretchen waving a hand in a way that exposed frosty pink fingernails. Allie weaved her way through jostling bodies and reached Gretchen just as the luggage carousel began to move. The two women embraced.

Gretchen stepped back first and grinned. "I told myself, that Allie, she's a smart one; she'll figure out where I'm supposed to be even before I do. And here you are!"

"It's good to see you again, Gretchen. You look terrific."

"That's my job."

"And I like what you've done to your hair." Allie in fact was intrigued by Gretchen's hair. She vaguely wondered whether her own mid-back, parted on the side, straight brown hair would look good highlighted in various shades of blond and cut in layers to frame her face, the way Gretchen's did.

Gretchen turned her head from side to side. "I began a full-scale makeover the second I found out about my new route." She lifted a hand, counting with her fingers. "Haircut, highlights, microdermabrasion, seaweed body wrap, infrared teeth whitening . . . Mm, what else, what else? *Oh,* and the tanning salon! Several trips turned my skin to gold." Her busy silver charm bracelet tinkled as she held out a sleeveless, smooth-tanned arm. "Plus I've been working out at Gold Digger's Gym. Does it show?"

"It does. You look fantastic."

"Thanks, but enough about me for now. What's new with you? Boyfriend? Dating anyone special?" With Gretchen, every conversation eventually included men.

"No. I don't have time to date. I'm too busy with work to meet anyone." Allie was surprised to hear herself say that, but it was true. Other than running, reading, and going to see the occasional movie, she focused her time and energy on making a name for herself at Horizon, not on looking for dates.

Gretchen clucked her tongue. "That's no excuse. You don't even have to make an effort. Los Angeles is *crawling* with prospects." Her take on men seemed to parallel her thoughts on pieces of jewelry: Collect as many as possible, be sure they're in style, and stay away from the cheap ones.

Keeping her eyes on the scuffed, beige linoleum floor, Allie slid a discarded gum wrapper back and forth with the tip of her running shoe. "I'm just not ready to get serious with anyone, that's all."

Gretchen lifted up on her toes and looked toward the far end of the carousel. "Hey, do you know of a good Chinese restaurant we could hit after I get my bags? I'm craving Kung Fu Chicken."

Allie looked up. "What kind of chicken?"

"You know, the stuff with the little red chilies and the peanuts."

"Oh, you mean Kung *Pao* Chicken."

"That's what I said."

* * *

Despite it being late afternoon, northbound traffic moved along the 110 Freeway without incident. The Chinese restaurant that, in Allie's opinion, served the best Kung Pao Chicken was Ah Chu's, located on the outskirts of Chinatown. But because Allie avoided driving through downtown L.A. after dark, she decided they would instead go to Madame Fung's Peking Palace, situated in safe and secure East Hills. On the way there, the two cousins chatted about how much fun Gretchen would have spending part of her time off in Hawaii.

"The beaches are bea-u-tiful. Oh, Allie, Waimanalo is one of my favorites on Oahu. It's hidden away from all the crowds."

"I hope to vacation in the islands someday," she replied, without mentioning that an all-expense paid trip to the tropics next summer would be part of the compensation for placing in the top ten at Horizon.

"Someday, schmumday! You'll come out there and visit *me*. We'll have a blast. And you know, in my opinion, the best time to go is November through April. It gets a little rainy during the first few months of the year, but it's much cooler and not as humid. Ugh. Humidity. That's one thing I will *not* miss about those hot Texas summers, thank you very much."

"But aren't summers in Hawaii hot and humid?"

"Yeah, I suppose so. But you're in paradise, so who cares?"

Not Allie. She didn't mind a little humidity. "Every year my company has a national awards trip for the reps who place eleventh through twentieth. I was one of the winners last year and guess where they sent us? San Diego. Funny, huh?"

"*Funny? Funny? That's insane! What is that, a two-hour drive for you?*"

"More like two-plus."

"You work your tail off all year and they send you down to *Sea World?* Unbelievable! Outrageous! What's wrong with those people? Why not Milan or Tahiti or somewhere else in the south Pacific? Even Guam is better than Southern Califor—"

Allie's jolting brake check did wonders to discourage the car on her tail. It also cut Gretchen off mid-sentence, giving Allie a chance to switch topics. "Do you remember my friend, Beth McKinley?"

Out of the corner of her eye Allie observed Gretchen's head tilting. "Light red hair, wavy or curly, I believe. Works in retail. Isn't she like eight feet tall?"

Allie smiled. "Five-foot-ten, but yes, that's her. She's renting her aunt's house in Malibu—it's half a block from the beach. Beth still manages the fragrance department at Rathman's in the Westside Plaza, but she's also a graduate student at Pepperdine University."

"Ahh, Malibu. *Too cool,*" Gretchen sighed, gazing out through the windshield. "Now, that's one of the better beaches in L.A. Very clean, beautiful homes . . . *and Pepperdine University!* Oh, Allie," she smacked her hands down in her lap, "I almost forgot to tell you about Joshua!"

"Who's Joshua?"

"Let's just say that back in Tayhoss we'd call him 'hot stuff.'"

As always, traffic on the 110 came to a grinding halt as cars connecting to the northbound 15 crawled through two tunnels then squeezed into two lanes. Allie used this pause to look Gretchen in the eyes. "Okay. I have another question. Who's Joshua?"

Once again, Gretchen sighed. "Ah . . . I remember it like it was yesterday . . ."

"When did you first meet?"

"Yesterday."

Even considering Gretchen's penchant for loquaciousness, Allie figured the Joshua story couldn't be too long or involved since it only happened the day before. And hearing it might be a way for Allie to add a little excitement to her life, if only by proxy. "Give me all the details, and don't hold back."

Gretchen exhaled a contemplative breath then went to work. "Okay, yesterday morning I opened my bedroom window to let in some air. I can't tell you how relieved I was to feel a cool breeze on my face. A cool breeze, I might add, that smelled like *dirt.* Pretty much everything in Texas smells like dirt. So, anyway there I am at the window and I see the moving van pull up as expected, at eight-thirty. Two men slide out of the truck's cab. They seemed fit and healthy enough for the job, but a third hand couldn't have hurt. I wasn't about to break a nail doing any heavy lifting."

Allie imagined the scene. Gretchen would have prepped for the casual event by wearing designer jeans, a form-fitting cardigan with faux fur collar, a pair of five-inch stilettos and an eau de toilette strong enough to revive the comatose.

Gretchen continued. "So I open the front door and see the face of the most gorgeous man on the planet: *Joshua Walden,*" she said with a breathy exhale.

"'Good morning,' he said to me, 'someone must be eager to get moving.'"

She let out sigh number three. "And then he smiled. Beautiful teeth, by the way, and the twinkle in his eye told me he was a big flirt. Just my type. So I smiled back, maybe even giggled and said, 'Kind of obvious, aren't I?'"

Allie laughed.

Gretchen grinned. "So he says, 'Hey, it's a big deal, relocating out of state and all. I hope this is a good move for you. That, you know, you're okay with it.' I told him I was, but I was asking myself, *why would he care?* I mean, he doesn't even *know* me. It seemed odd."

"He may just be a nice person. Kind and considerate." Allie checked the side view mirror while merging onto the 5. "I hear there are a few men out there like that."

"I hear that too," Gretchen agreed, even though she appeared confounded by the notion. "Anyway, he told me his name and introduced me to his brother, Steven." She fished an item out of her tote bag. "I had most of the easy stuff already packed in card-board boxes. I told him I was concerned about a large armoire in the bedroom. It was big and heavy, and I asked if it would be a problem to lift since there were only two of them. Well, it seemed Joshua couldn't resist a little more flirting. He said, 'The way I see it, with *you* that makes three. Shouldn't be a problem at all.' Allie, I tell you," Gretchen said as she pulled down the sun visor, "he looked downright adorable with those big blue eyes and that tousled sandy blond hair. But of course I hoped he was kidding. I didn't want to have to think less of him for making such an absurd statement."

She continued talking while dabbing frosty pink lip gloss on her mouth—the perfect complement to her nails. "Whenever you need a good excuse to get out of an unpleasant task, *Female in Fashion* magazine advises simply throwing down the beauty card." She shrugged, looking cutesy. "So I did. 'I just had a manicure,' I told him, 'I'm afraid I'll have to sit this one out.' He said that was fine, and that he and his brother would be happy to take care of every little thing. I just gave him a sultry look and confident smile—more foolproof advice from my fave magazine."

* * *

Andrew and his parents, Rob and Sue Gallagher, headed toward the sanctuary, picking their way through Valley Community Church's crowded courtyard. The pergola-covered area of stone, flowerbeds, and birdbaths had always been the social hub of conversation and visitation before and after services. So Andrew was not surprised to find that the courtyard could still become as densely animated as a teeming school of mackerel.

As the threesome neared the ornate concrete fountain in the middle of the courtyard, Jean and Harry Stuart, longtime family friends and patients of Rob's internal medicine practice, caught up with the Gallaghers. Jean interrupted Andrew's enjoyment of the fountain's cool mist.

"I don't believe it, Harry," she trilled. "Look, it's Andrew Gallagher, back from the military. And he's grown into such a handsome young man."

Jean looked so innocent and protective with her flushed round cheeks, sharp blue eyes and coy little smile that, for a moment, Andrew forgot what the woman was capable of. He tried not to cringe in pain when she began pulling on his cheek, pinching it hard with overzealous affection. He wondered why in the world people *did* such things. And even though Andrew had a tremendous fond-ness in his heart for the Stuarts, he also had a strong desire at that moment to be teleported from Jean's clutches and into the safety of the sanctuary—especially when the conversation turned medical and included topics such as Harry's phlebitis and Jean's aching bunions. Andrew looked to the crowd for an escape route. Relieved and surprised, he spotted a face from his recent past and he used the sighting to justify his separation from the group. "It's great to see you again." He touched both Harry and Jean on the shoulder. "But if you'll excuse me, I see someone I need to speak with."

Andrew walked away before Jean could protest. As he moved toward the young woman he'd spied a moment before, he found it ironic that he was grateful for the chance to talk to her. That hadn't been the story on his flight home three days earlier. He remembered thinking then, *Oh, how I wish she'd stop talking . . .*

Andrew had needed to say something to her. But what?

The young woman had introduced herself as Jennifer a microsecond after Andrew had taken his seat. She'd then begun offering her personal bio before the plane's wheels were up, adding details here and there throughout the flight's duration. She included the location of her birth in Colorado, and even the date, which was in late September, three months after Andrew's in the same year. He wasn't hugely perceptive when it came to women, but Jennifer was pretty easy to read, and it was obvious she was looking for something from him in return. However, Andrew wasn't exactly the type to pour his heart out to a complete stranger—especially not a woman sitting next to him on an airplane.

Not wanting to be rude he'd told her, "You look like someone I know."

Jennifer's slender, taller-than-average build and long, light reddish, wavy hair reminded him of Beth, a pretty girl he'd met at the lake the summer before tenth grade. But Jennifer's eyes, unlike Beth's, were a light brown color. And those eyes had sprung open at his comment. "Oh?" Her face reddened as she glanced down. "Your girlfriend?"

Andrew shook his head once and looked away. "The friend of a friend, you could say."

A sturdy blond flight attendant wearing a dark blue skirt and white blouse came to the rescue, pushing a heavy metal cart up the narrow aisle. She pressed her foot down on the brake pedal, stopping at Andrew's row to begin the second beverage service.

A small reprieve from Jennifer's constant chitchat.

Once the row had been taken care of and the cart pushed forward, Jennifer's tactic toward Andrew changed, and she began firing off questions at him.

"Are you headed to L.A. on business?"

He looked away from the land patchwork he'd been viewing out his window and set a cup of fizzy Sprite down on the tray table. "No. I live there."

"Oh, you're returning from a business trip, like me?" She explained how she worked at Fox Studios in Century City as a telecom assistant and was returning from a convention in Virginia.

Jennifer's gentle and keen eyes gave her face a look of earnestness, but the way she kept pressing her lips together and flicking her gaze to the side suggested an urgency Andrew didn't understand. He wanted to be nice to her, but he also needed to use the remainder of the flight to reflect on his life and collect his thoughts.

Still, he couldn't ignore her question. "I wasn't on a business trip. I've been away the past four years. Most recently, in the Middle East."

"Ah! How exciting." Jennifer shifted in her seat and her legs made a slight turn, like the needle on a compass. "I imagine you're thrilled to be coming home."

"I am. I've waited a long time for this day." And now that it had arrived, he couldn't help but remember the reasons he'd left in the first place.

"You must have been in the military."

"Yes."

"The Army?"

"No, Navy."

"What an admirable sacrifice."

Andrew laughed quietly, uncomfortable with the idea. "I thought of it more as a call to duty."

"What did you do in the Navy?"

"I oversaw flight deck operations aboard the *U.S.S Nimitz*. The launch and recovery of aircraft, basically."

"What an awesome experience." Jennifer smiled broadly, and Andrew noticed a slight overlap of her two front teeth. It looked kind of cute. She kept her attention on him, her eyes revealing a careful thought process in motion. The sweet scent of her perfume wafted Andrew's way as she swept reddish curls off her right shoulder. "Do you think it'll seem strange returning home after four years?"

Andrew had been entertaining such thoughts the entire flight. He wondered how much the Valley had changed, if he'd feel out of place after being gone so long, and whether or not his closest friends would still be in the area. Before joining the Navy, he'd had only a handful of true friends. As a rule, Andrew kept to himself as much as possible, so forming associations on a one-to-one basis wasn't something he did readily. But then again, a six-month deployment aboard a small mobile city known as an aircraft carrier, living in close quarters with and among a crew of five thousand, produced friendships, if only by necessity. Andrew was okay with the fact that he'd likely never see any of his shipmate friends again—most of whom lived out of state, anyway. And besides, being what was referred to as an "old soul" predisposed Andrew to having few friends in his own age group, preferring fellowship with those from the generation before.

"I don't dwell on what I can't possibly know," he answered.

A skeptical line knotted Jennifer's wide brow. "You don't? Ever?"

"I try not to." That wasn't a lie, but it wasn't entirely true, either. There were times when his thoughts trailed off into the dark and deceptive areas of the unknown. Just like now.

Most of the time, though, believing that God would take care of his daily needs helped Andrew maintain the inner peace he needed in order to function. "I have a strong network of family and friends. They help keep me focused—as does my faith. I've missed attending Sunday services back home. Our pastor, John McAndrews, is a terrific spiritual leader and an all-around great guy. You're welcome to come visit us anytime you like."

He had provided Jennifer with the service times and location details and left the rest in God's capable hands.

And now, here she was . . . in Valley Community Church's courtyard. Andrew knew he'd invited her to visit, but he honestly hadn't expected to see her again . . . or at least not this soon.

She smiled and waved when she saw him. He pointed to his right, toward a couple of wooden benches at the edge of the courtyard. When they reached each other, Andrew spent half a second admiring Jennifer's pink skirt. It was made out of some kind of swishy material, and it swirled midcalf around her brown boots.

"Hello, Jennifer."

"I'm so glad I found you." Her cheeks turned rosy. "I got here early and parked in a spot for guests. Is that okay?"

"Of course. You *are* a guest."

Jennifer immediately launched into small talk. Without saying much in return, Andrew listened. Every few moments he glanced in his parents' direction, waving them over when he saw that they had finally finished chatting with the Stuarts. Their faces filled with curiosity as they approached. His mother's face, in particular, took on a raised-eyebrow, wide-grin expression that made Andrew want to shake his head. Instead, he just grinned at them then at Jennifer.

"Mom, Dad, I'd like you to meet Jennifer . . ." He paused.

Jennifer smiled. "Campbell."

"Right, Campbell. Sorry about that. And Jennifer, these are my parents, Rob and Sue Gallagher. Jennifer and I sat next to each other on the last leg of my trip home, the one from DC."

"It's a pleasure to meet you both." Jennifer's voice shrank in on itself a bit and her shoulders hunched slightly as she shook their hands.

Was she nervous? Andrew wondered what made her feel uneasy.

Sue spoke first. "It's nice to meet *you*." She put more than the usual kindness in her steady voice, but as always, her burnt sienna eyes projected her warmth and caring. Andrew wasn't surprised. His mother somehow knew when people weren't perfectly comfortable, and she made it her business to help them relax.

"I hope Andrew didn't talk your ear off, Jennifer," Rob kidded.

Jennifer's brow creased. "Actually, I did most of the talking."

She didn't get the joke. She hadn't been around Andrew long enough to know he did more listening than talking.

Andrew smiled as he watched his parents, so happy and full of life. Rob, with his friendly blue eyes, short dark hair now graying at the temples, and amused grin had eight inches of height over five-foot-four Sue, whose brown hair streaked with natural blond highlights swooped upward at the shoulders. They both worked hard to stay in good shape, and Andrew thought they'd make great cover models for a magazine about baby boomer health—especially today. They were dressed in matching olive green oxford shirts (his dad's was paired with crisp khakis; his mom's was tucked into a slimming tan straight skirt). As a couple, they radiated an energy Andrew knew came from a pure joy of living. It came from faith, too. His parents had no doubts they were looked after by a benevolent God who loved them. They had always taken that love, magnified it, and shared it with everyone they met.

Andrew swallowed, suddenly overwhelmed with gratitude to be home.

Rob took Sue's hand. "We're going inside now to get a seat up front with all the other old folks. We'll catch you two after the service, okay?"

* * *

With the desire in her heart to find significance in Gretchen's sudden appearance in her life, Allie went to church. She hadn't been there in months. The appeal of congregating weekly to hear the same basic message over and over had somehow eluded her for the past few years.

Although she'd been labeled a "believer" after returning from summer camp, Allie had always felt something was lacking in her spiritual life. Sure, her newfound faith helped her to make sense of the tragedies she'd experienced in her youth—after the fact. But the "peace that passes all understanding" seemed to have passed over her as well. Allie wanted a deeper connection with God, and she knew she'd have to put forth the effort to make that happen.

Arriving at church as the evening service began, Allie stayed near the back. She took a seat between the end of a maple pew and a cherubic-faced woman wearing gray flannel slacks and a red suedecloth shirt covered in white fur, probably from a cat. Allie's eyes scanned the expansive yet modest sanctuary, which contained no stained glass windows, fancy ornaments, or distracting objects of any kind—just a rugged wooden cross, placed behind and above the pulpit. She didn't recognize anyone that evening, but she did notice a man and a woman several rows away sitting next to each other. They looked oddly familiar. The woman, with a face of classic features and skin as pale and smooth as an albino moth's wings, resembled Beth. Her hair was darker than Beth's, but it was styled in a similar manner, with lots of body and bounce.

Allie studied the woman's companion, a dark-haired man who had a strong jawline and a nose with a prominent bridge. Although she could only see him in profile, she realized he looked just like Andrew Gallagher. Allie almost laughed aloud at the thought. This man couldn't *possibly* be Andrew Gallagher because Andrew was still . . .

The opening prayer caught Allie's attention. Pastor John began the day's lesson by saying that many believe a great marriage is guaranteed if two people are simply in love. But he believed that wasn't enough. "Mutual deference," he said, "and the idea of considering others better than ourselves is something we must consciously choose to do. It may not be inherent in our thinking, but it is nonetheless a requirement for a healthy marriage."

Allie wondered if she might have a husband one day. She began imagining what he'd be like, how he'd look, and how she would feel about him. Her mind struggled to create an image of this man, familiar, yet still unknown. A form took shape, but without definition; she saw a face but couldn't see into the eyes. She sensed a block wall going up again, that same roadblock to some sort of memory or vision.

Pastor John's voice droned on, indistinct and hazy.

Maybe you're not meant to be married, Allison, she thought, growing impatient with her lack of emotional self-control. She admonished herself as tears stung her eyes.

Positive thoughts. Think positive thoughts.

Though she fought to overcome the feeling, despair crept back into her heart. Allie fluttered her eyelids, hoping the tears would evaporate before they streamed down her face.

She didn't know how much time had passed while her mind wandered, but a good portion of the message had escaped her. So much for getting guidance about the purpose of her time with Gretchen. If the help had been in Pastor John's message, Allie had been so mired in self-pity that she'd missed it.

When the hour-long service concluded, Allie bolted toward the exit. She barely made to the parking lot before bursting into tears.

* * *

The early evening air felt fresh and crisp on Andrew's face. As he and Jennifer left the sanctuary and strolled into the courtyard, his gaze surveyed the distant horizon, beyond the church property and all its activity. The sky was like a black velvet painting, studded with brilliant and remote stars; peaceful and calming but incomplete. Being with Jennifer made him feel off-balance somehow. Was it her eager openness, how powerfully *nice* she was? She was distinctly feminine, and he appreciated that in a woman. He'd missed it too. Spending the better part of the past four years in the Middle East aboard a massive nuclear-powered aircraft carrier, immersed in a complex and orderly system predominated by male energy, took its toll on a guy. Command and control. Demand and direct. Structure and sacrifice. The military offered a style of living where valuable lessons could not be avoided. It wasn't an easy life, and it wasn't for everyone, but if viewed as an opportunity for personal growth and a chance to embrace challenges not found in the civilian world, emerging on the other side a changed individual was a sure thing. Andrew was grateful for lessons learned and character built, but there were things the military couldn't offer, things he hoped to find back here at home.

A light breeze flowed through Jennifer's auburn hair. Reaching up, she pulled on a few strands that had been swept into her mouth. She certainly talked more than other women Andrew had known, but he was glad that in all her chatter he hadn't heard anything negative. She seemed good-hearted, spoke well of the people in her life, and when she'd brought up current events, she'd sprinkled her observations with optimism. Andrew admired that about her, something else she had in common with Beth. Though Jennifer was also similar to Beth in a physical sense, her personality—at least what he knew of it so far—reminded him more of Allie. And like Allie, Jennifer had a side to her that seemed to him to be vulnerable. But in Allie's case, it was more of a faint sliver; still, it was part of what made her so special: so magnetic and so indescribably one-of-a-kind.

31

Because he'd be interviewing the next two days at NASA's Jet Propulsion Laboratory in Pasadena, and also at Northrup Grumman in L.A., Andrew would have to wait until later in the week to go back to Allie's townhouse. He needed to find out what happened to her and why she hadn't called. None of it made sense; she knew he'd come looking for her and that he could be reached at his parents' house.

"*Andrew Gallagher!*" An excited voice shot through the crowd's murmur and speared Andrew, interrupting his thoughts. Good thing. He was being rude to Jennifer. For all he knew, she'd been talking to him for the last couple minutes. He didn't know. He'd checked out of his head and fallen into his heart.

Pastor John's wife, Laura, planted herself in front of Andrew and beamed at him. Four years hadn't affected her at all. Tall and thin, with chin-length, black hair, large root beer-colored eyes and an aristocratic nose, Laura looked every bit what she was: the daughter of an Italian father and Greek mother. She had a striking, almost exotic appearance and a capacity for enthusiasm, good will, and selflessness that was remarkable. She gave Andrew a welcome embrace and Jennifer a warm smile. After Andrew made the introductions, Laura called her husband over to meet the visitor. She seemed to think she hadn't missed the significance of Jennifer's presence at Andrew's side. The truth was, though, she was missing it entirely.

With the same intuitive grin Sue wore when she clearly knew something Andrew didn't, Laura said, "John, this is Jennifer."

Andrew's stomach did a small back flip. It felt as if he'd been sucked into a movie scene, which unfolded in surreal slow motion as Pastor John greeted Jennifer with something like a congratulatory handshake. Reading thought balloons wasn't one of Andrew's strong suits, and he knew it. But in the back of his mind, he was sure he could hear the orchestra section in this fantastic musical he'd landed in playing a tune with undertones of white and silver. His heart thumped and thudded against his chest wall, while a small lump formed in his throat. Oh boy.

Inquisitive bystanders turned, leaned, watched, listened, and smiled. Andrew had a feeling . . . No. That couldn't be. Was there a collective assumption that he and Jennifer were an item? *A couple?*

Not possible. He'd already decided how things were supposed to unfold once he got back home, having gone over the details in his mind a hundred—maybe even a thousand—times. His vision did not include Jennifer. And it did not include the conclusions people appeared to be drawing about the two of them. So how exactly did she get here? And why was everyone, including Andrew himself, confused?

Jennifer tossed her head back, laughing at something Laura said, but which Andrew missed because he couldn't hear a thing over the loud music inside his head. His failure to speak or even nod could have explained why his parents, standing arm in arm a few feet away, watched him with half-smiles and squints.

* * *

Whether they thought he'd lost his faculties or not, Andrew's parents were the ones who conducted the search and rescue. Taking his arm, Sue eased him away from the flock of well-meaning congregants. Rob placed a light hand on Jennifer's shoulder, and the four of them meandered toward the parking lot.

Andrew rubbed his hands together. The cool breeze, and the lack of circulation to his extremities that resulted from realizing he'd been summarily placed in "a couple" without his permission, lowered his body temperature noticeably. The previous fifteen minutes were jumbled up in his mind. He couldn't seem to recall anything concrete about them, other than the fact that he hadn't asked about Allie, or even mentioned her name, to John and Laura. And for that, he felt pangs of regret.

When they reached his parents' dark blue Lexus ES, Sue pulled a brass ring of keys out of her brown leather shoulder bag and deactivated the alarm. She handed the key ring to Rob.

Jennifer turned toward Andrew. She took a gentle hold of his arm and slowed down his pace. "It's still early." Her eyes expressed the same hopefulness Andrew had seen before. "Would you like to get a cup of coffee somewhere?"

Yeah, sitting down and setting her straight about a few things might not be a bad idea. The buoyancy he'd felt since arriving home was flattening out some, and he wasn't about to let this situation with Jennifer—whatever it was—interfere with his plans.

"Sure, a cup of coffee sounds good. But I didn't drive here. My car's at home."

Jennifer smiled. "We can take mine. I don't mind driving."

He agreed and walked with Jennifer to a silver Prius parked at the edge of the lot. "I need to get my wallet. I'll be right back." Andrew closed the door once she got inside, and returned to the Lexus.

He slid into the backseat and explained the revised plan. He lifted his backpack off the floor, setting it beside him on the smooth beige leather seat.

"Are you going to invite your new friend to the barbecue next weekend?" Sue asked.

Rob placed the key in the ignition and started the car. "She seems like a nice gal."

"And beautiful," Sue added. "She could be a model. Is she a model, Andrew?"

He glanced up. "Hmm?"

Sue pivoted in the front seat to look back at Andrew. "The lady you met on the plane." The thin gold chain and dainty cross Rob had given her years before sparkled in the sedan's interior light.

"Jennifer?"

"Yes, Andrew," she laughed, *"Jennifer."*

"What about her?"

Rob echoed his wife's question. "Are you going to invite her to the barbecue?"

Andrew clutched his wallet. "I doubt it, Dad. I barely know her. Besides, she wouldn't know anyone there. Why would she want to come?"

Sue's eyes creased as her smile widened. "Andrew, judging by the way she looks at you, I'm rather certain she'd be more than happy to attend."

"She's right, Andrew." Rob slid the gearshift down into reverse without moving the car. He flicked a glance over his right shoulder at Andrew. "That young lady seems very taken with you. I wouldn't be surprised if we see her at church again next Sunday."

Andrew studied his parents' faces. For the first time in a long time, he found himself questioning his whims. Inviting Jennifer to church may not have been God's plan after all. Because now it seemed that having Jennifer show up here—just for Andrew's sake—was not a good thing.

Not at all.

* * *

Allie pushed open the front door of Mo'Joes, relieved to see only Phoebe inside.

"You look terrible, Allie. Are you okay?"

"Phoebe, I don't know what to do with that question. If I look terrible, then how can I be okay? If I say I'm okay, then wouldn't I be lying?"

"How 'bout this? Stop analyzing the question and give me an answer."

Allie looked down at the narrow cables on her jade green sweater then at her sensible brown leather flats. She was being unreasonable. "Okay, fair enough. Here's your answer." Her eyes darted from the menu board to Phoebe. "A large iced Americano.

Decaf. I don't want to wake up tomorrow looking any worse than I do now."

Phoebe shook her head while entering Allie's order in the cash register, her glasses sliding down her nose a bit. She pushed them back up with an index finger. "One day I might understand what goes on inside that complicated little head of yours, Missy."

"When you figure it out, do me a favor and keep it to your-self, okay?"

"Whatever you say. You're the paying customer."

Allie watched as Phoebe placed a scoop of small clear ice cubes into a plastic cup and doused them with fresh brewed decaf espresso. She filled the cup with water then used a flat palm to press down on the lid until it clicked into place.

"One large, decaf, iced Americano." Phoebe slid the cup across the pick-up table toward Allie. "With room at the top."

* * *

Andrew and Jennifer arrived at Mo'Joe's at seven-thirty five. The parking lot was deserted except for a dark SUV exiting the driveway as Jennifer pulled into a spot near the door. She'd been talking nonstop on the way over, saying how much she'd enjoyed the church atmosphere and that she might like to attend services more often.

And Andrew might like to have his head examined.

Later. Right now, he had to be a gentleman.

He got out of the car and whipped around to the driver's side to hold the door for Jennifer as she stood. She smiled widely at him. Wincing when she turned away, he had a feeling he'd just done something more to add to whatever misconceptions Jennifer . . . and everyone else . . . had going. Swallowing a groan, Andrew led them into the empty coffeehouse, where a strong and bittersweet scent lingered in the air. Their footsteps clicked across the pale, dark brown, laminate floor. The only other sound in the place was the faint notes of piano music coming from a speaker across the room and a frothy hiss coming from one of the machines behind the counter.

After a quick glance over the menu board, Jennifer placed her order with the same dark-haired woman who'd been serving the day before.

"I'll have a medium, skinny, decaf vanilla latte, extra hot."

The woman began writing on a paper cup while glancing toward Andrew. "And for you?"

"A large decaf Americano, please."

"How would you like that?" Before he could answer, she said, "Wait a sec. You were in here yesterday, weren't you? You ordered two Americanos, one hot and one iced."

Andrew's heartbeat picked up speed when he remembered the reason why. "Yes."

Jennifer's eyes opened wide. "You ordered *two* coffees?"

"I don't think they were both for him," the woman said.

What difference does it make? Andrew made firm and direct eye contact with each of them. "I only drank the hot one. I really enjoyed it, but I think this time I'll have the iced." He opened his wallet and rummaged through his bills, keeping his eyes low. Jennifer took the hint and sat down at a small table near the front.

Standing by the pick-up counter, Andrew waited for their orders. When the dark-haired woman handed him the cups, he took the latte to Jennifer before carrying his Americano to the wide counter off to the side. He set his drink down and, when he reached for the stainless steel pitcher of cream, he noticed a small plastic card near his cup. He assumed it was a depleted Mo'Joes Coffee card; but when he flipped it face up, a wave of endorphins flooded his bloodstream.

It was a debit card issued by a local bank, bearing the name Allison E. Hendrickson.

Andrew stared at the card for several seconds. He glanced over his shoulder. Jennifer was fiddling with her latte cup. The woman at the front counter had her back to Andrew. Reaching for the card as if it was radioactive, he snatched it up and shoved it into the front pocket of his trousers.

Why had Allie left it behind? She wasn't absentminded or careless. *Was she okay?*

He glanced around again. He must have just missed her. He couldn't imagine the card had been there long. Someone would have seen it and either turned it in or stolen it.

If he asked the woman at the front about it, Jennifer might overhear and start asking questions again. He chewed on his lower lip. Then he straightened his shoulders. He had an idea.

If he could get Jennifer out of the room for a minute or two. . .

Andrew poured a dash of half and half into his cup. Using a long, flat wooden stick, he swirled the light and dark colors together, creating a milder-looking butterscotch tan. He replaced the lid without securing it and walked toward Jennifer. She was sitting in a chair, legs crossed at the knees. Her brown leather boots peeked out from beneath his target—her long pink skirt.

Right before he reached his chair, Andrew caught his right shoe on the leg of a nearby table. He took a couple hopping steps with his left foot and tipped his cup until the lid slid off to the side and the icy Americano splashed across the expanse of pink covering Jennifer's lap.

"*Ah!*" she exclaimed, half jumping from her chair.

Andrew gasped. "I can't believe I did that!" He took a step back while thinking, *Of course you can, Lieutenant Clodhopper. You just planned it!*

He set the cup on the table and offered Jennifer the handful of napkins he held. "I'm so sorry."

She directed her huge eyes at his, pressing the napkins against her skirt. "Don't worry, it's alright. But I think I'd better run cold water over the coffee before it sets."

"Sure. Of course. Good idea."

Jennifer turned away from the table. As she walked across the room, he wiped off his cup and snapped its lid into place.

The moment the ladies' room door closed, Andrew made a mad dash toward the dark-haired woman. She leaned against the front counter, watching him with obvious amusement.

"I saw the whole thing," she offered, as though relaying an eyewitness account of a traffic accident. "And you were at fault for reasons I won't go into."

Andrew's face heated up, but he kept his expression neutral. "I was wondering if a woman was in here this evening, at some point before we came in . . . about your height, brown hair, possibly long, I'm not sure, with soft gray eyes and a shy smile." Andrew spoke the words with haste, while keeping a close watch on the ladies' room door.

"*As a matter of fact, you just missed her!*"

Andrew cringed at the woman's loud voice.

She covered her mouth for a second, and then lowered the volume on her enthusiasm. "Something was bothering her, but she wouldn't tell me *what*."

The bathroom door began to swing open.

The woman lifted a hand, pressing the thumb and forefinger near the side of her mouth to whisper, "Typical of her, if you ask me."

Andrew wanted to ask more questions, but with precious seconds ticking off the clock and Jennifer advancing on her final approach, he never got the chance. In less time than it took to say *U.S.S. Dwight D. Eisenhower*, Jennifer had landed by his side.

"Is something wrong, Andrew?"

"No, everything's fine." He motioned toward their table. Gesturing at Jennifer's skirt as they sat down, Andrew said he hoped she was able to get all the coffee out. She said she had and he told her he was glad, and that, again, he was sorry. He wished he cared more than he did. But the only thing he cared about at that point was whatever was going on with Allie.

Chapter 3

Time Sensitive

Allie awoke to a pounding in her chest and a cold sensation on her leg. Entangled in a strange and distant netherworld, her mind continued drifting. She must have tossed the sheet and blanket off sometime during the restless night, exposing her leg to an early morning chill. She'd been having strange dreams over the past three nights. In this latest one, she feared she'd lost something important, but she couldn't recall what it was.

She didn't have time to think much about it though. From the time she opened her eyes to the moment she arrived at her storage facility at eight o'clock, she was 100 percent focused on work.

Allie entered the storage facility parking lot and drove toward her manager, Kevin, who stood next to his metallic silver Ford Explorer. As she pulled up alongside him, Allie noticed something different about Kevin. Either his suit was new or she'd never seen it on him before. It was dark blue and very flattering to his stocky, six-foot-four-inch frame. Normally, Kevin's thick, light brown hair fell across his forehead and into his slightly hooded hazel eyes. But not today. His hair had been recently trimmed, with the top section left longer, parted on the side and neatly combed into place. There was a contented and somewhat distant expression on his face, pulling at the corners of his wide mouth and enhancing his already high cheekbones.

They said their hellos and then took Allie's SUV to the Corner Café for a short breakfast meeting. It was something they always did before working together in the field, visiting the offices of Allie's top doctors. So, in a way, the Corner Café was almost like an office, albeit one decorated with items that had been salvaged from an old train depot.

A dingy, round-faced Victorian clock dangled on its wrought-iron bracket above the smoked glass door, which Kevin held open for Allie. Black-and-white photos in eight-by-ten inch frames covered the walls inside the waiting area: pictures of huge dilapidated barns, A-frame houses, churches with towering steeples, a dairy farm, an old fishing boat, and a rickety wooden carriage depicted life in America at the turn of the twentieth century. A scratched and scuffed train schedule blackboard hung high above the photos.

Kevin looked out through the large windows on the back wall of the restaurant. "Shall we sit outside for a change, Allie?"

"Sure. Fine. Let's do it."

The sinewy hostess with a long thick platinum blond braid grabbed two plastic menus. When she stepped around the counter, Allie took note of the woman's stylish outfit, a purple corduroy jumper over a knit blend white blouse.

"This way, please." The hostess took Kevin and Allie down the center aisle of the restaurant and toward the patio section. Half of the booths they passed were occupied, mostly with lone male patrons in business suits, sipping mugs of coffee while reading *The Wall Street Journal* or *The Los Angeles Times*.

"I like your jumper," Allie said to the woman's back. "The gold buttons are a nice touch. It's very cute."

Kevin agreed wholeheartedly that the outfit was a winner. The woman turned her head and smiled, saying, "Thanks, I got it at Self-Expressions."

Allie nodded. "I know the place; it's in the Westside Plaza. My friend Beth buys clothes there, too."

Once outside, they were seated at a white metal table near a pink camellia hedge in full bloom.

Their waitress, a gal about twenty-five with burgundy hair cut pixie short, medium-beige skin, and a pointy nose arrived in a flurry of activity, unloading napkins, silverware, syrup, bottles of ketchup, two kinds of hot sauce, and a multipurpose dispenser, containing tiny jam and jelly packets. She asked if either of them wanted coffee or juice, to which they both replied, "Coffee, please." Pulling a pencil out of her apron pocket, she scribbled on her bill pad, slowing down long enough to say she'd be right back with the coffees. She vanished as quickly as she'd materialized.

Kevin picked up his menu, flipping it over to look at the breakfast selections. With barely a glance, he set it back down and looked at Allie. "I have something important and time sensitive to discuss with you."

Oh, that tiresome corporate phrase: Time sensitive. Allie ranked it right up there with the worn-out family of business-related acronyms, including POA, ROI, FIFO and SOP. Allie knew they came with the territory, and even caught herself using corporate newspeak from time to time.

"Time sensitive, as in it's going to happen sooner rather than later?"

"Exactly. The company's new national sales director—and my new boss—Cassandra Hartwell, phoned me late yesterday to schedule a last minute two-day visit for Wednesday and Thursday of next week. That's October 24th and 25th."

"I got it, Kev." Whenever Kevin made a point of overstating the obvious, Allie knew something important was in the works.

"Good. She wants to meet with me and also observe how some of the more successful reps work in the field. Doug Wylie mentioned your name to her and I told Cassandra you're as top notch as they get."

Doug Wylie, huh? He was president of sales and operations in North America and a man Kevin spoke of often and with high regard. This *was* a big deal.

"You and Cassandra can work together on Wednesday, the twenty-fourth. Afterward, the three of us will meet up for dinner. Then, before she flies back to Atlanta on Thursday, she and I will spend some time together to discuss district business."

Allie nodded. "Okay then. Let your new boss know I'm looking forward to working with her."

"I'll do that." Kevin's typically mid-range voice suddenly sounded husky. "Also, Allie, I'm going to need you to do a presentation to our district at the National Sales meeting in Denver during the first week of November. Our breakout session will be on Wednesday. Since you have such great rapport with your key physicians and their staff members, I'd like you to share ten or so of your best practices. Start by making a list of what's been working for you in the field. I'll drop by your storage unit after I finish up with Cassandra, and we can go over your list at that time. That gives you a week and a half to prepare." He combed a hand through his hair. "You *will* put this on your schedule, won't you?"

Allie lifted her brow. "I haven't stood you up yet, have I?"

"No, no, you haven't. I just want to make sure we get you as prepared as possible for the meeting. I tell you, Allie, this Cassandra Hartwell is one terrific lady. I talked to her briefly during our manager's meeting at the home office two weeks ago, and wow! She has this fantastic voice—so smooth and self-assured. And her list of career accomplishments is impressive. We discussed our backgrounds on the phone yesterday, and I found out she comes from the medical device industry. I'd sure like our district to make a lasting first impression on her."

"Okay, Kevin, one topic at a time. The presentation?"

"Right. Let's see, uh, I'd also like you to handle sales objections. Again, I've seen how you work. When a doctor tells you he's not sure he should prescribe our products, you give him five great reasons why he should."

Various women had described the never-married, thirty-seven-year-old Kevin as poetic, sophisticated, dashing, super smart, or—Allie's all-time favorite—painfully adorable. And although she supposed he was all of that, in Allie's eyes Kevin was simply a kind and honest man. He gave her lots of support and room to be herself. For that reason, she felt enormous gratitude. "Thanks for the vote of confidence, Kevin."

"You're welcome, and thank *you* for always being such a trooper. Listen, later today I'll email you the itinerary for the meeting and for a few other items that might help you prepare. Oh, and before I forget, there's something else I think you should know. It seems congratulations are in order. I found out this morning you've got the best numbers in the entire western region."

Allie grinned and looked at the menu. She just might have to get an order of thick cinnamon French toast this morning . . . in celebration of the inevitable accomplishment of her goal.

* * *

It was just before nine A.M., and Allie was pulling the SUV into a parking space in front of the West Valley Medical Plaza in Encino when Kevin rubbed his palms together. "Okay, what's your plan of action?"

Allie turned off the engine and stared at Kevin. What was up with him? "You never ask me that question."

"I know. But I *should*. You need to be assessed on that kind of thing, remember?" His eyes, normally a golden hazel, had taken on a jade-green hue, which meant a shift into full-blown business mode.

"Okay, okay. I'll go along with it, but you know I work better when my ideas flow naturally."

Allie realized the reason for Kevin's sudden micromanaging. He wanted to be able to tell his new boss he was a "by the book" manager who made sure all his reps maintained accurate pre- and post-call notes on every visit to their physicians' offices. And even Cassandra herself would likely be checking up on Allie. In reality, Allie *did* do everything according to company protocol—just not always in the company's neatly prescribed and highly recommended order.

"My POA is to get some sit-down time with Dr. Miner and follow up on our discussion from my last visit, two weeks ago."

"And what did—?"

41

"First, I went over the Harvard clinical trial reprint with her. She was impressed with the results. Then I gave her feedback from other rheumatolotists who've gotten similar results with Advantol's pain relief and low sedation. Patients remain functional, and that makes everyone happy."

"How is Dr. Miner ranked among your anti-inflammatory prescribers?"

"Number fifteen. I've called on her for two months and left samples she says she's given to patients, along with new scripts. That's true; I noticed her activity on a recent data report. On my last visit, I passed her as I left the sample room. I asked if I could help her find anything in particular, and she laughed because obviously the *only* product I could help her find was one of my own. And guess what? She just happened to be looking for samples of a once a day, nonnarcotic, anti-inflammatory pain reliever. A top prescriber in the class, almost impossible to catch while she's seeing patients, and just like that," Allie snapped her fingers, "our paths cross."

Allie continued, "So," she reached into the backseat for her handheld computer, "I guess I'm still getting her warmed up. These docs mean well, but they're incredibly busy; and with twenty or more reps a day coming in bombarding them with info on so many different products, they forget a lot of it."

"It wasn't like this when I was a sales rep," Kevin reminisced with a headshake. "Now I hear about visits from three different reps per company per day."

"And *I'm* competing with all of them for one-on-one time with the doc." Allie powered up the device in her hand and looked over the information on the small screen.

"Be glad you have a computer, Allie. I remember when we did all our work on paper." Kevin made a little scoffing sound. "*Everything.* Like writing call notes and listing inventory; even getting the doctor's signature for samples. You guys have it easy these days."

"Easy? Using a computer has its own issues, don't forget. But thankfully, after almost five years I can practically do this job in my sleep."

In my sleep . . .

Painful details from Allie's recent dream flashed inside her head like a movie trailer. Actually, she couldn't say whether it was the dream that played on her inner viewscreen or the memory that the dream portrayed.

It's a cold and cloudy late-October afternoon. Thirteen-year-old Allie sits in her Grandma Mary's bedroom, monitoring her sleep, enduring her drawn-out death. Suddenly, Mary's heavy eyelids open, and she looks at Allie. "It's time for me to go now." Her voice is so weak Allie can barely make out the words.

"No!" Allie scoops up her grandmother's bony hand and holds it with a tight grip. "Don't leave me, Grandma. Don't leave me alone."

"Let me go, Sweetie."

Tears well up in Allie's eyes, burning them, blurring her vision. "No." She knows she sounds like a scared little girl.

Forcing a thin smile, Mary takes in a short, labored breath. "Don't be afraid to go to him, Allison. He loves you. He will take care of you."

"Allie?" Kevin gently grasped her shoulder.

Allie whipped her head around and blinked at him. As she involuntarily said, "What?," she realized where she was.

He frowned then laughed. "That must have been some daydream."

He had no idea. Allie shook her head. "Sorry. You were saying?"

Kevin opened the passenger door. "I asked if you were ready to go make a sale."

Chapter 4

Drama Queen

Tuesday morning at eight-thirty, Allie opened her front door to a lazy-lidded Bobbie Brennan bearing blueberry bagels, bran muffins, and an old-fashioned buttermilk doughnut for, as Bobbie called Gretchen, "the junk food junkie."

Allie hadn't seen Bobbie for a couple of years, the last time being at the surprise thirtieth birthday party Gretchen had arranged for Bobbie, but the differences between the two best friends remained.

Gretchen, on the one hand, was short and, although not over-weight, she was definitely more on the curvy side. Her overall look was one of high maintenance. She had a restless demeanor and always wore a sassy smile along with her fancy outfits. Bobbie, on the other hand, at about five-foot-eight, was built like a swimmer, lean with broad shoulders. She had a straightforward, uncompli-cated manner, shoulder-length, dark brown hair layered in a simple style, and nearly stock facial features that seemed to be weighed down by a permanent frown. Her casual attire most often consisted of blue jeans, tee shirts, and either flip-flops or sneakers. The contrast between the two women was stunning, so much so that Allie, not for the first time, marveled at their compatibility.

Bobbie tossed the brown paper bag of bagels onto the dining room table. After setting a small white bakery box next to the bag, she pulled out a chair, sat down, and looked at Gretchen. "FYI, your sugar fix is in here, away from the healthy stuff." As Allie and Gretchen took their seats, Bobbie pulled a napkin from the holder in the center of the table and removed a large bran muffin from the bag.

"Okay, Bobbie, here's what we have so far," Gretchen said. "Allie and I already measured everything and figured out what goes in the bedroom, what goes in the loft area at the top of the stairs, and what goes in the garage."

"I'm all ears." The words expressed in Bobbie's unrelenting monotone voice, were like a verbal "ho hum." She extricated a dark raisin from the muffin and tossed it into her mouth.

"Joshua left me a message this morning saying they'd be here by nine o'clock." Gretchen sighed. "Mm, that voice of his, so smooth and delicious . . . like fudgy European truffles." She shrugged. "What can I say? I'm a chocoholic."

Bobbie stared for a moment at Gretchen. "You're also a *talk*oholic."

"Okay, so I am. So what? I'm supposed to be quiet all of a sudden?" Gretchen said, making momentary use of an emphatic Bronx accent. She shook her head and reached for the white box. "Listen, Bobbie, I saved Joshua's message. You wanna hear it?"

"Well, let me put it this way . . ." Bobbie was practical, matter-of-fact and, for the most part, easily unimpressed. "No. I don't. I'll hear his voice soon enough, will I not?"

Gretchen wrinkled her nose and patted Bobbie's taut cheek. "Yes, you will, my crabby little Roberta Ramona Brennan."

Bobbie's face set in a hard stare. "Do *not* call me that."

Allie got up out of her chair. "Who's ready for coffee?"

Gretchen raised her hand. "Oh, I am. And I must get something into my stomach before the boys arrive. I'm going to need all the strength I can get."

Allie tilted her head toward a large truck's deep rumbling sound; it was obviously pulling up in front of the townhouse.

"Too late." Bobbie looked toward the front door. "Sounds like they're already here."

Gretchen was first out the front door, sashaying down the driveway like a petite clothing model on a catwalk, while Bobbie and Allie stood in the entryway and watched. Joshua grinned at Gretchen as he jumped down from the cab of the truck. The words *Walden and Sons Moving* were painted on the side of the long, white trailer. When Gretchen reached Joshua, she leaned in close and spoke to him in a voice so low that no one else could hear, but Allie already knew what was on Gretchen's mind. On the drive back from the airport, after she'd entertained Allie with the long story of her initial discovery of the magnificent Joshua, Gretchen had laid out in great detail her plans for him.

Joshua made his way toward the house with Gretchen sticking to him like blonde, flocked wallpaper. A good-natured chuckle belied his darting eyes and stiffened gait. Right away, Allie gave him extra points for high tolerance. He had straw-colored hair with a slightly wind-blown style, and he looked to be no more than five-foot-nine. His tanned, well-toned physique begged for a sunny beach on which to lie and a killer wave on which to ride. Gretchen was right about Joshua being handsome but, at five-foot-seven, Allie preferred much taller men, six foot or more. She also preferred a more understated look. And darker hair . . .

"Here we go again." Bobbie stretched out an arm in Joshua's direction, announcing, "May I present the latest flavor of the week—sea spray."

"Gretchen really seems to like him," Allie observed.

"Yup. She likes 'em all. She has to because she thinks if she doesn't find a man soon, she'll never be married."

"Really? I can't believe she'd have a problem finding a boyfriend."

"She doesn't have a problem finding boyfriends, Allie. She can't find anyone who wants her for a wife."

* * *

At twelve-thirty, with the move in its final stages of completion, all three ladies were up in Gretchen's room. Allie was tired but had volunteered anyway to unpack two giant cardboard boxes filled with angora sweaters and delicate things, such as silk scarves and camisoles. Because it looked to her like Gretchen had thrown everything into the boxes in sixty seconds flat, Allie took her time sorting through and folding the items before placing them in the armoire drawers. While inside the walk-in closet, arranging and rearranging her dresses, skirts, jackets, slacks, and blouses, Gretchen gleefully sang out a convoluted mash-up of several Christina Aguilera songs.

Directly behind Allie, Bobbie sat on the edge of the Gretchen's bare yellow-floral mattress, skimming through an issue of *Female in Fashion*. Allie turned her head in time to see Bobbie drop the magazine, stand up, and announce, "I want lunch."

Gretchen jumped out from the closet, gripping a fistful of white plastic hangers and promptly abandoning the almost unrecognizable lyrics to *Genie in a Bottle*. "Oh, me too! I only got a chance to nibble on half a bagel."

"Is that right?" Bobbie examined Gretchen with tapered eyelids. "And I was so sure that it was *you* stuffing a big ol' chunk of doughnut down your gullet when you thought no one was looking."

Joshua's face popped into view from the hallway. "I guess that about does it, ladies." He looked at Gretchen. "Is everything okay in here? Any changes you'd like us to make before we go?"

She froze, but a slight jittering of her eyeballs suggested brain wave activity. Allie figured Gretchen was sizing up Joshua for something other than furniture rearrangement—like carrying her toward the Honeymoon Suite and lifting her over a threshold. "Oh, uh no, everything is great, thank you, but Bobbie was wondering if you two would like to join us for lunch?"

"I was what?" Bobbie mumbled, not exactly under her breath.

Gretchen shifted her hips. "We could get sub sandwiches or pizza, whatever you like. You've been so helpful, and I, uh, we couldn't let you leave hungry."

"Thanks a lot. That's thoughtful of you." Joshua smiled and looked around, acknowledging everyone. "Anything you choose would be fine with us."

*   *   *

After Joshua and Steven left the townhouse to fuel up the truck, Gretchen asked Allie for the best place in town to get pizza. Allie would've named Caruso's, but Bobbie began an immediate protest against pizza, calling it "starchy dough slathered with tinny tomato paste, dotted with greasy pepperoni, and dripping with stringy melted cheese." She managed to make one of Allie's favorite foods sound surprisingly gross.

So, Allie instead suggested they get lunch at Subliminal. "It's a sandwich shop and deli, about a mile away. The floors and tables are always clean, and the food is good. I've never gotten sick from eating there," Allie added, figuring that might bolster her argument. She looked toward Bobbie, who shrugged and made a *"yeah, why not?"* face.

"Good." Gretchen stepped closer to the girls and, in a mock huddle, placed an arm across each of their shoulders, saying, "Now here's the plan." Assembling her impromptu panel of judges, she designated Bobbie as driver and first chair, and Allie as passenger and alternate second opinion. "We have a significant potential-boyfriend verdict to come to while we go get lunch."

Ten minutes later they arrived at Subliminal, located among a row of restaurants and shops set on a busy corner in mini-mall fashion. The family-run eatery offered the longest submarine sandwich in East Hills, as evidenced by an eight-foot plastic hoagie that had been mounted to the deli's roof. Finding parking was usually a nightmare because there were only eight spaces for as many businesses, but a spot became available as soon as Bobbie pulled inside the lot.

Bright sunshine poured through the deli's glass-paned front, reflecting off the white tile that seemed to line every inch of Subliminal's interior. The smell of cold cuts and potato chips helped cover up the slight bleachy scent that Allie detected as she stood in line with Gretchen and Bobbie. When they reached the front counter, Gretchen placed the lunch order for everyone.

"Okay, let me see if I got this right." The teen behind the counter appeared to be half-awake. "That's three large turkey, cheese and avocado, with mustard, no mayo, no onion, extra pickles and one Caesar salad, to go. Any chips with that?" He didn't bother looking up.

Gretchen waved a hand. "No."

"Cookies?"

"No."

"Drinks?"

Bobbie weighed in. "Look, junior, don't you think if we wanted any of that garbage we would've told you in the first place?"

Gretchen pulled a twenty and a five out of her brown Louis Vuitton wallet and handed them to the young man. His mouth dropped open in a gaping yawn he didn't bother trying to suppress. The cash register beeped with each press of a key until the mystery was revealed—twenty cents change due. He placed a receipt and two dimes in Gretchen's palm, thanking her with a complete lack of enthusiasm.

The three sat down in the only available booth to wait for the food. The conversation that started the moment they got in Bobbie's Jeep continued. Subject: To Joshua or not to Joshua. It was a topic Gretchen was passionate about. Allie, not so much. And Bobbie, even less so.

Gretchen wasn't easily deterred once set on a course of action. She made Bobbie list the pros and cons all over again. It didn't take long for the pros: He seemed to be a decent guy, and he was cute.

Everything else was a con. This category included the following facts, guesses, and outright assumptions: The man drove a truck for a living, and, as such, probably didn't have two nickels to rub together (although Gretchen pointed out that Joshua was in school studying, as she put it, "something or other," which she determined could mean that a better job with more money was in the cards—for *her*); he lived in a rental house at the beach, which, as Bobbie pointed out, made him a "beach bum" (however, Gretchen reminded everyone that Joshua was in school, but again had no clue as to why); and finally, Bobbie coughed up the coup de gras: Joshua was just too nice, which, in her words was, "kinda weird."

Gretchen tapped her red nails on the wood-grain Formica tabletop. "But I really like him. If I don't try *something*, I might miss out on an opportunity to find," she raised her hands, making quotation marks with her fingers, "my dreamboat. You know me. Miss Determination. I say, 'Where there's a will, there's a way.'"

"And I say, 'Where there's a will, there's a *won't*,'" Bobbie countered.

"Oh, excuse me for being optimistic, Gloom Hilda." Gretchen turned her back on Bobbie. "I'd like to hear what Allie has to say."

"*Three turkey, cheese, avocado and a Caesar, ready to go,*" announced a scratchy voice from beyond the counter.

Not a moment too soon.

* * *

Upon their return from the deli, Allie suggested that Bobbie park the Jeep in front of Gloria's unit. "As long as it doesn't leak oil," Allie cautioned, recalling Gloria's longstanding issue with her Firebird.

Gretchen cackled, sounding like a hen trying to lay an enormous egg. "Are you kidding? If that car of Bobbie's misbehaved by leaking oil, she'd push it over a cliff!"

Carrying the white plastic bag of sandwiches and salad, Allie lagged a couple paces behind Gretchen and Bobbie as they trooped toward Allie's unit. The moving van appeared at the top of Ridgeview, and Gretchen fluffed her hair. Bobbie shook her head. She turned toward Gretchen, offering what must have been Bobbie's version of encouragement: "Well, kid, you're on your own."

"Thanks, Sugar" Gretchen drawled. She perked up once the three were inside the house. "But you might be surprised to see a different side of Joshua before he leaves today. I haven't finished working all my angles yet."

Allie set her purse down on a wicker chair. "Can I help you sort out the lunch?"

"No, no." Gretchen took the bag from Allie and smiled at Joshua when he and Steven came through the front door. "I'll take care of it."

"Okay then. I'm going out in the backyard if anyone would like to join me."

"Count me in." Joshua grinned at Allie, who ignored Gretchen's quick scowl.

While Gretchen went in the kitchen and Steven made phone calls in the living room, Allie and Joshua went outside, where a warm Santa Ana wind breezed through the yard. They sat down and relaxed in two Adirondack chairs set out on the thick, Bermuda grass. Joshua noted that the plants surrounding the grass were still in bloom. Allie told him that she enjoyed tending to her garden and that she'd chosen the magenta bougainvillea, the roses with the variegated petals, and the orange and blue bird of paradise specifically for their brilliant colors.

49

Joshua was easy to talk to, Allie found. Within a few minutes, they'd discovered they'd both earned life science degrees—Allie had studied biology as an undergrad at UC Irvine, and Joshua majored in kinesiology as an undergrad and current graduate student at Pepperdine.

Allie chuckled softly to herself, remembering that during the ride home from the airport Gretchen mentioned how "stupendant" Joshua had looked in Dallas in his Pepperdine University tee shirt. "My best friend, Beth, is also working toward a Masters degree at Pepperdine," Allie told Joshua. "She'll be graduating next year with an MFCC," which Allie explained stood for marriage, family, and child counselor.

From school and career, they shifted to relationships. Joshua said that he'd experienced a revelation a week earlier, on his twenty-eighth birthday. Though not currently in a serious relationship, he felt he was at an age where his focus should be on finding that "special someone" . . . a woman to whom he could commit for the long haul.

"Honestly, I've never been one for casual dating." He explained how he'd had a steady girlfriend as a teenager and then dated a couple girls in college for over a year each. "When I was with them, I was *with* them; but when I realized my heart wasn't in it, I broke it off."

"And trampled their hearts in the process. Tsk tsk." Allie grinned and winked.

"Oh, no, my friend. Yours truly got the wind knocked out of him when his beloved high school sweetheart, Ronni Sue . . ."

"Ronni Sue?" Allie's grin widened. "You must not have grown up 'round these parts, son."

"Okay, okay," Joshua conceded, raising his right hand. "Her name was Veronica Susanne. I used to make her mad by introducing her to people as Ronni Sue and saying that when we first met she was missing her two front teeth."

"You didn't!"

"I did. And it was true. I just left out a couple facts, like that we were both eight years old and in the same Sunday school class."

"Oh, Joshua," Allie shook her head. "You are *too* much."

He laughed for a moment as he recalled the memory and then stopped grinning. "Hey, I've got an idea." He whispered something into Allie's ear that only she could have heard.

Allie nodded. "Let's do it."

They both stood. Quietly leaving the backyard, they entered the house and scurried upstairs.

* * *

Several minutes later, while Joshua washed up for lunch in the master bathroom, Allie descended the stairs. She glimpsed Steven seated on the living room sofa, writing in an appointment book. When she reached the bottom step, Allie heard Gretchen and Bobbie talking in the kitchen. She couldn't see them; from Allie's vantage point, she could only see the entrance to the kitchen. The two women were probably near the sink counter in front of the window.

"I've got some bad news for you, Drama Queen," Allie overheard Bobbie say to Gretchen.

Allie moved past Steven and headed into the dining room, pausing just outside the kitchen entrance. She peered in. With her back to Allie, Bobbie stood in front of the window, looking out into the backyard. Though Allie couldn't see her cousin, she knew Gretchen was next to Bobbie near the refrigerator. Allie watched Bobbie drop her left hand to a nearby sub sandwich on the counter and pluck out a piece of diced pickle.

"I think you'd better forget about Joshua." Bobbie popped the little chunk into her mouth.

Gretchen gasped. "Why? What happened? *Did he say something?*"

Allie still couldn't see Gretchen from where she stood, only Bobbie, who continued to de-pickle a sub as she said, "You know that I went to get a magazine out of your room a few minutes ago, right? Well, when I got to the top of the stairs, I happened to look to the left and I noticed Allie's bedroom was empty." Bobbie turned to glance in Gretchen's direction, saying, "Side note, not necessarily significant. Anyway, I then turned right and headed across the loft toward your bathroom. But when I got to the bathroom door, I heard voices behind me, down the hall. Your bedroom door was almost closed, making it difficult to hear what was being said. So I moved a little closer." Bobbie raised her hands flat in front of her, leaving a few inches gap through which to pretend-peek. "Looking through the cracked door, I could see Allie and Joshua standing in front of each other in the middle of the room."

Gretchen gave a quick exhale through her nose in a snort-like scoff. "Big whoop. So they were standing in the middle of my—"

"Holding hands."

After emitting a low growl, which reminded Allie of her childhood terrier, Freddie, she heard Gretchen retort, "If that's supposed to be a joke, I don't think it's very funny."

"No joke."

"*Bobbie! I don't understand!*" Gretchen nearly yelped.

51

"Well, it's like this, DQ," Bobbie reached for another pickle. "He and your little cousin were praying together over your room."

This time Gretchen hissed through her teeth, making a noise like a fuming mad teakettle. "*Oh, for crying out loud! What did Allie do to him?*"

* * *

Two days later, after an exhausting day in the field, Allie found herself seated in the faded pink vintage armchair in a corner of Gretchen's messy room. Before Gretchen's insistent invitation, Allie had been quite comfortable reading her murder mystery on the living room sofa. Allie knew Gretchen's request was for Gretchen's benefit. She needed something. Company? A willing (or even unwilling but captive) ear?

Allie had been looking forward to a couple hours of quiet time, and she loved to curl up on the wicker sofa with a good book. She realized the sofa didn't *look* comfortable, until you stretched out on it with a cushy jersey knit covered pillow behind your head. Actually, she enjoyed spending time in her living room because of the décor's soothing pastel colors. She had painted the walls herself, using a satin-finish paint called Sweet Buttercup. The sofa and matching chair cushions had been custom made in a misty heather cotton chintz fabric, while the colors periwinkle, spring green, and orchid could be found on the covers of three toss pillows—and inside a box of 64 Crayola crayons. The natural cream-colored floor brightened up the room, making it look bigger than its three hundred square feet. Allie thought the room reflected the professional woman she'd become, and it gave her a sense of accomplishment and satisfaction.

At the moment, though, Allie was *not* in her living room, calm and relaxed. Surrounded by Gretchen's knick-knackish belongings and being subjected to her obsessive nattering about men, Allie felt like she had gone back in time twelve years to hang out with a girlfriend and to discuss who was cute and who had passed a note to whom, saying, "Do you like so and so?" Before Gretchen moved in, Allie had used the spare room as her home office and study. It had been sparse in comparison to its current state, but like the living room, it had been a quiet spot where Allie could read or work on her laptop. She would sit at her simple oak desk and plan physician call cycles, fill out expense reports, or evaluate current sales data. An off-white metal filing cabinet and a couple of bookcases made from wood that was darker than the desk (probably walnut) had been the only other items in the room.

Allie, however, had asked Joshua to move the desk and an ergonomic task chair to the master bedroom, the bookcases to the loft, and the filing cabinet to the garage. Now, the ten-by-twelve foot spare room seemed overcrowded with Gretchen's bulky furniture, which was constructed from knotty pine and purchased solely because it matched that behemoth armoire bequeathed to Gretchen by her maternal, as she called her, grandmuh-ma. Gretchen had instructed Joshua and Steven to put her long narrow dresser along the doorway wall—on the left upon entering—and to set the four-post queen-sized bed directly across from the door. The pink chair and the armoire had been placed on either side of a picture window at the far left end of the room. Cosmetics, jewelry, and jars of potions, lotions, creams, and candles cluttered up every flat surface not already occupied by an issue of *Female in Fashion*. In some cases, the clutter sat on *top* of the magazine.

As if Gretchen's idle chatter wasn't intrusive enough, Allie's quiet time was soon to be interrupted further by a visit from Bobbie Brennan. Seconds after Allie had settled into the pink chair, Bobbie had called and announced over the speakerphone, "I'll be there when I get there. This traffic is a bearcat. I hate the 405."

Allie was holding out hope that she might eventually make her date with the book and her living room. Gretchen and Bobbie had plans to go to the Glendale Galleria to look for some new dance club fashions, along the lines of those featured in several magazine clippings spread out on Gretchen's rumpled aquamarine comforter.

"Let yourself in," Gretchen had told Bobbie, "I left the front door unlocked."

Allie's forehead tightened at that disconcerting bit of info, which now had her questioning the wisdom of allowing her cousin to move in with her.

After Bobbie hung up, Allie tried to return to her book while Gretchen finished painting her toenails bright pink. The sharp smell of ethyl acetate sparred with the sweet scent of a candle that burned on top of Gretchen's armoire. The candle was ahead on points, but the ethyl acetate was still on its feet.

With a pillow behind her head, one leg crossed over the other and foot bouncing, Gretchen now voiced her thoughts about what had taken place earlier in the week. "Okay, so maybe Babe Joshua is sort of religious. No reason to make a fuss over it, right? He seems really sweet. And he never tried pushing me into anything. *Unlike* frequent flyer, Alan from Fresno, who insisted he couldn't date anyone who hadn't been baptized. That nitwit almost drowned me in a Jacuzzi."

"Do you think I could borrow your nail polish sometime?" Allie knew her question might give away her total lack of interest in Gretchen's ruminations, but she figured Gretchen either wouldn't notice or more likely, wouldn't care.

Scrunching her face, Gretchen pointed at the small square bottle she'd just set on her glass-topped nightstand. *"That one?"* she asked, in a voice that implied Allie had taken leave of her senses.

The front door slammed shut with a sucking crack, sending vibrating ripples through the townhouse. Gretchen called out, "We're up here!" then tossed the bright pink polish to Allie. "Knock yourself out."

Not a moment later, Bobbie, wearing a black femme and fitted boyfriend blazer over a pair of black bootcut slacks, appeared in the doorway and paused. Her dark brown hair was pulled back with a claw clip, highlighting the angularity of her face. She'd mentioned in her call that she'd be coming straight from Hollister McMahan Mortuary, the place where she played the role of compassionate funeral director. This role constituted the other side of Bobbie's hard-to-define personality—a side Allie never would have believed existed had she not seen it for herself when her family used the services of Hollister McMahan.

The then twenty-year-old Bobbie had been assigned by the funeral home to handle the details of Grandma Mary's memorial service and burial. Gretchen showed up at the service to pay her, as she put it, "final regards." And it was there that she made the acquaintance of the young funeral director in attendance, Bobbie, thus beginning the most peculiar friendship between the two.

Lifting her chin toward Allie in greeting, Bobbie inhaled deeply and gestured toward the frosted glass votive atop the armoire. "Let me guess. Lite of the Party, Bodacious Berry."

Gretchen rolled her eyes. "Wrong."

"Amazing Grape? I always get those two confused," Bobbie muttered.

"No, silly. It's Blazin' Raisin."

"Well, I was close. Wasn't a raisin a *grape* before it became a *raisin?*" Bobbie entered the room.

"Come over here and sit down." Still propped up against a large aquamarine pillow edged in white ruffles, Gretchen patted her bed. "You're gonna *love* this month's exercise on Calculating Your Charisma Quotient."

Bobbie's left eyebrow popped up. Allie had learned from past observation this meant Bobbie was paying attention—or possibly even slightly interested. According to Gretchen, for the past several issues of their favorite magazine, *Female in Fashion*, she and

Bobbie had been studying the column, *How to Find the Man of Your Dreams and Make him Your Own.* So far, though, neither woman could claim victory in making the man of her dreams her own, or, for that matter, just locating him.

Gretchen began to read. "Okay, describe yourself as a dessert. Which would you be and on what would you be served? Be as descriptive as possible. See page 176 for an assessment of your answers."

"A dessert, huh?" Bobbie plopped down on a corner of the bed and tilted her head back, squinting up at the pale yellow ceiling. "I'd have to go with apple pie."

Gretchen nodded. "What kind of apples?"

"The sour green ones I guess. I don't know what they're called. Oh, and homemade, of course."

"With a thick crust and melted cheddar cheese. Sharp." Gretchen giggled. "And what would you be served in?"

Bobbie shrugged. "Some kind of earthenware bowl."

"Ooh, I *like* that!" Gretchen chirped, using a saucy British accent. "Spot on, dear girl, spot on." She patted finger pads to palm in an enthusiastic highbrow clap.

Though Allie had attempted to keep her nose in her book, she couldn't help but watch the spectacle unfold before her. Obviously, Bobbie and Gretchen grasped the personality theme implied by the article. Good thing Allie hadn't been invited to play. Comparing herself to a dessert would be like admitting. . .

"Okay, Allie," Gretchen piped up, as though suddenly acquiring ESP, "your turn."

Allie waved the book. "No, thanks. I'll pass," she said, trying to purge from her brain the image of a single scoop of vanilla ice cream—in a paper cup.

Gretchen stuck out her lower lip and huffed. "Fine then. I'll go next," she announced, taking center stage. "I already gave my answer some thought, so listen up, girls. I would be a rich and delicious molten lava cake, lightly dusted with cocoa powder and then topped with a dollop of freshly whipped cream, raspberries, and slivers of dark chocolate, served on an ivory china plate drizzled with raspberry puree."

Bobbie made a little *eh* sound. "Not bad. Way too much sugar, though. And I don't know about all that raspberry stuff."

"Good, I'm glad you approve," Gretchen said, not sounding very glad at all. "Now you wanna go down to the kitchen and get me a Diet Coke from the fridge?"

"Truthfully, I'd like nothing more." Bobbie didn't move an inch.

"You don't have to get snippy about it. Get yourself something, too. There's Diet Coke, Diet Pepsi, Diet Seven-Up or diet peach tea."

With the conversation intensifying, Allie watched Bobbie's reaction. "Do you know how many chemicals are in that stuff?" Her face pinched in like a dehydrated apricot.

Gretchen dropped the magazine on the bed and sat up, her eyes narrowed and the skin above her nose tweaked. "No, I do not. Nor do I care. But if you're afraid of a little asparticus why don't you stop by my bathroom on your way down and fill a Dixie cup with tap water instead?"

"Maybe I will." Bobbie shot off the bed and flounced from the room.

Allie bit down on her lower lip to contain her laughter over Gretchen's mispronunciation of aspartame. Mispronouncing, misusing, or simply making up words as she spoke was something Gretchen managed to do with the greatest of ease. She also had the peculiar habit—as did Phoebe Nagata—of using accents, both foreign and domestic, to emphasize a point.

"Hey, Allie." Gretchen's voice shifted so quickly from sharp to fawnlike and demure that Allie blinked several times and stared at her cousin.

Gretchen slid down the bed and sat on the edge, directly across from Allie. "Whatever happened to your friend, Andrew? The guy I met at your graduation party."

Allie blinked again. She was feeling a little like Alice, down the rabbit hole. She'd forgotten how dizzying it could be to get pulled into Gretchen's world. "You remember Andrew? I'm surprised."

"Oh, heavens." Gretchen waved a hand. "I always remember the best-looking men in the room." She'd traded in her saucy British for sweet Southern.

Allie once again wanted to laugh but was too hung up on the idea of "best-looking." The twenty-two-year-old Andrew at Allie's graduation party had been a skinny young man who was still dealing with a fairly respectable case of acne. He'd had long, surfer-boy hair and a distinct gawkiness about him. He was the nicest guy Allie had ever met, for sure, and he was, then anyway, a rock-solid friend, though no one Gretchen would have paid any attention to. What was she talking about?

"Are you sure you remember him from my graduation party?" Allie asked.

Placing a temporary hold on both the saucy *and* the sweet, Gretchen exclaimed, "Oh, absolutely! Tall, with great teeth and a beautiful smile. Strong and masculine, but also kinda gentle in the way he moved and spoke. And how could I forget those deep-brown, passionate eyes?"

Passionate eyes? *Andrew?* Allie shook her head. Gretchen had inhaled too many nail polish fumes. And Allie didn't want to be part of any more "he's so cute" conversations anyway. She just wanted to get back to her book. The story had begun heating up before Bobbie's arrival, and now the novel's main character was trying to find a biblical way to deal with a close friend who'd just stabbed her in the back.

Allie sighed and closed the book. Marking the place with her thumb she answered Gretchen's original question. "Andrew went into the Navy after college. I've only seen him once since then, two years ago. His folks invited me to a family gathering they had during his leave. I'd started dating this guy Carl, someone Andrew and I knew from school. Andrew's mom suggested I bring him, so I did." Allie shrugged.

"A *boyfriend?* Oh, do tell!"

"We dated for a while."

"And you took him to Andrew's parents' house, huh? *That* was a bold statement."

Allie had no comment, dismissing the ridiculous idea she'd been making a bold statement—or any kind of statement at all. Why was Gretchen making such a big deal about something that had happened two years ago?

"Where did you two first meet?" Gretchen asked.

"Who?"

"You and Andrew!"

Resigned to give in to the interrogation, in hopes of gaining a little peace, Allie sighed. "Elementary school."

"Wow. Really? What was he like way back then?"

Allie removed her thumb from her book. She marked her spot with a piece of scrap paper and placed the book on a table made from wood similar to the arms of the pink chair. "Shy and reserved, but everyone seemed to like him."

"So, you've been friends ever since you were tiny tots?"

"No, we were more like acquaintances, not actually friends. Not until the summer before tenth grade, anyway," Allie said, revisiting the turning point in her friendship with Andrew. "He'd invited me and a few other people from our school to a week-long youth retreat through his church."

"*His church?*" Gretchen fell back dramatically on her bed. "Oh, I can't take any more. Please do *not* tell me he's a Bible thumper like you and Joshua?" She sat back up. "No offense, Allie."

Allie shook her head. If she let Gretchen's frequent antichurch sentiments offend her, the two of them wouldn't have a relationship. "Yes, he is a *'Bible thumper.'*"

"Hmm. That changes things."

"What things?"

Gretchen once again waved a hand. "Um, never mind. Back to the story."

Did Allie want to go back to the story? She took a deep breath. Yes, she did. For some reason, she needed to pull it from its mental box and air it out. "Okay, well, Beth had recently transferred to our high school, and we'd become pretty close, so I asked Andrew if I could invite her. He said I could, and two weeks later we all boarded a bus and headed to Big Bear Lake." Allie caught herself staring at her lap and paused. She glanced up at Gretchen, who was now leaning forward, fully engaged.

Allie figured she might as well keep going. "I remember thinking, after arriving at the retreat location, how calm and peaceful it was up there, all woodsy and rustic with those huge pine trees, the beautiful lake, and the clear fresh air. We stayed in a group of cabins right off the lake, boys in one large cabin, girls in the other with the counselors in between."

"I'm curious about something." Gretchen's head tilted. "Why would you squander valuable summer time to go on a retreat with a bunch of church kids? It seems like it would be an utter and colossal waste of time, if you ask me."

The reality was that Allie had just wanted to get away. She'd been carrying around in her heart painful emotions like anger, grief, frustration, disappointment, and even shame, and she'd needed to find a way to escape it all for a while. But she wasn't going to reveal this to Gretchen.

Before Allie could figure out a casual response, Gretchen said, "Unless you went there to check out the guys."

After hanging around her "bad girl" neighbor, Karen Davies, for more than a year, chasing guys had been the last thing on Allie's mind, but trying to explain that concept to Gretchen would be nothing short of impossible. So Allie gave her the answer she expected. "The thought may have crossed my mind."

"Mm hmm. You were after Andrew, weren't you?"

"I didn't think of Andrew that way."

"Well, Sunshine, if you weren't after *him,* then he must've had a fancy for *you.*" Gretchen's sweet Southern drawl had returned.

"No. No fancies, on either part. Ask Beth; remember, she was there the whole time."

"Allie, why would he ask you to go on a romantic mountain retreat if he wasn't crazy about you?" The drawl disappeared once again, and Allie felt her eyes crossing for another trip down the rabbit hole.

"First, I never used the word *romantic*, and second—"

"Oh please. School's out for the summer. You're in boy-crazy mode, away from home for a whole week. The place is gorgeous, peaceful, *and right by a lake, for heaven's sake!* A guy invites you up there, and you don't think he's been dreaming about you, pining away for your love and devotion?"

Why did Allie need a novel? Gretchen was doing a good job of making up a fictional scenario on the spot. Allie blew out air and tapped her book against her thigh. "Look, I'm pretty good at reading peoples' motivations and intentions. Andrew was never one for secret agendas or skullduggery." She smiled to herself, finding the idea almost comical. Andrew Gallagher was more the old-fashioned type, if anything, and would never have behaved the way Gretchen was suggesting.

Gretchen pursed her lips. "It's not hard to figure something like that out, you know. You must have had some of the same classes."

"We had several classes together, but he and his friends were quiet and studious. We each hung out with our own crowds. Different kinds of people."

"Oh, you mean people like that troublemaker who lived down the street from you? What was her name again?" Gretchen giggled, forcing Allie to once again recall the close, and destructive, alliance she'd formed with Karen Davies.

The pain of dealing with her father's death and then her grandma's lingering illness had been too much for the barely teenaged Allie. So, in an effort to "run away" from the life she felt trapped in, she began emulating the behavior of her rebel neighbor. Karen was unlike any kid Allie had ever hung out with. She considered herself a grunge rocker, and she looked every bit the part, with thick black eyeliner, blue-black hair, and ear piercings galore. Karen had also sported the ultimate mark of rebellion, a small spikey-headed skull, tattooed on her hip by the brother of another neighborhood delinquent, Rachel Enriquez. Yes, Allie's new friends did whatever they pleased and cared little about what others thought. Tagging along with Karen promised to be a lot more interesting and much less painful for Allie than dealing with her own life circumstances.

Unfortunately though, smoking cigarettes—and occasionally something else—stealing munchies from the local 7–11, fooling around with much older guys, and drinking the hard stuff wasn't as fun as it initially sounded. When Allie's pain followed her into her new world, she finally realized that the solution to her problems would not be found in head-pounding hangovers, becoming a so-called "woman of the world," or letting her grades drop. In fact, with her self-respect in the tank, she hurt even worse. By the end of ninth grade, her friendship with Karen had showed signs of withering. Then, less than two months into their freshman year of high school, while in one of the restrooms, Karen picked a fight with a smart, pretty, and popular girl named Geniece Bertinelli. Karen shoved the petite senior so hard that the girl slipped and hit her head against the edge of a porcelain sink, sustaining a mild concussion. Only a bystander at the time, but deemed guilty by association (and truthfully, she felt guilty for standing by and doing nothing), Allie found herself being suspended for one week over the incident. Karen, however, was expelled from school and sent out of state to live with her father, leaving Allie to deal with the wreckage of what had been, before she'd taken a walk on the wild side, a halfway respectable social life.

Allie waved her hand through the air, as if she could wipe away the memories Gretchen's questions had brought up. "That was a long time ago. I was young and stupid, and I paid the price for it."

Gretchen rolled her head around. "Okay, okay. Sorry. Get back to the story already."

Allie straightened her back and gazed down at her feet. She thought about how Andrew had told her to pack for warm days and cool nights, and how she'd borrowed one of Beth's swimming suits, a one-piece with blue and white flowers. She knew Gretchen would have some comment about that. Gretchen often called Beth "the Amazonian," scoffing at Beth's height, probably because Gretchen wished she could have a few inches of it. Allie let memories of her days at Big Bear Lake play out like a mental slide show: The group discussions, receiving spiritual advice from the camp counselors, going on nature hikes, playing games, swimming, sitting around a campfire singing songs while toasting marshmallows, and—most important of all—finding a savior in Jesus Christ.

Allie stood. She wasn't going to share any of this with Gretchen, who would just have something disparaging to say anyway.

"Where are you going?" Gretchen demanded as Allie stepped toward the bedroom door.

"I have a headache. I need to lie down."

The conversation felt as though it had taken a sharp turn down a rough and bumpy road, depleting Allie of her desire to discuss the retreat any longer. Maybe what had happened at Big Bear Lake was a bigger deal than she'd thought it was.

Chapter 5

Rosebud, Scarlett, and the Mild-Mannered Mystery Man

Because he'd missed out on running into Allie at church, Andrew returned to her townhouse at 5:30 P.M. the following Friday. He wasn't in the mood to be polite and drive his car over to the visitor's parking area; instead he pulled the Mustang right up to Allie's garage door. This way, there'd be no chance of Allie coming or going without him knowing about it. He was on a mission, and it was time to be direct.

A lanky older gentleman in a camel hair overcoat strolled down the narrow street, making tapping sounds on the asphalt with his shiny wooden walking stick. He touched the brim of his green plaid Sherlock Holmes-style cap and nodded at Andrew. "Afternoon," the man said as he ambled toward the unit across from Allie's.

"Good afternoon." Andrew waved a casual hand before he trotted up Allie's front steps and pressed the doorbell. Cheerful-sounding sparrows chirped away from within a planter of sweet honeysuckle. Andrew enjoyed their songs for the twenty seconds that passed before he heard the locks being fiddled with. The front door opened, then the safety screen.

Fiery light from the setting sun shot across the first floor and into the entryway. It distorted Andrew's vision. He heard a small panting sound followed by a near whisper of his name. To his dismay, when he was finally able to focus, he did not see what he'd hoped to find: Allie's gentle smile.

He suppressed a sigh. "Hello, Gretchen."

"Hey there, Andrew." She swayed her hips to the right.

"Is Allie home?"

"Uh, no." Her eyes darted around. "You know, as a matter of fact, you just missed her."

And do you know, as a matter of fact, that's the second time in a week I've heard those exact words. He swallowed his impatience. "Okay. Do you know where she went or when she'll be back?"

"*That* I couldn't say." Gretchen pressed a finger to her upper lip. "Hey, would you like to join my friend Bobbie and me for dinner? We were thinking about trying that new restaurant down on Hillcrest. The Hummus & Hookah Hut. Why don't you come with?"

Andrew shook his head.

"You don't like Mediterranean food?"

"No, I do, but I—"

"Okay, we could go to the International House of Waffles and Falafels instead. Breakfast or dinner, take your pick. Their tandoori is the *best.*"

"Uh, no, but thanks anyway."

A brunette with an irritable voice and feathery hair that fell above her shoulders came into view behind Gretchen, dwarfing her by a good six inches.

"It's *tabouleh* not *tandoori,* and I'm hungry already. What's the hold up?" The woman jerked the door out of Gretchen's hand and squinted at Andrew.

"Bobbie, this is Andrew, the church boy I told you about. Remember?" Gretchen gave him such a big grin he gulped.

Bobbie glanced at her silver metal wristwatch. "Uh, well considering you just told me like ten minutes ago, I'm gonna go with *yes.*"

Church boy? Andrew shifted his feet. *I never talked to Gretchen about church. What has she been doing, following me?*

"Andrew, this is my best friend, Bobbie Brennan."

He hesitated then extended his hand. "Nice to meet you."

Bobbie leaned forward, offering a firm yet abbreviated handshake. "Likewise."

Andrew took a small step backward. "I need to get going now, so would you let Allie know I stopped . . ." He paused. "Better yet, why don't you give me her cell phone number, and I'll just call her."

Gretchen flinched. "Oh, wow, I'd love to, but I can't." She swayed her hips toward the other doorjamb on the left. "The only place I have her number is in my cell phone directory, and silly me, it seems I've misplaced my phone." She suddenly lost interest in looking at him.

Bobbie snorted and walked off while Andrew rubbed the back of his neck. Was this individual as confounded as she appeared to be or was he being played for a fool? And if so, why? Andrew's poor male brain didn't have the capacity to work out the kind of female machinations to which he had a feeling he was being subjected.

"But don't worry," Gretchen flapped her hand several times, "I'll leave her a note or something and let her know you were here. She's been super busy lately, in and out constantly. I never know where she is from one day to the next."

From one day to the next? How long had the woman even been living there? Less than a week, that much he knew.

Gretchen wrapped a small section of hair around her fingers, toying with the ends. She bent her head forward and smiled. "Are you *sure* you won't change your mind about the Indian food?" She kept her eyes locked on him, a vigilant hawk, scanning the prairie for any sign of life to latch on to.

After he turned down Gretchen's un-tempting proposal, Andrew politely excused himself, counting among his greatest victories that he made it back to his Mustang unscathed.

* * *

About an hour later, Andrew sat at one of Mo'Joes' small tables, sipping an iced Americano and fingering Allie's debit card. He'd been carrying it around since he'd found it five days before. The coffeehouse was packed, and he'd been lucky to grab a table. The hiss and spurting of the machines, the rabble of conversation, and the background jazz, which had been turned up way too high that late afternoon, created a disturbance that made it hard to think. But that didn't stop Andrew.

His successful interview on Monday and immediate job offer from JPL did much to put him in a more positive mood. But an unsettled feeling in the pit of his stomach was a constant reminder of the same painful story still unresolved.

He'd been back home for almost a full week now, and his erratic thoughts were driving him nuts. He was frustrated by his inability to connect with Allie. He was becoming highly suspicious of Gretchen. He was stressed about the ongoing misunderstanding with Jennifer, which he still hadn't cleared up. He'd been all set to straighten that out at the coffeehouse; but then his foolish espresso-dumping trick had rattled him so much he'd been unable to do much more than grunt, hopefully politely, in response to whatever Jennifer said. This was why he was back at Mo'Joes. He'd invited her for coffee so they could have that little talk he'd never gotten around to. Jennifer had sounded far too excited to meet him, which may have been the reason he kept turning the debit card over and over. Nervous tension.

Why did he tell himself he trusted God to handle the details of his life, and then interfere by second-guessing the results? What was it people liked to say? Let go and let God? To Andrew it had always sounded trite—yet strangely profound. However, he was neither letting go of his desire to control nor letting God lead the way. This made him wonder: Had four years away from the Valley been long enough? Had seven thousand miles away been far enough? Had he in fact escaped, or merely taken his troubles with him, relocating them to another part of the world?

The best answer he had to the last question was, ultimately, *no.* Being away had given him a chance to heal, to find the strength to persevere. He'd developed insight to see clearly, gaining the new and improved perspective he badly needed. Even so, a lingering ache remained, and he knew this would be his last chance to make it go away.

Forever.

Finding a job in engineering had been his post-military career goal. And being hired by one of the best firms in the aerospace industry was a profound blessing, one for which he felt immense gratitude. Deep down in his heart, however, he wanted more. He wanted to be with Allie.

To be *one* with Allie.

He hadn't even admitted it to himself up until now that he couldn't imagine being with anyone else. Though, one question still remained. Could Allie ever allow herself to feel the same way about him?

So what was he going to tell Jennifer? That he knew he was supposed to wait around for Allison E. Hendrickson to finally come to her senses and confess she found him intriguing, fascinating, and wonderful? That he was going to wait for Allie to figure out she loved him as much as he loved her and that she didn't mean what she said about him at summer camp twelve years ago?

Nah. Too much information. *Way* too much information.

Suddenly unable to take the noise and chaos inside Mo'Joes any longer, Andrew stood, intending to take his coffee to his car to wait for Jennifer. But a surge of adrenaline shot through his veins, and his legs refused to hold him up. He dropped back into his seat.

Allie!

She strode into the coffeehouse, followed by a well-hairsprayed blonde in a bright red business suit. The blonde was all dolled up, but she couldn't compare to Allie. Even dressed casually in a long sleeved white shirt and purple jogging pants with a hoodie of the same color encircling her small waist, Allie was breathtaking.

Her shiny brown hair was secured in a ponytail high up on her head. The ends of the ponytail grazed her shoulder blades as it swung from side to side in rhythm with her graceful walking gait. The same wispy bangs she'd worn since high school fluttered over her forehead. The last time he'd seen her, she'd worn her hair much shorter. He wondered what it looked like without the elastic band holding it back. He wondered how it would feel against his hands.

"Hi there, Allie," the dark-haired woman said when Allie stepped up to the counter.

"Hey, Phoebe."

Andrew's heart jumped at the sound of Allie's voice, the mere thought of which had always calmed his restless spirit, even when he was thousands of miles away. He wanted to call out to her and say something profound that might bridge the gap of their long separation, but his brain seized up, and the words caught in his throat. All he could do was look at her. That was okay. It was enough. For now.

Her face had a soft glow—the kind created by a flame flickering inside a candle. He'd memorized every inch of her serene face, including its smooth fair skin and the tiny freckles sprinkled across her nose. And her eyes—her eyes were indelibly inked behind his own. How he'd missed gazing into those lovely, dove gray eyes.

Allie. Easy-going and ladylike, but not afraid to stand up for herself. Sharp and intelligent, though never pretentious. Tough yet tender, bold yet shy. Most of all, maddeningly paradoxical and completely unaware of how incredible she was . . . and how much he adored her . . .

"*Andrew?*"

Allie's uplifted voice sucked Andrew out of the violins-playing, cherubs-frolicking, love-struck state he'd been in. How did she get from the counter to his table without him noticing? She stood not three feet away, looking down at him, holding a cup in her hand, gaping in disbelief.

He stared back, matching her look of astonishment. He willed his vocal chords to work. Swallowing, he managed, "Hi, Allie."

That sounded pretty good. At least he got the words out of his mouth, and they seemed to make sense.

She tilted her head and squinted. "You're back home?"

Speechless, Andrew reassessed the countless erroneous scenarios he'd envisioned over the past two days. For starters, it was clear Gretchen never told Allie about the barbecue. If she had, Allie wouldn't be standing in front of him saying with incredulity, "*Andrew? You're back home?*" and looking at him like he'd just ridden the interplanetary starship down from Jupiter. Or Mars. Or whichever planet men were rumored to be from.

65

"Oh, yeah, I, um . . ." Andrew inhaled to steady himself. "Yes, I'm back." He got to his feet with the intention of . . . what? Shaking her hand? Hugging her? What was the right thing to do in this situation?

Allie made it easy for them both. She leaned toward him and laid her arm casually across his shoulders in an embrace that was decidedly remote. "Welcome home." She stepped back. "It's good to see you. It must be wonderful being with your family again."

"Yes, it is. I mean, sure, we kept in close contact over the years. You know . . . phone calls, letters, online chatting, texting, birthday cards. Of course it's not the same as seeing them in person, but it was better than nothing . . ." He was babbling.

Her lips pursed slightly in an awkward smile.

Andrew piped down and stuffed his hands into his jacket pockets, suddenly realizing he still had Allie's debit card in his hand. Five days now she'd been without it. Had she noticed yet that it wasn't where it was supposed to be? Did Andrew have even thirty seconds to explain why it was in his pocket and not in her . . . whatever she carried it in?

"Are you going to drink your Americano here?" He pointed at the floor, envisioning Jennifer traipsing through the front door any moment and peppering him with more questions. "Or did you get it to go?"

"I'll drink it here. I'm meeting up with . . ." She paused, and her contemplative eyes narrowed a bit. "How did you know I ordered an Americano?"

Air became trapped in Andrew's lungs, making his chest muscles rigid. *He didn't know.* He just remembered that it was her favorite coffee drink. Actually, he remembered *everything that ever happened between them*, which was what made trying to communicate with her so difficult.

She got him off the hook. "Oh, you must've overheard me at the counter." She let out a small laugh, spontaneous and charming.

"So, you're meeting someone." Andrew reached for his coffee. "Okay. I was about to leave anyway."

"No, don't go. I'm waiting for *Beth*. She'll be here any minute, and I know she'd love to see you. Can't you stay a little longer?"

How could he say no, or why would he want to? He'd always had a special kinship with Beth, a sort of intuitive understanding. No one could read him as well, and yet never once did he feel uncomfortable by it. Kind, effortless, and genuinely compassionate, Beth was the kind of person who was a loyal friend in time of need, regardless of who had the need.

A cell phone's ring tone interrupted the momentary silence. Allie reached into her jacket pocket and answered the call. "Hey, Beth."

"Allie!" Andrew heard Beth's keyed up voice through the phone. "You won't believe what I'm looking at."

"Ditto."

"It's Andrew Gallagher's Mustang, here in the parking lot, with a *For Sale* sign in the back window. Isn't that odd? I hope nothing's happened to him."

Smiling, Allie shook her head. "Come on inside and see for yourself."

Fifteen seconds later, Beth pushed through the front door, dressed in a light gray skirt suit and an orange sherbet colored blouse. Poised and professional, she stood for a moment inside the entrance. Andrew certainly hadn't lied when he'd made the comparison with Jennifer, but Beth, like Allie, was super uniquely special, in such a way Andrew couldn't accurately put into words.

Beth's gaze flitted through the room and swiftly landed on Andrew. Crossing the space between them in four large strides, she wrapped her arms around Andrew's shoulders and hugged him tight. Now this was the hug he wished Allie had given him. He returned Beth's embrace, but when he tried to release her she held on and leaned back with a giggle.

"Andrew, Andrew. Just *look* at you!" She swung her head around toward Allie. "As handsome as ever, isn't he?" She faced Andrew again. "When did you get back? I hadn't heard anything from anyone, but I knew it was about time for you to return. You *are* back for good, aren't you?"

"Yes." He looked over Beth's shoulder at Allie. "I'm back for good."

"Now, that's the best news I've heard in a long time." Beth released him from her grip, looked over at his tiny, two-person table then surveyed the room. "How about we move to that booth over there?" She nodded in the direction of the rear entrance, adding, "Assuming you have time to spare for a couple of old friends."

"Of course I do. But . . ." He sighed. Like everything else related to Allie, this wasn't going the way he'd planned. Here he was with the chance to spend some time with her, and he had to meet Jennifer. "I can't do it right now, unfortunately. I have something to take care of first. It's important, otherwise I'd stay."

Beth shook her head. "That's okay. Let's try to meet for dinner soon. Just the three of us, so we can get all caught up on current events." Beth gave him another hug, shorter this time. "How does that sound, Allie?"

He glanced at Allie, who stood stiffly next to Beth. She flashed a brief smile. "Sure, that's fine."

"Let me give you my number, Andrew." Beth reached inside her purse and pulled out a little notepad and pen. "I'm over in Malibu now, renting my aunt's beach house. You know, the one with the mint green shutters?" She gave him a teasing grin. "And I'm sure you remember the pink flamingo on the lawn."

Covering his eyes with his hand, Andrew shook his head. He removed his hand and said, "You better believe I remember." He'd tripped over the beast and cut his foot on a sprinkler head. "That eyesore cost me four stitches and a tetanus shot, not to mention a whole month on swimming restriction."

Beth and Allie began snickering. "You know, Andrew, Allie and I were watching you from the living room window," Beth confessed. "You got so mad at that silly bird you tried to kick it, but couldn't . . ." Beth grabbed her midsection with both hands as she laughed uncontrollably, "because you were limping, and your foot was bleeding; so you ended up punching the poor thing in the head," she let out a gleeful yowl, *"more than once!"*

Andrew shook his head again, this time with more force. "I'm glad it amused you. I remember the ER doctor asking me if I'd been in a fist fight." He grinned. "I think I told him I had."

He caught a glimpse of Allie's eyes shining with amusement. Well, okay. If his clumsy past gave her pleasure, he was fine with that. He wished they had different past moments to talk about, but this one would do. "Well," he shrugged, "what else would you expect from a clumsy teenager?"

Beth wrote on a piece of paper and handed it to Andrew. He glanced at it and then slipped it inside his shirt pocket. "I'll call you about dinner," he looked at Beth while inching closer to Allie. He wanted to put his arms around her and hold her close, feel her heart beating next to his. But that wasn't going to happen. Not today, anyway.

So he bid them goodbye and did what he didn't want to do . . . he went outside to wait for Jennifer.

* * *

Allie watched Andrew leave the coffeehouse and disappear behind a white panel van parked just outside. Not sure of what she was feeling, she decided she felt nothing.

Beth set her gray nylon pocketbook on the table Andrew had vacated. She poked around inside one of the compartments and pulled out a five-dollar bill. "We might as well stay at this table. That booth," she gestured toward the back of the coffeehouse, "just got taken."

"Okay with me." Allie looked at the money in Beth's hand. "Can I get you a cup of coffee? Or tea, if you like?"

68

"A small green tea would be terrific. Thanks."

Allie took the money and returned to the counter where Phoebe had just finished waiting on a middle-aged bald man wearing baggy black jeans and a faded Aerosmith tee shirt. She batted her eyelashes at Allie.

"One small green tea for my friend Beth, please."

"Well, I declare." Phoebe's Southern belle drawl did nothing to complement her lacquered spiky hair and diamond nose stud. "It looks like ya'll been keepin' secrets from me, Miss Allie." She waved her wrist in front of Allie as though dangling a dainty handkerchief.

"Huh?"

"Why, you've already made the acquaintance of the fine and dandy, mild-mannered mystery man."

"*The who?*" Allie wrinkled her face. "Scarlett, would you *please* speak post-Civil War English?"

"Oh, all right, Rosebud." Phoebe's voice and demeanor returned to the present age as she worked the cash register. "That guy you were talking to was the one I told you about last Saturday. Remember? Tall, dark, and handsome? He ordered the two Americanos because he couldn't choose between hot or iced and then came in with his girlfriend the next night and dumped coffee on her skirt. Boy, was that scene a hoot!"

Allie stared Phoebe down while handing her the five. "Frankly, my dear, I think you've gone mad."

"No, I haven't. I know what I saw, and that was definitely the same guy. I asked him about buying the two coffees, and he admitted it. His girlfriend sure wondered why he bought two. He said he only drank one. I forget which. Anyway, he threw coffee on her skirt on purpose. I was watching him from here, and I almost died laughing."

Allie took the change due. "I'm lost, Phoebe. That was my friend, Andrew. He served in the Navy over the past four years and recently returned home." Glancing at the area behind Phoebe, Allie thought about her next words. "And, I'm *sure* he doesn't have a *girlfriend.*"

"*Are you, now?* Well, I'm telling you he came in with a pretty redhead. He deliberately spilled coffee on her skirt so she'd have to go into the restroom. Then he ran up here to ask questions about *you.* He wanted to know if you'd already been in. And you had, just a few minutes earlier. *Some coincidence, wouldn't you say?*"

"He asked about *me?* If *Allie* had been here?"

Phoebe twisted her mouth and looked up and then sideways. "Come to think of it, no, I don't think he called you by name. But he described you perfectly." Placing an elbow on the counter, she rested her chin inside her palm. She looked up at Allie with a raised eyebrow and a smirk, this time speaking like a Russian spy from a Bond flick. "Sounds like some kind of crazy American love triangle to me."

Allie smirked back. "Hardly."

Phoebe straightened and got Beth's order. She set a cup of hot water and a packet of jasmine green tea on the counter.

"Look, I don't know what to tell you." Allie collected the items. "I have more questions than answers at this point."

"Of course you do. I would expect nothing less."

Allie couldn't picture it. Andrew with a girlfriend? He hadn't mentioned anything about a girlfriend to her or Beth. Phoebe had to be mistaken.

Not that there was anything *wrong* with him, no reason why he couldn't have a girlfriend, she thought. She turned from the counter and nearly collided with another distracted patron whose eyes were locked on to his cell phone screen. Allie quickly apologized before heading toward Beth. Certainly Andrew was a terrific guy. He was smart, considerate, and self-effacing in an endearing sort of way. And besides all that, Beth was right. He *did* look handsome.

"Allison," Beth laughed, watching Allie dither in front of their table as though lost, "are you just going to stand there while my hot water gets cold?"

"No." Allie shook thoughts of Andrew from her head and sat down in the chair across from Beth.

* * *

Andrew flicked a glance at a white panel truck that was pulling away from the front of Mo'Joes. It had been shielding him from the inside of the coffeehouse, so he'd been confident Allie wouldn't see him meet Jennifer. Now, he'd be exposed.

He ducked down out of sight next to Jennifer's car and said through the open passenger window, "You know, this place is crazy busy. It's such a nice evening. How would you like to take a walk instead?"

Jennifer smiled. "Sure." She didn't seem to notice he was hiding behind her car.

James Bond, eat your heart out, Andrew thought. He wasn't half bad at subterfuge. Although it did turn his insides into something that felt like a smoothie churning in a blender.

Andrew looked over at his Mustang and back at Mo'Joes. He figured he could get to the car and pull away without Allie seeing him. "How about we take both our cars over to Wildflower Canyon

Park?" Allie and Beth knew he'd driven the Mustang to Mo'Joes. If he left it where it was or even if he moved it onto the street or to another part of the lot, they might spot it and wonder what he was up to. He reached into his jacket pocket to retrieve his car keys, but instead he felt something flat and smooth.

Allie's debit card.

He'd forgotten all about. It didn't help that he'd also lost all ability to think clearly as soon as he was near her. Great. He was going to have to go back inside. He wavered. Could he return it another day? No. He should do it now.

He was still crouched down on the asphalt, feeling the heat radiate from the engine of Jennifer's idling car. "I forgot something inside. I'll only be a minute."

* * *

The little bell hanging above the entrance door jangled, catching Andrew's attention. Funny he hadn't noticed that before.

The woman at the counter with the spiky hair . . . what had Allie called her? Phoebe? She tilted her face and raised a brow as Andrew headed to the table he'd vacated just a few moments earlier. He found Beth sitting alone, staring into a cup of tea. "Hey, there," he said.

She looked up. "You're back. Awesome. Can you stay a little longer this time?"

He smiled. "No, I'm sorry. I wanted to return something to Allie. Did she leave?"

"She's in the ladies' room."

"Oh, okay. Um, I need to get going. Would it be okay if I left it with you?"

"Of course."

"Thank you." He pulled the debit card out of his jacket pocket and placed it in her hand. "I found this on the cream and sugar counter a few nights ago. What are the chances of that happening?" He shifted his weight, suddenly feeling awkward. Then he remembered the barbecue. "I know this is short notice, but I'd like to invite you and Allie to my folks' place this Saturday afternoon, about one o'clock. We're having a family get-together. Another barbecue. Uncle Henry will be there; that's always good entertainment."

"I wish I could, Andrew. I'm sorry, I'll have to pass. I'm working tomorrow, ten to six, but I'm sure Allie can make it." She winked. "Why don't you ask her yourself?"

I've been trying to, he thought. "I will. And I'll call you soon about dinner." He started to walk away then pivoted to face her.

He grinned and patted his chest pocket. "Oh, and thanks for Allie's phone number."

* * *

Wildflower Canyon Park sat up high on the hill in the Verdugo Mountains, not far from Allie's home in the Valley Villas complex. The park provided a breathtaking view of East Valley and of beautiful sunsets, like the one Andrew and Jennifer watched as they approached the head of a flat winding trail. Murky haze across the city and above the Hollywood Hills produced a melding of intense colors. Coral, bright orange, and energetic shades of dark red and purple illuminated the sky in a blaze of glory. After walking no more than ten yards along the dirt path, Andrew felt a significant drop in air temperature. Overhead, a smattering of black birds cruised past, revealing their identity with a few telltale caws in an otherwise soundless journey.

Stalling to think of a kind way to tell Jennifer his heart belonged to someone else, Andrew shared the news of being hired by JPL and more detail than he'd ordinarily share about the type of work he'd be doing and the people he'd be working with. Although her responses sounded genuine, Andrew sensed something was wrong. She wasn't her usual sociable self.

"Jennifer, I want you to know I think you're terrific. A very nice person . . ." Andrew paused. He couldn't believe those words had come out of his mouth. They sounded like the beginning of a break-up speech.

"Andrew?" She didn't let him finish, which was probably for the best.

"Hmm?"

"I think you're very nice too, which is why I hope I can ask you for a favor."

Oh, no. This was *not* going as planned. Jennifer had already commandeered the conversation. He took a breath. "Sure."

"Well, since I'm new to the area, I don't know who else could help me. I hate to bother you with this."

Andrew stopped in his tracks, and she did the same. He turned his head to look at her. "Just ask." The red tones in Jennifer's hair and her rose-colored corduroy blazer looked soft and feminine against the backdrop of the orangey pinks saturating the sky. She glanced around then down to the ground before looking at Andrew.

"I begin a new lease for a little house in Glendale on the first of November. That's a Monday." She lifted restless hands, twisting the white gold band she wore on her thumb. "But because the house is vacant, the owner agreed to let me move in over the last weekend of October. I know it's short notice, and with you starting your new job . . ."

He gently clasped a hand over hers in reassurance, and to settle her fidgeting fingers. "It's okay; I'll be glad to help. I can borrow my dad's truck, and if he doesn't already have plans, I'm sure we can borrow *him* for a while, too. We'll get you moved in no time."

A small sigh escaped her lips. Through the diffused light of dusk, Andrew saw a slight glistening in her eyes. "Thank you so much," was all she managed to say before her voice began to falter.

In a way, Andrew had compassion for Jennifer. She didn't seem to have many, if any, friends in the area, nor did she understand yet that Valley Community Church was full of people who'd assist with moving, home repairs, and maintenance, and a whole host of other services without expecting so much as a dime in return. Yet he had to admit it was nice to feel needed by somebody. Would Allie ever need something that only *he* could give? He so wanted to be needed by her but wondered if she even understood the degree of their compatibility. *He* could see it, and without a doubt Beth understood it.

But Allie was different. She reminded Andrew of a modern day Rapunzel, isolated at the top of a castle tower with no way out and only a shoulder-length ponytail to pull someone else in. If he could just understand why she always kept him at arm's length, then maybe he could help her feel safe enough to allow him into her heart.

Andrew and Jennifer began walking again, taking a separate trail down through a densely wooded area, where the scent of damp earth and trodden pine needles lingered in the misty evening air. A weight appeared to have been lifted off Jennifer's shoulders, literally. Her posture was now more relaxed, and she seemed content with the stillness and quiet of their passage through the tree-shrouded canyon.

For ten more minutes, they walked in silence, and for once, Andrew wished she'd say something. The lack of dialogue wasn't a bad thing by itself, but rather an indication that no words were necessary. He and Jennifer had just crossed an invisible line, moving from unknown to known, from acquaintances to friends, from obscurity to commitment. How could he have that talk with her now? It felt like a relationship was forming in spite of himself. And he had no clue how to keep it from happening.

Chapter 6

A Snapshot of the Past

On Saturday, Allie was up and out of bed by seven-fifteen, beginning her day with a glass of water, a shower, and a few bites of a chocolate mint protein bar. Using her index finger as a shoehorn, she slid each foot into her running shoes.

Ready for the direct, two-mile trip over to Mo'Joes, she collected her cell phone, house key, and a small zippered pouch off a glass top table in the entryway and slipped them into the pocket of her shorts. As she stepped outside, Allie caught sight of her seventy-two-year-old neighbor from across the street, Gloria Danville. Seated in her red Pontiac Firebird, with her white hair swaddled in a neon pink silk scarf, and an enormous pair of dark sunglasses resting near the tip of her long nose, Gloria waved at Allie and tooted the horn, yelling out the passenger's open window words that sounded like "cheese and crackers."

With Gloria, anything was possible.

Allie trotted down Ridgeview until she reached Hillcrest, where she made a left, running the final mile and a half to the coffeehouse in less than twelve minutes. She took her place in line behind a woman who had questions about almost every item on the menu. After several minutes, the woman finally made her choice: A plain cup of black coffee.

"Next." The young man taking orders had curly hair the color of sun-bleached hay. His rather huge smile and close-set brown eyes fixed in a kooky stare caught Allie off-guard. She approached the counter and stood before him.

"What can I get you?" He tilted his head to one side, like a Cocker Spaniel with an ear infection.

"Oh, um, I'll have a large iced Americano, room at the top, please."

"Great choice." He gave Allie a thorough once-over while scribbling on the clear plastic cup.

"Beautiful day, isn't it?" he asked.

"Mm hmm."

"Name?"

"Rosebud." The line behind Allie began lengthening. Patrons grumbled. She swiped her debit card with deliberate swiftness.

She was happy to have it back in her possession, even though she hadn't realized it was missing until her return to Mo'Joes—the same day she'd run into Andrew. After placing her order and finding that the card wasn't in her little case, Allie concluded she must have left it in her purse. Leaving it behind at Mo'Joes was not like her at all. She was always responsible with anything valuable or important. Maybe Gretchen was rubbing off on her already . . . in the wrong way.

"Just finish a run?" the curly-haired man asked.

"Yes."

"I thought so."

The line grew longer. Allie heard rustling and more grumbling.

"Did my matted hair and flushed face give me away?" Allie asked, in hopes her straightforward rhetoric would put an end to the bantering.

He chuckled. "I like a girl who knows how to sweat."

"Uh, okay." Was that supposed to be a compliment? If so, she certainly wasn't going to thank him for it.

Allie took her receipt and sat down in a large reading chair. The soft jazzy music on the stereo system helped relax her a bit, but not enough. Unsettling thoughts ran through her head: What was it going to be like working with Kevin's new boss? Would she have enough time to prepare for the upcoming sales meeting? And why did it seem like Andrew Gallagher had just materialized out of thin air? Even Beth had been stunned over his sudden reappearance. Allie switched her phone on for the first time that morning. A few seconds later, she heard a chime. Connecting to voicemail she retrieved the new message.

"Large iced Americano for Rosebed!"

Allie stood up. "That's Rosebud." She took her cup over to a nearby counter and added sweetener and a little half and half while holding the phone to her head. Once she finished listening to her message, Allie slipped the phone back into her pocket and left Mo'Joes. She then headed home, sipping her Americano and wondering what to do with this unexpected information from Andrew.

* * *

75

Allie dropped her keys on the entryway table, set down her empty Americano cup, and connected her cell phone to the charger. She'd just offhandedly explained to Gretchen about Andrew's invitation to the barbecue, and now she heard herself reflect out loud, "I'm not sure I feel up to going. It's kind of short notice." Allie slipped off her running shoes and faced Gretchen, who sat cross-legged on the sofa. "Don't you think?"

"Uh . . ." Gretchen's gaze bounced around the room. Was she trying to find the right answer hanging on the wall or perched on a bookshelf? "I don't worry about things like that. An invitation is an invitation. Of course," she paused and shifted her mouth, "*Female in Fashion* says that a man should give at least three days notice before asking a woman out on a date."

"This isn't a date, Gretchen. It's a family barbecue."

"Oh, right. Well, then, I suppose you should go." She chewed thoughtfully on a pink nail, adding, "I could go with."

Allie grabbed the railing and took a step up the stairs.

"If you want me to go, that is."

Want you to go? thought Allie. *Why would I want you to go?*

"You know," Gretchen said, as though reading Allie's mind, "in case it turns out to be super boring. *Female in Fashion* says you should never go to a party without a party buddy. Just like you should never go swimming alone. Same concept."

Allie turned the idea over in her head. She was surprised to find herself concluding that Gretchen had made an excellent point.

If that was possible.

*   *   *

Andrew and his family spent an hour on Saturday morning preparing the backyard. By ten A.M., the barely hazy sky and bright shining sun were promising the perfect weather for a barbecue. While Rob mowed the lawn and Sue dusted off tables and chairs, Andrew and his brother, Luke, a senior at East Valley High, and their sister, twenty-one-year-old, Mary Anna, currently living in the dorm at San Diego State University, erected a ten-by-ten-foot canvas canopy. After Andrew and Luke placed a long buffet table underneath the canopy, everyone worked together to load up the table with supplies and then fill two large coolers with bagged ice, bottled water, and canned beverages.

Andrew wasn't as excited about the get-together as his parents were, but he looked forward to visiting with friends and relatives he hadn't seen in years. Even so, he felt awkward about the big fuss being made over his return. He voiced his concern to his mother as she laid a red, white, and blue striped tablecloth on top of the big redwood outdoor table.

"Oh, was this party supposed to be about *you?*" Sue put a hand over her mouth and pretended to look bewildered. "Don't worry. I'm sure Grandma will mention at least twenty times that her birthday is next week. And with Uncle Henry in the mix, people will forget all about you."

Andrew grinned at Sue's theatrics and decided he'd try to have fun. Especially if his Great Uncle Henry, Grandma Steven's younger brother by seven years, delivered one of his legendary monologues.

By two-fifteen, everyone had arrived. Everyone except Allie. Andrew had called her the day before and left a message on her cell phone, asking her to phone back if she couldn't make it. He was sure she would welcome the chance to see and visit with his family again. Or was that how he wanted her to feel? Having waited so long to see her, he couldn't imagine things not working out the way he'd hoped. The way he'd dreamed.

Andrew slid open the screen door for Sue, who stepped down onto the patio. She carried a large brown glass casserole dish filled with marinated chicken, hamburger patties, and Italian sausages over to the stainless steel gas barbecue. Rob placed the meat on the hot grill and fanned the fragrant wood chips inside the pit.

The backyard gathering had swelled to about forty family members, friends, and a few close neighbors. While most of the group played catch-up or ping-pong or simply relaxed in the shade of a giant Sycamore tree, Rob handled the barbecue detail and Sue mingled among the guests.

Still on the lookout for Allie, Andrew went over to talk to Grandma Stevens at the redwood table. He took a quick look at Uncle Henry, who changed course as soon as he saw where Andrew was heading. Henry limped across the patio then shuffled sideways around the table, steadying himself by holding on to the backs of the chairs.

"Doggone trick knee's actin' up again," Henry muttered, taking a wobbly stance behind his eighty-year-old wife, Victoria, whose hair and eyes coordinated well with the bluish color of her short-sleeved polyester pantsuit. Henry, being four years younger than Victoria, lovingly referred to his wife as "the Cougar."

The comment Henry made about his "trick knee" was in reference to a leg injury he claimed to have suffered during the Great War. The problem was that World War I—also called the Great War—ended almost twenty years before Henry's blessed birth. Another problem with his story was the fact that everyone already knew the injury had occurred within the last year. Andrew just assumed that, in Henry's mind, a cavalryman being thrown from a horse at full gallop sounded more romantic than a clumsy old fool falling off a stepladder while trying to change a light bulb.

"What are your plans now that you're back home, Andy?" Grandma Stevens asked Andrew.

Grandma Stevens had a cheerful and fun-loving personality, and Andrew loved everything about her. She was a slight five-foot-two, with determined brown eyes and soft gray hair worn in a bun at the top of her head. She was the feistiest octogenarian Andrew knew, but one with grace, poise, and charm.

"I start work at JPL on Monday, Gran."

"Good for you." She planted a light fist on the table. "Get right to work."

"JPL? Aren't they part of NASA?" asked Uncle Henry, a man primarily regarded as the family tattletale and gossip. He had an uncanny habit of talking about people "behind their backs," while making sure they were close enough to overhear every word. The scuttlebutt was that Henry did this because he was too lily-livered to come right out and speak his mind to the person in question.

"Every time I see NASA making headlines," Henry continued, "I think they finally made contact with aliens. But no, they've either blown something up or they need more money. Or both."

Victoria laid a bony forearm on the table. She turned her head, lowered her AmberVision sunglasses and peered up at her husband. "Henry, you need to find some new material on NASA. The launch has been canceled."

Ten minutes later, Andrew returned to the area near the barbecue to talk to Rob and to keep watch on Uncle Henry, who looked to be prepping for one of his infamous "Friends, Romans and Countrymen" speeches, in which he'd stir up trouble by artfully channeling Marc Antony. Taking a few steps away from the table, Henry moved into position. Dressed in his "lucky" tartan plaid golf pants, he stood before a small group assembled on lawn chairs near the redwood table. His waistband, as usual, had been pulled up high around his ample midsection, while one of his wife's flowered straw hats shielded his pudgy and flushed face from the afternoon sun. A light breeze drifted by, picking up the cool wintergreen scent of arthritis rub and briefly distracting two yellow jackets passing through.

Attempting to keep Andrew at his back soon proved futile for Henry. Because he'd figured out he was Henry's target, Andrew kept moving around, constantly keeping himself in Henry's line of sight. After shuffling and shifting enough to complete a near-perfect circle, Grandma indicated she'd had enough. "Oh, spit it out already, will you, Henry!"

Henry ignored the rebuke and reached deep into his pants pocket. His hands quavered as he fiddled with the small packet he'd procured. He tapped a few tiny black squares of licorice-flavored Sen-Sen into his cupped hand before tossing the tidbits into his mouth with enough force to send them straight to his stomach. The classic stalling tactic backfired, leaving him snorting and hacking for a good two minutes. No one ever accused Uncle Henry of being a wallflower.

"Well?" Grandma practically growled.

Henry adjusted his "sombrero" and cleared his throat. He then explained that by the time he was Andrew's age he was already married with a second child on the way.

"Yeah, well a lot has changed since then," Grandma said. "Kids these days don't need to leave the nest as early as we did. And even when they do leave, they often stay close to home—although Andrew did spend four years in the Middle East. You didn't do any traveling before you got married, now did you, Henry?"

"Ah, Andrew's a fine young man; I know that. I'd just like to see him with a nice girl, that's all." He made a halfhearted attempt to glance in Andrew's direction, avoiding direct eye contact. "Why doesn't he have a girlfriend?" Henry asked in a quieted tone. "He *does* like girls, *doesn't* he?"

"*Of course he does,*" Grandma said with a glare that made Henry stand at attention. "Give the boy a chance, will you? He just got back home."

By this time, Andrew was standing next to LAPD officer and neighbor Leroy Preston, a former pro football lineman of considerable stature and girth. Andrew was pretty sure Leroy had missed the revelation that at least one family member found Andrew's lack of a love interest to be abnormal at best. A brief chat with the light-skinned African American man gave Andrew a moment to regain his composure before he excused himself to once again scan the crowd for Allie.

* * *

"Your sundress is cute," Allie told Gretchen. And it *was* cute, in a dark blue cotton fabric with a sweetheart neckline and halter ties. But the only reason Allie mentioned it was to divert her attention away from the odd tingles at the nape of her neck. They were increasing, as she drove the SUV closer to the Gallagher's house.

"I'm glad you like it. I got it at Self-Expressions, a fun little boutique in the same mall where the Amazon woman works."

"Yes, I know the place. And her name is *Beth*."

Gretchen waved a hand. "Whatever." She gracefully lifted one of her short legs, propping a dainty foot on the dashboard. "And check these out."

Allie glanced over at five bubblegum pink-tipped toes squirming inside a cobalt blue platform espadrille. A thin leather strap with a shiny gold buckle snaked around Gretchen's ankle.

"I'm five-foot-five in these puppies," Gretchen announced. "And to make the outfit complete," she flicked a finger at large gold hoop earrings hanging from her small ears, "I added these beauties. And this." She held up her left arm so Allie could see the chunky wooden bangle encircling it. "Both are past birthday gifts from BFF Bobbie Brennan."

"Nice."

As desserts went, Gretchen's adorable dress and accessories were the equivalent of a hot fudge sundae—topped with roasted chopped almonds, whipped cream, and a maraschino cherry—served in a stemmed and fluted glass. Allie's ensemble, bought on sale at Sears and consisting of white Keds, white clam diggers and a lavender cotton baby doll blouse with embroidered hearts, was more in keeping with her vision of one scoop of vanilla ice cream.

Before leaving for the party, Gretchen had gone into Allie's room, keen on trying a spritz of her cousin's favorite fragrance. It was an expensive brand and the only perfume Allie owned. Gretchen claimed that having just one scent in your arsenal was almost criminal, and then suggested Allie invest in something more appropriate, like Jean Naté bath splash or Avon's Sweet Honesty. Allie had politely refrained from commenting on Gretchen's use of fragrances heady enough to unclog plugged sinuses.

A final right turn placed them on a tree-lined street of roomy single-family homes with circular driveways and wide, sloping front yards. The GPS voice prompt made the victorious announcement they'd arrived at their destination, but parking along the street was virtually nonexistent. Allie started to drive past the house, intending to find a spot on the next street over, but Gretchen made it clear she wasn't about to hike up anything steep wearing platform shoes and a mini dress. So Allie drove up the Gallagher's driveway, pulled as close to the front door as possible, and let Gretchen out. The sounds coming from the backyard indicated a party in full swing. Allie heard music (was it a Stevie Wonder song?) and lots of cheerful talking, interspersed with laughter. A large piece of paper taped to the front door invited guests to come in.

"I'm going to look for parking," Allie said. "I'll be right back."

"And I'll be joining the festivities." Gretchen waltzed up to the carved wood front door, pushed it open, and disappeared inside the house as Allie pulled away.

* * *

Andrew peered around the clusters of people in his parents' backyard. Allie was late. She was always on the *verge* of being late when they were in school. She'd rush into a class and flop down in her seat with the last seconds of the bell sounding. She always received stares, but she acted like she didn't care. In fact, she seemed to enjoy coming as close as she could to breaking as many rules as possible. A closet rebel, that's what she was, and Andrew found it intriguing—in a frustrating sort of way.

This is the last time I'll check, he promised himself. He stepped inside his parents' house and went into the kitchen. Picking his cell phone up off the counter, he closed his eyes before looking at the screen, willing the arrival of a new voicemail or text message. He paused, eyes still closed.

Was his mind playing tricks on him?

A faint, but wonderfully familiar scent drifted through the kitchen. It smelled like Providence, the perfume he'd given Allie as a birthday gift right before he'd left for boot camp. He bought it from Beth, who at first thought it was a Mother's Day gift for Sue, but because Beth was Beth, perceptive and discerning, she cracked the code before the transaction was complete. In truth, Andrew never knew if Allie liked the perfume enough to wear it.

He glanced at his cell phone. No new messages had arrived, so he left the kitchen and went down the hall, determined to find the source of the sweet smell. However, disappointment rattled his bones at what he encountered. It was Gretchen, standing before the floor-to-ceiling river rock fireplace, gawking at several photographs on top of the mantle. Andrew watched her grab a hand-decorated wooden frame with the words *Summer Youth Camp* painted along the bottom. He cringed as she gave the tormenting and unforgettable memory of his time at summer camp a close-up inspection.

"Hello, Gretchen."

Startled, she pulled the five-by-seven-inch frame to her chest, like she'd been caught doing something naughty. *"Andrew!* There you are. I've been looking all over for you."

"The party's in the backyard."

"Yes, I can hear everyone having a grand time." She displayed a generous set of teeth, her signature impersonation of the *Alice in Wonderland* kitty.

Andrew rubbed the back of his neck. "Um, where's Allie?"

"She dropped me off. She's scouting out a parking spot. The street's a madhouse, cars everywhere." Gretchen flung a hand, emphasizing the point before asking Andrew where she might find the sandbox.

"The what?"

"The lav. The loo. *The little girls' room.*"

"Oh, right," Andrew said, appalled by his lack of creative thinking. "Go into that room and turn right." He pointed toward the den, but Gretchen stayed put for another soliloquy.

"By the way, I *love* this room," she gushed. "It has such a friendly, modern feel to it."

Andrew glanced around at the copper, cinnamon, and burgundy decor. His mother was into interior decorating, and she'd carefully chosen the coordinating checks and stripes of the draperies and upholstery. He thought that aspect of the room was a little busy, but he liked the sturdy oak furniture, and he had to admit that the expensive, thick carpeting his dad had grumbled about when his mom had it installed did feel good underfoot.

"Allie's townhouse is clean and bright and everything, I'll give her that much," Gretchen went on, "but the French Provençal look? Gold-framed oil paintings? And all those prissy colors? No, thank you. Not my style. But that's Allie for you, living in her own little cocoon, all wrapped up in her outdated furnishings and old-fashioned ideas."

"I see," Andrew said, although he didn't see at all. Before Gretchen could wind up again, he said, "You know, it's interesting; I thought I smelled Allie's perfume. Or, at least I think I remember her wearing it once or twice before." He looked down. That wasn't even close to the truth.

"Once or twice? Are you kidding? It's the *only* thing she wears. The only one she owns, if you can believe it. I put some on before coming over here. It's called Providence." She sniffed her wrist, and her eyes rolled backward like a shark's. "And it's *delish.*"

Gretchen's attention returned to the picture, which she held up to examine. Andrew didn't have to see it to know what she was looking at. It was a shot of a bunch of kids, twenty-five or so, in bathing suits, and a few adults wearing coordinated tee shirts and shorts. They were posing on the shore of a lake, with nearly all the kids smiling, waving, or showing off in one way or another.

"Ha! I recognize that strawberry blond giraffe in the middle of the back row." Gretchen laughed derisively. "Braces and a sunburn. Good grief!"

He waited for her to notice the person standing *next* to Beth, the tall, skinny, dark-haired guy who wasn't smiling because he was distracted by something off to his right.

Gretchen took the picture over to the window to get a better look. She twisted the stick on the wooden Venetian blinds, allowing streams of sunlight to illuminate the photo. "I thought that was you standing next to the giraffe."

Andrew walked over and glanced down at the picture; his eyes automatically went to the end of the front row, where a blond kid wearing red bathing trunks and a goofy smile sat on the ground. His arm dangled lazily across the shoulders of the young teen next to him, a brown-haired girl in a blue and white flower print bathing suit.

"And is that *Allie* sitting next to that cute blond boy?"

"Gretchen? Is that you?"

If silk had a sound, it would be Allie's smooth and pretty voice—a definite and welcome distinction to Gretchen's nasal inflections. Andrew smiled, but as Allie entered the living room, his smile faded. Would he be able to explain The Cheshire Cat's devious deeds? Allie would notice he and Gretchen had met. Was it his place to tell Allie that she hadn't received the invitation to the barbecue because of her cousin's underhanded tactics?

Allie tugged on and adjusted the elastic band holding her ponytail in place. Just one time, Andrew wanted to see her hair down around her shoulders. He imagined how it would look lying against her sweetly flushed cheeks and framing her heart-shaped jawline.

She joined them near the fireplace. "I see you've met Andrew."

Gretchen handed her the photo. "We met before, remember?"

What?

Andrew's ribs froze up. They felt like Popsicles, keeping his chest from caving in, but also not allowing him to take a breath. Allie already knew he'd come by the house to see her and that Gretchen had been instrumental in keeping them apart?

Allie glanced down at the photo for half an instant. "Oh, yeah. I remember."

Andrew forced air into his lungs. It hurt.

* * *

"Be right back." Gretchen strolled from the room, rounding the corner at the end of the hall leading into the den. Allie placed the picture on the mantle.

Taking in a short, sudden breath, Andrew exclaimed, "I can explain everything."

Allie faced him and angled her head. Andrew suddenly looked feverish, and his gaze darted around the room. He opened and closed his mouth like he was catching flies. What was wrong with him? "Everything about what?" she asked.

"About," he motioned with a hand in the direction Gretchen had headed, "you know."

"I do?" Allie narrowed her eyes. "Something about Gretchen?" she guessed.

With a small nod, he leaned toward the fireplace to rest his arm casually on the mantle. But his elbow slipped off the edge, and he lost his balance. He staggered sideways then planted himself.

This time she lifted her brows.

Andrew cleared his throat. "Um, yes. About Gretchen. We met before. I can explain."

"What's there to explain? You were both at my graduation party. Gretchen said she remembers meeting you then."

"No, she doesn't." Andrew's eyelids flew open as though trap doors in a haunted house. "Uh, I mean, *oh, she does?*"

"You don't remember meeting her?"

His elbow finally made firm contact with the mantle. "How could I forget?"

Allie glanced at the picture near Andrew's arm and smiled. How funny, she thought; everyone looked so odd during that transitional phase called adolescence. "I don't know how anyone could forget meeting Gretchen. She leaves quite an impression."

"Yes, she does. Similar to a Yeti footprint, I would guess."

Allie laughed. Whatever was making Andrew act so weird seemed to have passed. He was relaxing, which was helping her relax. Maybe this barbecue would be more fun than she'd expected.

* * *

After Gretchen finally emerged from the sandbox, Andrew escorted Allie and her cousin to the backyard. He took them first to Grandma Stevens, who had a special fondness in her heart for Allie; his grandma knew how much Allie missed spending time with her own grandmother. While the two of them chatted privately, Andrew introduced Gretchen around. She immediately took center stage, commanding, Andrew noticed, male admiration and female annoyance.

When she finished talking with Grandma Stevens, Andrew stole Allie away to visit with Rob.

"Well, if it isn't Horizon Pharmaceuticals' shining star." After he removed a hunter green apron from around his neck, Rob passed off a spatula to Andrew's cousin, Mark Gallagher, a hulking, prematurely gray-haired thirty-four-year-old investment banker from Duluth. Rob then extended his arms toward Allie.

Standing on her tiptoes to reach his height, she wrapped her arms around his broad shoulders, giggling. "Did your son plant that seed in your head, Dr. Gallagher?" Stepping back Allie looked at Andrew with a suspicious grin.

"Dr. Gallagher? It's Rob, Allie, and I don't need Andrew's help in recognizing a fantastic drug rep when I see one. You've detailed me plenty on your products in the past, my dear—once right here in this backyard. You know your stuff."

Andrew recalled that Allie had impressed everyone at the first barbecue two years earlier. She'd discussed her products with self-confidence, handling a myriad of polysyllabic and odd-sounding Latin-root words like a pro.

"Oh, and by the way," Rob added with a happy chuckle, "I talked with Joe Stevenson not long ago. Apparently he's pretty excited about starting his new venture with your company."

"New venture?" Andrew asked of his dad.

"I don't know if you remember the intense conversation Allie had with Joe and me during the last barbecue. It was in reference to a brand new drug called Advantol."

Yes, Andrew did recall overhearing the conversation. Allie had gotten into a serious discussion with Rob's long-time friend and pain management specialist, Joe Stevenson. "From what I remember, Joe was unfamiliar with the product and kind of skeptical about prescribing it."

"That's it, Andrew." Rob patted his son on the back. "Good memory."

Oh, if he only knew just *how* good it was.

Allie jumped in the conversation and finished the story. "So, during my next visit to Dr. Stevenson's office, I went over the results from our clinical trials of Advantol, which showed a greater effectiveness and safety over other products in the same class. I also shared feedback from the field. Dr. Stevenson agreed to obtain consent from a few patients to conduct his own trial. After seeing excellent results, he became a believer."

Andrew knew a lot of the guys he'd served with had a problem with assertive, powerful women. Not Andrew. He'd always found Allie's proficiency and determination to be very attractive.

Allie beamed with contentment. "It took me a year and a half to convince him to become an advocate speaker for Horizon, and my manager and I are thrilled he finally agreed to it. I attended one of his speaking engagements not long ago and saw how well the other physicians responded to him. He has another lecture coming up in about a month, addressing a group of neurologists at their annual pain conference in Palm Springs. I know he'll be a huge success."

"I'm sorry he couldn't make it today. He had a prior engagement to attend back east, his granddaughter's baptism." Rob looked at Andrew. "By the way, he wants you to swing by his office one day. Grab a bite to eat or get a cup of coffee, whatever works for you both."

Nodding, Andrew rubbed his thumb and forefinger against his chin. "Yeah, I should give him a call soon."

Meeting up with his father's friends wasn't a big priority for Andrew after his return. Even reconnecting with his best high school friends, Scott Doyle and Ryan Alexander, had barely crossed Andrew's mind; but Joe Stevenson wasn't just a family friend, he was, actually, more of a spiritual mentor. Visits with Joe always proved helpful and constructive for Andrew, even during the most casual conversations. And now, with a great job and, he hoped, Allie close by him, Andrew could finally relax and expand his attention to include the many other important people in his life.

Chapter 7

The Hurricane

Allie arrived at the airport at nine A.M. on Tuesday. She pulled into a white zone, alongside an individual matching Kevin's description of Cassandra Hartwell. "Look for a tall, dark-haired woman of timeless class," Kevin had intoned to Allie during an obsequious voicemail message from the day before. "Her face," he'd said, "is serious but stunning, and her gaze is intense and hypnotizing." Wonderful, thought Allie. I'm meeting up with Elvira. Or maybe Morticia—in dark designer sunglasses, no less.

The grave and mysterious-looking woman opened the rear passenger's door of the SUV and slid two items across the bench seat. One was a black Coach shoulder bag in python-embossed leather and, the second, a red and black Victorinox weekender with wheels. Nice—and expensive, too. Allie had seen similar bags while fantasy shopping at the Westside Plaza with Beth.

After Cassandra eased into the front seat, Allie introduced herself. "I know you had a long flight. Would you like to relax a bit and have a cup of coffee before we get started?"

Cassandra lowered her square black Coach sunglasses. Kevin wasn't kidding about that intense gaze. "I don't think so, Allie. I'd like to make the most of my time out here."

So, without another word, Allie drove to her first stop, the Pasadena medical office tower located next to Huntington Memorial Hospital. She pulled into a spot on the parking structure's roof just as the sun disappeared behind dark gray clouds. Exiting the SUV, she glanced up at the sky and sighed, hoping that the suddenly gloomy weather wasn't a portent of things to come that day.

Street-level traffic sounds became amplified from where Allie stood on the top level. A gold Mini Cooper's shrill alarm blared for several seconds until it was deactivated by the owner's key fob. Allie waited while a white service truck with a loud clanking engine passed by on the way to a lower level. Acrid diesel exhaust lingered in its wake.

After several moments, Cassandra stepped out of the SUV. She came around the back to watch Allie lift the hatch, extract a computer from its nylon case and then turn it on. Pointing to the screen, Allie explained the relevance of the data. "These are the physicians we'll be calling on in this building. This column over here shows how many samples I've left with each office in the past." She slid her finger across the screen. "And this column shows the doctor's ranking, which may have an influence on the number of samples I leave. A higher ranking usually means he or she writes more prescriptions. I like to encourage a sampling of the product along with a new script. That way, in case there's a delay in getting to the pharmacy, the patient can begin a course of therapy immediately."

Cassandra studied Allie's face for a moment before asking, "Do you and Kevin work together often?"

Allie set down the computer. "Once a month or so." She continued talking while placing small blue and white boxes of anti-inflammatory samples in her black roller bag. "The doctors and staff are receptive to Kevin and our occasional two-for-one special." She grinned. "That reminds me. I call on one practice with five docs, which is a huge selling opportunity, especially on Tuesdays and Thursdays when all of them are in. The office manager only allows one rep to go in at a time to wait in the sample room until a doctor passes by or shows up to get samples for a patient. The other reps have to wait in the hallway, outside the office, until the one inside is finished."

"Is there a time limit to how long you can stay in there?"

"No, not really, which is why I make it a habit to take a waiting rep in with me when it's my turn. That way I get to help them out, and I don't have to worry about another rep's day ticking by waiting for me while I'm in there gabbing with a doctor."

"I see." Cassandra nodded. She continued studying Allie, who felt a twinge of self-consciousness, but tamped it down.

"I applaud your creativity in the field and shrewd nature in handling people," Cassandra said. "Consideration for your colleagues is a commendable trait."

Something about the edge in her voice made Allie glance over at Cassandra to look for a muscle or eyebrow twitch, or some other confirmation of cynicism, but she detected nothing. Cassandra's chiseled face, with its regal nose and sharp bones, remained placid.

Allie closed the flap on her black detail bag then slid open a drawer in the plastic storage unit she kept next to the sample boxes. "Once I started, I saw other reps doing it, and I wanted everyone to see how being considerate benefited us all."

A strong breeze picked up and began scattering leaves and debris along the concrete surface of the roof. Cassandra's A-line skirt clung to her legs like a tenacious toddler, while wisps of dark hair that had slipped out of her hair clip became tiny lassos, whipping about in the constant blast of air. "What's in there?" she nodded toward the open drawer.

"Stuff," Allie answered, not knowing how else to put it. She removed ballpoint pens, yellow and pink highlighters, self-sticking notepads, and two clear Lucite clipboards—all bearing the brand names of her products. "The office staff and nurses love these things. They give us time with the doctor and we thank them with, I guess you could call them, 'goodies.'"

"You mean *quid pro quo.*"

"Kind of, but without any negative, political connotations. We only provide items that benefit the patient in some way. For instance, pens or pads are used to make notes or take phone messages, and a clipboard holds a patient sign-in sheet. And I consider these highlighter markers to be aromatherapy everyone can appreciate. Lemon and strawberry scented." Allie removed the caps from one yellow and one pink pen, handing them to Cassandra, who sampled the fragrance of each.

"And how might *this* help a patient?" Cassandra held up a squishy, palm-sized foam replica of a pill she'd taken from one of the drawers before Allie closed the hatch.

"That little guy is a helpful product reminder for the prescriber," Allie said, rolling her bag toward the elevators. Cassandra walked alongside.

"Plus, it can be squeezed by the patient while having blood drawn," Allie added. "Ingenious, huh?"

A tall, flaxen-haired rep with model good looks, piercing blue eyes, and a canary-yellow shoulder bag emblazoned with bright orange and red flames approached them from the left. "Yes, let's not forget to show appreciation for those marketing geniuses whose job it is to make our lives more difficult," the rep said. "They dream up these fantastic ideas and then we become schlep reps, hauling all their precious treasures around trying to find them homes."

Allie forced a small laugh. "Hey, Kathryn."

Kathryn Sheppard and the name of her company were embossed on a nametag she wore on the lapel of an impossibly wrinkle-free, indigo blue linen pantsuit. Her golden mane had been parted in the middle, gathered at the nape of her neck and then spun into a harshly coiled bun.

"Good morning, ladies," Kathryn nearly stated. The elevator bell dinged; the doors opened up onto a blue-carpeted box with wood panel sides. Strains of Barry Manilow's *Looks Like We Made It* greeted the three women as they stepped inside. "Going to see Dr. Tanaka?"

"Tanaka, Hawthorne, and Lew," Allie replied. "How about you?"

"Only Tanaka."

"Okay, we'll call on Hawthorne first, Tanaka last."

The elevator made a whirring sound as it took them down several stories to the ground level. The enclosed space smelled of chicken soup and pine cleaner. Not a pleasant combination. Allie was happy when the doors separated with a small jolt. Kathryn stepped out first, turning around to look at Allie. "Thanks, and I'll see you around." Her words sounded almost like a dare. Or maybe even a threat.

Cassandra watched Kathryn take a right off the elevator and disappear down the corridor. "I detected some kind of vibe. Territorial, perhaps?"

"Well, I've learned that people with a take-no-prisoners attitude like hers don't discuss work matters casually."

The two walked straight ahead and through a frosted glass door marked Rushton L. Hawthorne, MD—Internal Medicine. "What else have you learned from reps like Kathryn, Allie?"

Allie scanned the room for other reps who may have arrived before them. "To always keep my eyes and ears open when I'm in the field. Did you see the symbol on her tote bag—the fire? She promotes our competition. And she's one of the best at it."

Cassandra raised a questioning eyebrow, and Allie squared her shoulders. She didn't intend to think about Kathryn anymore. She was here to show her boss's new boss how good she was at *her* job. It was time to focus.

* * *

They finished the day with a trip to Allie's storage unit. Since Cassandra's past work experience hadn't included the distribution of samples or, as she called the giveaway items, "trinkets," she'd expressed interest in seeing how and where Allie kept such things.

"What time are we supposed to meet Kevin?" Cassandra's voice sounded hollow as she and Allie walked down the concrete stairs of the drafty, mausoleum-like building.

"He made reservations at Damian's for six o'clock. The restaurant's about fifteen minutes from here." Allie checked her watch and saw it was already five-thirty. "That gives me ten minutes or so to show you around."

Cassandra removed a shiny gold lipstick compact from her shoulder bag. "Then let's get on with it." She eyed herself in the small mirror while pressing the enclosed powder puff against her forehead and chin. After applying a generous coat of dark red lipstick, she removed the claw clip from her hair. Shaking her head back and forth, she held the compact at arm's length, studying the results.

Allie fiddled with the padlock until it clicked open. The roll-up door rattled and shuddered as it slid upward, revealing an eight-by-ten-foot area containing two metal storage cabinets and three stacks of cardboard boxes. Stepping inside, she flipped the wall switch and an overhead fluorescent light flickered to life with a faint buzz. Cassandra misted herself with perfume, and the damp, musty smell in the air was suddenly replaced with a strong and spicy fragrance. She then followed Allie into the unit and went straight to one of the storage cabinets. The intent expression on her face hid a motive Allie couldn't quite identify. Cassandra twisted the handle and swung the door open, stepping back to examine the contents inside.

Allie watched her close the doors without a word then move over to a magnetic clipboard secured to the exterior of the cabinet. Cassandra maintained her unsettling silence while flipping through the first few pages of inventory, looking them over with what appeared to be superficial interest.

Finally, with nothing left to inspect, she handed Allie the clipboard. "I've seen enough," she said without expression, but what her face didn't reveal, the hint of sharpness in her voice did. "I'd like to go to the restaurant now. I wouldn't want to keep Kevin waiting."

Allie tensed. All afternoon, Cassandra had been cordial and respectful, but now her demeanor was putting Allie on edge, reminding her, in a unsettling way, of a languid lioness relaxing after consuming a fresh kill . . . not immediately threatening, but not safe to be around either. Why did Allie have a feeling she'd be better off with a barrier between her and the woman at her side?

* * *

Allie brought the SUV to a stop in front of Damian's, the area's finest steakhouse. A red-vested valet opened the driver's door and handed Allie a claim ticket. After Cassandra emerged from the passenger's side of the vehicle, the valet slid behind the wheel, driving off into the crowded parking lot. Allie and Cassandra passed through a vine-covered trellis archway. It led to a wooden bridge that stretched across a large koi pond and ended at the front door of the well-known restaurant. A tall, trim silver-haired businessman entered first. He held the door open with the back of his hand when he realized Allie and Cassandra were behind him. The man then walked straight ahead and turned into a room on the right.

"Reservation for three at six o'clock," Allie said to the young hostess who greeted them at the podium. The woman's long, pale blond hair and clear blue eyes seemed luminescent against the background of the lobby's dark wood paneling and restricted lighting. When the incredible scent of the restaurant's famous garlic cheese bread drifted by, Allie's mouth watered. She swallowed and said, "Um, it's under the name Rafferty."

The woman ran a French-manicured fingertip down the name roster then looked up. "Oh, yes. Mr. Rafferty has been here about ten minutes. He said he'd be waiting for you." Several metal bangles made a jingling sound as she gracefully stretched out a well-toned arm and indicated the way with an open palm. Her gaze followed her hand, and a curious smile appeared on her face. She focused in on something, or someone, at the far end of the room to the right, a low-lit lounge, which Allie and Cassandra entered into. A long bar in the center was surrounded by several barstools, all occupied. There were four booths on either side of the room, each illuminated by track lighting and a candle in a dark red jar. Several small round tables filled in the rest of the area. Despite it being a Wednesday night, the restaurant seemed particularly busy.

Having recognized Kevin's excitement over Cassandra's visit, Allie knew how he'd react as soon as he laid eyes on his boss: like a hyperactive ten-year-old trying to get the teacher's attention. As she and Cassandra wove through the tables to reach Kevin's booth, his hand shot up above his head with a frantic wave that shouted, *Pick me! Pick me!* Allie clamped a hand over her mouth to suppress her laughter; now she understood the hostess's smile and what, or rather who, she'd been looking at.

Since Kevin was a relatively simple man at heart, Allie could always establish his mood by simply looking into his hazel eyes. When he was serious, all business, the green tones in his eyes stood out. When in a more casual, fun-loving mood, the yellow-gold aspect would be prominent. Allie made a note-to-self to perform a color check on his irises once they got to him.

Kevin stood up well before they made it to the table. He gave Cassandra an eager double handshake then motioned for her to slide into the high-back, burgundy leather booth. How ironic, Allie thought, taking her turn to greet him, that his eyes, even under dimmed lighting, appeared to be the same golden-amber color of a caution light warning off a potential head-on collision.

Allie observed the exchange of amusing and ingratiating conversational pleasantries taking place between Kevin and Cassandra. Kevin said he'd arrived early enough to order a drink at the bar. He got distracted with checking messages on his phone and didn't realize until he took a sip that the bartender had given him a Shirley Temple by mistake.

Allie smiled but said nothing. Kevin's odd behavior was making her skin itch.

Cassandra revealed that her career in medical equipment sales spanned nearly three decades. Kevin noted this was difficult to believe considering she didn't look a day over thirty-five.

Allie's smile dissolved. She stifled an urge to clear her throat.

Cassandra then confessed that the stress caused by a contentious divorce, corporate downsizing, and an increased workload with no promotion or pay increase all contributed to her need for a change of scenery, better working conditions and more authority. After all, she felt she deserved it. Besides, she claimed, after working her way to the top without a single break or helping hand, she wasn't the type to give in easily—to anyone.

Allie assumed Cassandra had made quite an impression on Doug Wylie by marketing herself with mastery and foresight, and by using the same skill set that had Kevin beguiled this very minute. As Cassandra continued sharing her in-depth autobiography over the course of dinner, Allie noticed a couple important points. One, the woman clearly had the brains and the brawn to get her way; and two, nothing got past her. Playing favorites was a big no-no in Cassandra's book, unless, it seemed, she was the one at play.

Definitely a lioness to be watched carefully.

If Kevin had come to the same conclusions, he didn't seem to be concerned, but why should he? He had bragging rights. And brag he did. He waxed eloquent on how second quarter numbers placed the L.A. District in the top three nationally.

Allie still hadn't said anything more profound than, "Could you please pass the steak sauce?" when Cassandra moved the conversation closer to home.

"After reviewing total volume data, I was impressed with your district numbers, Kevin. Also, with the way they helped the mediocre performance of the region as a whole."

"Yes, once again," Kevin added, wearing humility like a fuzzy angora sweater, "it's the first-rate performance of the L.A. district keeping the entire South Western Region afloat."

"Doug told me as much," Cassandra purred, giving Kevin's hand a gentle squeeze.

Releasing her coal-black hair from the tortoiseshell shackle had certainly given Cassandra a more relaxed and less intense look, but the ebony turtleneck sweater and those bright red pouty lips of hers gave the raven-haired seductress the uncanny resemblance to a black widow spider.

Without allowing Cassandra's less-than-subtle gesture to register, Kevin shifted gears. "I'm sure you two went on some great calls today." He turned away from her to grin at Allie. She smiled back, noting in her peripheral vision, but not liking, the stiffening of Cassandra's facial muscles.

At that point, Allie finally spoke up, sharing with Kevin the results of the afternoon visits. She kept her voice strong and confident despite feeling the weight of Cassandra's heavy stare.

After dinner, Cassandra ordered a snifter of Remy Martin cognac, which she claimed could "elicit the most subtle hint of orange."

Whatever.

Kevin rested his forearms on the table and steepled his hands, bouncing his fingertips together. "Did Allie happen to mention her new goal for this year?"

"Ah, yes," Cassandra recalled, "she has aspirations to reach the pinnacle of sales success and be number one in . . ." she paused, "the region, is it?"

"No," Kevin replied, "the *nation.*"

Cassandra's eyes widened. Allie knew the surprise was feigned.

With the eagerness of a new father ready to hand out cigars, Kevin's face shone with pride. "According to the latest report, her numbers are unbeatable in the region, and she easily places in the top five nationally. Barring any major disruptions to her current sales trends, and if she continues to put forth the effort, she's right on track to reach her goal."

Cassandra's shoulders shifted. Dropping her head she glared at Allie. "Is that right? Well, then I suppose you've got a great shot at winning the title *and* the crown." Her voice sounded as coarse as sandpaper. *"Don't you, Alexis?"*

Alexis? Why did she call me that? Allie wondered. *She normally* would have set Cassandra, or anyone else, straight about her name. However, Kevin had stooped over to pick up his dropped napkin and didn't even notice the faux pas; and at that point, Allie only cared about getting through the evening ASAP, so she kept quiet.

"My original plans had me visiting your district after the first of the year." Cassandra spoke, peering over the rim of her glass. "But I changed my mind." She took a sip of her navel-essence liqueur, swallowed then leaned in close to Kevin. "I couldn't wait that long to see you in action." Could he smell that subtle hint of citrus she'd been crowing about? Allie supposed he could.

"I was honored to be the first on your list," replied Kevin.

Though Cassandra was someone rumored to be all work and no play, her gleaming dark eyes, and her cheeks, now reddened with a teenage blush, proved otherwise. The semi-seclusion of their dimly lit booth offered all the trappings of a made-for-TV epic romance— minus the unfortunate presence of a certain drug rep .

She's beautiful, Allie admitted to herself, watching Cassandra execute her juju. However, she was also cold and uncompromising, like a carefully sculpted block of ice. Allie was sure she'd just crossed over into the *Twilight Zone* when Cassandra took another sip of brandy and said, "I'd like to sit in on a few of your district presentations during the national sales meeting."

Without hesitation Kevin said, "That works for me."

Oh boy. He was soaking up Cassandra's attention the way a fluffy paint roller absorbs latex primer, but Allie knew Kevin *had* to cooperate with his new supervisor—in whatever manner that required. If not, it could spell trouble for any number of innocent bystanders caught in the eye of Hurricane Cassandra.

Summoning the waiter from across the room with a lifted hand, the hurricane ordered her second cognac. The edge had been taken off, but she was still as sharp as a razor, using sugarcoated words and beguiling Kabuki body language to play Kevin Rafferty like a one-stringed Stradivarius.

The meal that Allie had just eaten gurgled in her belly as a horrendous thought smacked her upside the head. *To what lengths would this power maven be willing to go to get what she wanted? And what would it mean for Allie and her goal?*

* * *

On Thursday afternoon, Kevin stopped by Allie's storage unit. She thought he'd come by, like he'd told her he would, to discuss her action items for the upcoming meeting. Instead, he shared the disturbing details of his private discussion with Cassandra. The topic: Allie's abysmal job performance.

By the time Kevin left the parking lot, Allie was on the verge of angry tears. Fortunately, a DEFCON 3 text message to Beth soon had help on the way.

"Where are you now?" Beth asked, after telling Allie she was behind the wheel of her Ford Focus, using her Bluetooth. One of Beth's pet peeves was people who broke the law prohibiting cell phone usage without a hands-free device. Another was people texting while driving.

"I'm sitting in my car in Mo'Joes parking lot," Allie lowered the volume on her stereo, "listening to KKLA and waiting for my best friend and spiritual advisor to get here and calm me down."

95

"Don't worry, I won't be long. It's ride-share Thursday. Traffic's not bad, especially for 5:30."

"Thanks for coming over on such short notice, Beth."

"You're welcome, but it's no biggie. We'd just finished a department managers' meeting, and I planned to head in your direction anyway. I need to return the research books on parapsychology, precognition, and psychokinesis I checked out from the East Hills Public Library."

"Uh, okay. How's that thesis coming along, by the way?" She wasn't really in the mood to discuss Beth's studies; but it offered Allie a distraction from the chaotic thoughts that had turned her head into a hive full of agitated bees.

"Better than I expected, thanks for asking. Listen, Allie, why don't you give me a rundown on this crisis situation."

"Mm, it's not exactly a crisis *yet*, but the atmospheric pressure being exerted by my boss's boss is about to make mincemeat out of my career."

"Allie?"

"What?"

"Could you be a *little* more specific?"

"Okay, here it is in a nutshell. A power-hungry woman named Cassandra Hartwell recently took over as national director of sales. This makes her Kevin's boss. You remember my manager, Kevin, right? You saw him at Rathman's that time he bought a bottle of cologne. Midnight Cowboy, I think. Or was it Danger Zone? Anyway, Cassandra flew out from Atlanta two days ago to work with me in the field. Afterward she met with Kevin. I talked with him today, and he said she was displeased—that's how she put it, *displeased*—with my inventory management, the way I interacted with people in the field, and my disposition as a pharmaceutical rep. Kevin was stunned, and told her as much, which he said seemed to *displease* her even more.

"He also told me he's confused. Well, *I'm not* confused. Not at all. I think that woman is out to get me, if you can believe it; and I think she's jealous of my alliance with Kevin. I suppose either he can't see it or he doesn't want to admit it. The worst part isn't just her displeasure. It's what she's planning to do. She's going to make changes to our sales goals, retroactive to the start of the fourth quarter. Kevin argued it would negatively impact certain territories, such as mine, but Cassandra insisted that it would create a more level playing field for everyone. I just love that. *Level playing field.* Ha! More bureaucratic mumbo jumbo."

Allie's pulse quickened. After so many years of having things flow along as she desired, her life seemed be returning to its old pattern of moving in unpredictable directions. The thought sickened her. She needed to maintain control. "What do you *think?*"

Beth was silent for several seconds, before saying, *"That's your idea of a nutshell?"*

"I was hoping you'd say something with a more spiritual or psychological flavor. I'm not sure I can come up with the best solution to fight this, this . . . this *thing.*"

"Relax, Allie," Beth said, using a calming voice. "I'm sure you'll look at both the positives and the negatives before taking action. I have faith in your ability to make reasonable judgments."

"Oh, come on. Don't make me sound so wise. I'm anything *but.*"

"That's not true."

Frustrated, Allie said, "Remember back when the most important person in my life was *me?* I sure wasn't thinking about consequences then."

"Yeah, and I also remember what brought that on. You had more than enough trauma for an eleven-year-old, and then you got the double whammy just a few years later."

"Two and a half years to be exact," said Allie.

But who's counting?

"Don't be so hard on yourself," Beth maintained. "It was a normal period of sadness and defiance on the part of a grieving adolescent. The unfortunate thing is that most people in your life didn't recognize it as your silent cry for help."

"I know, but you did, Beth." Allie would never forget how Beth's protective instincts had kicked in, how Beth had nurtured Allie like an injured bird until she began to heal. "You're an awesome friend and counselor." Her voice caught, and she cleared her throat. "Which is why I need your input on this."

Modest as usual, Beth chuckled. "Look, I'm coming up on my exit now. I'll be there before you know it. So go on inside, get yourself a cup of coffee, and find a good place for us to sit, okay?"

Allie said she would and ended the call. Taking a deep breath, she got out of her SUV. Maybe she'd feel better after an iced Americano.

If only life's problems were as easily solved.

* * *

With Phoebe off for the evening, Allie gave her order to the blond fellow with the kooky stare. Like last time, he seemed interested in discussing life beyond Caffé Americanos. And, as before, customers accumulated behind Allie like rush-hour traffic piling up at the East L.A. interchange.

The credit card transaction device on the counter was broken—according to Kooky. So Allie handed over her debit card, then began absently tapping on the screen of her cell phone, keeping her gaze down.

"Enjoy that Americano," Kooky said, holding up the card after he'd swiped it.

"Thanks. I will." Allie tried taking the card from him, but he held on with a playful tug until she broke down and gave him a smile.

A simple little smile.

It was something Gretchen would have done without even thinking. Smile, chatter, make a ridiculously amusing remark, just plain bubble over with charm and enthusiasm. It all came so easily to Gretchen, someone who oozed vitality and charisma. Someone Allie *never* would have thought she'd one day have the desire to emulate.

The commotion caused by a young barista-in-training interrupted Allie's thoughts. As though witnessing a comedy skit or play, Allie watched the flustered plump girl distress onlookers by cross-pollinating their orders. She placed caramel drizzle in a mochaccino, chocolate syrup in a caramel macchiato, and who knew what in a vanilla chai latte. The final act had her squirting defenseless patrons with ribbons of whipped cream when she unintentionally hit the nozzle while shaking the can.

The spectacle gave Allie a chance to see her own work situation in a new light. Her compassion for the barista eased Allie's mounting aggravation over Kevin's questionable loyalty. She prayed that no more than the required amount of espresso would be added to her large Americano, lest she morph into a human jackhammer.

Eventually, Allie got her drink and dropped down into a seat at a table near the front. Not five minutes passed before Beth showed up, wearing an ivory blouse tucked into a knee-length black silk skirt, both from *The Loft*, inside the Westside Plaza. It was the usual type of minimalist outfit she wore to work. Beth spotted Allie and pointed to the front counter. Allie nodded, relieved to have a friend who not only was willing to rush to the rescue but also had wisdom to share.

A few minutes later, Beth slung her black suede shoulder bag over a chair, set down her cup, and took a seat at the table. "I gave this some thought on the way over."

"And?"

"And I'd have to say that with Cassandra calling the shots, you should expect trials, difficulties, and a testing of your faith."

Maybe soliciting Beth's advice hadn't been such a great idea after all. This wasn't exactly what Allie wanted to hear.

"Are you sure she has the power to make changes that could impact your numbers for the *entire* year?" Beth dunked a tea bag into her cup of hot water while eyeing Allie.

"Oh, I'm sure, all right. I watched with my own two eyes as she turned Kevin into an obedient wad of Silly Putty."

"Yikes, Allie, that's harsh."

"Kevin said Doug Wylie . . . he's the president of sales in North America . . . told him at their recent manager's meeting that Cassandra had a 'backbone of titanium and the resolve to make things happen.'" Allie huffed. "*A backbone of titanium? I ask you, who talks like that?* I'll tell you who, someone who's either very impressed or very deceived. Plus, at dinner last night, Cassandra referred to me as *Alexis. Right in front of Kevin.* He didn't even notice because he was too spellbound, but still, *how rude is that?*"

The corners of Beth's mouth turned upward ever so slightly. Her face became what Allie called *intensely pensive,* and her bottle green eyes reflected unease and the desire to tread with care. "Let me ask you a question."

Allie had learned to spot Beth's end-around approach, but that didn't make the process any easier. She knew Beth was about to suggest Allie take a hard and objective look at the circumstances at hand, be fair in her assessment of the facts, and then come to an honest conclusion about the reality of her wants versus her needs.

She hated this part of problem solving.

Beth folded the little paper jacket she'd removed from her tea bag and looked up. "How important is all of this to you?" Her voice was tempered with concern, but at that point it didn't matter—Allie's objective was nonnegotiable. Would she be able to explain that in a way Beth could understand?

Allie pictured the little girl at the storage unit, spinning through the air in a perfect cartwheel, then skipping toward her father, eager to embrace him in love and receive his affirmation. Allie stared at the name, *Rosebud,* Kooky had written on her cup. A crushing sadness settled in her chest, while pooling tears blurred her vision before spilling down her face.

"I think I need to prove I can do this," Allie said at last, imagining how proud this accomplishment would have made her father. "Prove I'm strong, and resilient, a fighter who doesn't back down. I gave in once before, you know. I buckled under the pressure and let tough circumstances determine my path. I won't let that happen again." She glanced up at Beth, whose eyes exposed her own touched and torn heart. "So how important is it? Very."

Without a word, just the understanding touch of a true friend, Beth laid a gentle hand on top of Allie's.

Chapter 8

Beach House Dreams

Late Saturday morning, one week following the barbecue, Andrew left the house to purchase a day planner for his new job. He drove over to Ledgers-n-Things, an office supply store located in East Valley's largest outdoor shopping center, which happened to sell more than just office-related items; it had an aisle of party supplies as well. Seeing the paper plates, cups, and napkins, he remembered Beth's dinner invitation. So when he returned to his car, he phoned her.

"Why not tonight?" Beth immediately suggested. Andrew heard bottles clanking and crisper drawers being opened and closed. It sounded like she was gathering the makings of a meal. "Allie was already planning to come over."

"Sure." See? This was how he would love for God to run his life . . . smoothly and easily.

"It gets dark by six," Beth said, "so why don't we meet here at, say, three? I'll put the chicken on the grill after we've relaxed a little while."

"Great. I can't wait." Andrew watched a small spider scurry down the Mustang's windshield then dart across a wiper blade, disappearing over the side of the car. "What can I bring?"

"Just bring yourself, thank you. And an appetite."

"Easy enough. We're a traveling pair these days."

Andrew grinned. Here he was, soon to be hanging out with two of his favorite people at one of his favorite places. Years ago, he'd loved being at Beth's Aunt Ginny's beach house. He and his friends had spent countless hours in the summers there during high school. Aunt Ginny, the most patient and thoughtful person Andrew had ever known, opened her cozy home to as many kids as would fit inside at any given time.

Andrew thought about the Saturday nights he'd stayed over; hanging out with Beth's older brother, James, and at least one of their cousins, sleeping in sleeping bags on the living room floor while the girls stayed in the spare bedroom, talking and giggling until well past midnight. They'd all wake the next morning to the aroma of sizzling bacon, and the incredible scent of Aunt Ginny's buttermilk pancakes fresh off the griddle.

After breakfast they'd go down to the socked-in beach. The fog usually lifted by noon, and the sun's welcome warmth helped to offset the water's chill. At the end of the day, Beth's fair skin had always been burned. The bright pink hue would become an angry red right about the time they all piled into James's Toyota minivan—the ultimate summertime shuttle—for the forty-five-minute drive home.

"I should call Allie," Andrew said. "See if she wants to carpool."

"Mm, I think she'll drive over by herself. She's spending the night. I told her I'd help her pick out an impressive power suit tomorrow for her district presentation at an upcoming sales meeting."

"Oh." Andrew tried picturing his sweet Allie wearing a power suit. "She didn't mention the meeting to me when we spoke at the barbecue, or while she was talking shop with my dad."

"There've been some new developments with her job, and she's pretty upset about a particular work-related incident. I'll see if I can get her to explain it to you in her own words."

He thanked Beth for the advance warning. "The way Allie operates, I never would have guessed there was a problem."

But that was part of her infinite charm, and what caused Andrew the most frustration; Allie kept her deepest emotions hidden under lock and key.

After saying goodbye to Beth, Andrew thumbed off the phone and noted the time on the stereo. He was ready to be at Beth's place right *now*. Or anyplace, really, as long as Allie was there.

* * *

Andrew brought the Mustang to a stop in front of a cottage-like, off-white house with mint green shutters and a brown shake roof. He pressed the gearshift into first, turned off the engine, and looked at his watch. It read fifteen hundred on the dot, which was a relief. Before the Navy, Andrew hadn't been such a stickler about punctual arrivals. But in this instance, it probably had more to do with the company he was about to be in than with military training. He glanced around for Allie's SUV but didn't see it. Well, so much for the company, he thought, getting out of the car and smiling to himself.

Still, it was a beautiful, cloudless, breezy afternoon, with much to look forward to and be thankful for.

Beth scampered out of the house wearing tan pants and a long-sleeved pink shirt, greeting Andrew as he entered the enclosed front yard. A round glass top table and four white powder-coated steel chairs sat in the center of the small area of light red concrete paving stones.

As soon as Andrew stepped through the front door and into the living room, Beth began pointing out all Aunt Ginny's recent upgrades. A flat stone ledge had been built in front of the raised fireplace, replacing the original worn brick hearth. The same sofa and love seat from their teen years had been reupholstered in a soft light blue denim fabric, which Beth called chambray. Leading Andrew through the dining area and into the kitchen, Beth told him how the old Formica countertops and speckled gold linoleum floor no longer kept the house stuck in a bygone era. The plain boring kitchen, Beth said with a look of relief, had been transformed by soft pastel colors and bright reflections. The sunshine, filtering down through the new skylight, brought to life the subtle color of marbled green granite and the brushed sheen of stainless steel appliances.

Beth glanced at the floor. "This beautiful pale green tile was my favorite part of the upgrades. See how well it blends with the granite? Aunt Ginny also had it put in the bathroom. *Oh, Andrew!*" Beth shuddered. "Remember that long shag carpet in the living room and bedrooms?"

Andrew chuckled. "Kind of a golden moss color, as I recall. Your brother used to say it was originally plant life from the sea, washed ashore, and brought back here by Aunt Ginny."

"Along with a thousand and one seashells, sand dollars, worndown glass chunks and anything else that looked interesting."

Andrew observed the new beige carpeting in the living room and dining area. "Well, this carpet . . . what do you call it?"

"Berber."

"It looks good. I guess the flat weave is more practical than shag; there's no chance of dropping something in it and never finding it again."

"Yeah, like the little Black Beauty charm I got for my sixteenth birthday. I'd only had it a short time before the clasp on my gold chain broke, and the charm disappeared. I know that old sea monster swallowed it up."

Andrew grinned. Not only had the shag carpet looked like something dragged in from the sea, but it had smelled like it too. It had given off a distinct "beachy" scent, which may have come from all the accumulated sand, brought into the house on damp beach towels, crusty flip flops, and in between bare toes. Andrew was just deciding that making such an observation out loud might be rude when he heard a short knock on the front door. It opened slightly, and Allie poked her head into the house. "Hey there." She came inside, closed the door behind her and dropped a lavender cardigan and a pink and yellow striped canvas tote bag onto the loveseat. Her wide-set and perfect eyes, the gentle arch of her brows, the slight width of her nose with its graceful point, matching that of her chin, and the cupid's bow on her upper lip made her face look so sweet and angelic Andrew almost sighed.

Although already familiar with the remodeled house, Allie joined Beth and Andrew as Beth continued the tour. Andrew insisted Allie step ahead of him. He did this because he was a gentleman, but also because it gave him a chance to inhale the soft and clean scent of her freshly washed hair, which was pulled up into that dratted ponytail and still a bit damp. Her shoulders looked sculpted and squared in her white long-sleeve Henley, while the denim fabric of her plum-colored pants gently hugged her long legs and narrow hips. Andrew found that he was far more interested in the details of Allie than in those of the house.

* * *

Just after four-thirty, Beth came into the kitchen through the back door; she carried a red and white checked platter of chicken, hot off the grill and smothered in barbecue sauce, over to the oval solid oak table; the same table Andrew recalled dining on during their youth. Surrounding the chicken were accompanying side dishes of coleslaw, potato salad, and cornbread. The air was filled with the comforting and delicious scents of the wonderful meal ahead of them, and of the soothing seaside setting. From the table came the spicy tang of the barbecue sauce, the sweetness of the slaw and the cornbread, and the rich egg and fragrant mustard aromas from the potato salad. The salt-tinged air and faint smell of the ocean from the onshore beach breeze created a feeling of relaxed ease. Andrew felt his heartbeat slow in response.

Beth had seated Andrew at one end of the table and Allie at the other. Behind Andrew was the entrance to the open kitchen, and behind Allie, a sliding glass door leading out to a small patio. Beth took a chair near the wall, behind which was the short hallway to the bedrooms.

Smiling, Andrew gave thanks for the meal and for their time together that evening. He couldn't remember the last time he'd offered up grace so passionately. Life couldn't have been much better.

Andrew eyed the chicken, recalling aloud how Aunt Ginny prepared it the same way, served it on the same platter, and placed it on the same table.

"Though back then," Beth added to Andrew's observation, "it would have been piled much higher either with grilled chicken or hot dogs and hamburgers—enough food for first *and* second helpings."

"Is it me, or does it seem like we're back in high school, hanging out, chowing down, and preparing to discuss life's more profound issues?" Andrew asked.

Allie snickered. "The only profound issue in my life at that time involved keeping my grades up enough to get into college." She reached for a chicken leg, saying, "Pardon my hands." After setting it on her plate, she licked her fingers.

Beth bit her lower lip, stifling a big grin. "Oh, Allie, I remember how angry you used to make Mr. Ellis. I thought for sure he'd throw you out of English Lit, or at least give you a lousy grade."

Allie shook her head. "He couldn't do either. That man was just plain irascible. I never did anything to justify being thrown out, and my test scores were so high he had no choice but to give me an A." Wearing a playful smile, she dished up some potato salad. "And don't think it didn't almost do him in."

"I didn't have Mr. Ellis for English Lit." Andrew scanned his memory for his own former teacher. "I don't recall who I had."

"Let's see." Allie glanced at the ceiling fan above them. "It would've been either Butler or North."

"That's it," he said, "Mr. North. And what a character he was. He knew the sound of every fire engine and truck in the department. He'd be sitting at his desk, fifteen feet from the window, but whenever any fire vehicle drove by, Engine 13, Truck 11 or whichever, he'd name it—and get it right every single time."

"From what I remember, he also recognized the booming sound of someone's vintage muscle car," Beth's eyes crinkled at the corners, *"Andrew."*

Andrew grinned. "Yeah, the good ol' days." He piled his plate with food then signaled Beth with a discreet nod in Allie's direction.

She immediately took the hint. "It sounds like your new sales director and your old English teacher have a thing or two in common, Allie." Beth spooned coleslaw onto her plate. "I believe there's a lesson to be learned here."

"What? That if I don't behave myself around Principal Cassandra Hartwell, she'll have me expelled from school?"

"Are you being feisty, Allison Elizabeth Hendrickson?"

"No, I'm not, Bethany Maude McKinley."

Andrew's laughter caught in his windpipe, and he almost choked on his mouthful of iced tea.

"Hey! You promised you wouldn't tell anyone!" Beth's cheeks flushed bright red.

Allie made an "oops" face then asked, "Isn't there a statute of limitations on keeping middle names a secret?"

Andrew chuckled. "Aw, it's not so bad, Beth. My grandma's older sister was named Maude."

"Yes, *exactly.*" Beth threw her hands up. "Thank you, very much. Now do you see why I only use the initial M? Why on earth did I ever tell you that, Allie?"

"It was at summer camp, remember? You had to either reveal your middle name or go into the boys' cabin at midnight and say you were scared and wanted to go home."

"Oh, now I remember." Beth clicked her tongue, rolling her eyes upward. "Truth or dare. I should have taken the dare. When was that, anyway?"

Andrew knew the answer. He also knew what Allie had said about him one night during that trying week in the mountains, when interloper Carl Lansing never left her side.

"You and I had only been friends a short while," Beth said, "so it had to be our second year of high school—or, the summer before anyway."

Allie slid a forkful of potato salad into her mouth. "Mm hmm."

Andrew had no desire to relive his nightmare memories from youth camp. Although he'd been overjoyed to witness the spiritual change take place in Allie, the only other worthwhile memory was when everyone boarded the bus to leave.

"Boy, we *do* sound like high schoolers, don't we?" Andrew looked at Beth to make his point. "Can't seem to stay on one topic for more than ten seconds at a time."

"Right. Where were we, Andrew?"

"Um, Allie was saying something about her new sales director—"

"Okay you two," Allie chimed in, "I see what's going on here; but I've already made up my mind, so don't try talking me out of anything. I'm going to fight for this. No power-hungry corporate schemer is keeping me from a top sales spot and a big bonus check. I plan to use that money for Erin's and Edward's college expenses. They need my help, and I'm not going to let them down. Period."

Andrew recognized the set of Allie's jaw. Her severe determination often erupted so suddenly it took him by surprise. It seemed so inconsistent with her usually mild and composed demeanor, and he'd noticed that it only came to life when something significant troubled her.

"Speaking of the twins," Andrew interjected, "how are they doing these days? And how's your mom?"

"They're all well, thank you. Mom still works at K&L Flooring, and the twins are making things happen at East Valley High. Erin's playing the lead female part in *Fiddler on the Roof,* and Edward was recently voted in as ASB senior class president.

"And by the way, Andrew," Allie continued, bringing the conversational focus back to her job, "remember me talking to your dad about Dr. Stevenson?"

Andrew nodded.

"My current quarterly data shows that he's written more prescriptions for Advantol than anyone else in my territory, which is great. Except that Cassandra Hartwell wants to see to it that all the reps in our division lose the entire Pain Management specialty. No more calls to their offices and no more credit for any Advantol sales they generate. After all the effort we've put into growing their business, we have to hand them over to another sales division. Effective immediately, if Cassandra gets her way."

There was something about this whole thing with Cassandra that was bigger than Allie was letting on. He didn't understand it all, but he knew she was taking what could have been just a setback in her career as much more than that. Oh boy, did he want to rescue her somehow. Where was that knight suit when a guy needed it?

* * *

After dinner, the three sat around the table, relaxing and reminiscing. Andrew was comfortably stuffed, and normally, he might have been drowsy, but being around Allie had all his nerve endings on red alert.

"I've got a suggestion." Beth stood and began loading her arms with empty plates and dishes. "Why don't you two go down to the beach and take a nice stroll along the bike path while I clean this place up?"

Andrew glanced over at Beth. Her twinkling green eyes made him feel like he was on the receiving end of a top-secret transmission. It was like she was signing without hands or sending Morse code messages without the dits and dots.

Allie got up. "Oh, Beth, I don't want you to have to . . ."

Beth shook her head, hands too full to be raised in protest. "Don't say another word. Andrew, please get this girl out of here before Maude throws another ugly fit."

"Consider it done." Andrew motioned Allie toward the back kitchen door.

Allie shrugged then said to Beth, "Okay, you win." She pulled her sweater off the loveseat and threw it around her shoulders as they stepped outside. Even so, she shuddered from the sudden cool air. Andrew wished he had a jacket to give her, but he only wore a long-sleeved polo shirt. He'd have taken it off and handed it to her if he hadn't thought suddenly going bare-chested would have sent her running back inside the house.

Allie dropped her head back and inhaled deeply. "I love that smell."

"Which one? The sea or the salt?"

"Neither. The musky one. I think it's just all the moisture. The fog maybe?" Her gaze was directed at floodlights at the edge of the yard. A brisk breeze swirled wispy tendrils into knots in the yellow beams.

Andrew and Allie walked toward the sound of the sea. After reaching the end of Aunt Ginny's street, they descended two flights of concrete steps to the sandy beach. Music echoed down from the top of the bluff behind them. It sounded like some kind of country song; Andrew didn't recognize it. He figured it came from a car radio. He could imagine someone's Chevy parked near the edge of the cliff, overlooking the water. Two people lost in thought and emotion, clinging to every second they had in the company of the one they loved.

He glanced at Allie, but she wasn't focused on him. She gazed out at the water. He shook his head, embarrassed by his sentimental thoughts, even though no one could hear them.

The nearly full moon was bright enough to vanquish the fog and light up the bike path near the water. Andrew and Allie walked up and then back down the shoreline, chatting about nothing in particular. Andrew had the feeling she wasn't entirely there. Uncharacteristically, he did most of the talking.

It only took thirty minutes to get to the end of the bike path and back to where they started. Reluctant to go inside, Andrew led Allie to a concrete bench set in the sand just off the path. She smiled, seemingly liking the idea.

As they settled themselves, the car on the bluff drove off and the music faded away, leaving a soothing lull in its place. The waves continued their unending cycle, rushing up to the shore like a curious child and then quickly retreating back to the safety and familiarity of their mother, the sea. The moon hung low in the sky, casting a glistening glow on the water's surface—as though prepared to illuminate unknown or hidden secrets.

Allie buttoned up her sweater and leaned forward on the bench, resting her forearms on her thighs. She watched the waves as they flowed in and out, in and out.

So constant. So reliable. So trustworthy. *Like you,* thought Andrew. *How could we have been so close our entire lives, and you never felt this special bond between us?*

As if able to read his thoughts, Allie turned her head to look at him. He gazed into her soft and soulful eyes, feeling as though he was finally making a tenuous connection with her spirit. He wasn't going to pass up this opportunity. Unable to hold back his love any longer, he reached for her right hand lying on top of her left. With a slow and gentle motion he slid his palm against hers, opening her hand flat and lacing their fingers together. She didn't pull away.

Andrew's pulse quickened. The contact felt magical.

He reached up with his right hand and brushed back from the side of Allie's face strands of hair tossed about by the crisp onshore breeze. Her hair felt as satiny as it had always looked.

When she didn't flinch, he lightly stroked the length of her cheek with the backs of his fingertips. She looked directly at him, and their gazes locked together. He felt like their eye contact said everything that needed to be said in that moment. Or at least he hoped so. He wanted to believe she was finally allowing herself to feel for him what he'd felt for her all along.

* * *

It was so weird. Allie couldn't figure it out. One moment everything was as it was supposed to be. She and Andrew were walking along the beach and talking like two old friends. The next moment he was looking at her with an unfamiliar intensity, with the eyes of a stranger. But Andrew was no stranger. She'd known him most of her life though had never imagined having feelings for him like this.

Or had she?

Then it hit her. From some vague recess in her mind, she heard Grandma Mary's voice, saying, "Trust him." After Allie's acceptance of Christ, she assumed that her grandmother, a believer, like Andrew, had meant that Allie should put her trust in the Lord, but now there seemed to be more coming to the forefront of Allie's memory. What about her fear that she had lost something of great value? Had that been a kind of subconscious message? She thought about the man she'd envisioned, the one whose face she couldn't see clearly—and then in one quick burst of clarity everything came into focus. The dreams she'd been having over the past few months had been about Andrew!

About *her* and Andrew.

But *this* was not a dream. This was real, and nothing like this had ever happened to her before—with anyone.

Allie sensed that the tide was bringing each wave further up the shore, but she didn't look. She couldn't look at anything but Andrew's face.

He continued to gaze at her, taking her in, absorbing her presence, her essence, her being. His eyes seemed to be overflowing with longing and devotion, and Allie felt herself falling into them, drowning in them, not wanting to be rescued. Her breathing became shallow, constricted with anticipation as Andrew brought his face closer.

A thousand thoughts bounced around inside her head, like silver balls zinging through a pinball machine. Things were happening too fast, and the intensity of it suddenly generated unanswered and confusing questions: When did Andrew return home? Why hadn't he contacted her or Beth before they ran into him at Mo'Joes? Who was the woman Phoebe referred to as his "girlfriend"? And most important, how could Allie become emotionally involved with him yet remain committed to her career goals?

Needing to ground herself and turn down the amps on the electrical currents flowing between her and Andrew, Allie leaned away slightly. She said the first thing that popped into her head. "Thanks again for keeping my debit card safe for me."

Almost imperceptibly, Andrew's demeanor changed. He stiffened ever so slightly. "Sure." He looked away from her, staring straight ahead toward the advancing waves.

Allie took a few seconds to study his profile. It was so distinct, with its high bridged-nose, pronounced brow, and slightly squared jaw. He had such strong facial features, but his appearance was so gentle and nonthreatening. And Gretchen was right about Andrew having deep-brown, passionate eyes, but how did she remember that from seeing him only once before, when Allie had never even noticed?

"I'm just glad I was the one who found it." His voice sounded tight and edgy.

Unsure of what her words had triggered in him, Allie unlaced her fingers from Andrew's, placing her hand back on top of her leg. "My friend, Phoebe—she's works at Mo'Joes—short black hair, blue-framed glasses?"

Andrew's eyes shot to hers, almost in defense. He licked his lower lip. "I know who she is."

"She um, told me you bought two coffees last Saturday, and then went back the next day . . ."

Say it, Allie, she thought. *With your girlfriend!*

Why couldn't she get the words out?

She knew why. What if it was true? Could she handle it?

Huh? Could she *handle* it? What was she thinking? Why *couldn't* she handle it? Why did any of this even matter? Less than an hour ago, Andrew had simply been a good friend.

Andrew watched her, not saying anything. He wasn't making this easy.

Oh, get it over with, she told herself.

"That you were there with a young woman," she finally said before shifting her gaze to the waves. She waited, hoping he'd tell her Phoebe was mistaken. He didn't; he stayed quiet, and Allie felt a stirring sensation in her stomach, which she recognized all too quickly. She felt caught between her emotions for Andrew and her two worst enemies, denial and ignorance.

The uneasy moment lingered until Andrew's cell phone rang. He reached into his jacket pocket, engaging the speaker while trying to extract the phone.

"Hello? *Hello?* Andrew?"

Frown lines bisected the space between his brows. "Yes?"

He disabled the speaker function but the caller's voice echoed loud and clear. "Hi, Andrew, it's Jennifer."

Jennifer?

Andrew turned his head away from Allie. "Hello."

"I thought once we get everything moved into my place tomorrow, we could order Chinese take-out for dinner and then watch a movie on DVD. I have hundreds of them to choose from."

Get everything moved into her place? Chinese take-out? Watch a movie? Together? Allie's self-control began to slip away again, and she was getting tired of it. Anger, frustration, and a profound sense of unfairness welled up inside her while tears flooded her eyes. She'd vowed that nothing like this would ever happen to her again, and she meant it. There was too much at stake—her pride, her heart, her career—and she wasn't about to let Andrew Gallagher do what Carl Lansing had done to her two years before. No way.

Allie pushed off the bench and nearly ran toward the beach house, expecting Andrew to call to her.

He never did.

* * *

Allie managed to get to bed that night without seeing Andrew again and without saying more than a few words to Beth. Going to sleep saved her from having to sort out all her thoughts and feelings. But morning came soon enough, and she had no choice but to face it.

She entered the kitchen and cringed at the bright sunlight perpetrating a full on assault on the room. Beth, standing near the window, wearing a much too cheerful blue gingham apron, appeared undaunted by the sun's invasion. She flashed a jolly good morning grin that Allie was in no mood to reciprocate, and then held up a batter-splattered index card. "Look what I found inside a cute little tin box in the cupboard."

Allie slumped into an iron chair at the small round café table near the back door. "Hmm, let's see? A recipe for humble pie?"

Beth squinted, proceeding with caution. "Nooo. Aunt Ginny's buttermilk pancakes. I thought I'd make some. What say *you?*"

Rubbing the heels of her hands back and forth across her eyelids probably made Allie look like a little girl waking up from a nap; whereas, in reality she felt more like a scared child waking up from a nightmare. With unfocused eyes and attention, she answered the question. "Sure. Fine. Whatever."

Beth dropped her arms by her sides, her sunny smile gone. "All right, what's going on?"

"Nothing. I didn't sleep well, and I guess I'm worried about work stuff."

Beth laid the card down on the counter and took a seat next to Allie. "A pastor once told a story about an elderly woman in the congregation who worried about any and every little thing. He told her that most of what we spend so much time worrying about never even happens, to which the woman replied, 'You see? It works.'" She grinned.

"Okay. I get your point." Allie tried sounding gracious. "Instead of worrying, I could be, I don't know, *praying?*" Her question was more of a self-rebuke than an attempt to find an answer, especially from Beth. They were too like-minded to play games with each other.

Beth took Allie's hand. "Let me."

Allie's head drooped down further, and her chest began to spasm in anguish. Under the circumstances, there didn't seem to be any need to pretend. She was in terrible pain, and Beth knew it because Beth was Beth. For that matter, God knew it, too. And He already knew what was in Allie's heart. That thought unleashed the tears. Allie let them come. They flooded out of her eyes and splashed onto her arm as Beth said, "Lord, please place your gentle, loving arm around Allie's shoulders, giving her the kind of peace only You can offer. Help her to stay strong, self-controlled, and sincere while facing adversity and seeking Your truth. We trust *You*, and we know You only want what's best for us."

Now Allie's forehead rested on her wet, salty arm. Her tears had become sobs, the sobs of a heartbroken child—scared, confused, hurt, and angry—but not defeated, not without hope. She knew she would be okay. She just needed a few more minutes to release her sorrow, a few more minutes to miss her father and her grandmother.

And a few more minutes to grieve for the short time on the beach when she thought she had found someone to love.

Chapter 9

Mr. Sunbeams and Merriment

*S*he fights against me and then I fight against God, Andrew
determined—which was exactly what he'd made a point of
telling himself he would not do.

Andrew slipped the Mustang into the spot next to the white-
haired lady's red Firebird, after which he sat staring at a sign on the
tan stucco wall—a warning that only guests could park there. In the
absolute sense of the word, he knew he didn't qualify. Tough. He
had something to say, and Allie would hear him out whether she
cared to or not. Andrew didn't want to fight against God, but that
didn't mean he couldn't stand up to Allie.

It was his own fault for trying to be so considerate. Why should
he even care what she thought? Nothing had changed. She was still
stubborn, willful, and difficult; too cool, too calm, and too collected;
distant, remote, and inaccessible. She was Andromeda in a power suit.

And he couldn't get her out of his mind.

He walked around the flowerbed in front of Allie's unit. Dried
Crepe Myrtle blossoms crunched under his shoes. Bright headlights
from a car entering the main driveway illuminated the private street,
and Andrew bolted down the short walkway toward Allie's front
door. Trying to jump onto the porch, he caught his foot on a step
and fell flat on his face. His keys flew from his hand and clanged
against the metal screen door.

Andrew leaned sideways to reach for them as he picked himself
up off the unbelievably scratchy welcome mat. He was brushing
some hay-like debris off his brown canvas jacket when the door
swung open.

"Andrew! What a wonderful surprise!" Gretchen's high-pitched
greeting and wide smile helped alleviate the embarrassment of his
unplanned aerial stunt.

"Hi, Gretchen," Andrew said calmly, as if he hadn't just sprawled himself across Allie's front porch.

"Come in, *come in.*" She half-dragged him through the entryway by his jacket sleeve then rushed toward the kitchen. "Make yourself at home. I need to get these fat-free fudge brownies out of the oven. The side of the box said that baking them for more than twenty-three minutes might make the edges hard and crusty. Or something like that."

The white wicker sofa in Allie's living room creaked softly as Andrew eased down on it. He inhaled the chocolate aroma that filled the house while Gretchen continued her jabbering. "Can't have hard edges. Precautions must be taken to protect my pearly whites. No one in their right mind would pay good money to have a flight attendant offer a glass of champagne while smiling with a mouthful of cracked and broken teeth."

Andrew looked around the room with curiosity. An oil painting hung above the small fireplace. It depicted a lonely lighthouse perched on a craggy cliff and overlooking the bluish green ocean. It was calming, yet in a way sad. Both the whitewashed mantle and a white wicker bookcase in the corner contained books, hardcover and paperback. He stood and stepped to the shelf to investigate their titles, finding a mixture of mystery novels, classical literature, and medical reference books, such as *Gray's Anatomy, The Merck Manual,* and a current edition of the *Physician's Desk Reference.* He called out behind him to Gretchen, "Is Allie here?"

"What?" The sound of an oven door closing came from the kitchen. "Oh, these look amazing. I've been craving chocolate for I don't know how long now."

Andrew heard the guttural idling of a car's engine out front. It was too loud to be the Firebird. Was it a different neighbor's car? He returned to the sofa and continued studying his surroundings.

Much of the light colored artwork, two tall candleholders and even the base of the glass top table in the entryway had a certain look. *What did his mom call it?* Andrew remembered only that the name was an oxymoron and that the first word was "shabby."

The doorbell rang.

"I'll be right there," yelled Gretchen, loud enough to be heard in the nearby City of Glendale. She darted out of the kitchen like a Dungeness crab running for its life, opened the front door, and gasped. *"I don't believe my eyes!"*

From Andrew's catbird seat on the sofa, he saw a light-haired man standing on the porch holding a small gold gift box.

"Joshua Walden! You look utterly magnificent." Gretchen smoothed her blouse and fluffed her hair.

114

"Hi, Gretchen. Long time no see."

"Indeed." She folded her arms across her chest, sizing him up with a nod. "Come on in."

"Thank you." He peered inside the house before entering.

Who is this guy, Joshua? Andrew wondered. Gretchen knew him, but not well it seemed. As Joshua came through the doorway, Andrew checked him out . . . *not*, of course, in the way he might notice a woman, but more in a way that, as a soldier, he'd assess a threat. To accomplish such a task on a national level, Homeland Security used a color-coding system. It went from low-level green to high-level red, with blue, yellow, and orange in between. Joshua stood only a head taller than that squirt, Gretchen. Andrew's six-feet-two-inches could easily go up against Joshua's five-feet-nine-inches, give or take an inch. So no threat detected in the height category. As Joshua stepped down into the living room, Andrew evaluated the man's physical condition. It was admirable, admittedly. He looked like he worked out or did heavy labor, but even that didn't pose a threat to Andrew in the physical fitness department. Having first picked up heavy weights during boot camp, Andrew never put them back down.

"Hey." Joshua reached forward and offered his hand to Andrew, who'd by then stood up. The smile on Joshua's boyish face could only be described as enormous and cheerful. Like mind-reading, overt cheerfulness was not one of Andrew's strengths. His mood turned cautious. The threat level had just gone from green to blue.

Andrew nodded. "Hi." He grasped Joshua's hand. The smiling man's grip was firm but not lingering; he released before Andrew, and the threat level stayed put.

Joshua sniffed once. "Mm, smells like chocolate."

Gretchen's head bobbed. "Yeah, I whipped up a batch of brownies."

"Homemade brownies, eh? Impressive."

"Oh, well I love to bake. It's one of my hobbies." She eyed the gift box.

"This is for you." Joshua placed it on his flat palm as if showcasing an item on *The Price is Right*. "But I imagine you already know what it is. I thought you'd be worried sick about it by now."

"Worried? About *what?*"

"This." He lifted the lid and tilted the open box toward her.

Her eyes bugged out. "Well, if it isn't that *absurd* little stick pin."

"It sure is sparkly," Joshua noted. "I figured with all those tiny diamonds inside the letters, it was valuable. Plus it's gold. What does the H stand for?"

Gretchen looked at him as though he had a long spiraling horn projecting out from his forehead. "First, it's gold-*plated*, not *gold;*

second, those are *cubic zirconia*, not *diamonds;* third, the G stands for Gretchen, obviously, and the H stands for Helene; and *fourth,* the W stands for a name I'm more than ready to trade in, thank you very much."

Joshua ignored the snippy tone in Gretchen's voice and kept talking, clearly exacerbating her displeasure. "I found the box in a corner of the trailer a few days ago when Steven and I were in Kalamazoo, Michigan."

"And kept it safe for me all the way home." She managed to sound surprisingly sincere even though her expression read something like, *you should have ditched it in one of those big lakes in the area.* "Joshua, you are *so* considerate." Taking the box from him, she tossed it on the entryway table with more than a little bit of English.

"My apologies. I imagine it slipped out of one of your tote bags on the drive over from Dallas."

"Mm. Could be." She placed the tip of her index finger on her chin. "Listen, how would you like to go out tonight with Bobbie and me? You remember Bobbie. She helped me move in."

"Sure, I remember."

"We're going dancing on the West Side. Monday Madness— ladies get in free."

He chuckled. "I'm not much of a dancer, so no thanks, but I appreciate the invite. You two girls go out and have some fun. Is Allie home yet? I'd like to say hello to her."

Before Gretchen could answer and convey what looked to be profound disappointment in Joshua for turning down the offer of an exciting night of dancing and madness, the doorbell rang—again. Gretchen opened the door to a dark haired man in his thirties. He was wearing a charcoal gray suit and the kind of blank expression Andrew had seen on the faces of trick-or-treaters about to receive a handful of their least favorite candy. Andrew's guess would have been black licorice. Or those red and white peppermint discs.

"Hi," the man said, "is Allie home yet?"

Gretchen blew out a puff of frustration. "She's not here."

"I'm her manager, Kevin. We talked on the phone a short while ago. I told her I wanted to make a quick stop here to discuss our upcoming sales meeting."

"Okay. Wait inside if you like. I'm her cousin, Gretchen, by the way. I live here."

"Nice to meet you." Kevin shook her hand then eased past her as Andrew noticed the wheels start spinning inside the impish little blonde's head.

116

Gretchen grabbed Kevin's forearm, leading him over to meet Andrew. Joshua added his introduction to the mix and then, at Gretchen's insistence, the three guests sat down on the sofa.

"So, who's up for some dancing tonight?" She ignored Joshua and, hands on hips, waited for a reply. "How about you, Kevin?"

"Who me?" He pointed at himself. "Oh, no. My dancing days are behind me. Besides, I have important business to discuss with Allie."

Gretchen's eyes rolled around like marbles. *"Yeah, I heard you the first time."*

She glared at Andrew. "I suppose you're going to say no, too."

He shrugged and nodded. "Sorry."

Andrew made polite conversation with the men while trying to figure out why, before storming into the kitchen, Gretchen had them all sit on the sofa when two chairs remained unoccupied. Did she have plans to move the coffee table and entertain her small audience with a song or a little tap dancing?

When the talk died down, the men stared straight ahead in uncomfortable silence, like apprehensive middle school truants waiting their turn outside the principal's office. *Could the circumstances get any more uncomfortable?* Yes, Andrew decided, they could. And they did when Gretchen answered the doorbell for the third time and walked to the edge of the entryway with her "best friend, Bobbie Brennan."

"I got a part-time job," Bobbie said to her.

"You've already got a job. A good one. You need more money all of a sudden?" Gretchen said, using a New York accent reminiscent of Rocky Graziano and flapping her wings like a chicken in distress.

"It's not for the money. It's more," Bobbie cocked her head, "recreational."

"Recreational? What does that mean? You took a job as a lifeguard?"

Or a *bodyguard,* thought Andrew.

Bobbie glanced toward the men, her face neutral. "Nope."

"Oh, I know," Gretchen nodded, "they offered you something at the firing range."

"Nein."

Andrew's stomach growled. *Or maybe on the firing SQUAD?*

Bobbie tried to step down into the living room, but Gretchen restricted her passage with an outstretched arm. "What's the job, Bobbie? Just tell me, I can't *stand* the suspense."

"A telemarketer."

"A *telemarketer?* That's a horrible job! People yell, hang up, get angry that you interrupted their dinner. I know this because I've done all of the above more than once myself."

"Yep. I love that kind of stuff."

"Hmm. Okay, now I see it." Gretchen dropped the roadblock and let Bobbie pass through. "I should have guessed." Then, as if addressing the latecomer's adoring fans, she introduced her friend's arrival with the enthusiasm of a professional boxing announcer. *"Here's Bobbie!"*

The men stood up simultaneously. Bobbie walked toward the sofa looking like a kid going to get her braces tightened. She allowed Joshua to initiate the greetings. He raised his hand in a casual wave-salute combo. "Hi, Bobbie."

"Hey."

Kevin offered Bobbie his hand. "I'm Kevin Rafferty, Allie's manager."

"Mr. Rafferty." Her expression of indifference unchanged, Bobbie shook his hand.

Now Andrew felt like a self-doubting contestant on a late-night re-run of *The Dating Game*. He thought back to the day he first met Bobbie, almost two weeks ago. "Unremarkable" was how he would have described her then; but tonight, she looked different. Very different.

She was dressed in black pants and a red tank top covered with shiny beads; around her neck hung a black velvet choker with a dangling silver object that looked like a goat. She'd pulled her brown hair back, exposing her face now brightened up with a pinkish color on her cheeks and a glossy shellacking on her mouth.

He reached out to her, preparing himself for another curt hand-shake. "I suppose you remember who I am."

She nodded. "Yeah, you're *The Little Drummer Boy*. I forget your first name, though."

"Andrew."

"Right." She clasped his hand with a gentle grip, shaking it more than a few times and gazing at him in a way that felt almost telepathic. "Nice to see you again," she said, in a much softer voice. "Andrew."

"Same here."

When she released his hand, Andrew saw a look in her small dark eyes bordering on bashfulness, and a slight smile forming on her lips, but before he had a moment to digest what had taken place, the door from the house to the garage flew open.

* * *

Allie wanted nothing more than to savor the peace and quiet of her home then go upstairs for a long, hot bath. She entered the house and walked through the dining room, rolling her shoulders as she dropped her purse on the kitchen counter. She inhaled chocolate and noticed a pan of brownies sitting on the stovetop. Mm. That sounded good, too. A bath and some chocolate just might bring her back to life.

After exiting the kitchen, she turned left toward the stairs and froze. Her first thought was, *Why is there a row of men sitting on my sofa?*

Her second thought, when her eyes locked on Andrew's profile was, *Why is HE here? Does he think I'm going to be nice to him just because there are other people present? Ha! That's not going to happen!*

Allie sighed then stepped toward the crowd assembled in her living room. "Hello Bobbie, Gretchen, Kevin." She made sure her eyes didn't migrate toward Andrew. "And Joshua!" Allie mustered as much enthusiasm as possible. "What a pleasant surprise."

"Hey, Allie," Joshua said. "How've you been?"

"Just peachy. And you?"

"Better, now that I returned Gretchen's fancy diamond pin."

Gretchen let out a snarky laugh.

Joshua chuckled. "She's a spitfire, that one."

Gretchen took a couple of purposeful strides toward the sofa and hovered over Joshua. "And you wanna know *why?*" she asked, a challenging look on her face. "Because I'm a Leo with an Aries moon and Sagittarius rising." She raised her hands toward the ceiling, tilting her head back as she spoke. "A glorious trifecta of fire signs. Unlike Bobbie, who's a Capricorn with a Virgo moon and Taurus rising. *That,* my friends, is *the Sahara Desert."* Gretchen exhaled her distaste. "For a woman, it couldn't get any worse. Might as well be the plague."

From a nearby wicker chair, Bobbie lifted an eyebrow in slow motion, watching Gretchen unravel like a spool of thread. "Hey, DQ. In case you hadn't noticed, I'm sitting right here."

Gretchen continued unraveling. "Unless house signs and planets indicate—"

"I don't think anyone else is interested in that." Allie walked into the living room and stood behind Joshua. She had the feeling her cousin would give them all a crash course in astrology if she wasn't stopped.

"Hmm. Okay." Gretchen tossed her head to the side and blond hair over a shoulder. hair over a shoulder. "I just think all of you should be a little more open-minded. Expand your horizons, try something different for a change."

Wearing a shining grin, Kevin looked up at Gretchen. "I had my palm read once," he proclaimed, as though he'd just announced the cure for the common cold.

Gretchen wrinkled her nose. "That's ridiculous." She shook her head, disparaging him with a huff. "Whatever were you thinking?"

Kevin fumbled to give her a logical response. "I suppose I thought I might learn . . . I mean, at the time it seemed . . . It *was* quite a while ago . . . I was at one of those carnivals . . ." He swept a hand through his hair and looked down at the floor. "I guess I *wasn't* thinking."

Allie spoke next. "What is it you wanted to talk to me about, Kevin?"

Kevin stood up and reached into the interior pocket of his suit coat. He pulled out a folded piece of paper and handed it over. "I added a couple suggestions to your list. Include them in your district presentation on Wednesday if you like."

Allie glanced at the page. "They look good. I'll make the changes while I'm in the air tomorrow morning."

Kevin nodded, hesitated, and then said goodbye to everyone as he and Allie walked toward the front door.

* * *

Andrew's mind buzzed with distressing thoughts while he waited in silence for Allie to return.

So this was how it was going to play out, huh? He had finally come home, after flying thousands of miles thinking about nothing but Allie—well, almost nothing, he did have one minor distraction, but that wasn't his fault. *And now she was treating him like he had leprosy?*

Here's a question for you, Allison, he thought. *WWJD? Hmm? Yeah, I think we both know the answer to that one. Even lepers got respect from Jesus, but from you, who knows!*

With a square baking pan of brownies and a dinner knife in hand, Gretchen stood at the bottom of the stairs and made an announcement. If anyone needed her, she'd be in her room making an important phone call and giving Bobbie a magazine quiz. She motioned for Bobbie to follow her, and surprisingly, Bobbie did.

This left the two men alone to discuss the latest pro football scores, the weather and, what turned out to be Andrew's least favorite topic of the evening: Joshua's plans to ask Allie out for an early dinner.

Dance music boomed and echoed from upstairs. Andrew didn't see how that helped Bobbie concentrate on the answers to her quiz, or how Gretchen could hear herself speak on the phone, but it did give Andrew two more items to add to the ever-growing list of unsolved mysteries related to women in general.

God, I know You have a sense of humor, but at the moment I don't think any of this is funny, humorous, or amusing in the remotest sense. Please, Lord, help me keep my emotions in check and give me the words I need to communicate effectively with this exasperating creature named Allie. Amen.

Andrew and Joshua stood up when Allie returned to the room. Her face registered her own growing frustrations, compounded by at least two unannounced guests—one welcome and one leper, her boss adding to what seemed to already be a very stressful workload, and her cousin behaving like a spoiled child.

"How about a quick bite to eat, Allie? I'll have you home in time to get plenty of rest before your busy day tomorrow." Joshua tilted his head, grinning big time while Andrew wondered if anything ever bothered the guy—Mr. Sunbeams and Merriment.

"Oh, Joshua, I don't know. I've got so much on my mind, and I don't think I'd be very good company." Allie glanced toward Andrew, their eyes meeting at last, and her tired expression turned to defiance. She jutted out her pretty little chin and stiffened her shoulders. "Oh, why not? *Let's do it.*"

"Super. I've got to give Steven a call about a move tomorrow. You take your time here," he nodded toward Andrew, "and I'll wait for you outside. I parked the Baja Bug over in guest parking."

* * *

"I shouldn't be a minute," Allie called to Joshua as he trotted down her front steps. She wanted to make it clear to Andrew the clock was ticking.

Stepping back inside, she swallowed, took a breath and turned to face him; but as annoyed as she felt in that moment, she had to admit Andrew *did* look adorable. Watching her in anticipation with those beautiful brown eyes, their sadness framed and enhanced by his thick, dark hair and lashes, he waited for her to make the first move. His stature seemed withered, and his shoulders slightly slumped, perhaps in an unspoken admission of wrongdoing.

Gretchen's stereo music, turned off for a moment, began again, punctuating the silence with a burst of high volume energy and reminding Allie of the task before her.

Allie crossed her arms. "I suppose you have something to say to me."

121

Andrew slid his hands into the front pockets of his blue jeans, raising his shoulders out of their slump and into a confused shrug. He averted his eyes away from her demanding stare and asked in a quiet voice, "Who's Joshua?"

Unbelievable. *Who's Joshua?*

"You're asking if he's my *boyfriend*, right? Isn't that what you're implying?"

"I wasn't implying *anything*," he said, barely making eye contact.

Irritated by the denial, Allie snapped, "They say defensiveness is the first sign of guilt."

His jaw dropped slightly. Good.

"Oh, yeah?" He straightened up, leaning his face toward Allie. "Well, they also say *indignation is a signed confession.*"

"Who's *Jennifer?*" she countered.

Andrew's dark eyes flared, like a cat's being hit with a flashlight beam. "She's a friend."

"Great. Joshua's a friend too, and just like you had dinner with *your* friend, I'm going out now with *mine*. Any more questions?"

"Allie, I think there's been a big misunderstanding."

"On my part?" She pressed a hand against her chest. "No, I don't think so."

"Why won't you even let me explain?"

"There's nothing to explain, Andrew. You have your life, and I have mine. End of story."

"You're being stubborn."

"No, I'm not."

"Now you're being contrary."

"I hardly think so."

"*Skeptical.*"

"I don't have time for this."

"*Impatient.*"

"I'm not saying another word."

"*Uncommunicative.*"

"*Andrew,*" she hollered, grabbing the doorknob and yanking the front door open, "*just leave me alone!*" A thunderous shudder resonated throughout the downstairs as Allie stormed out of her house and slammed the door shut behind her.

* * *

"And now," Andrew sighed, "you're gone."

Then it occurred to him that Allie hadn't simply swung a large flat piece of wood with hinges and a peephole at him.

"She's shutting me out! Again," he yelled aloud. He figured the empty room would not be offended by his rarely-used, super-angry voice. "I don't need this nonsense," he mumbled. "Who does she think she is, getting all petulant and huffy, storming off in a snit and slamming the door in my face?"

A horrified gasp cut through his fury. Andrew stiffened.

He turned to watch Gretchen bound down the stairs. Oh boy. Had she heard him? If he'd been aware she was listening, he would've kept his irreverent thoughts to himself—or better yet, not had them in the first place.

"I agree with everything you said, Andrew!" Gretchen proclaimed, bouncing to the floor from the second step. She clutched his arm with one hand while patting his shoulder with the other.

Stunned, he jerked his head back and forth in one quick shake, trying to wake himself from the nightmare he'd just experienced while fully awake.

"I can see how much you like her, but you're wasting your time. She's into Joshua now; and before him, I think she was still hung up on that guy Carl. The one she wanted to show off at your barbecue a couple years back."

"*What?* She told you she wanted to *show him off? She actually said that?*"

Gretchen nodded. "Uh hmm, something like that, I'm pretty sure."

"Well, how do you like that?" Andrew muttered.

"I don't. I think it's awful, just terrible."

"Good ol' Carl Lansing, the pride of East Valley High—Mr. Varsity football, class president and, as far as I'm concerned, *class clown*. We used to be the best of friends."

"Yeah?" Gretchen's green eyes widened. "What happened?"

"I invited him to youth camp the summer before tenth grade, that's what happened! He knew how I felt about Allie, but I guess he wanted to have a big laugh at my expense, and then at Allie's. So he attached himself to her like a barnacle on a ship's keel."

Andrew knew he'd regret telling Gretchen this—he'd never told anyone else about it—but he was losing his bearings, and he needed to vent. "And if that wasn't bad enough, Allie brought him to my parents' house when I came home on leave two years ago."

"Did she date him that whole time, I mean since summer camp?"

"No, no, no. The two of them got together before I came home on leave. I suppose it was just a coincidence, her dating him right at that time, which was even worse because he told me something he'd overheard Allie saying to Beth at camp." Andrew looked away and said in a quiet voice, "It was about me."

123

"What'd she say?"

He stared at Gretchen. Boy did he want to get this off his chest. "She said that she could never . . ." He paused and closed his eyes, then slowly inhaled. No. He wasn't going to tell Gretchen any more. "It's not important." He shook his head. "Anyway, at this point, it looks like Carl was telling the truth. I'd hoped that he'd made the whole thing up or just misheard her, but it all seems to make sense."

"What makes sense?"

Andrew shook his head again.

Gretchen lightly chewed her lower lip. "So, you're going to let her go, right? No more running after her?"

He looked down at the floor, rubbed his neck then looked back up. "You think I've been chasing her around—like a fox running after a rabbit?"

"Kind of."

"Hmm. Now that I think about it, you not telling her I came by the first time is the reason I kept looking for her."

She gazed up at him, pressing a hand to his forearm. "And now do you see that I was only trying to help?"

He wasn't sure about that, but perhaps she'd helped *without* trying. Maybe God had it all under control after all.

Maybe he and Allie just weren't meant to be.

Chapter 10

Killer Tomatoes

Allie awoke the next morning and crawled out of bed at o'dark hundred on the dot. She took a hot shower, got dressed then hauled her navy blue canvas suitcase downstairs. While Mr. Coffee finished his work with a few final sputters, Allie grabbed a banana off the kitchen counter and a strawberry yogurt protein bar out of the pantry. The second she snapped open the ripe banana, the singing began . . . soft at first, then louder.

Much louder.

Allie shook her head at the inharmonious rendition of *Battle Hymn of the Republic*'s familiar refrain. The second go-round of "Glory, Glory Hallelujah" began before Allie could abandon her meal prep, run to the entryway, and wrestle with two sets of locks. Flinging open the door and screen, she beheld Gloria Danville belting out the song at entire-neighborhood-waking volume.

Gloria stopped singing and stood motionless in smug silence. Her flyaway alabaster hair was illuminated from behind with a halo of light created by a post light's glow. Allie sighed, grateful for the intermission.

"Howdy!" Gloria's voice conveyed more cheer than should be allowed at a time of day that still qualified as night. She'd obviously been awake for a while.

"Hey, Glor, come on in."

Clad in a lime green velour tracksuit with matching headband and white deck shoes, Gloria walked in and headed straight for the kitchen. "Ah, that coffee smells divine." She sniffed at the air in the way a raccoon might react to a scent that warranted further investigation, and then said, "Do I smell nuts? Hazelnuts, maybe? Macadamia nuts? Oh, heavens, don't tell me it's *peanuts!*"

"None of the above," Allie said while wondering if Gloria's sense of smell should be put on the now-defunct list. The coffee beans she'd used were plain old French Roast. "I started peeling a banana right before you arrived."

"That must be it." Gloria waved a hand, satisfied with the answer. "Would you like a cup?"

"Oh, I shouldn't. I've already met my three cup quota."

"Okay then."

"But it smells so good. I doubt half a cup would hurt. What flavor is it again?"

"Banana nut," Allie deadpanned. She backed up toward the kitchen with slow, small steps, as if luring a skittish animal into a safe enclosure. "Sit down, and I'll get it for you." She waved her open palms downward so Gloria knew she was serious. "We've got about fifteen minutes before we need to leave."

Gloria sat and happily picked at a cuticle with all the concentration of an artist sculpting a masterpiece. Allie turned away to get the coffee and found herself, in spite of the ridiculously early hour, pondering the choices she was making in her life. Gloria occasionally had that effect on her.

Gloria was a great inspiration, even if she didn't know it. Impervious to others' judgments, she could honestly claim absolute satisfaction with her life, and with who she was. But Allie had a job that required a certain level of performance and an even higher level of emphasis on superficial appearances. To some degree, she needed to be what people wanted or expected her to be. It had been so much easier during her rebel phase to not care about what people thought. Lately, though, it seemed her life had swung, wrecking-ball style, in the opposite direction.

Even her driving goal to be the best at her job was based on the approval of others. Yes, she wanted the satisfaction of it, but if no one knew about the accomplishment, if she wasn't *recognized* as the number one rep, would she want it as much?

"Are you meditating over there?" Gloria asked.

Allie jumped.

"I thought I heard you say something about a cup of coffee."

"Sorry." Allie reached for the pot.

"If you're going to gather wool, we should knit a sweater."

Allie poured the coffee. "I've probably accumulated enough for several sweaters," she said, handing Gloria the cup, "but we just don't have time."

* * *

Risking life and limb before the break of dawn, Allie allowed herself to be whisked to the airport by the highly caffeinated driver of a V8

Firebird, which even so was still the preferred form of transportation. With Beth on the other side of town and Gretchen sleeping in on her day off, the other available options would have been either a taxi or an airport shuttle—neither of which sounded appealing for a cold, dark, early November morning.

They made it to LAX in record time, and when Gloria sent Allie off with a small prayer for her safety and a heartfelt bear hug, Allie knew she'd made the right ride choice. Her neighbor's genuine caring and concern made Allie smile and helped usher her into the bustling airport with a surge of dynamic energy. With a send-off like that, her flight had to go well.

And it did. An uneventful two hours and forty minutes later, Allie arrived safely in Denver, Colorado. Fortified with a good breakfast and Gloria's warmth and charm, Allie had gotten a lot of work done on the plane. And even though a behind-the-scenes battle raged inside her weary heart, she felt ready for whatever the powers that be at Horizon Pharmaceuticals dared to throw her way.

* * *

Allie's neutral mood lasted until she got outside the airport.

Denver's ashen and overcast sky might as well have been a soiled wet blanket hanging over the city. Then, making Allie's arrival even more dismal, was the appearance of Roy Beckham, an expressionless Towne Car driver of middle age, middle height, and middle weight. His only distinctive feature was a plucky little soul patch beneath his full lower lip. He opened the rear passenger's door for Allie just as a soft spritz of rain landed on her face. She slipped into the back seat of the vehicle, immediately catching a five-day weather forecast on the radio. Rain, strong winds, and possible sleet were indicated in the Denver area for the next few days. Would the environment at the hotel be as inclement?

Allie hoped not.

For the first time since she'd gotten up that morning, her mind fluttered with thoughts and images of Andrew. She exhaled a heavy breath. Now wasn't the time for that. She needed to concentrate on what might take place at the cocktail reception that evening.

After a ten-minute drive through the city, they pulled into the circular driveway in front of the TriStar Metropolitan Hotel. At the building's entrance, a uniformed doorman wearing a red cap greeted Allie with a smile. Grabbing hold of a long, shiny brass handle, he swung open a thick glass door. Warm air met Allie's exposed skin with a soothing embrace. Entering the crowded lobby, she was immediately overtaken by echoing murmurs and by the heavy sweetness of a gigantic vase full of Stargazer lilies. Throngs of Horizon employees, and all other hotel guests trying to check in, turned the lobby into a mini Grand Central Station.

With her heels tapping on the shiny blush-colored marble floor, Allie stepped and sidestepped her way through the crowd, rolling her suitcase along behind her. While inching closer to the registration desk, she ran into several out-of-state reps interested in her take on the recent events at Horizon. They asked questions like, "What do you think about our new National?" "Do you actually believe Doug Wylie is dumb enough to agree with Hartwell's half-wit plan?" And, "My manager says *your* manager is trying to move to the head of the class and become the new Teacher's Pet. Is that true?"

The answer to the last question was a definite *yes*, but, since Allie was wary of being too forthright with people whose motives she didn't know, she avoided making statements that might be taken out of context and used against her later on.

So, she just told everyone she spoke with, "Let's see how things play out." That way, she had the option to adjust her strategy as events unfolded.

Allie's hotel room was barely distinguishable from the countless others she'd been in. It was decorated in the standard neutrals of beige and brown, with furniture that could only be described as modernly functional. It wasn't her style at all, but its simplicity was, in a way, comforting. It gave her a nice uncluttered and sedate backdrop for all the thinking she'd probably be doing within the room's walls.

Soon after settling in, Allie received a text from Kevin: "6:30 at the reception entrance. Don't B L8." She complied with the request, but then waited outside the Mile High Banquet Room for ten minutes. Kevin was nowhere in sight.

A large poster board set on an easel and bearing the company's name, stood outside the entrance of the banquet hall. A young man wearing a well-tailored black suit and a smile as bright as Betelgeuse attended the nametag table nearby.

As Allie approached, the man's hand jutted forward. "Welcome. I'm Lon Reynolds, from marketing." His slicked back, thick blond hair and dimples made him look twelve years old, but Allie guessed his actual age to be closer to thirty.

She took his hand. "Allie Hendrickson, from Los Angeles."

Lon perused the dozens of nametags in front of him. "Ah, yes, here we are." He handed Allie her tag.

She secured it to the backside of her jacket lapel while asking, "Do you still have Kevin Rafferty's nametag? He's my manager."

Lon shook his head. "No. I gave it to him a few minutes ago."

"Okay, thanks." Allie started to walk away, but then stopped and looked back. "Was he alone, do you remember?"

With a lopsided grin, Lon said, "Oh, I remember all right and, no, he wasn't alone. Cassandra Hartwell was with him. They took their nametags and I don't know where they went; but they definitely didn't go into the banquet room."

That came as no surprise to Allie. Actually, she expected such behavior from Cassandra—especially if Kevin mentioned to her that he'd made plans to meet Allie right at six-thirty.

Giving up on seeing Kevin any time soon, Allie decided to join the reception, entering a large banquet room lined with cream-and-gold-striped wallpaper, and carpeted in a brown and beige plush cut pile. Two massive chandeliers, dripping with sparkling glass diamonds, dangled from the ceiling. Allie took her time mingling amongst her local and out-of-state co-workers before stopping by the bar to request a ginger ale. A steady flow of customers kept the cute Italian-looking bartender occupied, as did his obvious penchant for the pretty ladies. Allie overheard him chatting up two different women on two separate occasions. He assured them both that given the chance he'd have taken each one out on an unfor-gettable date to Sal's Pizza and Pins, for a New York-style pepperoni pie and some serious bowling, but because hotel management frowned on employees dating guests, he'd apparently defaulted to Plan B, flirting with reckless abandon.

A gaggle of five females, unwilling to stray too far from either the open bar, or perhaps the bartender himself, gathered nearby to converse. It had been more than a half hour since the reception's inception, and blood-alcohol levels were on the rise for everyone it seemed but Allie, who gave up drinking in her youth.

Puerto Rican rep and former lady mud-wrestler Regina De Luca, representing the Queens territory and sporting peacock-blue eye shadow, had preceded Allie at the Bar. While Allie took a sip of her ginger ale, Regina put on a show. She was holding a glass of something red in one hand and waving the other in the air as though riding a mechanical bull. This began her solo gyration to the music's thumping techno beat. It was a rather inappropriate thing to do, considering the nature of the event and the fact that no one else was so much as tapping a toe. Allie remained a fly on the wall as bar-side conversations among some of the newer recruits became comical.

"So where exactly in Nebraska is your territory?" Stephanie Taylor, a bubbly redhead from Charleston, South Carolina asked Debbie Jensen, the plain-looking, yet attractive, milk chocolate brunette from Indianapolis, who was clad in a taupe pantsuit and equally taupe low-heeled pumps. She coordinated well with the room's earth tones.

"I have the Omaha territory, which runs along the border with Iowa," Debbie said.

"I heard a news story about Nebraska the other day on the radio," added another rep, this time from Northern California, in a voice several decibels above the legal limit. "Something about killer tomatoes."

The first two reps exchanged expectant glances, waiting for "The rest of the story" to arrive in a Paul Harvey-type follow up.

Miss Omaha spoke first. "Do you mean killer *tornados?*"

Northern California squinted. "Eh, yeah, I guess that's possible."

Allie suppressed a smile and wandered away from the group. She shared mindless chitchat with at least a dozen people while awaiting Kevin's arrival. When he finally showed up—forty-five minutes late—he had a distracted look in his eyes and a conniving national sales director draped over his arm. Smiling and waving, the pair sauntered through the room. Had they been chosen as prom king and queen? Allie wondered. And if so, who would have been dense enough to vote for them? Allie watched the theatrical performance, feeling almost entertained, until her gaze met Cassandra's. The crafty woman's left eyebrow arched up, like the spine of a cat ready for a confrontation. Allie had a sudden urge to hiss in response.

The royal couple made it to the far end of the banquet room and back, but Allie intervened before they had the chance to begin their second victory lap. "I was getting a little concerned about you," she said to Kevin, adding a cool, "Cassandra," while giving a nod toward the only woman in the room dressed in scalding crimson red.

"Concerned?" Cassandra feigned incredulity. "Are you his mother?" She squeezed Kevin's upper arm, chuckling in sarcastic amusement.

Allie hesitated only long enough for a half-smile. "No. *I'm* not old enough."

Cassandra curled her upper lip, looking down on Allie with help from her sharp-heeled sky-high shoes. "You remind me of someone, Allie. A foolish little girl who, like you, thought she had all the answers."

Kevin jumped into the shark-infested waters and tried to calm things down. "One of the southeast managers told me Doug Wylie should arrive soon. Looks like bad weather delayed his flight by about an hour, but he called from the Denver airport saying he should be here by 7:30."

All three glanced at their watches.

"Good," Cassandra said, "I have something to talk to him about."

And so do I, thought Allie, as her cell phone purred inside her tiny black shoulder bag. A new voicemail message. "Excuse me." Brushing past Kevin, she meandered through the crowd and exited the banquet room.

Walking across the subdued lobby, Allie looked around for a private place to listen to the message. As she passed in front of a framed mirror near the elevators, she glimpsed her reflection. Her step faltered; she wasn't happy with what she saw. Her gray eyes looked gloomy, and her face appeared drawn and weary. True, she hadn't gotten much sleep the night before, but there was much more to it than that.

Allie had attended nearly a dozen national meetings over the years, and she had always been full of energy, excited to learn different sales strategies, listen to motivating guest speakers, or prepare to launch a new product. Fast-paced and oftentimes hectic scheduling made the experiences all the more exciting, with numerous activities jammed into the few days set aside for company business. This time though, she felt disconnected and disconcerted. In short, she didn't feel like being there.

She spotted a small sitting area off to one side of the lobby. It looked like a cozy rustic cabin, inviting her in for a short retreat. So she sat. The moment she dropped down into an overstuffed chair across from a glowing stone fireplace, the cavernous room behind her all but vanished. The ambient sounds of garbled voices, ringing phones, and various footfalls suddenly became far away and muted.

Allie stared at the flames, entranced by the random bouncing and flickering. She felt herself being pulled into their warmth and wonder. The distinct crackling and scent of a burning campfire filled her senses. In her mind's eye she saw a group of kids relaxing in a circle. They were laughing, singing, toasting marshmallows, and having a great time—all except for one.

Andrew.

She remembered how he'd sulked and brooded the entire week of camp. Such uncharacteristic behavior for Andrew had caught everyone's attention, and the subject came up one night in the cabin Allie shared with the other girls. Beth, concerned as usual, took Andrew's side—though from what Allie recalled, no one else did.

"I don't blame you for sitting here and enjoying the fire, instead of rubbing elbows at the reception," a calm yet commanding male voice said.

Allie blinked, leaving Big Bear Lake and returning to Denver in a hurry. She started to stand.

131

"Don't get up on my account."

Allie looked up to see a lean man in his fifties standing before her with a "stay" palm held out in front of him. "Hello, Mr. Wylie."

Doug Wylie took the chair next to hers. While she studied him, she shifted so she was sitting forward in her chair.

He had an easygoing face, slightly weathered, yet handsome in an undeniable way. His hair contained more salt than pepper, and his well-groomed moustache more pepper than salt. Allie recalled the last time she'd seen him—at the Vegas meeting earlier that year. He'd taken a special interest in her because her achievements the year before had, as he'd phrased it, "set her apart from the rest of the sales force."

"I'm glad you weren't delayed long," Allie said.

He grinned. "You heard about it, did you? Good news travels fast in this business. I guess you could say the same for bad news as well."

Allie, realizing she'd forgotten her manners, extended her hand. "It's nice to see you again, Mr. Wylie."

"You too, Allie." He took her hand and shook it briefly. "And please," he pretended to wince, "call me Doug. 'Mr. Wylie' makes me sound like a stern old man. I hope that's not how the sales force sees me."

"No, of course not, but I can't speak for the managers." Allie kept a straight face during her delivery and for two seconds afterward. Long enough to get Doug's attention and then send him into a fit of jovial laughter, the likes of which she'd never heard from him before.

While Doug regained composure, Allie calculated a plan. She'd invite him to watch her district presentation the next day, where he could take note of her abilities to lead and train her counterparts. That might give her the extra leverage she'd need to plead her case against Cassandra's efforts to sabotage Allie's goal of finishing the year in first place.

"Thanks, Allie. I needed a good laugh."

"Yes, Allie's a brilliant comedian, isn't she, Doug?"

Oh, no.

Cassandra's radar must have registered Doug's arrival. Allie turned toward the source of the interruption, noting that the wily national director had abandoned the lowly district manager. She'd replaced Kevin Rafferty with a whole squadron of reinforcements. Two east coast regional managers, a PhD from R and D, and a marketing wizard famous for sending the reps giveaway items, then issuing their subsequent recall, all flanked Cassandra, one pair on each side for balance.

Allie knew if she didn't get Doug to commit right then, it would be too late. She smiled, acknowledging Cassandra and her followers, then turned her attention to Doug. "I don't know if you have plans for tomorrow's breakout sessions, Doug, but I'm doing a presentation to my district and I'd like to invite—"

"Oh, I'm so sorry, Allie, but I've already promised him to the Miami district." Cassandra raised her brows in a gloating expression as the saccharine-drenched words seeped from her mouth.

Doug gave her a questioning look. Unfazed, she batted her eyelashes. "But in the meantime," she slithered up to him and placed a coaxing hand on his shoulder, "we need to plan our strategy to implement the new fourth-quarter parameters." Glassy dark eyes and a pleased sneer warned of her underhanded motives. She looked down her nose at Allie, who was still seated in the armchair. "Don't we?"

Why are you making fourth quarter changes in early November? Or at all? Allie thought. *Leave the goals intact until the beginning of next year and stop messing with numbers that are going to completely alter the annual bottom line for some of us. Okay, for me.*

Couldn't anyone else in the room see how preposterous Cassandra's plan was?

Allie kept her thoughts under control for the moment, knowing a better opportunity would reveal itself if that was God's will. Jesus speaking out in anger only proved necessary on select occasions, and the current circumstances didn't seem to correlate with any she recalled from biblical times.

The small group mingled among themselves for a moment while Allie mused. A conspicuous buzzing sound caught her attention and reminded her why she'd chosen to sit down in what *had* been a quiet and comfortable setting until Cassandra appeared, rattling her saber.

Allie took out her cell phone and connected to voicemail. Doug caught her eye and smiled. He gave a quick nod in the direction of the banquet room, signaling his departure. Allie raised a hand, offering a feeble wave as he and the others moved out of sight.

Taking a deep breath, Allie listened to the message, which brought up all the thoughts and feelings she'd deliberately set aside. Dramatic scenes from the previous evening replayed in her mind. The accusations she'd exchanged with Andrew, the frustrations she'd expressed, her demand to be left alone. She'd been the one to instigate a confrontation by ignoring him and then she made things worse by leaving without giving him a chance to explain himself.

Andrew's message shouldn't have caused such a sudden and unexpected sense of regret, but it did. The conviction in his voice rang hollow as he told her she was right—they each had their own lives and friends and were free to spend time with whomever they wanted. He said he valued their friendship and he understood she needed to focus on achieving her career ambitions.

He could have ended the call right then, and Allie wished he had, but he didn't. His final words made his intentions perfectly clear and hit her like a tidal wave returning to the shore it had once abandoned. He felt he needed to be honest with her about something she already suspected. He said there was a woman he planned to see more of. She was the one who'd phoned him at the beach, and yes, she was the same woman he'd taken to Mo'Joes. Jennifer.

Frustration and anger overcame Allie, and she jabbed at her phone in response. She thought for sure she damaged the screen, but after taking a steadying breath, she checked the phone's function and it worked fine. Thankfully, she thought, as she caught herself squeezing it tightly inside a clenched fist.

Chapter 11

Downpour

At five-fifteen on Thursday, Andrew pulled up to the curb in front of Jennifer's new place on Maple Street. The Mustang idled while he studied the details of the house: white stucco, steel blue trim, a cobblestone pathway leading up to a small Spanish-tiled porch. The owner had upgraded both the interior and exterior without altering the original structure of the classic postwar, single-family home. The inside measured approximately eleven hundred square feet, which included two bedrooms, one bathroom, marginal closet space, a decent size kitchen with a breakfast nook, and hardwood floors throughout.

On Saturday, Andrew and Jennifer had brought over most of Jennifer's clothing and smaller household items, packed in boxes and easy to carry. On Sunday, Rob and Sue pitched in to help finish the task quickly.

Andrew slid the gearshift into first and shut off the engine, taking a moment to evaluate whether what he was doing here was right. So much had happened in the short two and a half weeks that he'd been home, and much of it had been emotionally intense. Almost as intense as catapulting Super Hornets off the flight deck of the *Nimitz*. Andrew had felt a sense of urgency each time he pushed the fire button and sent a plane and its pilot screaming down the runway. In the words of a fellow lieutenant working launch and recovery, shooting planes was ". . . rowdy, risky, and just plain mad physics." In retrospect, it all seemed to Andrew like a fun day at the zoo—at least in comparison to the logistics of handling two women at once and all the feelings that went along with it.

The Navy had been simple. Think and act. All he'd had to do was what needed to be done, which was usually pretty obvious. He'd seen things that had torn him up inside, but unlike some of his buddies, he'd been able to handle the traumas and tragedies because he believed, unreservedly, in God's plan.

Now, though, it seemed that much of that certainty, along with his strength and focus, had deserted him since coming home. Andrew felt like a dinghy wallowing in a destroyer's wake. He needed to batten down the hatches on all this emotional stuff and figure out what was real and what was not. It wasn't even that he knew in his heart—like he thought he'd known with Allie—that Jennifer was *the one*; all he knew for sure was that after four years of being denied the companionship of the woman he'd loved for as long as he could recall, he'd come to a clear-headed conclusion about their chances as a couple—and they weren't promising. That could only mean one thing: That it was time for Andrew to change course and head off in a different direction.

Andrew's first priority in life was honoring God, which meant releasing the tight grip he had on how he believed his future ought to unfold. Allie had her life and he had his; they agreed on that fact. And why shouldn't they? It was the truth, and if you didn't embrace truth, you'd soon become confused and heartbroken. He'd already had enough of both confusion and heartbreak since falling hard for Allie in ninth grade.

Watching while she struggled with the loss of her father had been difficult enough for Andrew. He remembered how her dad's death had been talked about in school and around town; he even remembered seeing a dispassionate, stiff-haired news anchor report the details: David Hendrickson, a twenty-one-year veteran of the East Hills police department, had been shot and killed in the line of duty, leaving behind a wife and three young children.

Once Allie's mom realized that caring for toddler twins and a distraught preteen was too much to handle alone, Allie was sent to live with her paternal grandma, Mary. Soon after moving in, resilient Allie overcame her grief by forming a close bond with Mary. Andrew recalled the envy of their classmates over the special treatment Allie received from her grandma. The two became the best of friends, and through that relationship, Allie's spirits, like the dark clouds that had been lingering above her, lifted, giving her the chance to feel hopeful and secure.

A few years later, though, tragedy struck again when Mary passed away due to complications arising from a stroke. This time Allie's grief turned to anger. Andrew's young emotions had also been strongly affected, going from sadness to frustration. He saw his distraught friend do things he knew she'd never have done if her circumstances hadn't been so extreme. It was painful for him to watch Allie, who'd been such a genuinely nice girl, turn into a toughie. The smoking and truancy wouldn't have been so bad, but then things got worse.

Still, it was a period of time, Allie later admitted to Andrew, which allowed important changes to take place in her attitude and perspectives. He learned a lot from that. In fact, it helped him get through his time in the service. He saw how what could seem harsh and entirely wrong could plant the seeds of growth and transformation that otherwise couldn't have occurred.

Andrew smiled as he recalled Allie's decisive moment. Whereas her friendship with Karen Davies had provided the unfortunate incentive for acting out, summer youth camp had offered a much-needed impetus for change. A few simple days of fun and fellowship had fertilized Allie's innate desire to grow into a different person, a new creation. Sometime before they graduated high school she'd talked about her renewed ability to trust. It helped her to see life as a journey of unknowns, a series of interconnected and meaningful incidents—sometimes tragic, like the deaths of her father and grandmother—often taking place with little or no influence on her part. She shared with Andrew her newfound insight: that having mastered the art of speaking, she felt she finally learned how to listen, although that didn't mean she always heard the message.

Could the same be said about Andrew? Was Allie trying to communicate some kind of message to him, and if so, what was it? That she had to prove something to herself? That she needed more time? Maybe both? Andrew had used the past four years for his own personal growth; perhaps now it was Allie's turn. She'd already been through hardships and trials he couldn't come close to understanding. He had no right to demand something of her she didn't have the capacity to give.

Andrew closed his eyes and opened them; as if his mind were a dry-erase board he could just wipe clean with a slow blink. He refocused on his surroundings.

Withering orange, gold, and rust-colored leaves drifted downward as a gust of wind shook them loose from a large tree, scattering them chaotically along the street. Andrew got out of the Mustang and inhaled the fresh air, noticing for the first time the advent of autumn. All traces of summer had finally melted away. For the next two months the days would be getting shorter.

He approached the white wooden gate off the sidewalk. It creaked on its hinges when he pushed it open. As he walked up the stone path through the front yard, the living room curtains shifted and Jennifer's face appeared in the window.

She greeted him at the front door wearing a broad smile, a beige fisherman's sweater and faded blue jeans. "Your timing is perfect. I placed the order ten minutes ago, so it should be here soon." She closed the door behind Andrew. "I hope you're hungry. I got us one spicy and two not-so-spicy entrees, plus all the standard goodies on the side: egg rolls, paper-wrapped chicken, and fried shrimp. It'll be an official celebration feast in honor of your awesome kindness and generosity."

"Thanks, but you didn't have to go to all the trouble."

"What trouble? It's the least I could do to thank you for your help. I'm sorry we finished too late on Sunday for the dinner I promised you." She pressed the tips of her fingers against her lips, knotting her brow. "I need to find a way to thank your parents."

Andrew shook his head. "Jennifer, you already thanked them. I heard you, and I know you were sincere. We were glad to do it." He looked around the room for help in changing the topic. "The place looks great. Is there anything else I can do while I'm here?"

She moved her hand away from her face. "Yes. One thing." With a deep sigh, she gave his forearms a light squeeze. "Help me eat the Chinese food. Please." She laughed. "I think I ordered enough for six people."

Andrew smiled. He didn't feel like eating even *one* portion, but he'd certainly try his best. Although he'd always enjoyed Chinese food in the past, it had suddenly lost its appeal.

Twenty minutes later, their dinner arrived with a knock at the door. While Jennifer handled the transaction with the deliveryman, Andrew's cell phone rang from inside his jacket pocket. He checked the caller ID. It was Beth. He slipped out of the room, hurrying through the kitchen and into a generously sized back yard. "Hey, Beth."

"Hey yourself. How's everything with you?"

Andrew toed a clump of straggly, yellowing grass. Jennifer's new yard needed some work, some mowing and trimming. Its planter beds were choked with a tangle of plants he couldn't identify. At least the patio was in good shape; it was big, and just off it was a great brick firepit. He crossed the Spanish tiles and sat down on a black wrought-iron chair next to a white resin table.

He wanted to ask Beth if she'd heard about what happened on the beach last Saturday. However, with Jennifer a mere eggroll's throw away, it was neither the time nor the place for a drawn out exposition on his failed attempt to reason with that mythical individual otherwise known as Allie Hendrickson.

"Everything's fine. Just fine," he told Beth. "The people at JPL are terrific. They've got me working with a seasoned team of engineers, some of whom even have personalities." He laughed at his own bad joke, wondering if Beth bought into his canned enthusiasm.

Her reply said it all: "Hmm."

Nope. She didn't buy it.

"Andrew! Soup's on," Jennifer called out, her head appearing through the back door. "I got us war wonton, I hope that's . . ."

Andrew looked up at her, and surprise widened her eyes. "I'm sorry," she whispered, pointing over her shoulder and retreating into the kitchen.

"War wonton, huh? Good choice," Beth said. "Sounds like you're busy."

Yeah, I am. I'm busy contemplating ditching this super sensitive cell phone and replacing it with two tin cans and a string.

"Thanks for checking in, Beth." Andrew's fingers grazed his chin, now textured by a slight five o'clock shadow. "By the way, have you heard anything . . ." He paused, his flow of words cut off in mid-sentence as though a faulty cell tower had sliced through the call.

"We talked yesterday afternoon." Beth's usually buoyant voice went flat. "She said she tried to invite Doug Wylie to watch her presentation, but couldn't make it happen. Then she approached him twice the next day to discuss the new goals, but again to no avail. All three times Cassandra intervened and now it's too late to do anything about it. Mr. Wylie went back to Atlanta earlier today. Allie says he's a stand-up guy—honest, straightforward, ethical—and he'd have reconsidered implementing the plan if she'd gotten a chance to show him how unfair it is."

Andrew grasped that whatever was going on with Allie's work was bad for her career goals, but he didn't understand the specifics. Not really. What exactly was so unfair about this plan?

"Look, I'm not in sales like you and Allie, and I never have been, so my knowledge on the subject is limited." He glanced back at the house. Jennifer was probably anxious to dig into the food. "I need to know if Allie is making a bigger deal out of this than she should be. Do you think Cassandra is out to get her? Because, to be honest, it sounds to me like a plot in a bad soap opera, or, I don't know, a cheesy spy novel."

Beth laughed. "You're right; it does sound extreme, but this is how real world corporate politics play out. Sales in the phar-maceutical industry, or any other, is just a numbers game where frequent changes in goals, territories, and in the types of products promoted are a common occurrence. Allie gets that, but between Cassandra's sly comments and the drastic and sudden changes she's proposed—which happen to be especially damaging to Allie's L.A. territory—it seems this new director's actions are intentional. That said, I don't think it's Allie's place to make any enemies over it."

That was a relief. Sort of. At least it appeared that Allie had a legitimate reason for standing her ground. Though Andrew himself had been in situations in the Navy where he could have, and probably *should have*, received honors for things that others took credit for. To him, it hadn't been worth getting all worked up about . . . but then again, he didn't have Allie's go-getting temperament.

"The next time you talk to her, Beth, please let her know I hope things work out the way she wants them to. Okay? I'll be keeping her in my prayers."

"Oh, don't tell me you two aren't speaking to each other."

Oops. Dead giveaway. *What was he thinking?* He heard Beth sigh, and he paused to think of a response. She'd been on this roller coaster ride with him before over the years, and the last thing he wanted was to drag her along on another trip to the amusement park. "Okay, I won't tell you that."

Beth snorted. "Right."

"No, really. I think we're both going through a period of self-identification and introspection, where we need to analyze the situation and see things as they really are." Could he have sounded any duller or more insipid? he wondered.

"That's impressive, Andrew. I may have to let you help me with my thesis paper."

"Beth, I'm serious. I've been focusing on pursuing something I'm not sure was part of God's plan for my life. I need to stop fooling myself. The dream may not have been real, just a self-imposed illusion."

"All right," she said at last, "I can accept that. You both need some time to think about what you want . . ." She interrupted her thought. "Well, well, well. Guess who's calling me on the other line?"

"You should take the call. I'm sure she's on a tighter schedule than either of us."

"She'll leave a message. I can call her back."

"No, it's okay. I should probably get going anyway. Soup's on, remember?"

Andrew and Beth said goodbye, and he stood, straightening his back and shifting mental gears to focus on a different female than the one who had dominated that call . . . and the one who still, in spite of his best efforts, dominated his thoughts.

* * *

"*Allie.* I'm glad you called." Beth's voice sounded breathy in Allie's ear.

"I can't talk long." Allie ran a bristle paddle brush through her hair, scanning the closet in her hotel room for the appropriate evening attire. "I'm meeting Kevin in the lobby in forty-five minutes."

"I just got off the phone with Andrew," Beth said, using a tone that seemed much too self-satisfied for Allie's liking. "He asked me to give you a message."

Another one? What more could he possibly add to his unexpected and rather disturbing voicemail message? Allie wondered if he'd told Beth about what happened Saturday night. Probably not, but with a district dinner to attend at a local landmark restaurant and no time for idle chatter, a detailed explanation of what had taken place on the beach would have to wait. There wasn't much to explain, anyway. Andrew had a girlfriend. That was it. No big deal.

Allie pulled a black-and-white wool skirt still encased in the plastic covering from the dry cleaners off the closet rod; she hung it up on the hook inside the bathroom. "So, what's the message?"

"He said he hopes things work out the way you want."

"Should I wear a black cashmere turtleneck or a white blouse with my houndstooth skirt? The restaurant's fairly upscale from what I hear."

"Either one, Allie. I'd probably go with the blouse, as long as you have a warm coat to wear outside. Did you hear what I said about Andrew?"

"I heard you."

"Do you have a response? Now that it looks like I've become your official intermediary."

"No response. He's got a girlfriend, you know." Allie went back to the closet to retrieve her cotton jacquard blouse and a pair of calf-high black boots. All the while, Beth kept quiet. "I'll take that as a *yes*, Bethany."

"It's not a *yes*, Allie, I don't know *anything*."

"You must have known *something* at *some* point or else why did you encourage Andrew to take me down to the beach for a walk? But we didn't just walk. *Oh, no.*" Allie dropped her blouse on the king-sized bed and started pacing. "Apparently Andrew thought it would be amusing to play with my emotions, touching my hands and face with all kinds of tenderness and affection and staring into my eyes like we were the only two people in the universe." Hadn't she decided a detailed explanation would have to wait? Evidently her mouth had other ideas. "I felt myself falling for it. Falling for *him*." Frustrated with herself, Allie sighed. "And then his cell phone rang. Guess who called?"

A couple seconds passed before Beth said, "He never said anything to me about—"

"*Jennifer* called, Beth. Her name is *Jennifer*."

"What did you do after he got the call? Did you ask who Jennifer was? She could just be a friend. Didn't you guys talk about it?"

"I left him there and went back to your place. You know what I went through with Carl. And no, I didn't ask. I saw the look on Andrew's face, and that said it all."

Beth clicked her tongue then took an audible breath. "I'm sorry. I had no idea. I know you're dealing with enough stress as it is, but I still think there's an explanation that will make sense of it all. Jennifer might be a neighbor or a friend of the family."

"Talking about ordering in Chinese food and watching a movie together?" Allie shook her head with force. "I highly doubt it."

"Uh oh," Beth said in a low voice. "War wonton."

"Huh?"

"Oh, nothing."

"Anyway, even if I didn't know about it then, I do now. Andrew left me a message my first night here. He told me flat out that he's dating her." Allie stopped pacing and sank down onto the bed.

"I just don't know what to say, Allie. Other than I still think you should have talked to him. It's so out of character for Andrew to do something like that. I mean, not that he couldn't have a girlfriend, but if he did, he wouldn't have—"

"Look, I have enough going on in my own life as it is." Allie made a sound somewhere between a laugh and a small sigh. "I honestly don't even know what I was thinking. *Andrew and Allie, a couple? What an absurd idea.*"

"Actually," Beth said, "it's always made perfect sense to *me*."

* * *

"I'm sorry, but that makes no sense." Allie's pulse throbbed at her temples while Kevin attempted to explain Cassandra's last-minute change of plans for the evening. They stood near the comfortable nook in the lobby, the one with the fireplace, but its charm did nothing to soothe Allie. In the last hour, she'd managed to calm her frazzled nerves and forget, or at least pretend to forget, her conversation with Beth about Andrew, but already her so-called Zen state was evaporating.

"She worked with me, met with you, and then had dinner with both of us only one week ago," Allie snapped at Kevin. "Then she sat in on half of our presentations and now she wants to join our group again tonight? Enough already. There are countless other district dinners she could attend. Why choose ours?"

Kevin crossed his arms over the narrow lapels of his blue pin-striped suit jacket. "Now, I see what Cassandra meant when she told me she picked up a territorial vibe from you."

"A territorial vibe? *From me?* What's that supposed to mean?" Allie started tapping her foot.

"It means you don't want anyone getting too close to what you think is yours." Kevin ran a hand through his hair. "She said you were being aggressive in the field with other reps who were only trying to be courteous. She also said she thinks that *you* think you've got *me* wrapped around your finger."

Impossible, thought Allie. This can't be happening. She inhaled and exhaled through her nose once, trying to hold on to the last of the Zen. "Kevin, you can't believe any of that."

"Are you saying she's lying?"

Yes, that's exactly what I'm saying, Allie thought. *Only, if I use those words, I'm finished.* If she went to Doug saying Cassandra was a liar, even though he may have wanted to believe Allie, he'd side with Cassandra. Head honchos always stuck together—the dutiful clan of company back scratchers, looking out for one another in times of crisis. Allie had seen it happen before; no use trying to kid herself about it now.

There wasn't time to, anyway.

The overpowering scent of a perfume, no doubt named Corporate Venom or Envious Elixir, preceded Cassandra as she entered the lobby. Dressed in a leopard print silk blouse tucked into black velvet pants, she made her presence, and her intentions, known. "I only have room for one other person in my rental car," Cassandra said with mock regret. She placed a hand on Kevin's forearm and began leading him away from Allie.

Wearing a benign expression that Allie knew masked a surly sneer, Cassandra glanced back over her shoulder. "Oh, and Allie, like I told the others, make sure you wait for us *outside* the restaurant. We'll meet you there." She smiled up at Kevin. "Ready, Kev."

Allie simultaneously clenched her fists and her teeth. *Well, dear Kev, it might interest you to know that you're about to ride shotgun with a woman who's losing popularity among the sales force at breakneck speed.*

To illustrate the point, Regina De Luca approached and stopped, hovering over Allie like a shady eucalyptus tree. She looked in the direction of Cassandra and Kevin. "What did she rent, a golf cart? Or how about a wheelbarrow? She sits, and your boss pushes her. What do you think, Allie? That would basically accommodate two people."

Allie fought back the urge to burst out laughing, until she saw Cassandra picking lint off Kevin's jacket sleeve as though preening her young. "My boss doesn't get it. He's nothing more than a pawn in that woman's sinister chess game."

Regina threw her chin toward the odd couple. "I can't figure this Cassandra bird out at all. The stuff she wants to do right away can wait until first quarter next year. Advantol's just starting to pick up in the northeast, so for me, it's no sweat, but I suppose you guys in California are gonna feel this the most."

"You guys?" Allie turned toward Regina and shook her head. "No, Regina, believe me when I tell you none of the districts aside from mine will be hit hard. The majority of pain management doctors in the entire western region are in my territory. Plus, I have the highest market share of Advantol *in the nation.* The bulk of my total volume sales is from that product alone—the one that used to be our main focus until Cassandra materialized and decided to foul everything up."

Regina used both hands to grab hold of her hair, making a thick ponytail of the tightly wound frosty brown curls. She widened her eyes and dropped her hair back in place. "You're pretty high up in the national rankings, Allie. What's gonna happen to your numbers if Advantol loses priority and we say *adios* to the PM docs?"

Allie touched Regina's shoulder, leaning in as if to whisper but then raising her voice. *"Total destruction."*

"Hmm." Regina's dark eyebrows spiked up. "You'd almost think Cassandra planned this just to take you down," she said, shaking her head as she strode off to meet another rep on the far side of the lobby.

* * *

Less than a minute after Regina moved away, Allie met up with two of her L.A. district counterparts, Marty Jackson and Isabelle Perry. Marty, the short Milwaukee native with a shiny shaved head and a joke for every occasion, and Isabelle, a gangly Jamaican gal with near perfect corn rows, spearheaded a wade through the crowded lobby to get to the front door. A bone-chilling wind bore down on the three as they stepped outside to wait for the next available cab. Angry-looking charcoal gray clouds swirled above the early-evening Denver skyline, a gathering storm making preparations to release its wrath.

Like Cassandra.

After a quick wait, the reps hopped into a heated green cab. The moment Allie pulled her door shut, the downpour began. Zigzags of electricity crackled and flared in all directions while clamorous peals of thunder bellowed in their wake. Gregarious Marty, who'd opted to sit in the front seat, immediately began a dialogue with the driver, a heavyset man with a walrus-like mustache and an Eastern European accent as thick as old paint.

144

"We don't usually get storms like this so early in the season," the driver said, glancing in his rearview mirror, "but it does happen on occasion."

The cab pushed through dense traffic and up a winding road, which the driver explained was the only way to get to the four-star restaurant, The Lodge. He told them that it was set high atop a mountain, overlooking a rural landscape filled with evergreens, aspen, and an abundance of wildlife.

Isabelle looked at Allie. "Did you hear Cassandra say we should wait outside the restaurant?" Concern marred her usual lilting voice.

"Yes. I heard her." *Never mind the little fact about the weather. Why am I even here?* Allie wondered. *I'm losing Kevin's confidence, and I've all but lost the battle with Cassandra. Am I only thinking about myself and my own needs, as Kevin said, or am I right in trying to fight this? I wanted to be successful, but is that a good enough reason? Certainly my father wouldn't have wanted me to become demanding and selfish just to prove a point . . .*

"That must be you, Allie."

"What? Oh." Startled by Isabelle's tap on her shoulder, Allie fumbled to slide open the zipper on her handbag and answer her cell phone. "I didn't even hear it ringing."

The call was blocked, a private number, and she hesitated a second before answering it. "Hello?"

"Allie?"

Andrew. Why was he calling *now?* "Yes?"

"Oh, hi. It's Andrew."

Without responding, she looked out the window at the blurry shapes of cars going by in the other direction.

"I, I, I . . ." Andrew drew in a breath, releasing it with deliberateness. "I hope you weren't in the middle of something important."

Seriously regretting taking the call, Allie blew out an aggravated sigh. "As a matter of fact I am. I'm on my way to a district dinner."

"I won't take up too much of your time. I talked to Beth earlier. I guess you know that."

"I do."

"She said you missed out on meeting with the company president."

"Yep."

"You won't get another chance to talk to him before it's too late? Can't you call him or try to set up another meeting without ol' What's-her-name knowing about it?"

What was he so interested for? And why had Beth told him Allie's business in the first place? It wasn't like they were a *couple* or anything.

Andrew kept pressing the issue. "I mean is there *nothing* you can do?"

Besides end this senseless conversation with YOU? thought Allie. "No. Nothing. Just continue to work hard and hope the changes don't go through. They're not official yet, but it doesn't look good. We may not even know before the end of the fourth quarter, if you can believe that bizarre bit of logic . . ." *Shut up, Allie! Why are you telling him all this?*

The driver slowed the car. "Okay, folks, this is it." The cab came to a stop near a lone cluster of reps huddled together at The Lodge's front entrance. Before exiting the warm, dry cab, Allie studied the group through the window. Their overhead shelter, a simple canvas awning under which they all barely fit, combined with a smattering of open umbrellas, did little to shield them from the downpour, or protect them against the cold and furious wind.

Marty paid the driver, then forced open his door against strong buffeting gusts.

"We're at the restaurant now," Allie told Andrew. "Give me a minute, will you?" Without waiting for a reply, she dropped the phone into the pocket of her black swing coat. Using the sole of her boot, she pushed open her own door. The back seat turned into a cyclonic wind tunnel as she forced her way out of the cab. Snapping her umbrella open and gripping it with tight fists, she trotted as fast she could after Marty and Isabelle, toward the rain-soaked reps. Once nestled among the huddlers, Allie retrieved the cell phone from her pocket. "I'm here."

"It sounds like you're in the middle of a hurricane," Andrew practically shouted.

"That about sums it up," Allie said, raising her voice and turning sideways to evade a headwind.

Andrew let out a small disbelieving laugh. "Well, I can wait until you're inside the restaurant."

"We're not going inside. Not anytime in the near future, anyway," Allie just about hollered.

"Why not?"

"I don't know. Orders. I suppose if we go inside, we may lose our jobs."

Isabelle gave Allie a tight-lipped nod. Several of the other reps glanced at Allie then tucked their heads back down to look at their feet. It could have been chagrin, or it could have been an attempt to keep rain out of their eyes.

"Lose your jobs? How can you lose your jobs?" Andrew demanded.

"Because you-know-who told us to stay out here until she and my manager arrived."

"That's stupid," Andrew scoffed.

"Tell me about it."

"I don't have to tell you about it; you already know. I'm just wondering why you're still out there. You aren't exactly the type to let someone walk all over you."

Is that what she was doing?

Yeah, that's what she was doing.

And to have it pointed out by Andrew, someone who'd already gotten away with making a fool of her on the beach, was more than she could stand.

"I was just about to lead the troops indoors," Allie announced into the phone. "Wait on the line and you'll see for yourself!" She again dropped her cell into her pocket.

Allie approached the South Bay rep, John Carpenter, a football-player-sized, thirty-something guy with a squared jaw and a white-blond crew cut. He had the look to run interference for her. Unfortunately, he didn't have much in the way of a personality to complement his imposing size. Still, he was positioned furthest from the front door. So she said to him, "Let's get out of here," then took his arm, tugging a little to encourage him to vacate the miserable scene.

John began to move, then resisted. "I don't know, Allie. The Viper said, 'Stay outside until we get there.'"

"I'd hate to see anyone get sick over this." Allie pointed in the direction of Kris Szychek, a petite, small-boned woman who'd recently undergone a tonsillectomy. "Does Cassandra know about Kris's health issues? Would she even care?"

"Kevin knows," countered John, "and he didn't say anything about waiting inside."

"Kevin's not thinking clearly these days," she said, becoming more insistent they get out of the rain. "What do you say, John?"

He scowled and shook his head in disgust. "You're right. This is ridiculous." He plowed an opening so he and Allie could get to Kris.

Wearing a short, lightweight coat and trying to keep the rain off her face by using an oversized purse as a shield, Kris stood shivering in the center of the group. Allie's umbrella provided protection against the elements while she convinced her small counterpart to go inside. The rest of the group agreed with the decision and followed suit willingly.

Once all twelve reps had assembled in the waiting area and started shaking off water and straightening wind-mussed clothing, Allie remembered her phone call from Andrew. "Are you still there?"

"Of course I am. I was listening, but most of the words were kind of muffled."

Several reps found seats on a bench running along the front entrance wall. They craned their necks as they watched for Cassandra and Kevin through the large window behind them. Allie stood nearby, realizing with each passing moment how having Andrew on the line made her want to be back on the beach with him where, if for only a moment, she'd felt safe and loved.

Bright lights flashed across the windowpane when the driver of a fancy silver coupe slid the vehicle underneath the parking attendant's canopy, nearly grazing the valet podium. The small car's headlights illuminated the rain, which was now coming down with even more ferocity, creating a thunderous pounding on the restaurant's roof. A yellow slicker-clad valet assisted Cassandra, who emerged from the passenger's side then dashed toward the front door.

"Cassandra's coming in now," Allie said, though not specifically to Andrew. Remaining in front of the window, Allie observed a discussion between Kevin and the valet attendant, who was frantically waving his hands, probably perturbed over Kevin's erratic driving.

In the meantime, Cassandra waltzed into the waiting area wearing a frosty glower and holding a brown leather attaché case. She swept water droplets off her long black leather coat with the back of a free hand tipped in burgundy-lacquered nails. After surveying the reps, she gave them a look of self-satisfaction. Allie interpreted that as a sign Cassandra had already assumed they'd disobey the order. The only thing left to do was identify the culprit who led the charge.

"I'm glad to see you all made it here safely." Cassandra's face was relaxed and neutral, even cordial. Most of the reps responded favorably, giving her grateful and reassured smiles—but not Allie. She had already experienced Cassandra's I'm-a-nice-person façade, having fallen for that ruse within the first few hours of meeting the devious director. Not anymore.

"However," Cassandra intoned, "I am *not* glad you decided to ignore my request to wait out front and instead come inside." She leered. "Whose idea *was* that, by the way?"

The smiles and tranquil expressions disappeared from the reps' faces as Cassandra performed a retinal scan on each of them.

"Aren't you going to say something?" Andrew's voice sounded off in Allie's ear. Somehow, he'd become more worked up from a thousand miles away than anyone else in Allie's group. "She probably thinks it's *you,* and she's expecting you not to have the guts to say so. You should admit it was your idea. That would show her you're not intimidated."

Allie raised a hand, interrupting Cassandra's power play. "It was *my* idea."

"Good job," Andrew congratulated her.

Kevin entered the waiting area, and Allie once again dropped the phone in her pocket. She looked at him, hoping he might back up her decision to bring the group inside, but alas, no. The strained look on his face made it clear he would not be coming to her defense.

Sighing dramatically Cassandra said, "Just as I told you, Kevin."

"You guys couldn't wait outside for two minutes?" Kevin held up two fingers to illustrate the seemingly simple request.

To Allie's surprise, John Carpenter arose from the bench and responded. "Why not wait in here?"

Cassandra glared at him. "Because with all of you loitering in the waiting area, there is no room for any other patrons to sit, or even stand." The edginess in her voice gave away her mounting indignation. "We are guests in this town, are we not? How do you think that makes Horizon Pharmaceuticals look?"

"For coming indoors, out of a typhoon? Pretty smart, I'd say." John fixed his gaze on Kevin while answering Cassandra's rhetorical question. "There's no one else around but *us.* And it was more than two minutes, Kevin."

Allie wanted to give John a standing ovation.

He continued. "We were waiting outside for at least ten minutes before Allie got here and—"

"Oh, don't tell me." Shamefaced, Kevin shook his head. "This was *your* idea?" He looked at Allie, who found his lifted eyebrow expression blatantly patronizing.

Allie tightened her lips, torn between fury at Kevin and Cassandra and rage at Andrew. She really couldn't say with whom she was more upset. Why did Cassandra have to be so . . . *wicked?* And why did Kevin have to be so . . . *weak-willed?* And *why* had she let Andrew talk her into defying Cassandra's stupid orders? It was easy for him to be assertive. He had nothing to lose.

"I already said it was my idea, Kevin." Allie ground her teeth together.

A gray-haired maître d' with an English butler's stoic face peered cautiously around the corner, trying to get the brunette ringleader's attention. "Excuse me, ma'am. Your table is ready, if you'd like me to seat you now." He spoke using a pleading tone, which Cassandra paid little attention to.

"Kevin, I'll let you handle *her,*" Cassandra's head jerked in Allie's direction, "while the rest of us go sit down and relax."

The reps moved out, trailing Cassandra in one large mumbling mass. If Allie had kept quiet, she wouldn't need to be "handled." This was a perfect example of why Andrew's presence in her life was nothing more than a hindrance to her. She pulled the phone from her pocket and held it up to her ear. *"Are you still there?"*

"Of course."

She knew he would be. He was always there—just not in the way she needed.

"I have to go. My boss is about to punish me for being unruly, which doesn't make sense considering *none of this was my idea to begin with.*"

Andrew cleared his throat then offered a cautious, "What's he going to do?"

"I'm not sure. Give me a time-out and stand me in a corner for twenty minutes. Or maybe send me back out in the rain."

"Would he really do that?"

"Who knows? Anything's possible," she said before saying a terse goodbye.

Allie faced Kevin, ready to receive her penance. Nothing he could say would be worse than everything that had happened already in the last couple of weeks, making her wonder, *How did my life get so complicated?*

Chapter 12

A Covert Operation

"He'll be free in about five minutes. He asked me to have you wait," Dr. Stevenson's longtime receptionist, Mandy, said as she walked Andrew down the familiar blue-carpeted corridor with its nature-photo-lined walls.

"Thanks, Mandy. That would be great."

Andrew hadn't had to think very hard or very long to come up with a plan to help Allie. The real mind power had been required for the question of whether or not to try to help her in the first place. It had taken a full week to work that out.

After the restaurant phone call fiasco, he'd spent two hours sitting on his parents' back patio, watching the stars and arguing with himself about rushing to Allie's rescue. It was bad enough he'd cut short his dinner with Jennifer, telling her he'd had a long day and was exhausted. Even though the Chinese food had been good and Jennifer's company pleasant, Andrew hadn't been able to concentrate on anything but what Beth had said about Allie's work problems. That's why, as soon as he left Jennifer's house, he'd called Allie. He was trying to be helpful and supportive. Instead, he'd gotten her in trouble.

Although he reached no conclusions in his parents' yard, after days of chewing on the issue, he finally decided that since he'd helped make Allie's problem worse, he needed to try and help fix it. Hence the plan he was now putting into play.

Mandy ushered Andrew into Dr. Stevenson's office. "Here you go, kid."

He thanked her again and turned toward the oak shelves lining one whole wall of a tasteful but somewhat messy office decorated in burgundies and creams. The shelving held medical books, of course, but mostly it was packed with photos of Dr. Stevenson's family and

151

friends. Looking at the pictures, Andrew's mind flashed back to the days of his youth and all the fun times he and his family shared with the Stevensons. Whenever Rob Gallagher and Joe Stevenson got together for social gatherings or vacations, which included all immediate family members, the med school anecdotes would abound. The two had become close friends during high school, with each claiming to have had a profound influence on the other's decision to receive his medical training at UC San Diego, where Rob decided on immunology as his specialty, and Joe, anesthesiology.

Moving away from the shelves, Andrew crossed to the west-facing window of Joe's spacious, fifth floor corner office. He gazed out at the panoramic north-south view of East Hills, which included Interstate 5 packed with commuter traffic and big rigs; the Empire Center, the city's newer large outdoor mall; and a dozen or so high rise office buildings. Andrew spotted, about five miles out, the bright green patch of Forest Lawn Memorial Park flowing up into the Hollywood Hills and separating the Valley from the west side of L.A.

No more than ten minutes passed before the office door swung open and tall, hardy Joe Stevenson walked in, offering Andrew a friendly smile and a fatherly hug. Joe looked good. He'd dropped some weight around his midsection and added a few gray hairs to the light brown, thick mass already on his head; but the Boy Scout charm he claimed he'd never lose was still with him, as evidenced by a mischievous glimmer in his lucid blue-gray eyes. After an exchange of warm greetings, Joe removed his white lab coat, hung it up in a small closet in the corner then turned to look at Andrew. He gestured at a pair of burgundy-and-cream tweed armchairs that sat in front of a nearly aircraft-carrier-sized desk buried beneath mounds of medical files.

As Joe sat, he asked, "How's the job-hunting going? Your dad mentioned you had an interview lined up at JPL."

"Done deal." Andrew settled into the chair opposite Joe.

"Fantastic. When do you start?"

"Three weeks ago."

"You're not working today?"

"Nope. I'm working four-day shifts of ten hours a day."

"That's terrific! I only work mornings on Fridays and I'd be glad to treat you to lunch."

"Sure, Joe. That'd be great."

For the next several minutes, the two addressed the more personal aspects of life, ranging from Andrew's last two years in the Navy to the recent baptism of Joe's granddaughter; but with thoughts of Allie weighing heavily on his mind, Andrew quickly steered the conversation toward the real reason for his visit.

"I understand there's a new face on the Horizon," Andrew quipped.

Joe laughed and leaned back in his chair, clasping his fingers behind his neck. "And you know who I have to thank for that, don't you?"

"Yes, I do. Someone you won't be seeing anymore."

His relaxed position short-lived, Joe sat upright, a look of concern creasing his eyes. "Did Allie quit?"

Andrew shook his head and leaned forward. As succinctly as possible, he went over the pertinent details, beginning with Allie's goal to become number one in the country and ending with the arrival of new boss, Cassandra Hartwell. He briefly outlined Cassandra's recent antics, including her plan to omit sales generated by pain management specialists and the result that would have on Allie's totals for the year; he also described Allie's thwarted efforts to have a private discussion with Doug Wylie and the incident at the restaurant a week earlier.

"I know Doug Wylie." Joe picked at a loose thread on the arm of his chair. Plucking at furniture or his clothes or doodling on a pad if he was behind a desk was a habit he had when he was listening with care. "He's a good man. I'm surprised he'd allow this kind of thing to happen."

"From what I understand, Cassandra's quite a force to be reckoned with. Do you think he's intimidated by her?"

Shaking his head and looking thoughtful, Joe said, "No, I don't think so."

Andrew continued. "Allie used to think of herself as an asset to the company, and to her manager, who hasn't been backing her up lately. I'd hate to see her give in and give up on her ambitions, which I admit I don't completely understand the importance of. I haven't lost faith in her ability to see this through, but to be honest, Joe," Andrew shifted uncomfortably in his seat as he glanced out the window to the right, "I think she might need some help." The expression on his face made Joe lean forward.

"Oh? What did you have in mind?"

* * *

Part one of Andrew's plan, visiting Joe, had gone better than Andrew had hoped. Part two got off to a smooth start as well.

Early the next morning, Joe Stevenson arrived at the Gallagher house to pick Andrew up for a two-hour drive down to the low desert. After a stop at a nearby gas station to fill the tank of Joe's dark green Ford F-150 truck and to get a cup of coffee, they were on their way. Their destination? The National Neurological Pain Conference held annually in sunny Palm Springs. Their objective? To have a friendly chat with Doug Wylie, who would also be attending the conference.

Actually, Andrew couldn't take credit for part two of the plan. His plan mostly had consisted of part one, visiting Joe and asking for his help. It was Dr. Joseph Stevenson, respected physician and occasional mischief-maker, who had come up with the real strategy. Although Andrew had been skeptical about it, Joe had done a marvelous job of convincing him that it was not unusual for a doctor participating in an out-of-town speaking engagement to enjoy a relaxing game of golf with a company VIP. And after a quick phone call to Doug, Joe's suggestion to play a round on Saturday had been met with enthusiasm, as had Joe's request to include Andrew. Joe was sure this golf game would be just the thing to solve Allie's problem.

As they cruised down I-10 and through Cabazon, a town known for its ever present, low-pressure cloud cover, Joe admitted he didn't have *all* the details of his scheme worked out, but the main goal of securing some face to face time with Doug had been achieved. Joe seemed confident everything else would easily come together.

Andrew, on the other hand, had doubts. "So, where do I fit in all this?" he asked Joe. "I just show up on the golf course with you and start talking business with the head of a company I don't know anything about or have any vested interest in?"

"You don't have a vested interest in *Allie's welfare? In her future?*" Joe shook his head. "Andrew, you've been telling me for years that you and Allie are just friends, but you're not. You're in love with her." He took his eyes off the highway long enough to look at Andrew's face. "I admit I've always suspected it, but I'd say the fact you're here with me right now proves it."

Andrew thought up until then he'd succeeded in fooling everyone, including, sometimes, himself, about his true feelings. Everyone except Beth, of course, but Beth had a gentle touch in handling the situation, never becoming confrontational enough to force Andrew to openly admit that he really didn't know how to deal with Allie.

Looking out the window, Andrew saw a giant dinosaur lurking off the highway—a restaurant or museum or some other kind of roadside attraction. "I've kind-of started seeing someone else." He almost felt guilty about saying the words aloud. "Allie's been dealing with a lot of . . . I mean I don't want to get in the way . . . I guess I, uh . . ." Frustrated, Andrew sighed. "It's complicated."

Joe inhaled and held his breath for a few seconds before exhaling with a soft chuckle. "I guess so."

"Don't get me wrong, Joe. I think Allie's terrific. She's funny, sweet, smart. The most beautiful girl I've ever seen in my life." He stopped talking abruptly, not willing to allow Joe to see the battle he was waging inside. All the sadness he'd been able to hold at bay while he'd served his country overtook him, not because of what he'd seen when he was in the Navy but because he couldn't stand the thought of Allie struggling to stay strong, fighting to achieve a goal that might elude her.

She'd pushed him away and welcomed Joshua's companionship instead, which only made things worse because it forced open a porthole to another fact—that Andrew was jealous. He hated feeling like Allie was rejecting him for someone else. He wanted to be the one giving her encouragement and support. And he was, in a way, but he wanted to do it *with* her, not from someplace off in the distance.

Joe repeated Andrew's claim. "But you're seeing someone else."

"Yes. I tried showing Allie how I feel about her. Twice. Suffice it to say she shot me down both times, but like I said before, it's complicated." So complicated even Andrew didn't understand it.

"I think I understand what you're doing," Joe said.

Relieved, Andrew laughed. "What *am* I doing?"

"You're letting go. And I assume you've given this over to God."

"Absolutely. I couldn't handle it by myself anymore."

"Maybe that's the point. Turning something over to God doesn't have to mean you're giving up. Like in this case, you're not giving up on being in a relationship with Allie; you're accepting the situation for what it is . . . for now." He glanced at Andrew with an earnest look on his face. "Give it time. I believe she'll come around."

Blood rushed to Andrew's brain at the mere thought. "I don't know about that." He used his thumb to press open the plastic lid on the empty coffee cup in his hands; he pushed it closed again. "I thought when I came home that maybe I had a chance. I can't get my hopes up again."

"Now, this other gal . . ."

"Jennifer."

"Jennifer. Does Allie know about her?"

"Yes. This is where things get complicated. See, I took Allie down to the beach one evening after the two of us had dinner at our friend, Beth's, house. Up to that point in the evening, everything had turned out perfect, and it seemed like the right time to . . ." Andrew's head started spinning as he pictured himself sitting on the bench with Allie, near her alluring warmth.

"Anyway," Andrew flushed, "then out of nowhere, Allie starts asking questions about this woman her friend saw me with at a coffeehouse—Jennifer."

"How do you know each other?"

"We met on my flight coming home; we talked about this and that. I don't remember most of it, to be honest. Though I do remember inviting her to Valley Community Church. It was just a casual invitation. So she showed up one evening, and after the service, we went out for coffee. That was when Allie's friend saw me with Jennifer and reported back to Allie." Andrew shook his head then dropped it back against the headrest. "I probably shouldn't even be seeing her right now." He was beginning to see how denying his strong feelings for Allie would interfere with his ability to relate to another woman.

"How do you feel about her?"

Andrew turned toward Joe. He'd already told him how he felt. Hadn't Joe been listening? "I'm crazy about her; she's all I think about. I barely have an appetite. I have trouble concentrating at work—"

"Now I see why this is complicated, my boy." Joe chuckled. "I was asking about Jennifer."

Andrew looked out his window and rubbed the back of his neck, now hot with perspiration. "Oh, I, uh . . ." He shook the cobwebs out of his head and grinned. "What was the question again?"

* * *

Joe had told Andrew that the National Pain Conference occurred yearly in midfall and was currently in its second day. Joe was scheduled to speak the afternoon of their arrival at four P.M. on the adjuvant use of Advantol in the treatment of mild-to-moderate headaches, and as a prophylaxis in the management of migraines.

As they neared Palm Springs, Andrew, who had been reading from a program listing all lectures taking place that day, said, "I have no idea what any of this means." Okay, so he was slightly exaggerating. But the topics ranged from poststroke contractures to the new advances in Alzheimer's research, and most of it was way beyond him. "Ask me about fly-by-wire flight control or planetary rovers and we can engage in some meaningful dialogue, but medical nomenclature is a foreign language like no other, except Cantonese, I suppose."

Joe took his eyes off the road for a second and laughed. "Don't worry about any of that. Our strategy is to start a conversation about the reps in general. I'll mention that the representative who calls on me has proven herself invaluable and is, in effect, the reason I became a speaker for the company. We can work in your association with Allie as well, and you can be a character witness, so to speak."

"Do you think he'll care? Most CEOs are all about the bottom-line. Business is business to them; they're not concerned about what the employees think." Andrew didn't like hearing himself speak that way. He'd always tried to be an optimist, someone who expected the best from people, but he needed to keep his hopes from soaring through the air like a lost helium balloon.

"My guess," Joe said, "is Doug *will* care. I don't know if we'll get him to change his mind, but it's worth a try. At least if we get him talking about these new policies, we might better understand the logic behind them. And who knows, that might give Doug the chance to think twice about making any changes at all."

That made sense to Andrew. The Navy had taught him to break obstacles down into solvable pieces, all the while remaining flexible enough to see solutions in unusual places. So he nodded. And he blinked in surprise when the truck came to a stop. Andrew looked around a crowded parking lot lined with bright green flowering shrubs and dotted with humongous palm trees.

"We're here?"

Joe grinned and nodded. "You look like a sailor on the way to his court marshal."

Andrew laughed.

Joe got out of the truck, and Andrew followed suit. As they both opened the cab's rear doors to get their bags, Joe said, "I'm sure that whatever happens here in the next day or two, Allie will appreciate your efforts and concern." He grabbed a brown-and-tan overnight bag.

Andrew stiffened. "Allie doesn't know anything about this."

Joe, who had been moving away from the truck, stopped in his tracks and gave Andrew a sideways glance. "Okay. Hmm." He nodded in the direction of the hotel and resumed walking.

Andrew joined him.

A doorman wearing a red jacket and an expression solemn enough to earn him a job guarding Buckingham Palace stood near the automatic front doors. He gave Joe and Andrew a nod as they entered the hotel. The area around the registration desk reminded Andrew of the wild mural painted on the exterior of Mo'Joes. Tall, spindly rubber trees planted in a sand pit shot up through the center of the lobby. Their heavy leaves were laced with dark green vines, creating an umbrella of camouflage, while the water from a volcanic rock waterfall splashed down into a little lagoon. Andrew stayed on high alert to the possibility of rambunctious spider monkeys hiding out amidst the floppy leaves.

"After you came up with your master plan," he confessed to Joe, "I thought it would be best to keep it to myself. I wasn't sure how Allie would react." *As per usual*, he thought, without mentioning that part to Joe.

"Hey, am I being implicated here?"

"Okay," Andrew chuckled, "I'll admit I did come to you for help."

"And?"

"And I did ask if you knew of a way to get to Doug Wylie."

"And?"

"And that's it. You came up with the golfing scheme."

Resting his elbow on the front counter, Joe snickered. "It *was* a clever idea, wasn't it?"

A woman who looked to be of Native American descent straightened her light green suit jacket and asked, "How can I help you?"

Joe smiled at her, and Andrew said to Joe, "I'll have to get back to you on that."

Whether it was clever or not would depend on how it worked out. Andrew was more than a little concerned that this mission didn't have a satisfying conclusion coming.

* * *

In the elevator on the way to their rooms, Andrew protested Joe's insistence on paying for Andrew's room and meals. He'd tried arguing against it at the counter, but to no avail. And because Andrew didn't want to attract attention, he'd saved his concession speech until they were by themselves.

Now, being assaulted by the elevator's bright green leaf-patterned wallpaper, and listening to a canned piano-version of *Achy Breaky Heart* but trying not to take the music personally, Andrew said, "You really didn't need to pay my way."

"It's not a big deal, Andrew. Horizon is paying for all of my expenses, so I'm free to pick up yours. You've got to save up your money to buy a house for your new bride." He clapped Andrew on the back.

Andrew smiled tentatively. "I'm one step ahead of you on the house, Joe; but you're two steps ahead of me with the part about the bride."

"So you're getting a house? Good for you. Have you found something?"

"No. I'm not even going to start looking until after the holidays. In the meantime I'll save up a little more money for a down payment. I should be good to go by early spring."

158

The elevator doors slid open on the sixth floor. They stepped out into a hallway lined with more exotic wallpaper, this time shades of brown and orange joined the same loud apple green color.

"Okay, it's eleven-forty now," Joe said, approaching the bright yellow door to room 618 and glancing at his watch. "Go on in and get settled. I imagine you're hungry by now, so do whatever you like. Get room service or go to one of the eateries downstairs. There's a fantastic Jewish deli right off the pool area. They make the best corned beef on rye I've ever had. I think there's a little coffeehouse somewhere around here, too. Charge everything to the room, Andrew. Promise."

Andrew hesitated then nodded. "Sure, Joe. Thanks." He opened the small green folder he'd been given at the front desk and removed the card key for room 620.

"I'm going to change into something more presentable," Joe tugged on his comfortably-worn gray polo shirt, "then go over to the conference room to set up during the lunch break. I'll be in touch afterward."

* * *

One hour later, Andrew was back in the first floor tropical rainforest in search of a restroom. He pulled a schedule of events out of the back pocket of his jeans and quickly looked it over. The doctors' lunch break ran from 11:45 to 12:45. It was 12:35 now, which explained the throngs of attendees whooshing past Andrew. He felt adrift in a sea of individuals even nerdier-looking than the engineers at JPL. How many pocket protectors could there be in one room? Andrew walked an orderly search grid around the perimeter of the lobby, seeking a "Men's Room" sign. He didn't spot one, but he thought there might be one near the main conference room. He began politely working his way through the folks wandering aimlessly and congregating in various-sized clusters.

These were the faces of some of the brightest doctors on the planet, many of whom weren't known as *brain surgeons* for the fun of it. Andrew thought it was funny how smart people rarely looked as smart as they were.

Case in point: a couple of stick-thin women with thick glasses and uncombed hair (or maybe that was a style . . . Andrew couldn't have said), shoved past him gesticulating so wildly that they knocked him back against a table. The corner of it prodded his thigh as he rotated to keep his balance. When he turned, he found a white-haired woman with clear blue eyes and a patronizing smile watching him. She sat in a folding chair behind the table, which held nametags and a box of file cards.

"Are you just arriving?" the woman asked as though she already suspected as much.

"Uh, yes, I am, actually."

"You'll need a nametag in order to get into the lecture hall." The tiny woman sat tall as it was, but she straightened her spine and repositioned her body into a more authoritative position. "Under which name did you register?"

Register? Did Joe register *both* their names?

He didn't have time to find him and ask. After gulping down two large glasses of passionfruit iced tea along with one of the heralded corned beef on rye sandwiches at the Jewish deli, Andrew didn't have a moment to spare. "I need to take care of some business first," he said, at once regretting his unfortunate choice of words.

"It'll only take a second," the woman insisted. "Give me your name, and I'll give you the nametag. You put it around your neck like this." She grabbed a stray off the folding table in front of her and demonstrated the process, bringing to Andrew's mind an image of Mrs. Longfellow, his sprightly yet rather elderly third grade teacher.

"My name is Andrew Gallagher."

The Mrs. L look-alike thumbed through a long narrow file box of three-by-four inch cards, stopping several times to pull one out for closer inspection, only to replace it again. After four such false alarms she came to the one that put a satisfied grin on her soft wrinkled face. She then tucked it into the plastic pocket of a model like the demo. Before turning the whole enchilada over to Andrew, she gave him a short verbal recap on how to fashion it around his neck, name card facing out.

"We want the other doctors to be able to see who you are." Her grin was as emphatic as her nod.

"Right." His dire need of a bathroom mounting, Andrew slung the strap over his head. "Thanks for your help, ma'am," he said in a rush. "Now, may I trouble you for the location of the nearest restroom?"

"Certainly. It's right over there." She pointed a bent finger in a nonspecific way toward an area somewhere behind Andrew. "Near all those people."

Andrew turned to look, but there were people everywhere. Her information was useless. "I'm not sure where you mean."

The Mrs. L. look-alike bobbled her head back and forth, searching for a helpful hint. "Oh, Dr. Bruner just came out. Do you see him?"

See him? Ha! "I don't even *know* him."

"How about Dr. Kirkpatrick? He's talking to Dr. Bruner and the others. They're all right outside the men's room."

Andrew shook his head. He didn't know any of those doctors. And to make things more confusing, they all looked the same to him—like a massive cookie cutter collection of geniuses.

"Dr. Marshall?"

"No."

"How about Dr. Dettweiler? He's wearing a tan sport coat."

No need turning around for that clue. Every male in the room had on a tan sport coat, except for Andrew.

"I don't know what else to tell you." She sounded noticeably frustrated by Andrew's ignorance. "Everyone knows Dr. Dettweiler. And besides, you can't miss him. He's standing next to that huge potted palm."

Huge potted palm? Now that was something he could work with. "Got it." Andrew spun around and raced toward the large plant. It was the first thing in the room he'd noticed but the last thing the little look-alike had bothered mentioning as a point of reference. Andrew remembered seeing it on one of his circuits through the lobby, wondering at the time if spider monkeys had an affinity for that variety of palm tree. After darting past Dr. Bruner's entourage, then around a corner and through an entryway, Andrew made it into the men's room at last, where a few stragglers still remained. Paying just enough attention to his surroundings to notice that nearly every color imaginable was probably included in the parrot-shaped tile mosaics on the walls, he got down to his "business" as fast as possible.

A couple minutes later, Andrew tossed away a paper towel and exited the restroom. A short man with wire glasses, thinning brown hair, and a cleft chin approached as soon as Andrew was through the swinging door. The man thrust his hand forward. "Glad you could make it," he said in a British accent. His baritone voice seemed incompatible with his slight stature. "I'm Philip Bruner, but among colleagues, Phil works just fine."

"Andrew Gallagher." Andrew shook the man's undersized hand, impressed by the strength of his grip.

"Nice to meet you. Do you prefer Andy or Andrew?"

The only person who ever called him Andy was Grandma Stevens. "Andrew."

"Andrew it is. I was about to go inside. I'm quite interested in the one and four o'clock discussions by the pain management boys. Join me?"

"Sure. Dr. Stevenson's lecture is at four. He's a personal friend of mine. We're playing golf tomorrow, which is the main reason I'm here."

Dr. Bruner nodded. "Ah, yes. Joe. We met during lunch today. Nice fella. He mentioned bringing a chap along for the game. I'm an avid golfer, myself. Twenty-two-handicap," he added, inflating his chest and standing as tall as he could under the circumstances. "I'm the golfer, and my wife's the shopper. She's here somewhere." He took a quick look around the room. "Or perhaps she's at one of those local outlet malls with Dr. Dettweiler's wife.

"I must say, Andrew," he continued, "I thought you'd be a bit older, but then again, when I meet people who've read one of my books they sometimes let slip they envisioned me being over six feet tall. Funny isn't it?"

Andrew laughed at Dr. Bruner's observation, having no idea at all what the man was talking about or why he'd asked to be addressed as "Phil." He and the good doctor were not exactly colleagues.

"It looks like we've only got a couple minutes left to find a good seat. Shall we get going?" He nodded toward the dwindling crowd that funneled through double doors the way anxious steer enter a cattle squeeze chute.

Andrew and Dr. Bruner entered the large conference room. It had three sets of stairs running alongside and between a good thirty rows of cushy, dark blue seats. The room was surprisingly sedate given the rest of the hotel's psychedelic décor. They accepted from a young woman with a freckled face and straight brown hair a folder containing lecture notes and dosing information on various products. The old adage "When in Rome, do as the Romans do," came to Andrew's mind as he and Dr. Bruner scouted out then settled into their fourth row amphitheatre seats.

The first two lectures highlighted painful myoclonic spasms and cervical dystonia, neither of which Andrew had heard of . . . but that didn't stop him from taking notes. He then dedicated his full attention to Joe's forty-minute lecture and fifteen-minute follow-up Q & A. By that time, Andrew felt fairly confident in his ability to diagnose and treat tension, cluster and pre-migraine headaches, though he was doubtful the opportunity would ever present itself.

Joe concluded his time at the podium with a joke about neurologists, which got a huge response of laughter and a hearty round of applause. As soon as the racket died down, Dr. Bruner, who'd been taking copious notes and frantically jotting down arrows, stars, exclamation points, and circled numbers, stood up and stretched his back. "Jolly good show!" he said with unbridled excitement.

He gestured to Andrew to follow him. Andrew did, and they took a different set of stairs back down, using those that ran through the center of the room. At the bottom, they encountered two doctors from the potted palm entourage ready, willing, and now more able than ever to discuss the highlights of Advantol.

Right about the time the discussion became clinical enough to remind Andrew that he was an engineer among doctors, an unfamiliar face caught his attention. A tall woman wearing a bright yellow pantsuit and a menacing gaze came striding toward the group like a SCUD missile. The woman shot Andrew a hard-edged look of disapproval. His pulse rate sped up, and a chill worked its way down his spine. He could almost hear the Wicked Witch of the West theme from *The Wizard of Oz* playing in his head.

Was she one of the speakers? Or Dr. Bruner's wife, angry she'd lost him in the crowd and thinking Andrew must have had something to do with it?

"Don't tell me you sat through my entire boring, pedantic shtick?" called out a voice from behind Andrew.

He turned and grinned at Joe, who had appeared just in time. Andrew quickly excused himself from Dr. Bruner's clan, taking a few steps to the side and out of the line of female missile fire.

"I know this is going to sound crazy, Joe," Andrew said through clenched teeth, "but I'm getting a weird feeling all of a sudden, like I shouldn't be here."

"That's absurd. You're here as my guest. Doug Wylie knows that. Oh, and speaking of which, I'm sorry to say, but the golf game's off for tomorrow. Doug's got to fly back to Atlanta first thing in the morning."

Andrew's heart plummeted toward his shoes. The trip would be a complete waste of time if they couldn't talk to Doug.

"So, with my speaking duties out of the way," Joe continued, seemingly unaware of Andrew's disappointment, "we can either hit the course as planned or head home first thing tomorrow morning. That way you'll have your whole Saturday ahead of you." Joe glanced at Andrew's face. "Oh, but don't worry." He apparently got a whiff of the smoke coming from Andrew's hopes burning up. "We'll still get the chance to discuss Allie. We're meeting Doug and another fellow from his office for dinner tonight. Six-thirty in *The Terrace* restaurant, just off the main lobby."

Dinner with Doug Wylie? Andrew brightened. Rubbing his chin against the pads of his middle three fingers, he nodded slowly, allowing the idea to come to life. "You know what, Joe?" He smiled with guarded optimism. "I believe that's even *better* than a game of golf."

Chapter 13

Tee-Off

Allie and Beth were at the midway point of a late Friday afternoon walk. They were tackling the steepest incline of Walnut Street, which paralleled Wildflower Canyon Golf Course. The area, like Allie's townhouse, was at the base of the Verdugo Mountains.

Recent rains throughout the hillside had encouraged new growth of poisonous sumac shrubs, tall willowy weeds, and a widely scattered flowering groundcover that smelled pungent and medicinal when crunched underfoot.

Allie gathered her hair in her hands. Twisting the elastic band around it, she lifted the mass up into a shoulder-length ponytail. "My mom and the twins are staying in Kansas for Thanksgiving, visiting my Uncle Brent and Aunt Ava. I told you that already, didn't I?"

"Yes. And I told *you* my folks will be in St. Paul visiting my brother, right?"

"Your parents will be out of town?"

"Yes, Allison."

"I don't remember you telling me that."

"That doesn't surprise me. You can't seem to focus on much of anything lately." Looking past Allie on her right, Beth smiled, keeping her gaze on a portly, puffy-faced man who was struggling to get up off the green after aligning his ball for a putt. Leaning on his club for support, he hefted himself to a standing position. "You must be in love."

"What should we do? Where should we go?" asked Allie, disregarding the comment. "I don't feel like cooking a big dinner. Not this year."

"Haven't you gotten any invites yet? What about your cousin Gretchen? Doesn't she have family in the area? Thousand Oaks or Agoura Hills?"

"Gretchen? Hmm. I don't know about that."

"Why not? It works for me if it works for her. At least ask. She may not even have any plans; then we orphans could make a go of it. Hang out in Malibu or wherever."

Allie pictured the scene in her mind. Thanksgiving dinner at Uncle Larry and Aunt Linda's split-level ranch-style house in Thousand Oaks: The guest list would likely include Linda's outspoken Danish kin from Wisconsin; Allie's first cousins—and Gretchen's younger brothers—Gunther and Gerhardt; and, for good measure, one BFF by the name of Bobbie Brennan.

Uh boy.

"Or I could call Andrew instead." Beth smiled coyly and bobbed her head, making her strawberry blond ringlets dance. "See if they could use a couple of party crashers over at his—"

"Okay, okay." Allie raised both hands, palms facing out. "I'll ask Gretchen. If she says yes, then of course that means you should spend the night at my place. Happy now?"

"Mm hmm. *Oh!* I almost forgot. All the stores in the Westside Plaza are having *incredible* Black Friday sales. Let's do some shopping while we're at it. Okay?"

"Whatever you say. I don't have it in me to argue: Not with you, or anyone else."

"So, does that mean if I decide we're going to the Wok of Fame for dinner tonight you won't protest?"

"The Wok of Fame?" Ugh. For obvious reasons, Chinese food had lost its appeal for Allie. "I was thinking we could get tacos at El Cubano, or how about a grilled chicken salad at that new—?"

"So much for you not having the energy to argue with anyone," Beth teased, poking Allie's shoulder."

"Yeah, well."

"Okay, we'll go to Caruso's instead. Pizza and salad. What say you?"

Allie said okay. It was her new mantra: Okay. Since nothing was going as she wanted it to, she figured the only way she could stay sane was to agree to whatever was going on. Perhaps that was the lesson God had in mind for her anyway.

So she'd ask Gretchen about Thanksgiving dinner, even though she would have preferred to spend the day tucked into her bed with a book that had nothing to do with medicine or pain or men. A nice all-female comedy would be acceptable. She'd go shopping too, even though she dreaded the idea of wading through a crowded mall full of fanatical bargain-hunters. And tonight, she'd eat pizza, even though she hadn't had a decent appetite since she'd inadvertently become the satisfying meal for a certain corporate viper.

* * *

Andrew dressed for dinner, choosing a brown sport coat, light-colored slacks, and a cream-and-brown striped shirt. Choosing clothes wasn't at the top of his list of talents, not even close. He was used to having Uncle Sam decide how he should be dressed, and when he was on liberty, he usually just wore jeans and tee shirts.

His attire clashed with the purple and bright blue wallpaper and upholstery in his vivid hotel room, but after he'd inspected himself in the huge bathroom mirror, he decided he passed muster. With several minutes before Joe was supposed to be by to get him, he figured he might as well sit. Andrew lowered himself onto his king-sized bed. The too-soft mattress sucked him into a well-worn pit, while the slick palm trees and bamboo print bedspread chilled his "rear admiral" (a phrase Andrew learned from Ensign Donny Smithers, in generic reference to that particular posterior body part). Andrew squirmed into a semicomfortable position and looked over at his cell phone, which he'd set on the rattan nightstand.

All of a sudden, he *needed* to hear Allie's voice again. He wanted to talk to her, but he didn't pick up the phone. He was so energized about having dinner with Doug Wylie, he wasn't sure he could keep from mentioning it to her if he called.

In truth, he didn't want her to know about what he and Joe were doing. Knights didn't need credit. They just needed the victory. He only wanted to see Allie back in the position to realize her dream, without Cassandra Hartwell's interference. Joe was right about him having an interest in Allie's welfare and in her future. No matter what happened between the two of them, he cared about what happened to *her*. He finally understood he'd always love Allie unconditionally and want her to be happy.

A few seconds ticked by in the silent room. Andrew eyed the phone as if he was desperate for it to start ringing. Finally, unable to resist the urge to hear her voice, he grabbed his phone. After pulling up Allie's name in his directory, it occurred to him she might not be alone. It was, after all, Friday night, and Gretchen had said . . . What was it she said? "Allie's into Joshua now."

Andrew chewed the inside of his cheek. He frowned. Allie told him she and Joshua were just friends, but what if she *was* dating Joshua? He seemed like a nice guy, which made the thought that much worse because it also made it more likely that what Gretchen said was true. Andrew knew Allie would never date someone who didn't treat her with respect, someone who would treat her like a lady. He got the feeling Joshua was that kind of guy.

Andrew needed to figure this out. He'd tried to release Allie to find out what she really wanted, but his heart held on. He missed her. It had only been three weeks since he last saw her, but it felt like he was back overseas, counting the days until he could be near her again.

Was he simply wasting time and energy on something that was never meant to be? He took a deep breath and pressed the telephone icon on his phone. Well, he'd soon find out.

He listened to rhythmic ringing that was a mere tenth of the pace of his racing pulse.

* * *

Beth shifted on the red vinyl-covered bench she and Allie shared in Caruso's waiting area; she looked at the ringing cell phone in Allie's hand. "Aren't you going to get that?"

Allie stared at the phone. It was Andrew.

Now why couldn't she and Beth wait for a table in peace? Allie sighed and, to avoid the phone, she watched the servers and bus boys hustle around. The tan-stone floored, roomy trattoria was so packed with diners and the wait staff was so busy, it seemed like trays were flying past under their own power. The sounds of clinking glasses and plates being hastily cleared off tables combined with the rumble of conversation and accordion-dominated Italian music to create a clamor nearly loud enough to drown out the ringtone.

Allie returned her gaze to her phone then looked away again. With contrived interest she studied the restaurant's creamy orange faux-cracked plaster walls and various remakes of Michelangelo's artwork.

The phone kept ringing. If she answered the call and Beth knew it was Andrew—and she definitely *would* know—she would want Allie to ask him about Thanksgiving.

Not gonna happen.

But if she didn't answer the call, Andrew might try calling Beth. That could be worse.

Allie stood. "I'll be right back. Or I'll find you at a table." Before Beth could reply, Allie scurried off. She dashed between tables crowded with families and couples practically inhaling Italian salads, pizza, and mounds of spaghetti and meatballs. Smelling the aromas of tomato and basil and cheese, Allie ignored her suddenly growling belly and ducked into a darkened bar area. After passing by a large, wall-mounted television, she paused near a swinging door leading to the kitchen and answered the call. "Hello?"

"Oh, uh, hi, Allie," Andrew stammered, sounding surprised to hear her voice. "I didn't know if you were going to answer or not."

167

That makes two of us. Three, with Beth.

"Yeah, well, sorry about that." She glanced at the TV screen, where a rabid crowd of fans packed into a college football stadium exploded to their feet in response to a pass interception. The crowd's roar competed with the clatter coming from the restaurant's kitchen. Even so, it was quieter here than it had been in the waiting area. "I had to get away from a noisy crowd."

"Oh, if you're busy, we can talk another time. It's nothing important. I only wanted to . . ."

A few feet from Allie, a heavily-muscled man pounded his table and yelled at the TV, "Are you blind, ref?"

Allie turned her back to the man and cupped her hand over her phone. "I didn't get the end of that last sentence," she said, disgruntled that she had to try to have a phone conversation in the first place. "You were saying you wanted something?"

Andrew raised his voice considerably. "I wanted to see how you're doing and say hello."

Well, Allie wanted to ask how Miss Jennifer was doing, but she refrained. Given the mood she was in, she'd probably come across as snide, and there was no reason to be mean-spirited or petty.

"I'm great." She forced a smile . . . as if he could see it.

"Anything new on the job front?"

Yes, Andrew, there is. I'm working harder than ever to achieve my career goal, while battling malevolent forces on two fronts. I've got a fair-weathered Kevin on one, a tyrannical Cassandra on the other, and a double-crossing YOU in the middle! "No, same old baloney," Allie said, not allowing Andrew the chance to delude her with deceptive concern for her welfare, the way Kevin, Cassandra, and even Carl Lansing had. "I'm just taking it all in stride."

"Really?"

"Yeah. What else can I do?"

"Oh, nothing, I suppose." His cavalier tone only served to irritate Allie further.

"So, uh, what's new with *you?*" she asked, trying to sound like she couldn't care less, even though she knew that she cared far too much. "How's work? Your mom and dad doing well? Don't you have plans for tonight?" She instantly cringed. *Why did I just ask him that?* Was it because she was wondering why he was calling *her* on a Friday night and not on his way to pick up . . . *Jennifer?*

"I have a dinner date," he boasted.

"Oh yeah? *Well, so do I.*"

She heard his breathing quicken. She'd struck a chord. Good.

Allie spotted Beth coming toward her. "I have to go."

"Okay. I, uh, I hope you have a nice evening."

"I'm sure I will." She pressed a finger against the screen of her phone.

Beth flicked the back of Allie's ponytail. "Anyone I know?"

"Andrew."

"Hmm, no kidding. Did you ask about Thanksgiving?"

Allie smacked an open palm against her forehead. "Ah! I can't believe I didn't mention it."

Beth twisted her mouth into a lip-pretzel before saying, *"I can."*

"What should we do, Bethany, invite ourselves to every turkey dinner in the Valley?"

"No, Allison. That would be rude." Beth took a step forward, allowing a server to pass by and enter the kitchen.

"I'm sure his girlfriend will be there," Allie challenged.

"You don't know that. He may not be seeing her anymore."

"Sorry to disappoint you, but they've got a hot dinner date tonight." Allie's own derisive smile made her wonder whose side she was on.

"Oh, *phooey* on both you knuckleheads. Why can't you two make up, get married, and live happily ever after?"

Allie put her hand on Beth's shoulder, looking her straight in the eyes. "Because this isn't *Never Never Land* and stuff like that just doesn't happen."

"That's the spirit." Beth raised a clenched fist and jabbed the air in a make-believe show of victory. "Six points for cynicism." She made fake crowd noises then gave Allie a dry smile. "Now before you go for the extra point, let's get something to eat."

* * *

Andrew sprang up off the bed ready for a fight.

"Who does Joshua think he is?" Andrew blasted into the empty room. "Allie's *my* girl!"

He began pacing, trying to calm himself, but images of Joshua and Allie together wound him up so tight he was nearly running back and forth in the confined space. He stopped, recognizing that he was experiencing a nearly crazed adrenaline rush. This was not good. He needed to cool off before Joe arrived.

Think, Andrew. Think! Stay focused, stay calm, and don't lose sight of the target. This is not about you; it's about Allie. The person you care about, remember? The person you love unconditionally.

Frustrated beyond words, Andrew smacked the wall with the flat of his hand. *"Why does this have to be so difficult?!"* he exploded.

Someone knocked on the door of his room. "Andrew? Are you okay in there?"

Andrew rubbed his stinging palm and shook his head. He quickly marched to the door and opened it.

Joe peered at him. "Everything okay?"

"Fine. I was just talking to myself."

"Sounded more like shouting than talking; but hey, your relationship with you is none of my business." He winked.

Andrew clenched his fists then relaxed them. "Let's forget about it, huh?"

"Works for me. You set to go?"

"Sure." Andrew slid his card key off a round table by the door and placed it in his jacket pocket along with his cell phone. He swiftly scanned the room, not knowing what he was looking for and almost certainly stalling for time. Convinced he was as prepared as he'd ever be, he flipped the wall light switch and joined Joe, already five paces ahead of him down the hall.

Throughout their ride in the colorful elevator and their brief walk through the lobby to *The Terrace*, Andrew worked on calming his breathing. He nearly had it under control by the time he and Joe approached a mahogany hostess station. While Joe spoke to the hostess, a dusky woman about thirty with short dark hair and pale blue eyes, Andrew deliberately looked around, hoping his surroundings would distract him from his stirred up thoughts.

The spacious restaurant held thirty or more tables, each covered in a crisp white cloth. Precisely arranged cutlery and gleaming stemware sparkled under the restaurant's recessed lighting. The classy establishment seemed out of place in a resort with a real-life *Gilligan's Island* in the lobby and potentially-contagious jungle fever in the elevators; however, the moment he detected the charbroiled aroma of grilled steak, Andrew lost all interest in the hotel's inconsistent décor. Thankfully, his appetite appeared to be triumphing over his troubles.

When the hostess informed them that the rest of their party had not yet arrived, Andrew and Joe sat down on a black leather bench to wait. Andrew was pleased that his pulse felt normal.

Five minutes later, Doug walked in—alone. He greeted Joe before introducing himself to Andrew, who noted how fatigued the man appeared.

Doug then rocked back and forth a couple times, pursing his mouth in the same classic CEO lip grip Andrew had seen on the faces of stressed-out high-powered television show executives. "I'm sorry I'll have to miss out on the golfing tomorrow," Doug said with the regret of someone on the verge of shedding a tear.

"Me too." Andrew agreed, although in his opinion, missing out on the opportunity to swat a little white ball around a pristine, ego-challenging expanse of grass dotted with holes, sand traps, and tall trees was hardly reason enough to become morose. He wondered if overseeing the activities of hundreds of sales reps was the reason for the slight dark shadows under Doug's eyes, and for a lack of energy in his general demeanor. Or was it due to the work of a certain someone high up in the ranks, waging her very own crusade of destruction and acting as a bloodletting thorn wedged in Doug's side, slowly draining him of his life force?

Or was Andrew's sudden hunger making him melodramatic so he saw things that weren't there?

After a moment of small talk, the three men followed the hostess through a shrimp scampi-scented cloud that left lingering aromas of butter and garlic in Andrew's nostrils. They crossed the main dining room and entered a semi-enclosed terrace. It overlooked the eighteenth hole and was indirectly illuminated by a series of floodlights. The hostess seated them at a rectangular table that had been pushed up against a Plexiglas partition. Andrew lowered himself into a plush armchair, the legs of which conveniently had casters, allowing him to roll with ease into position at the table.

Once they were settled, the hostess handed Andrew a menu card. It was printed in fancy script and slipped into a heavy cardboard base covered in burgundy vinyl, which was the same color as the armchairs and the cloth napkins.

A busboy arrived and filled the stemmed ice water glasses set at the right edge of each place setting. After he was gone, Andrew absently gazed out at the fairway.

With no allowance for any more small talk, Joe cut right to the chase, using a conversational knife so sharp that it caught Andrew by surprise. "I hear I'm going to lose the wise guidance and direction of my Advantol rep, Allie Hendrickson, the same lady who helped bring me on board." Joe glanced up while unfolding a napkin, laying it purposefully on his lap. "Any truth to that rumor, Doug?"

If Doug was surprised by the topic, he didn't show it. He tended to his own napkin before addressing Joe's straightforward question. "I understand your concern. It's always tough losing a trusted resource."

A trusted resource? Andrew thought. Was that what Allie had become in Doug Wylie's eyes? A resource? Nothing more than a medical journal or a section from a textbook? A nameless, faceless individual who conveniently possessed valuable pharmaceutical information but whose heart and soul didn't merit consideration?

Oops. There he went getting worked up again.

"Allie told me that there's a strong likelihood of a sudden shift in personnel, which, as she put it, 'may become effective immediately.'" Though Joe made his point with surprising force, it seemed to work.

The skin above Doug's commanding nose tightened, and he pressed his lips to the side. His forehead creased as he began attempting to explain the reasoning behind the recent changes at Horizon. He used football terms such as "fourth and goal," "two-minute warning," and "hail Mary pass," all of which only served to further confuse Andrew, making him wary of joining the conversation, even though he knew this was the opportunity he'd been hoping and waiting for. How would it help the cause if he continued to sit on the sidelines?

Pushing from his mind the disturbing image of Allie and Joshua sharing a candlelit dinner, Andrew made the decision to put himself in the game. "For the record," he began, leveling his eyes on Doug's, "I also know Allie. She's a great gal. Hardworking, dedicated to her job and, quite frankly, a little confused about this new company policy Joe mentioned." Andrew picked up his water glass and took a sip, trying to calm his jittery nerves.

Pressing a cupped hand against his face just under his nose, Doug stroked downward on his gray moustache. "Yes. Hmm. Well, you see, this sort of thing is not uncommon. Happens all the time, actually."

Their waiter breezed past, eyeing the empty fourth chair as Doug finished his thought. "Nothing that's been done can't be undone, you know. We're talking about a very dynamic industry here."

Andrew took Doug's wavering as a good sign, but he'd hoped for something more concrete in terms of a possible policy reversal. Maybe that dastardly Cassandra Hartwell had been practicing her mental jujitsu on him, creating confusion over the best course of action to take. Andrew's mind raced to think of a clever way to introduce the topic of her recent inexcusable exploits.

Joe cleared his throat then looked at Doug. "What happened to your associate?"

He shrugged his shoulders. "Can't say for sure. Perhaps being detained in the lobby by a chatterbox scientician trying to charm his way onto the speaker panel." Doug pondered the notion for a split second then shook his head in apparent amusement. "Then again . . ." A less than warranted snicker escaped from his mouth.

Joe grinned in expectation. "Then again, *what?*"

A childlike smile formed on Doug's face. He leaned across the table toward Joe and Andrew, his eyes wide with delight—like a little boy with a big secret to tell. His voice dropped down to a near whisper as he took a quick peek in the direction of the entrance.

"Charming Ms. Cassandra Hartwell into doing *anything* would be like trying to fly across the Atlantic wearing a red cape." His amused snicker morphed into laughter. "That woman's a regular bare-knuckles street fighter camouflaged as a classy corporate diva. She's a vixen in Versace, a barracuda in Blass, a piranha in Prada."

Oh no, thought Andrew. He felt his intestines rearrange themselves into a series of sea-worthy slipknots.

No, no, no!

"Yes, indeed," Doug said, as though the point hadn't been adequately emphasized. "Our new national director of sales is not one to be pushed into a corner. If she doesn't like your way of doing business, she'll let you know—in no uncertain terms. And at that point you'd best head straight for the door."

Andrew and Joe looked at each other, knowing they'd come to the same conclusion. Cassandra Hartwell was not only at the pain conference, but she would also be present during the discussion in which they planned to lament the very issue Doug was touting as her greatest virtue.

A low-level murmuring began emanating from various sections of the restaurant. Hushed tones escalated to a hum-like resonance; it was a sound similar to the one made by wedding reception guests, anxiously awaiting the arrival of the bride and groom. But there had been no wedding ceremony, and a jovial crowd's anticipation of its beloved and newly-wed couple was not the reason for the unexpected whispers and mumbles.

"Oh, there she is now." Doug's face glowed like a pre-lit Christmas tree as he watched his guest—accompanied by the hostess—head toward their table.

From a distance of thirty feet, Andrew spied a head of shoulder length hair, pitch-black and voluminous. From twenty feet, he saw a face, exhibiting the same harshness of a black-ink drawing, beset with menacing eyes perpetrating a sub-zero glare. Stunned and astounded, Andrew watched the woman cross the room with the stealth and force of a German U-boat cutting through the icy depths of the sea. Her long sleeve V-neck top in a dizzying peacock print (which admittedly went well with the hotel's wild jungle theme) was gathered at the waist and buttoned up the front with a few gleaming gold medallions. Factor in black leggings and a pair of patent leather shoes with ice picks for heels, and it was no wonder the room had the energy and buzz of a high voltage electrical tower.

The three men got to their feet when the gap between Cassandra and the table narrowed to less than eight feet. The next few moments were a blur for Andrew as he struggled to make sense of what was happening. He had a faint recollection of the waiter swooping in to pull out Cassandra's chair, even though Doug had put a hand on the back of it one second beforehand, thus creating a literal tug-of-war situation over who'd do the honors. The waiter, having a leverage advantage due to the fact he was in position *behind* the chair, won.

"Sorry I'm late," said Cassandra irritably, as the waiter eased her closer to the table and the men reclaimed their seats. She moved her water glass to the left above her forks. Then, before looking across the table at Joe, she set a small shiny black purse next to her knife and spoon.

Andrew's respiration rate was holding steady at around one breath per minute, which seemed odd considering he could feel his heart fluttering around inside his ribcage like a hummingbird on a sugar rush. He wondered whether, if he remained very still, he might not be noticed.

"Cassandra, this is Dr. Stevenson," Doug said, nodding in Joe's direction from his seat to her left. "He's one of the more recent additions to our illustrious panel of speakers. Dr. Stevenson, Cassandra Hartwell."

Joe reached across the table. "Please, call me Joe."

She took his hand, saying, "It's a pleasure," though Andrew heard just the opposite in her smug tone.

"And this is Andrew Gallagher, a family friend of Joe's."

So much for not being noticed.

"He recently returned from a tour of duty in the Middle East," Doug said. "The three of us were supposed to bat a few golf balls around tomorrow, but I have to take a rain check on account of that emergency board meeting." He wrinkled his nose. "It's always something, isn't it?"

Because of his diagonal position and lack of proximity to Cassandra, Andrew felt it necessary to half-stand, reaching across the table to make the acquaintance official with a handshake. He realized, though, too late, that a salute would have been the safer (and, dare he say *more appropriate?*) gesture the moment his coat sleeve grazed the top of the newly positioned water glass, sending a clinking flood of water and ice cubes flowing in Cassandra's direction.

"*Ah!*" she gasped. Shoving her hands against the edge of the table she plowed the back of her chair into the front of the waiter, still foolishly standing by. Cassandra jumped to her feet, escaping the stream of cold water seeping through the white tablecloth and making an unseemly dribbling sound as it landed on the carpet.

"That was a close call," Doug said, using yet another inane sports cliché and looking cautiously relieved. "No harm, no foul," he added, demonstrating a much more grateful perspective than the unintended victim herself.

"*No foul?*" repeated Cassandra, her eyes shooting laser rays of disbelief. "What do you call *this?*" She lifted the little purse off the table high enough so pretty much everyone in the restaurant with at least 20/100 vision could appreciate her plight. Water mixed with black dye trickled from the corner of the bag as she held it up on an angle, facilitating the run-off.

"This isn't some off-label vinyl clutch from Wal-Mart," she hissed, strangely enough at Doug, whose only crime had been a couple of overused and underappreciated one-liners. "It's a custom-made silk shantung handbag I purchased at Dolce and Gabanna," she looked directly at Andrew, "during my last trip to London."

Oh, yeah? he thought. *Well, I picked up my durable khaki backpack on base in Dubai—at the Military PX. That, sweetheart, is one store you're not even allowed to enter.*

This time, the hostess swooped in, presumably on behalf of the injured waiter. She offered to seat the four of them at another table.

Doug deferred to Cassandra. "Would that be okay?"

She rolled her eyes. "Naturally."

The group moved to a nearby table. As soon as they settled, the waiter arrived to take their orders. Andrew was grateful; it gave him a moment to rethink. He had to at least apologize to Cassandra. He *was* the one responsible for damaging her vida loca purse, or whatever she called it. It was a silly-looking thing to begin with and too small for practical use but, nonetheless, it was still his fault for giving it a cold shower.

He waited until Cassandra had finished dabbing most of the remaining liquid from the purse. She'd quickly used up the multitude of napkins bestowed upon her by various concerned individuals, including the hostess, their waiter, and two unidentified male patrons.

"I'm very sorry for spilling water on your purse," Andrew said at last, making use of the tact and diplomacy skills he'd acquired while at officer candidate school.

Unmoved by his sincerity, Cassandra narrowed her eyes into a frozen and calculating stare. "Is that all you have to say on the matter?"

What else *was* there to say . . . that he was a ham-fisted klutz? Wasn't that part obvious? "Uh, the purse is pretty?"

"Well," she snorted, "if you're not going to offer to pay for a replacement, I'll simply expense the cost to Horizon Pharmaceuticals." She tightened her mouth, glancing in Doug's direction with an arched brow.

Without missing a beat, Doug smiled and nodded. "That should be fine." He held a warm roll in one hand and a knife in the other. He concentrated, far too intently, Andrew thought, on extracting whipped butter from a small crock the waiter had placed in the center of the table.

Cassandra eyed Doug as he slathered an artery-clogging dose of trans-fat and triglycerides on his little bun. "It cost twelve hundred dollars."

"What?" Doug's knife slipped from his hand and hit the bread plate below with a startling clatter.

"Is that going to be a problem?" Cassandra's tone dripped with daring defiance.

Doug reconfigured his flatware. "No, no problem." He gave her a plaintive look. "Do what you have to do."

She jerked her chin in proud satisfaction but Andrew knew that if Doug hadn't cooperated with her, she'd have gone above his head, in all likelihood to the mayor's office, or even the governor's. *Because after all, "if she doesn't like your way of doing business, she'll let you know—in no uncertain terms. And at that point you'd best head straight for the door."*

Andrew wondered if Doug realized how prophetic his own words had become at that moment.

"So, what was the topic of discussion before my arrival?" Cassandra asked, of no one in particular.

Doug popped the tail end of his roll into his mouth then did that hand-cupping thing again with his moustache. "Let's see," he said after swallowing, "we were talking about work. I know that much."

Joe and Doug both laughed at the irony, but not Andrew. He feared the worst . . . that Doug would pick up where they'd left off, talking about Allie.

Doug stroked his face for the umpteenth time. "I know it had something to do with you, Cassandra."

Adrenaline once again shot through Andrew's body. The evening's events were spiraling out of control, and he needed to *do something* . . . create a disturbance, yell *fire*, knock over another glass of water. *Anything.*

Cassandra's penetrating eyes crept around the table. *"Oh?"*

"What was it? Joe? Andrew? Help me out, boys; I can't put my finger on the specifics."

Huh uh. No, sir. You're not getting any help from me, Andrew thought.

Doug squinted in thought. "Wait a sec, I think I remember. It was something about . . ."

Andrew held his breath.

"I know!" Doug snapped his fingers and looked at Joe. "You and Andrew were saying some nice things about the representative who encouraged you to become a speaker. Allie Hendrickson."

The waiter interrupted the subsequent excruciating pause by setting a plate of garden salad in front of each of them. Andrew exhaled, hoping a crisis had been averted. But before he could so much as stick his fork in a crouton, Doug started talking again.

"Cassandra and Allie worked together not long ago." He inserted a superball-sized cherry tomato into his mouth. It made a popping sound when he bit into it.

"And how did it go?" Joe asked Cassandra, with a hint of a challenge in his voice.

Tilting her head in mock curiosity, she met his stare and smirked. "Not well, actually."

"Yeah? And why is *that?*" Andrew knew he should be quiet, but he couldn't help himself.

Cassandra seemed keen on playing her little game. She leaned forward and placed her elbows on the table, clasping her hands over her salad plate. "The girl shows a blatant disregard for fellow pharmaceutical sales representatives. She's disorganized in her daily activities, *and* she has a distracting attachment to her district manager."

"That's an awful lot of dissing," said Joe.

Andrew smiled at the appropriateness of Joe's word choice, but he figured Joe probably didn't even realize that dissing meant *being disrespectful* and could be found in any urban dictionary.

Before Andrew could come to Allie's defense, Doug spoke up. His voice was sharp. "I never saw any of that. She's had high rankings in recent years. You don't get to the top by being ill-mannered and inept."

It worked for *her,* Andrew thought, looking at Cassandra's mask of a face turn to hardened steel over Doug's remarks.

From out of nowhere the hostess appeared, planting herself next to Cassandra like a dessert cart. Cassandra glared at the poor woman. *"What is it?"*

"I'm sorry for the disturbance, but there's a gentleman here to see you. He'd like just a moment of your time."

Cassandra sniffed. "Where is he?"

"At the front. I'll take you to him."

Grabbing hold of the soggy black purse, Cassandra curtly excused herself. She launched out of her chair like Apollo 14 and then followed the hostess from the table. Andrew watched the women's progress through the restaurant and to the area near the hostess stand, where Dr. Bruner stood waiting. Catching sight of Andrew from across the restaurant, Dr. Bruner smiled and stood up on his toes. When he waved in friendly acknowledgement, Andrew returned the gesture. Cassandra looked back to see who was being greeted, before beginning an exchange of words with Dr. Bruner. The two periodically glanced in Andrew's direction until the doctor's disposition downshifted noticeably.

The conversation regarding Allie resumed in Cassandra's absence. Joe, clearly not willing to give up on their mission yet, expressed his appreciation for Allie's hard work and dedication. Doug was so receptive Andrew began to relax, encouraged by the prospect that Doug would reconsider the changes.

Ten blessedly calm minutes passed before Cassandra returned to the table. Strangely, she was smiling broadly and behaving in an almost civil manner. Under different circumstances, this might have been a welcome relief; however, in Cassandra's case, Andrew knew it meant one thing and one thing only.

She was up to something, and it didn't look good.

Chapter 14

The Burnt Bean Confessions

J oe pulled his truck into the Gallagher's driveway early the next morning. With ominous rain clouds swirling overhead, it looked like the decision to abandon the scheduled golf game and beat the storm home had turned out to be a good one. It gave Andrew a chance to run a few errands, after which he'd take the Mustang in to have it serviced. He didn't know *why*, but he had a funny feeling about a potential buyer for the car showing up in the near future.

Andrew opened the rear door of the truck and grabbed his duffel bag. "So, what are your thoughts on how things went?"

"All things considered, I'd say it was a worthwhile trip," Joe said, adding that Cassandra revealing the sinister side of her personality had given Doug "cause for pause."

Yeah, and everyone else a headache.

Andrew agreed, in spirit at least. He *wanted* to believe it had gone well. Even so, he still had an odd lump in his gut. He couldn't help but sense that something weird had happened before Cassandra returned to the table.

Once settled inside the house, Andrew went to the kitchen. It was empty and quiet, but he knew it wouldn't be for long. The coffeemaker held a full pot. The coffee's vanilla scent added to the sweetness of Sue's trademark Saturday morning cinnamon rolls, now warming in the oven. Andrew took a deep breath, grateful to be back in calm, and not tropical, surroundings. He stretched forward to look out through the bay window over the sink. Well, okay, maybe a little tropical. He watched heavy water drops slap against a small Sago palm on the other side of the glass.

"Good morning."

Startled, Andrew straightened and turned his head. "Hey, Dad."

Rob removed a large, blue pottery mug from the bamboo dish drain and filled it with steaming hot coffee. After taking a seat at the table, he slipped the morning paper out of its protective plastic sleeve and briefly scanned the front page. "I expected you back later today."

Andrew sat down across from him. "One of the guys in our original party had to cancel. And besides, we didn't want to chance getting rained out." He extracted the real estate section from the pile and absently flipped through it. "I've been considering looking at houses up in the Montrose area. Maybe La Cañada or La Crescenta."

"That would make an easy drive to work. Good schools up there, too." Rob raised an eyebrow and lifted his mug to take a drink. "Do you have a realtor yet?"

Andrew ignored the schools reference. "No."

"I could recommend one or two. A couple of my patients are agents. If you're interested."

"Sure. Thanks, Dad."

"What's your timeframe? Of course, you can stay here as long as you need to, Andrew. I'm not in a hurry to kick you out."

Andrew appreciated the comment, but as much as he enjoyed being back with his family, he did feel a pressing need to get a place of his own. After years of either living at home, with a roommate, or in barracks or crew quarters, he was ready for some freedom. "I'd like to stay until after the holidays. Start looking sometime in January, February at the latest. It's a big decision; I don't want to rush into it."

Sue entered the kitchen. "Rush into what?"

"Getting married." Rob pulled the newspaper down and watched Sue with big eyes, waiting for her reaction.

"*Married?* Andrew, are you thinking about proposing?" Sue's voice was high and loud. Her eyes lit up. Then she pressed her lips together. Her voice returned to normal. "Or is your father testing my early morning patience?"

"*Early morning?* It's eight thirty-five, good woman."

Paying no attention to Rob, Sue gave Andrew an expectant look. "I thought I'd been seeing stars in your eyes lately. Are you in love with Jennifer?"

"*Jennifer?* No, Mom. And you were right the first time. Dad's testing your patience, or something." Andrew narrowed his eyes at Rob and shook his head.

"Only trying to keep things interesting around here; that's all." Rob frowned, pretending to be hurt. He shook the paper dramatically as he turned the page.

"What is it you don't want to rush into, Andrew?" Sue reached up into the cupboard near the sink, pulled down a mug that matched

Rob's and filled it with coffee. "Or is it top secret?" She looked over her shoulder and winked.

"Buying a house, in the Verdugo Mountains. La Cañada, Montrose, someplace around there."

Sue took a sip and nodded. "Nice area. Great school districts, too."

There was the school thing again. Andrew continued to ignore it.

"You should know, Teach," Rob said, using the nickname he often called his wife, a fifteen-year, twelfth grade English teacher at a private high school in Sherman Oaks.

Rob and Sue began a discussion on the elective courses offered in public schools versus those available to them "back in the day." Andrew stood up, giving his parents a short wave on his way out of the kitchen.

"Will we see you later?" Sue asked.

"I doubt it. I'm going out with Jennifer. A movie and then to dinner."

Sue smiled. "That would be Jennifer, the person you are *not* starry eyed over, correct?"

"That's right."

"Okay, Hon; whatever you say."

Andrew walked through the den and past a bookcase full of trophies he'd won while playing basketball in high school. Entering the garage, he wondered why his mom still kept those out on display. But more important, *What did she mean by "starry eyed"?* When he looked at himself in the mirror, he didn't see anything different about his eyes. He liked Jennifer and enjoyed her company, but that was all. And besides, he'd already traveled the "madly-in-love, I-can't-live-without-you" route once before in regards to a beautiful, brown haired girl named Allie. It was a journey that had led to a painful, albeit valuable, lesson learned about trying to force the hand of God.

After the stress of the previous day's events, Andrew was ready to conclude that, without a doubt, being starry-eyed and in love was just not worth the effort. Not for him, and not with anyone.

* * *

Allie sat at the eating counter between her kitchen and dining room, making a list of her stops for the day: Grocery store. Dry cleaners. The library, to check on the arrival of Sue Grafton's latest mystery novel.

"It's better if you forget about him," Gretchen advised, from pretty much out of the blue, which was where most of her thoughts seemed to originate.

Allie looked up and blanched at the mess in her usually spotless kitchen. She'd left the counters clean and tidy the night before, but they weren't that way now. The perpetrator of the disarray, Gretchen, stood before the stove, dusting cinnamon over a saucepan of warm milk. A sticky honey bottle sat on the granite counter, amidst a scattering of debris akin to that of a breakfast tornado: toast crumbs, orange peelings, and a trail of Lucky Charms cereal, that began with a yellow moon near the microwave and ended with a green clover by the sink.

"Andrew and I are still friends," Allie replied. "You don't just abandon friendships that have spanned an entire lifetime." It sounded reasonable enough, though Allie only said it in an attempt to throw Detective Gretchen off the case.

"I wouldn't have a problem kicking someone to the curb if they aggravated *me*."

Allie bit down on her tongue, keeping her thoughts from becoming words. If she lived by that rule, Gretchen wouldn't be in Allie's kitchen right now, creating mayhem under the guise of preparing a meal.

Although Allie had thought having Gretchen around would be a good experience, so far, it wasn't working out that way. Gretchen just didn't fit in with Allie's orderly life. Or then again, maybe she did, because Allie's life wasn't as orderly as it used to be.

Gretchen poured the steaming milk into a cup. "And, no kidding," she said, squirting in a blob of honey, "I just read an article in *Female in Fashion* on this exact same subject. Their advice: Kick 'em *all* to the curb. Especially the people who borrow your clothes and never return them."

"That advice is extreme. And it doesn't even apply here. Andrew's got things going on in his life, and I'm busy with work. That's it," Allie said, in an effort to curtail the conversation.

"That's not the impression I got the night he came over here to see you. I heard the screams, and I felt the heat in the room after you left."

"Screams? What screams? Who was screaming?"

Suddenly flushed, Gretchen looked away. "I'm not sure. I was upstairs the whole time. I think it was Andrew."

"No. Andrew was not screaming."

"Okay, then it was *you*."

"Well, I may have raised my voice a little before I left, but I certainly wouldn't consider that 'screaming.'"

"You slammed the front door!"

Allie winced. "Did I?"

"Shook the whole house." Gretchen raised her arms, making a gesture that looked like jazz hands. "I thought it was an earthquake. I lived in California when the last big one struck, so I remember the feeling. That baby was over ten points on that, that, that scale thingy."

"Richter," Allie said before attempting to segue over to a discussion on natural disasters. "I remember it too, but I'm pretty sure it was only a six-something. Most of the damage occurred in Northridge, which is why they called it the Northridge earthquake."

"Okay, whatever." Gretchen flicked her wrist. "But like I said, that's what I thought was happening when you stormed out of here screaming."

"I wasn't screaming."

"Well, *somebody* was."

Allie removed a whole wheat bagel from a bag on the counter and wrapped it in a paper towel. She grabbed her purse, brushed past her cousin, and marched through the dining room. Gretchen had mentioned Andrew's name twice since Allie's return from Denver. Both times, Allie managed to redirect the conversation. Talking and thinking about Andrew had been causing her to feel that same sense of loss she'd experienced before—first in her dreams, then in the days after the incident on the beach. She'd made up her mind that revisiting those feelings was not going to happen. Not if she could help it.

Stepping down into the garage, Allie looked over her orderly shelves and pegboards with satisfaction. She also felt a sense of gratification in maintaining the exterior of her Ford Escape, with its jet-black paint and gleaming finish. Allie prided herself in driving a clean vehicle and having clean surroundings. At least that was something she could control.

She punched the lighted button on the wall.

The automatic garage door ticked upward with a rumble. As it rose, it slowly revealed bright white leather sneakers, purple polyester knit pants, a safety orange nylon vest, a multi-colored turtleneck sweater, and a lavender knit cap, atop which sat a floppy white pom-pom. All of this eye-catching attire encased a smiling Gloria. "What's up, kiddo?" she asked.

Allie stared in fascination at Gloria's mouth, which was smothered in candy apple red lipstick. "Kind of a lot, to tell you the truth."

"I wouldn't want you to tell me anything *but*. Wanna come over for a cup of Joe? I found a company on the web that sells the same delicious banana nut flavor you brewed the other day. This outfit claims to use robust Panamanian beans along with imported banana extract. From Jamaica, mon." She gave Allie a happy smirk and did a little dance step that Gloria might have thought was reggae. It wasn't.

"Ah, thanks. But I've got a bunch of errands to take care of before the storm hits. You know how people around here drive when it's raining."

"Yup. The exact same way they drive when it's *not* raining—like maniacs. Come by afterward if you wanna talk." Gloria looked up at the gloomy sky. "You're right, it's moving in fast." She whirled a bright yellow compact umbrella around her wrist by a loop on the handle. "I better try to squeeze in my power walk before it's too late."

"Good idea." Allie opened the door to the SUV and slid her bottom onto the chilly leather front seat. She placed the bagel inside her purse before tossing the purse in the seat behind her; this placement was the way she'd broken her bad habit of fiddling with her cell phone while driving. Starting the engine, she backed out of her garage and headed away from her townhouse.

After she made a right turn at the end of her street, Allie saw the power walking purple and orange blur nearly two blocks away. Pressing the button on the SUV's armrest, Allie lowered the passenger's window and slowed down, calling out, "I'll be by later for sure, Glor."

Maintaining her brisk pace, Gloria gave a thumbs-up sign, then vanished down a side street that circled back through the complex. Allie focused on the road ahead of her.

A moment later, a faint beeping sound interrupted the gentle crooning of Harry Connick, Jr. on the radio. Allie extended her right arm behind her. She groped around for the purse. Unable to reach far enough to retrieve it, and unable to wait until arriving safely at her first stop, she detoured into her storage facility. Other than the dented and scratched red truck she'd seen several weeks ago, the parking lot was empty. Allie pulled into one of the spaces facing the gray cinder block wall surrounding the building.

She grabbed her purse and took out her phone, surprised to discover that part of her—maybe a big part—hoped the call had been from Andrew. But no, it was from Kevin, the person who'd spent ten minutes scolding her in The Lodge restaurant's waiting area, and the same person with whom she hadn't spoken since that scolding. Kevin was, in fact one of the people she least wanted to speak with . . . ever again. He was a reminder of a day that had begun badly and had ended miserably.

After his lecture that evening, Kevin had finished with a warning that Cassandra wasn't the kind of person who suffered fools well. Allie hadn't been sure which angered her more . . . that his comment implied Allie was a fool or that he thought Allie was too stupid to notice what kind of a person Cassandra was. Where Cassandra was concerned, Allie wasn't the one wearing blinders. She'd held her tongue though, and the two had joined the rest of the group for the district dinner, an event that had turned out to be the most somber and depressing of Allie's career.

It had started with Cassandra usurping Kevin's authority by sitting at the head of the table, in effect holding court over the Los Angeles district like an evil Queen of Spades. She'd even coordinated the seating in a boy-girl, boy-girl arrangement before Kevin and Allie arrived, leaving two chairs vacant—one to her right and the other at the far end of the table. Of course, the latter was for Allie. It was right near the entrance to the kitchen. Allie could barely hear the conversation at the table because she spent the whole meal listening to clattering, clanging, and a French-accented chef shouting orders at his "eenept" sous chefs.

Not having much of an appetite to enjoy her chicken fettuccine alfredo, Allie had stayed quiet and out of trouble, mindlessly twirling pasta around her fork and feeling alone in the world. Cassandra's right-hand man for the evening more than made up for the table's glaring lack of conversation. Kevin kept the group entertained with a self-serving anecdote about how quickly he'd worked his way up from sales rep to district manager. Fortunately for Allie, the kitchen cacophony had drowned out most of Kevin's posturing.

As Allie expected, the district dinner charade had ended in grand finale style. With narrowed eyes and a tight smile, Cassandra brandished photocopies of a newly compiled fourth quarter list of the national top twenty reps. The decision to exclude fourth quarter pain management sales numbers hadn't even become official, but that didn't stop her from sharing the new and unapproved standings. It was no surprise that, in Cassandra's revised and phony list, Allie's numbers had tanked. She'd gone from being in the top three to being nowhere in sight. At one point, Allie had looked up from her pasta to find Cassandra sneering at her in triumph.

A sprinkling of rain droplets splashed down on the SUV's windshield, yanking Allie away from the image of Cassandra's contempt. Staring at her phone, Allie pondered whether or not she wanted to listen to Kevin's message. Even though she hadn't spoken with him in recent days, she had heard his voice. He'd sent out a district voicemail message the day after the disastrous dinner, seeing fit to copy Doug Wylie and Cassandra. The message sounded like a mini pep rally—full of company rah rah rahs and blah blah blahs. It was the typical corporate fare served after all meetings, but particularly those on a national scale.

Sighing, Allie accessed her voicemail.

185

"Hey, Allie, it's Kevin," the message began, "just following up on our conversation at the restaurant in Denver."

"What conversation?" Allie asked the SUV's empty interior. "I listened, you talked. This does not constitute a conversation."

Kevin, since he wasn't there and couldn't hear her, continued blathering. "I just heard about an unfortunate incident that took place at the pain conference in Palm Springs. It concerns you." Several seconds of silence passed. "Call me back as soon as possible. It's urgent."

An unfortunate incident in Palm Springs that concerns *me?* Call back ASAP; *it's urgent?*

Distracted by his coded communication (which was the equivalent of a bright neon sign flashing an important message—in Mandarin Chinese), Allie called Kevin back. He didn't answer, so she left a message. Exiting the parking lot, she cut the corner too sharp, and the SUV lurched over a curb. She admonished herself and tried to concentrate on driving. But it was a losing battle.

What was Kevin trying so hard not to say?

* * *

"I forget how you take your coffee," Gloria said, entering her dining room and setting a pink ceramic coffee mug on the table in front of Allie.

Each room in Gloria's house—the dining room being no exception—had its own distinct look and "feel." None of the furnishings matched, in either color or style. The decor ranged from estate-sale hodgepodge in the living room, to early twentieth-century Edwardian in the dining room, to country bumpkin farm animals in the kitchen. Somehow, though, Gloria's *extreme-eclectic* style worked. Allie had always felt not only comfortable in Gloria's home, but also curiously uplifted. There was nothing stiff or restricted about Gloria Danville's approach to interior decorating . . . or her approach to life.

"Oh, and just so you know," Gloria said, "this stuff tastes a little sweet to me. Of course, my sense of taste isn't what it used to be. Neither is my sense of smell, for that matter. And, my vision's going down the tubes. I can't hardly hear worth a whit—"

"Milk or half and half would be great," Allie said. "Whatever you have."

"You got it, Cupcake." Gloria ducked into her kitchen and returned a moment later. She set a teaspoon, a small red and white milk carton, and a matching hippo-shaped mug for herself on the table. As Gloria sat down, Allie's cell phone began to ring.

Muttering an apology, Allie jumped up and dashed into the living room. She dug her cell phone from her purse, sank down on an orange mid-century modern reading chair, and answered it.

"*Allie,*" Kevin barked in her ear. "I'm glad I reached you. I was afraid we might end up playing phone tag all week."

"What's up, Kevin?"

"Well, I understand one of your doctors spoke at the Palm Springs pain conference yesterday."

"Yes. Dr. Stevenson."

"Mm hmm. That's right, Dr. Stevenson."

"So what's the big emergency? Did he have an accident or something? Is he all right?"

"Oh, he's just fine. But apparently he brought someone along to play a game of golf with Doug Wylie. Doug then invited Dr. Stevenson and this individual to join him and Cassandra for dinner last night. I spoke with Cassandra earlier today, and she is *livid.* She claims the doctor's guest tried to pass himself off as a neurologist to get access to the conference hall and lectures, and that he ruined one of her expensive handbags when he spilled water on it."

"Okay." Allie shook her head, clueless as to what this could possibly have to do with her or why Kevin was so keen on interrupting her weekend over it. "Why tell me? Did Cassandra convince Doug it's *my* fault because I arranged for Dr. Stevenson to become a speaker? *Is that it?* She's now going to blame *me* for every bad thing that happens in the world?" Allie's frustration erupted into more honesty than she'd intended to spew: "Kevin, I can't stand her!"

Kevin sighed. "Let's not start *this* again."

"Start what?" she nearly shrieked. "Start being honest about the fact that Cassandra Hartwell is just plain evil and out to get me? Start talking about how she'd love to destroy my reputation—*and* my career?" Allie knew she sounded shrill, but she didn't care.

Kevin didn't say anything. Allie tried to calm her breathing. She slipped off her shoes and attempted to receive a little soothing from the shaggy faux red fur of the area rug beneath her feet. The silence between them stretched out into a tense standoff.

Finally Kevin inhaled, letting the air out slowly. "Cassandra said this man and Dr. Stevenson discussed *you* at length. She believes you set this meeting up so the two of them could quote, 'work Doug over' regarding the new goals."

"I don't know anything about any of that." Allie gritted her teeth and nearly squeezed the life out of her phone as she said, slowly, deliberately, and as steadily as she could, "That woman is completely insane."

Kevin groaned. "Allie, you need to consider yourself warned. Next time something like this happens, you'll be written up for noncompliance and insubordination. Now, perhaps you weren't aware that encouraging contracted physician speakers to influence company policy on your behalf is not allowed. If that's the case, I can try to talk to Cassandra for you, but as it stands now, you're being watched very closely. Therefore, I would suggest you give Cassandra, and *me*, for that matter, your full cooperation. Understood?" He ended the call without waiting for a response.

It didn't matter. She had no response to give him.

Allie looked at the phone in her hand. It was funny . . . she could see the phone, but she couldn't feel it. She'd gone numb. *What was happening?* Had she been thrown, against her will, into a time machine and transported back to her youthful days of anger and hopelessness? Why had she been trying so hard these past years to get right with God by staying on the straight and narrow? If people were determined to push her up against a wall, the way life had pushed her before, why not rebel?

Again.

Allie threw her cell phone at her purse, which she'd set on Gloria's oak barrel coffee table. The phone bounced off a side pocket and landed in an octagonal ashtray. It was black, covered with small white bull horns, and its interior bottom read, "Steer Your Butts Here." Gloria had returned home with it the previous year after visiting a dude ranch in Midland, Texas. She claimed it was a parting gift. And though Allie couldn't be sure, whatever it was, it made her want to reach for a "smoke" to calm her nerves—the way she used to in her teens.

It was a good thing Gloria didn't have any cigarettes in the house.

* * *

By midafternoon, the storm had passed, and enormous white cumulous clouds were floating against the azure sky backdrop. Andrew parked the Mustang in Jennifer's driveway and got out. He inhaled deeply. The air smelled clean and felt invigorating, filling his weary spirit with a sense of newness and hope.

Before he could head toward Jennifer's front door, she came through it then shut it behind her. Skipping across the front porch she hopped down onto the driveway. "You look different," Andrew said. He rounded his car and opened the passenger's door.

Jennifer took hold of a handful of auburn hair and ran her fingers down the strands. "It's my hair. I flat-ironed it."

188

"That must have been awkward. Did you use an ironing board?"

Jennifer giggled and gave the side of Andrew's arm a light punch. "No, silly. Not *that* kind of iron. You know, a *straightening* iron." She joined her opened hands at the palms then clamped them together like a snapping crocodile.

"Oh, right, right, right. My mistake." Andrew pressed his fingers to his forehead. "I thought they called that thing a fravisat."

Before getting into the car Jennifer paused for a second to play along with Andrew's silly game. "Oh, what do they know?" she said, giving him a perplexed look and a shrug.

Andrew gently closed the passenger's door and walked around the back of the Mustang. He removed a few wet orange and yellow-tinged leaves from the trunk lid and tossed them onto the street among thousands of others. He slid into the driver's side. Hanging out with Jennifer seemed to be good therapy for Andrew. It helped take his mind off the sobering fact that he'd been viewing his life as segments of time ticking away without Allie by his side—without knowing if she ever would be.

And even though letting go of his dream scared Andrew, what scared him even more was the idea that he'd been trying to mold Allie into what he wanted her to be, instead of allowing her to be who she was.

Andrew shook his head, disappointed with himself for wandering back into Allie-land, especially while he was with Jennifer. He glanced at her to see if she'd noticed his mind had taken a little detour.

She pulled her seatbelt strap downward and clicked the buckle securely in place. "Are we staying in Glendale?"

"If you like. Do you have something in mind?"

"How about the Americana on Brand? We could catch a late matinee and afterward get some Mexican food at Tacos de los Gatos."

The Americana? Yeah, why not? Andrew might be able to get Jennifer to go into the Sport's Specialist with him. Would she mind it if he looked around for a new fishing pole? He and his dad had already been talking about going camping at Lake Arrowhead in the spring. Andrew could also take a few minutes to look over the store's huge selection of hiking boots, but if he bought a new pair, he'd have to break them in a little before attempting a challenging hike up in Wildflower Canyon Park . . .

Jennifer interrupted Andrew's satisfying daydream by jabbing an elbow in his direction. "We could even check out the Americana's cute dress shops and boutiques while we're at it."

"Or maybe," Andrew said with a straight face, "we should just forget about dinner and the movie and go shopping instead. I could use a new ensemble or two." He raised his hands with fingers fluttering.

"Oh, *you*. Okay, forget the boutiques. After we eat, we'll get you some coffee. An Americano at the Americana. *Your* favorite coffee drink in *my* favorite shopping center. Now, how can you pass that up?"

The irony of her words jarred Andrew out of his jovial mood and brought him back to his painful reality.

"I guess I can't." He sighed, started the car and then backed out of Jennifer's driveway. When he put the Mustang in first gear and pressed the accelerator, the gearshift popped into neutral. The engine revved.

Great. Was this some kind of sign or a warning he should heed? Maybe it was God showing Andrew that instead of moving ahead in the way and in the direction he'd said he wanted to, he just kept idling on thoughts of Allie.

* * *

The Americana, Brand Boulevard's ultimate shopping, dining, and entertainment center, was already decorated for Christmas, even though Thanksgiving was still five days away. Andrew found that depressing, as if retailers were conspiring to hurry his life along.

Andrew and Jennifer arrived at the movie theater in time to catch the four-fifteen showing of a film Andrew couldn't seem to concentrate on long enough to know what was happening at any given moment. By the time the picture ended, he was totally lost.

Fortunately, though, it didn't matter. From the second the show let out until they walked to the restaurant and were seated, Jennifer did a thorough job of critiquing the entire film.

The interior of Tacos de los Gatos was decorated in blaring yellows and reds, its walls covered in multi-colored sequined sombreros. The look was bold and in-your-face, and so were the aromas that filled the lively restaurant. It smelled of grilled onions and peppers, and Andrew knew that no matter what he ordered he'd leave there that evening smelling like a deep-fried chimichanga. But that was the price one paid for eating in a place that brought a smoking hot cast iron pan of sizzling fajitas right to your neighbor's table. After looking over their menus, Jennifer chose the chicken tostada salad, and Andrew opted for an enchilada and taco combination plate.

"What did you think of the movie?" Jennifer asked just as a server showed up at their table. He wielded a red, green, and white basket filled with fragrant tortilla chips, a small white melamine bowl of salsa, and two glasses of ice water.

After removing the items from his round serving tray, the server set them down in an orderly manner. He threw in two straws wrapped in clear plastic, then vamoosed.

Andrew considered knocking over his water glass (he was good at that) or unobtrusively flipping the basket of chips—anything that might help change the subject—but he did neither as both ideas seemed in poor taste.

"I, uh . . . I like what *you* said about it."

Jennifer seemed content with the answer. She reached for a chip and dipped it into the salsa bowl right when their waiter arrived to take their orders. He was about Andrew's age, medium build with short brown hair. His face was pulled downward by a weighty frown, an expression that could have signified concentration, or it might have reflected his desire to be someplace else. Andrew could relate. He wanted to be someplace else, with *someone* else.

"I know this line will sound familiar," Jennifer said, once the waiter had departed, "but he reminds me of someone I know."

Line? She thought his comment on the airplane about Beth was some kind of line? Oh, man.

Jennifer tugged on the straw's plastic cover, struggling to release it. Once successful, she plunged the straw through the ice. Her hands shook slightly as she removed a lemon wedge from the rim of the glass. She gave the lemon a quick squeeze, set it aside then leaned forward, taking an extended drink. Andrew inhaled the tart spray the citrus had released into the air; he scooped up a small amount of salsa with a warm chip, thankful for a distraction from his own uneasy emotions. For several moments, he continued to munch on chips and salsa, keeping an eye on Jennifer's glass as the water level dropped precipitously.

Finally, she removed the straw from her mouth and pushed the glass away from her. Focusing her big round eyes on Andrew, she sat up straight and pressed her back against the tangerine orange naugahyde booth.

"I was engaged recently." Her face suddenly looked like a New Year's Eve balloon after a long night of celebration. "But I'm not anymore."

Andrew didn't see that one coming—obviously—so he stayed silent, more out of surprise than good manners.

Jennifer waved a hand in the direction of the departed waiter. "He looks so much like my fiancée—former fiancée," she added glancing away from Andrew. "His name is Michael."

"I'm sorry." Andrew didn't know what else to say, but sorry seemed appropriate. Jennifer's expression had taken a turn for the worse.

"I called it off. The wedding, I mean. We had a date set, guest list made out, honeymoon reservations. We'd even purchased . . ." Her voice faltered, and her head dropped down. She left the sentence unfinished. Using her left hand, she twisted the white gold band she wore on her right thumb.

As the moments slipped by, Andrew thought back to his first contact with Jennifer on the plane, when he'd seen her constant questions and comments as a disturbance. He'd thought she was just being chatty, but maybe she had wanted to talk to someone, anyone. He realized now that what Jennifer had needed was a friend. Lately he'd been taking for granted her interest in him by spending the time with her he couldn't spend with Allie, time that should have helped take his mind *off* Allie, but didn't.

Festive Mexican music being piped through the PA system delighted an eclectic group of eight, contentedly crammed into a large corner booth. They were having a blast . . . laughing, singing, and shaking imaginary maracas. Andrew noticed how the mood at *his* table paled in comparison. With Jennifer close to tears, and his own mood taking the double hit of pining for Allie and having no clue how to comfort his dinner date's distress, they needed less mariachi and more rhythm and blues.

"I hope I did the right thing." She once again reached for her water glass then shoved it away. "He was devastated, as I'm sure you can imagine." Her voice was sharp, as if she was berating herself. "But I couldn't go through with it, living a lie and pretending to want something that wasn't in my heart. Do you know what I mean, Andrew?"

He nodded. Jennifer's sentiments paralleled the circumstances of his life in a strange and coincidental way. In Andrew's case, though, he'd found that he couldn't pretend to *not* want what was in his heart. And look where *that* had gotten him. He was in the painful place of accepting that he had no right to demand something of Allie she didn't have in her own heart to give him.

"I know in my head it was for the best, ultimately. Michael knew he wanted to get married more than I did. He told me that; he really did." Jennifer sniffled, lifting up the napkin she'd placed on her lap and pressing it lightly against her cheeks.

Andrew found himself wondering if Jennifer's woeful tale of lost love wasn't about to top his own. Not that he wanted to compare the two. "Do you mind if I ask how long ago that was?"

"No, I don't mind, not too long ago. Early September, Labor Day weekend, in fact. We were at my old apartment, painting the second bedroom, which we'd planned to use as a shared office once we were married. I don't even know how it happened; but one minute I was rolling sage green paint on the walls, and the next minute I was telling him I couldn't go through with marrying him. It was dreadful. I don't know what I was thinking. I *wasn't* thinking; that's the problem. I was just blabbering away."

"I know someone like that," said Andrew, as a vision of the Cheshire Cat danced in his head.

"I guess in truth I'd known it from the start," Jennifer continued. "We'd dated for almost two years, but all along I'd felt that I was settling for companionship, instead of holding out for true love just because I didn't want to be alone." She breathed in deeply through her nose. This seemed to relax her a bit. "Please don't misunderstand me. I still care about him and want him to be happy. It wasn't meant to be, that's all."

Their waiter arrived, balancing a large round black tray high up on one hand and, in the other, carrying a stand on which to place the tray. Jennifer looked away as he set their meals down on the table with a warning that the plates were hot.

After the waiter left, Andrew didn't know what else to do, so he made insignificant small talk while Jennifer absently extracted sliced olives from her tostada. She made a pile of them on the side of her plate and poked at her food. She was silent for the entirety of the meal.

How long had they known each other? About six weeks now, and that was the first time she'd spoken of a former fiancée.

After fifteen minutes of an unnervingly one-sided conversation, the waiter reappeared. Andrew observed the man giving Jennifer a visual nudge, probably in an attempt to evaluate his customer's level of satisfaction. She ignored his unspoken appeal, avoiding even a quick glance in his direction.

"Can I get you anything else?" the man finally asked Andrew, giving up on trying to rouse Jennifer's attention.

"No, thanks. We're good," he replied, though, truthfully, he knew they were anything but.

* * *

After dinner, Jennifer perked up enough to insist they try The Burnt Bean coffeehouse next door to the restaurant. It was a roomy establishment with wood cabinetry and flooring as rich and earthy as the hearty scents inside. Jennifer ordered a sweet, icy, caramely beverage, complete with whipped cream and yet more caramel drizzled on top, while Andrew threw caution to the wind and chose a pumpkin spice latte. They sat across from each other at a small round table in the back corner, an ideal spot for a long, meaningful talk. Andrew, however, wasn't in the mood for such a talk, but then, just like that, it happened. He finally stopped pretending.

He leaned toward Jennifer. "I know how it is when you love someone who doesn't love you back the same way."

Jennifer's brows creased together, and her eyes flickered. Before she could react further, he figured he should get to his point. Quickly.

"I met her a long time ago, in school."

"Ahh." Jennifer nodded. "It's the girl you mentioned on the plane, the one I reminded you of."

"Oh, no, no. That's Beth. She's a friend, a great friend. No, this is someone else. Her name is Allie." Andrew rubbed the side of his face. "She's seeing some guy named Joshua." Even saying the man's name made Andrew's teeth hurt.

"Were you in love with her? Or did you love her because she was special to you? There's a big difference, you know. When you're in love, you want to be with that person all the time. That's all you think about. Whereas, loving someone and caring about them because you have a special fondness in your heart . . . well, it's not the same thing. I learned that the hard way."

Andrew shrugged and shook his head, wishing he hadn't brought up the topic at all. Jennifer didn't seem to get it. There was no past tense about this situation. It was happening right then, right there, in real time, forcing him to accept the facts for what they were.

Before he could think it through, he said, "Jennifer, I'm *in love* with her. *And* I love her." Andrew sat back and breathed out all the tension he'd been carrying around for days. He looked at Jennifer, and was relieved to see understanding in her eyes.

"And I've felt that way for as long as I can remember," he said, finally telling himself, and Jennifer, the truth about his feelings for Allie.

Chapter 15

Let's Talk, Turkey!

At one-thirty in the afternoon on Thanksgiving Day, Allie and Beth sat on Allie's living room sofa. They'd been discussing a plan to do all or most of their holiday shopping after church the following Sunday. Once Beth finished outlining what the Westside Plaza called its, *Employees-Only Black Weekend Blowout*, Gretchen's unexpected exclamation made it obvious she'd been eavesdropping.

"Whoa! *An extra thirty percent off everything in the entire mall?* Now that's what I call an employee discount."

Allie and Beth shushed and looked over at Gretchen, who stood on the imaginary line between the kitchen and dining room, scraping a metal spoon across the bottom of a pint container of *Chunky Monkey.*

"So, what time will you be hitting the mall to buy the goods? I wanna come with." Gretchen's eyes bounced open wide as she maneuvered a frosty, heaping spoonful of ice cream into her mouth.

Allie got to her feet. "Remember, we're due across the street in half an hour. Don't you think ice cream will spoil your appetite for dinner?"

"No."

"It won't?"

"No, I mean it's not ice cream."

"It looks like ice cream."

"It's frozen yogurt."

"Okay, then don't you think frozen yogurt will spoil your appetite?"

"That's the idea." After discarding the empty container into a trashcan sitting at the base of the eating counter, she dropped her spoon in the sink with a clink then reemerged from the kitchen with a package of Oreo cookies crinkling in her hands. "I get a voracious appetite when I'm smitten with a new love interest, and I simply cannot have Joshua's darling little brother, Steven, watch me pig out over at Glenda's."

"Gloria's," Allie corrected. Knowing her neighbor's unpredictable side, Allie had already prepared herself for a Thanksgiving meal capable of causing culinary shock. Who knew what they'd be eating. It could be anything from Mama Mia's frozen pepperoni pizzas to a Charlie Brown-style Thanksgiving feast consisting of marshmallows, popcorn, and buttered toast.

Gretchen clamped an Oreo between her teeth while she removed a handful from the package. She strolled over and plopped herself onto the sofa with a sigh. Then she bit down, crunching loudly as she chewed.

Allie cleared her throat. "I hate to tell you this, but Steven will not be joining us for dinner."

Gretchen stopped shoveling food hand to mouth and blinked at Allie with wide eyes.

"He moved a family to central California yesterday by himself," Allie tried to sound sympathetic, "and is staying up there to have Thanksgiving with one of the Waldens' cousins."

Gretchen glowered. With her mouth too full of Oreos to speak, she puffed out a snort of discontentment through her nose instead.

Welcome to my world, Allie thought. *What did that song say? "You can't always get what you want."*

* * *

Standing at her kitchen sink, Sue Gallagher plunked her hands into a bowlful of water and lettuce. She was dressed in festive Thanksgiving attire, which this year included a pair of burnt orange wool slacks "with an elastic waist to create room for seconds," a tan cotton sweater patterned with knitted turkeys, and a brown apron with two pilgrims on the front and the words, "Got turkey?" Andrew passed through the kitchen and chuckled to himself at his mother's sweater and apron, two among many less-than-serious gifts Rob had given her over the years. He smiled as he inhaled the combined aromas of roast turkey, cornbread stuffing, and candied yams baking in the oven. He also enjoyed the erratic chopping sounds filling the room. These came from Jennifer's efforts to help with the meal. She was busy at the pullout wooden cutting board in the center island, mincing several cloves of garlic. Her intense frown and clumsy motions suggested she hadn't done a lot of cooking in her time.

"You want me to put all the garlic into this little bowl of olive oil, right?" she asked.

"Right," Andrew answered. "This special salad dressing is a tricky recipe to remember, Jennifer. It's olive oil, garlic and—"

"Fresh ground black pepper," Sue added before Andrew could finish the short list. "Sometimes I include a touch of coarse salt, but usually it's not necessary with the crumbled bleu and shredded Parmesan cheeses already in the salad itself. It's important to make the salad with leaf lettuce—butter, red, or green leaf work the best."

"It sounds yummy." Jennifer used a whole piece of garlic to slide the remaining chopped bits off the butcher's knife and into the bowl of oil. She wore one of Rob's barbecue aprons, a red one with "The Grillfather" written in black across the front. The apron clashed with Jennifer's slender coral skirt and matching sweater set.

Passing through the slider in the den, Andrew stepped down onto the covered backyard patio to retrieve a chair that he'd taken outside to clean. The moment he picked it up, his cell phone, which of course he'd left in the kitchen, started ringing.

Hopeful it might be Allie, he called out, "Mom, could you get that?"

Then he remembered . . . her hands were as full as his own. He scrambled through the slider, raced awkwardly toward the dining room, dropped the chair on the floor with a loud thud, and dove toward his phone.

It was too late.

"Hello?" Jennifer said, pressing the phone against her ear.

* * *

Beth had insisted they call Andrew to wish him a Happy Thanksgiving. "I'll use the speaker function," she said then began dialing the phone set in its usual spot on the eating counter.

From the short hallway near the entrances to the garage and downstairs bathroom, Allie watched Beth. "Go ahead, but the speaker in that phone distorts voices; so don't be surprised if Andrew sounds like Kermit the Frog. Or Deputy Dog. Or . . . ."

Beth looked over her shoulder and frowned. Allie gave her an innocent shrug then took a few steps forward to sit in a chair at the dining room table.

A woman answered the call. "Hello."

Beth tilted her head. "Mrs. Gallagher?"

"No, this is Jennifer."

Allie felt her knees go weak and her heart jump into her throat, but she kept her face neutral . . . or so she thought, until she saw Beth glance at her with a wrinkled brow and compressed lips. Beth shook her head as if to say, "I didn't know."

Gretchen popped up off the sofa at the sound of the stranger's voice. "Who's Jennifer?" she asked, rushing toward Allie.

Beth shook her head, swatting at Gretchen. She pressed a finger to her lip and shook her head again. Then she said, "Oh, uh, hello, Jennifer. This is Beth McKinley. I'm a friend of Andrew's."

Beth kept her gaze on Allie, who started to get up but then stopped, unable to bring herself to leave the room.

After a brief hesitation Jennifer said, "Yes, of course, Beth. Andrew's mentioned you before."

"Who's Jennifer?" Gretchen whispered to Allie.

Allie ignored her.

Beth twisted her body and leaned backward. Her green eyes sparkled as she push-poked Allie's shoulder while mouthing out, "And I'm sure he's mentioned *you, too.*"

Allie rolled her eyes.

Unaware of the silent drama on the other end of the line, Jennifer prattled on through the speakerphone. "I'm helping Andrew's mom in the kitchen right now. She was washing lettuce when you called, and Andrew was bringing in a chair from out back; he's here now if you'd like to speak with him."

"Uh, sure. That'd be great. Oh, and Happy Thanksgiving, Jennifer." Beth gave Allie a playful wink.

Allie glared at her.

"Same to you. Here he is."

"Who is that girl?" Gretchen hissed in Allie's ear.

Allie turned and put her lips near the side of Gretchen's head. "That's Andrew's girlfriend," she whispered, in a near bark. "Now, would you please put a lid on it?"

"All right, already." Gretchen flung herself back on the sofa like a chastised puppy. "Don't get all fussbudgety."

"Hey, Beth." Andrew's voice blasted from the speaker and seemed to resonate throughout the entire downstairs.

Allie pointed to the phone and wriggled her nose. "There. You see, what I mean, Beth?" she said, barely above a whisper. "Kermit."

"Hi there, Andrew." Beth stepped around the counter and into the kitchen to keep an eye on Allie. "I've got you on speaker, and Allie and Gretchen are here as well. We're all going across the street shortly to Allie's neighbor, Gloria's, house."

"Is she the one who drives a Firebird?"

"That's her."

"Interesting lady."

Beth laughed. "You got that right."

Their conversation continued, and Allie's imagination went into overdrive as she placed herself in the Gallagher kitchen. She saw

Jennifer helping Sue peel potatoes, tuck tiny pimentoes into olives, or chop garlic for that unique salad dressing Sue was famous for. Or was Jennifer only capable of boiling water and handing Sue utensils. Allie didn't know anything about Jennifer except that her voice sounded as fragile as a croissant. She hardly seemed the type to hand-knead enough dough for three different kinds of bread, bake a cheesecake and a pumpkin pie from scratch, and then stuff a twenty-three pound turkey all by herself—feats Allie could perform with ease.

"Is Allie still there with you?" Andrew asked.

Beth waited for her to answer. When Allie didn't, Beth scrunched up her face at her then said, "She's here, Andrew. Would you like to speak to her privately?"

Allie shook her head and waved her hands.

Andrew didn't hesitate. "Sure."

Beth lifted the handset off the base unit. She placed in firmly in Allie's hand, along with a look of suspicion, a warning for her to behave herself.

"Hello. This is Allie."

Beth rolled her eyes. *"Oh, please."*

* * *

Hello, this is Allie? Andrew thought. Why not just say, *"Good afternoon, this is Allison Hendrickson. How many I help you?"*

Sweat seeped from Andrew's forehead. More games, was that it? Hot, cold; yes, no; start, stop; push, pull. Why couldn't he and Allie *for once* be in sync?

Why did she have to make everything so difficult? Was it too much to ask that they engage in friendly discourse?

Suppressing a frustrated sigh, he overlooked her forced formality. "Hi there."

"Good afternoon."

A muscle began to twitch at his jawline. He kept his voice steady. "So, you're going to your neighbor's house for dinner. That should be nice."

"You think so?"

"I do. I met her, you know. Your neighbor."

"Oh?"

Could she have sounded any more uninterested? "The first time I came to your place, I pulled up next to her Firebird in guest parking. You know, it was the day I brought the two Americanos . . ." He stopped, his last words hanging in the air like an anvil over his head.

"Andrew," Allie's tone was as chilly as the one she'd used in her arctic greeting, "Gloria *does* drive a Firebird, but I don't remember you bringing over Americanos. Are you sure it was to my place and not *Jennifer's?*"

Ouch. Below the belt.

More important—*oops!* He'd just unintentionally mentioned his first trip to the townhouse. If Allie found out about the visit, she might get upset that someone had been playing with her social schedule—namely Gretchen. Or Allie might become miffed at Andrew for not telling her beforehand about Gretchen's misbehavior. He feared that at any moment the Chesire Cat herself would come leaping out of a bag, exposing him for the fraud Allie believed him to be.

And leap Gretchen did, but instead of unveiling him, she made a cacophonous announcement in the background that Joshua had arrived.

"You were saying, Andrew?" Allie prodded.

"I'm sorry, what was the question?"

"Never mind. You'd probably give me some made-up answer anyway."

What? Andrew's temper flashed. How did that woman know which combination of buttons to push to get his pulse racing—like a catapulted F-18 Super Hornet—from zero to a hundred and thirty miles per hour in two seconds flat. For better or for worse, no one in his life had ever affected him the way Allie Hendrickson did.

Before he could think twice about his next words, he blurted, "I was just wondering if Sir Joshua knows about your dark past. Or does he think you've *always* been sugar and spice? Perhaps he'd be interested in a little history lesson." Oh man, had he just said that out loud?

"All right then, professor," Allie snapped, "why don't you give him the lesson yourself?" Andrew heard a muffled and echoing sound as Allie reengaged the speaker function. Her voice switched from edgy to soft and sweet. "*Joshua*, would you please come over here. You remember Andrew Gallagher, right? He'd like to say something to you."

Great, Andrew thought. *Just what I need to be dealing with at the moment, Mr. Sunbeams and Merriment, back to spend more time with MY woman.* The regret he'd felt a second before evaporated. It would serve Allie right if Andrew did tell Joshua all the nitty-gritty details of her troubled youth . . . the truancy, the cannabis smoking, the shoplifting, the vandalism. Oh, the list went on and . . .

"Hey, Buddy, Happy Thanksgiving," Joshua said. "How's it going?"

No, Andrew could no more badmouth Allie than he could kick a dog. Not even a rabid, junkyard dog. So he tempered his response. "Just fine, thanks. And with you?"

"Can't complain."

No, of course you can't. You're with Allie.

"You know, I've got a question for you, Andrew. Remember that night I took Allie out for an early dinner?"

Are you kidding? How could I forget? "Not really. Refresh my memory, please. *Buddy.*"

"Uh, let's see. You'd come over to talk to Allie, and then a bunch of us came by after that."

"Oh, yes. As I recall, Allie was," Andrew raised his voice, "in quite a state and *fit to be tied.*" She deserved that one, putting Joshua on the phone out of spite over Jennifer. Andrew snickered softly as Allie made overt scoffing noises in the background.

Joshua pressed on. "So when I went outside to wait for Allie, I noticed the Mustang. She said it's yours."

Leaving the warm kitchen because he felt his core temperature beginning to redline, Andrew headed out onto the back patio. He inhaled the brisk afternoon air; its scent was an odd mix of musty leaves and roasting turkey. "That's right. She's mine."

"Still for sale?"

"Yes."

"I'd like to take a look at it sometime. Are you local?"

"I'm about ten minutes from Allie's place."

"Okay, uh, I live near the beach, but I could come back here this weekend sometime, if that works for you?"

Before Andrew could give his answer, Allie piped up, practically shouting. "Make it Saturday afternoon, Joshua. Then afterward you and I could go to that new Middle Eastern restaurant I've been wanting to try."

"Hey, you mean The Hummus & Hookah Hut? I wanna go too," whined a discordant nasal voice. Gretchen. Andrew could identify her irksome intonations anywhere. "I still haven't made it over there," she pouted.

"Saturday's good for me," Joshua said. "How 'bout you, Andrew? Say, four o'clock?"

"Oh, rats," Gretchen exclaimed, "I *can't* go. I have to work that day."

Joshua had already gotten the girl of Andrew's dreams. Shouldn't he give the man a chance at the car as well? "Sure, why not."

Chapter 16

KFC and Cocoa Crèmes

On Saturday, déjà vu struck Andrew with intensity.
Eyeing one of two vacancies in guest parking, Andrew drove past Joshua's bright orange Baja Bug, now occupying the place of honor in front of Allie's garage. He pulled into the end spot and turned off his engine. A second later, Allie's white-haired neighbor lady parked her Firebird in the spot alongside the Mustang.

What was her name again? It started with an L. Maybe. He couldn't remember.

Jennifer was checking her makeup in a small handheld mirror when Andrew turned toward her and asked, "Do you want to go inside or wait here? I imagine it won't take long, once I get Joshua to tear himself away from Allie's side."

Jennifer continued looking in the mirror. "This whole thing bothers you a lot doesn't it, Andrew?"

"What? Selling the car? My baby."

"No, I'm talking about Allie's relationship with Joshua. That must be painful for you."

Yeah, of course it was painful, but more than that, he just felt aggravated and discouraged by how difficult it had become to communicate with people. He felt like the whole world was on some other radio frequency, bandwidth, or Wi-Fi.

Keys tapped against Andrew's window. The neighbor lady peered through the glass. She waved one hand with gusto and used the other to shield her eyes from the sun, now perched on the mountain crest. Andrew gave a quick salute, which she returned before throwing a grinning nod in Jennifer's direction. The woman then stepped around the front of the Mustang. Andrew watched her canter up her porch steps like a filly at the state fair. Could it be that her get-up—denim jeans, brown suede vest, and straw cowboy hat—had been the inspiration for her energetic giddyup?

"Who's that?" Jennifer smiled as the woman disappeared then snapped the hinged mirror closed.

"Allie's neighbor. I can't remember her name. I think it starts with a W."

"Wanda?"

"Yeah, maybe. I don't know."

"Andrew, are you okay?"

Another tap on the window. It was Joshua this time, wearing a blue and orange hooded sweatshirt with Pepperdine Waves printed across the chest. *Pepperdine Waves? How appropriate for a sun-tanned dude sporting a sand-colored five o'clock shadow.*

"Hey, there," Joshua said. The waning afternoon sunlight bounced off his big toothy grin, nearly blinding Andrew.

Jennifer stepped out first. She dashed around the car with a wide smile and an outstretched hand, while Andrew's own hand slipped on the door release, trapping him in the car and leaving Jennifer on her own. He tried the handle again, with success this time, and hurried to get to his feet, closing the door gently behind him.

Joshua grinned as he shook Andrew's hand. "Good to see you again."

"Same here. Thanks for driving all the way in from the beach just to see the car."

"Well, after this, I'm taking Allie to get a bite to eat at some Lebanese restaurant she wants to try."

"Oh, right." Andrew absently gave one of the Mustang's tires a light kick. Had he forgotten the rest of that story on purpose?

"You're welcome to come along," Joshua said to Andrew while turning his head enough to make eye contact with Jennifer. She didn't hesitate in answering.

"That'd be great. I adore Middle Eastern food. Tahini, falafels, keftkes, baba ghanoush—it's all good."

"Whoa!" Joshua held up a hand and grimaced. "I don't think I could eat a baba ghanoush. Whatever that is. I might have to hit the drive thru at McDonald's on the way over."

The two of them laughed jovially while Andrew abstained.

"It's not that bad." Jennifer tilted her face up toward Joshua's. "It's like an eggplant dip or a relish."

"Sorry, little lady, but that doesn't make it sound any more appetizing." Joshua clamped his mouth closed and shook his head, like a toddler refusing a spoonful of strained peas and carrots. "Uh uh."

Jennifer gave him a coy little smile. "Okay, I'll tell you what."

What, Jennifer? What will you tell him? A rush of blood to Andrew's head made stars flash before his eyes. Now Joshua was flirting with Jennifer? Wasn't Allie enough for him?

"I'll let you try some of my baba ghanoush. You eat it with pita bread."

A sudden cold breeze swept through the complex. "Are you still interested in the Mustang?" Andrew didn't even care if his impatience was evident.

Joshua pried his eyes away from Jennifer. "Yeah, sure," he muttered, finally turning his attention to the car.

* * *

Allie paced back and forth between the dining and living rooms, awaiting Joshua's return. He should have already finished looking at the Mustang. *What was taking him so long?*

With her cell phone to her ear, Allie listened to Gretchen rambling on the other end. Standing near the kitchen sink, Beth, sipping a cup of jasmine tea, shot amused looks in Allie's direction.

"Why can't I meet you at the coffeehouse after you do," Gretchen sighed into the telephone, "*whatever* it is you do in church?"

Gretchen's scheming little brain had come up with a new plan for Sunday morning. She'd decided to spring it on Allie before her flight left Honolulu airport, but Allie wasn't interested.

"Because that's not what we agreed on," she told Gretchen. "The plan is that we'll go to the early church service, *together.* I'll drive the two of us, and Beth will take *her* car. Afterward, we'll go to Mo'Joes, get our coffees and *then* go to the mall. That way Beth can head straight home when we're finished buying all our Christmas gifts, using *her* generous discount."

Gretchen argued the point, using a weak defense. "My flight won't land at LAX until at least ten-thirty tonight."

"Then that should give you plenty of time to drive back here and get some sleep."

Silence.

"The service starts at nine," Allie said. "*Okay?*"

"Oh, all right," Gretchen huffed. "*Good bye.*"

Exhaling, Allie touched her cell phone screen, ending the call. With her cup in hand, Beth laughed softly and leaned back against the kitchen counter. "Is Gretchen backing out?"

"No. She's trying to maneuver around someone she thinks will interfere with her Christmas shopping."

"You mean Jesus?"

Allie checked the time on the clock above the sink then looked at Beth. "Exactly."

The front door opened and Joshua walked in. He'd been outside since a little after four, and it was now almost five. Allie watched him trot through the living room, moving toward her with haste.

"Sorry it took so long." He stopped a few feet from Allie. "I wanted to take her for a test drive." His face flushed. "The car, I mean."

Allie felt relieved Andrew had left, and she'd been able to avoid seeing or talking to him. "That's okay, no problem. What about the Mustang? Are you buying it?"

"I am." He did a little fist pump. "Andrew wants a week or so to get the paperwork in order and to find some other wheels; he's thinking probably a truck. He'll let me know when he's ready. I'm stoked."

"I'm happy for you." Allie smiled in spite of her frustration. She told herself everything would be fine and tried to relax. "Okay then. Dinner?"

"Absolutely. I'm excited to try this place."

"Me too." Allie turned to Beth. "You're coming with us right?"

"No, but thanks for the offer. I've got some studying to do for a psych final week after next. And besides, it's no fun being the third wheel." She raised her cup with a genial wink.

"Actually, you would've been the *fifth* wheel." Joshua grinned and slipped both hands into his back pockets.

Allie and Beth stared at him.

He shrugged, "Andrew and Jennifer are meeting us at the restaurant."

* * *

What did I get myself into? Andrew wondered.

Bringing Jennifer along for the ride had been a bad idea—a *really* bad idea. Andrew had thought it might help ease the discomfort of having to see Allie and Joshua together, but he'd never considered it would lead to the offer of a double date.

In silence that Jennifer didn't seem inclined to interrupt, Andrew drove to the bottom of Ridgeview and pulled into the gas station on the corner. They were supposed to meet Joshua and Allie at The Hummus & Hookah Hut at five-thirty, which left Andrew exactly twelve minutes to ponder his ill fate and fill up his tank—literally and figuratively.

While Jennifer sat quietly watching cars drive along Hillcrest, Andrew played soldier . . . on the lookout for enemy combatants. The area was devoid of activity, at least on his side of the mini market.

Elsewhere in the large parking lot, engines revved and someone shouted out a request for directions to the nearest Kentucky Fried Chicken. Although not a big fan of greasy fast food, Andrew wished he could just leave the gas hose sticking out of his car and join whichever vehicle was on its way to KFC. He had a bad feeling about the impending dinner date with Allie and Joshua, which was an orange-alert situation if he'd ever seen one.

After filling the tank and securing the gas cap, Andrew decided to buy a lottery ticket for that evening's Mega Millions drawing. He imagined for a moment a sprawling Frank Lloyd Wright estate set high up on a secluded bluff, overlooking the Pacific Ocean. Would a house like that get Allie's attention? Would he want it to?

He stooped down to look at Jennifer through the open driver's side window. "I'm going inside. Can I get you anything?"

She furrowed her brows in thought. Andrew waited.

"Yes!" She dug around inside her purse as she spoke. "Would you please get me the latest issue of *Female in Fashion* magazine? I saw it when I was in the market recently and should have grabbed it, but I got distracted. Make sure it's the December issue. I believe the cover story is something like, "How to Ring in the New Year without a Ring on Your Finger."

Oh, great.

She pulled out some money and tried handing it to Andrew, but he waved her off. "It's okay. I got it."

* * *

What in the world had Joshua gotten her into? Allie wondered. *Dinner with Andrew and Jennifer, that's what!*

Allie would almost rather be meeting Kevin and Cassandra at The Hummus & Hookah Hut than Andrew and his croissant.

Almost.

Joshua's smile faded as Allie glared at him. He shifted his stance again then kicked at the dining room's tile floor. "I hope you're not mad, Allie."

When she didn't say anything, he looked over at Beth with pleading eyes, as if asking, "What did I do wrong?"

Beth set her teacup on the counter. "Oh, Allie, it's no big deal. You'll have fun, and you know you're dying to try that restaurant's kebabs and rice pilaf."

"And I wouldn't be surprised if they make a spectacular baba ghanoush." Joshua's face flushed. "You eat it with pita bread," he added, glancing down at his big feet.

Allie pursed her lips at him then shook her head. Was she getting exactly what she deserved for trying to irritate Andrew? Was a double date with him and Jennifer God's way of showing Allie that she was being selfish and unloving?

She took a deep breath, removed her twill short coat from the back of a dining room chair then exhaled. "You're right."

Joshua's face brightened, as did Beth's.

Allie slipped her arms through the sleeves. "It's no big deal." At least, that's what she'd been telling herself all along, right? Andrew had a girlfriend. So what.

They said goodbye to Beth and went outside. The brisk evening air was lightly scented with the smoke from a wood-burning fireplace. Allie looked up before getting in Joshua's car. Countless stars in the clear evening sky twinkled at her as she prayed for strength, courage, and self-control.

Joshua started up the Bug with a loud roar, put the car in reverse, and backed up. He slid the gearshift into first, zipping out of the driveway and making a right turn onto Ridgeview.

"Is there a convenience store nearby?" he asked. "I need to pick up a *Recycler*. I told Andrew I'd help him with the Mustang's pricing. We didn't come to any kind of firm deal, but I'm sure he'll be fair." Joshua glanced in the rear view mirror. "Not sure what was going on when I was checking out the 'Stang, but he couldn't seem to keep his attention on the car. Guess he's got a lot on his mind these days."

Yeah, like Miss Jennifer.

Allie pointed at the windshield and toward the right. "There's a gas station at the bottom of the hill. They'll have a *Recycler* in the store. I'll run in and get it for you. I want some gum anyway."

A minute later, Joshua entered the parking lot of the gas station. He drove past a couple of shaggy-headed teenage boys in droopy jeans. They were talking to the driver of a red Gran Torino. Allie knew the model of the car because it looked exactly like the one in *Starsky and Hutch*. It even had the same white swoosh detail on the side. After Joshua dropped Allie off at one of two opposing entrances to the mini market, he rolled his Bug forward, out of the way of the gas pumps. It idled noisily. As Allie pushed through the glass door, she heard the driver of the Gran Torino yell out, "Thanks, man. I'll tell the Colonel you said hey," before he went screeching out of the lot.

Inside, a swarthy man with glasses and a short gray beard stood behind a long cluttered counter. Allie watched him for a brief moment as he rang up the purchases of two men in flannel shirts and blue jeans. She then scanned the area inside the door and down the first two isles in search of a standalone rack of *Recyclers* or the magazine section.

"What is it you need, young lady?" asked the attendant once he'd finished with his customers.

"Gum." Allie gestured with her chin down the aisle to her left. "But I also need a *Recycler*."

The man pointed over the side of the checkout counter. "Right here."

"Thanks. I'll get my gum first." Allie turned down the candy aisle. The second she did so, a desire for Reese's peanut butter cups suddenly hit her. The combination of the chocolate and peanut butter was always one of her favorites. And besides, it would make a nice after dinner treat—assuming she had enough of an appetite to make it through the first course.

* * *

Andrew's cell phone rang just as he grabbed the gas station store's glass door handle. He pulled the phone from his pocket and glanced at the screen to check the caller ID. Before taking the call, he opened the door and stepped back. Two workmen in buffalo plaid shirts and jeans thanked Andrew as they carried hot dogs and fountain sodas out of the store. The pungent smell of sizzling meat by-products caught in Andrew's nose as he entered and put the phone to his ear. "Hey, Joe."

Joe's voice sounded rushed. "Have you talked to Allie?"

"Briefly, but not about anything important." Andrew stepped to the side so he wouldn't be in anyone's way. Why had he come in here in the first place? He couldn't recall. "Why? What's up?"

"Did I mention I'd be out of town this past week, spending Thanksgiving at Diana's Mom's in Spokane?"

"No, I don't think so. You may have. I can't remember much these days. Why, what's going on?" Andrew saw the Mega Millions sign and snapped his fingers. He started toward the counter to buy his lottery ticket then remembered Jennifer's request for *Female in Fashion*. He began a loop around the store, on the lookout for the magazine section.

Joe blew out a breath so loud Andrew almost felt it in his ear. "I don't know how else to say this," Joe said, "so I'll just tell it to you the way Doug Wylie told it to me."

Andrew had walked halfway around the perimeter of the store and was now standing in front of the doors opposite the ones he'd entered. Oblivious to his presence, a short, round Latina appeared just outside, forcing one of the doors open with her backside. Andrew jumped out of the way. The woman slipped into the store, fingers tapping hastily on the screen of her iphone. She bustled to the soda dispenser without once looking up.

"I would've contacted you sooner," Joe continued, "but I just received word myself from my answering service about Doug's phone call earlier in the week. There was some sort of mix up the afternoon of our arrival."

"Mix up?"

"Yeah. Apparently, while I was preparing for the lecture, you checked in at the registration table outside the conference hall?"

"Yes?" He turned the word into a question. Joe's tone was making Andrew feel like he should refuse to answer questions without an attorney present.

More customers filed into the store, opening and closing the door in front of Andrew's face. He strode past the entrance and down a side aisle until he spotted a built-in magazine rack along the wall. *Female in Fashion* immediately caught his attention with that crazy-making cover headline. Several males loitered in front of the rack; they skimmed through magazines such as *Armchair Quarterback, Mega Muscle,* and *Mechanically Inclined.* Andrew walked carefully around a burly, bearded biker. Wearing a red bandana on his head and dressed in a worn-out black leather jacket, the man made small grunting sounds as he flipped through a stout issue of *Rode Hogg.*

Joe continued. "Now, this is where I think the mix up occurred. Doug claims you were most likely given the nametag of a Dr. Andy Gallagher, from Houston, who didn't arrive until later that day. By that time, his name card was missing."

Andrew took a deep breath. In one quick swipe, he peeled the fashion magazine off the rack, rolled it slightly then secured it under his arm. He retreated to the back corner of the store, glancing over his shoulder to see if any of the men reading manly periodicals were laughing at him. They weren't.

"I suppose that's possible," Andrew said quietly into the phone. "I never looked at the nametag the woman gave me. I just put it on. I still have the thing at home. I can check it out and get back to you, although I don't see what difference it would make."

Joe sighed. "At this point, Andrew, it wouldn't make *any* difference because we're being subjected to the power and determination of one irate Cassandra Hartwell. She believes you were trying to impersonate a doctor."

Andrew, who'd started working his way along the back aisle, suddenly froze in front of a cardboard display of nacho cheese flavored Doritos. "That's ridiculous, Joe."

"Of course it is."

In a hurry to get to the front counter and out of the store, Andrew began moving again. He brushed past a section of coolers. "How about Doug Wylie? What does he have to say about all this?"

"He thinks it was simply a mistake, but he's not the one with the vendetta. Add the purse incident to Cassandra's discovery that we'd been discussing Allie, and your little mix-up became the torch that set that woman's hair ablaze. Doug said she believes it was all Allie's doing." Joe snorted then sighed again. "I *am* sorry, Andrew. I should have kept my great ideas to myself."

"No, it's okay, Joe. It's not your fault. I'm the one who got us into this. I'm just afraid it's going to mess things up for Allie." He turned down the next aisle and nearly dropped his phone when he found himself face to face with the last person he expected to see.

Stunned to have Allie standing before him, Andrew's legs came to a stiff halt, while his arms went limp. He managed to maintain possession of his phone; however, the magazine fell free from his arm and tumbled to the floor, cover side up.

"*Allie,*" he croaked, his throat suddenly as parched as a freeze-dried pineapple. "What are you doing here?"

Glaring at him, she shook her head. "Finding out what a sneak you are, I suppose. Is that Dr. Stevenson," she pointed to his cell phone, "*your accomplice?*"

"Andrew, what's going on?" Joe asked. "Where are you anyway?"

Andrew pulled the phone away from his ear and gaped at it. Continuing the conversation with Joe could only make things worse, so Andrew did what he had to and disconnected the call—without so much as a "sayonara."

"Who? *That?*" Andrew shoved the phone into his pocket and stooped down, keeping Allie distracted by staring into her eyes. He casually collected the magazine and slowly straightened. "That was nothing, nobody important."

Allie took a step closer, breaching Andrew's personal space and practically forcing him up against a cooler filled with energy drinks. "You're lying!"

Now she was angry. Angrier than he'd ever seen her or imagined she could be.

"You said, ' . . . it's going to mess things up for Allie.' I heard you. I also heard you say, 'Joe.'" Her eyes narrowed to a smoldering glare, and her jaw pulsed as she clenched her teeth.

Andrew's stare widened.

"And just what *things* were you referring to?" The scorn in her voice said she already knew and that she'd probably heard most of his conversation with Joe. Andrew panicked and tried re-rolling the magazine but the movement caught Allie's attention. She plucked it from his grip and glanced at the cover.

"For your girlfriend, I imagine," she sniffed. "Or were you interested in the story on *Winning Your Man Back Through Texting?*"

"Allie, I know this is going to sound crazy, but we were only trying to help you."

"Oh, you helped me all right. You helped destroy my good standing at Horizon. Now I'm *this* close," she held her hand up to Andrew's face, thumb and forefinger a half inch apart, "to being written up for something I didn't do, or even know about."

The store began filling up with people at an alarming rate, many of whom made tracks to the back of the store, where the situation with Allie was set to go nuclear. Andrew spotted a group of tight-clothes-wearing, gum-popping teenage girls watching Allie with interest. He wanted to make a dash for the exit but couldn't. He was trapped, caught between a frosty glass cooler door and a shelf full of snack cakes displayed at the end of the very aisle he now regretted turning down.

He ran his hand along the back of his neck. Looking up, he tried to assess the odds of giving Allie a coherent and satisfactory explanation. "Going to the pain conference was *my* idea. I sort of roped Joe into it. I'd rather you only be angry at me over the consequences."

"That shouldn't be a problem."

"Thank you."

Allie shook her head. "I don't believe you! Thank you? *Thank you?* There's nothing to thank me for, Andrew. You *betrayed* me! You made a mockery of our friendship and my trust in you. I don't know why or how you decided you had the right to interfere in my professional life, unless . . ." She stopped and squinted at him, apparently oblivious to their growing audience.

Andrew glanced at the eager gazes locked on them. He wanted to move Allie to a quieter spot, but he knew if he so much as took a step toward her, she would probably drop kick him into the next county. Before he could figure out what to do, Allie wiped out all thoughts of their audience with her next accusation.

"Unless you were just looking for kicks," she challenged. "Like, like the night we were on the beach."

Andrew's discomfort turned into disbelief. *"What?* What do you mean?"

She curled her upper lip and laughed. "You can't remember something that happened, what, a couple weeks ago?"

"Four weeks, exactly," Andrew corrected, as though he'd been chicken-scratching the days on his cell wall. He glanced away from her, embarrassed about giving the answer so readily.

"And in that time, you've accomplished so much." She returned the magazine to him with a thrust and began enumerating her many grievances. "Let's see, first you show up at my house unannounced, insulting and antagonizing me while I try to get ready for a date, with *Joshua*. Then there was that incident on the phone while I was outside the restaurant in Denver, when you *coerced* me into telling my counterparts to go inside, which got me in trouble with Kevin and Cassandra. And of course, now we have your latest caper, a secret field trip to Palm Springs with Dr. Stevenson, after which my career is left in ruins."

Apparently uninterested in the drama blocking his way, an elderly man with stringy gray hair and a ruddy face loitered for a moment near the troubled twosome. "Pardon me," he said.

Allie whirled to glare at him.

The man's glassy eyes widened so much they looked like glazed donuts. "Sorry," he said. He reached between Andrew and Allie and removed a rectangular box from the snack cake display. Holding his breath because the man's dilapidated wool sweater smelled overwhelmingly of mothballs, Andrew prayed in earnest that Allie might simmer down during the interlude.

Unfortunately, though, the shelf life of Andrew's reprieve turned out to be as short as his adversary's temper. As the old guy shuffled safely away from ground zero, tasty treat in hand, Allison Hendrickson reignited her blowtorch.

* * *

Allie spared a glance at the little man who had just braved her ire to get a box of Little Debbie Cocoa Crèmes. She felt like snatching the carton from him, ripping it open, and pelting Andrew in the head with a few of the chocolate-covered, cream-filled rounds.

Dismissing the thought, as satisfying as it was, she pinned Andrew with a hard gaze. "Did I leave anything out?"

"I hope not."

"You *hope* not?"

"I mean I *hope* there isn't anything else to add."

"Oh, I'm *sure* I can think of something . . . now that you mention it . . ."

"Now that *I* mention it? *I* haven't mentioned anything. I'm not the one standing in the middle of a convenience store wailing and gnashing my teeth."

212

Allie snorted. "Nice. Is that what I'm doing? Well, let's not make it sound like I don't have reason to."

"Allie." Andrew wedged his girlfriend's magazine up into his armpit and inched forward, eyes cast downward. "Do you want me to apologize?" He hesitated then laid a hand on top of her shoulder, like he was trying to create a bridge between them. Well, it was a bridge she wasn't about to cross.

"So, you'll only apologize if *I want you to,* not because you think you did anything that warrants an apology?" Allie threw an arm up and took a step back, knocking Andrew's hand away.

She opened her mouth to continue the lambasting, but then looked at his face. She hadn't noticed, until now, that his skin color had gone from light tan to a shade resembling a medium rare slice of prime rib. She also hadn't noticed that his forehead glistened with sweat. Now she saw that it nearly gleamed in the overhead bank of fluorescent lights. His lips were pressed together in a hard line, and his nostrils flared slightly.

Allie had never seen him look like this. He was furious. For a second, she felt uncertain. Andrew's rage unsettled her. Not for long, though. She was furious too!

And what did he even have to be so upset about anyway? *He* was the one who'd been sneaking around, *wreaking havoc on her career!*

"Okay, let me get this straight," Andrew said, rubbing his fingers across his chin with vigor. "You won't let me explain anything. You won't accept an apology. *And* you keep insisting on *living in a cocoon."*

"What?! A cocoon? What's that supposed to mean?" Allie kept her voice high and emphatic but, inside, she faltered again. She knew what it meant. And, though unwilling to admit it to Andrew, she knew it contained some truth—but she wasn't about to let *him* know that. Keeping her gratifying fury going, she nearly spat, "That sounds like something *Gretchen* would say."

Andrew leaned closer. "She *did* say it. And I agree!"

Before Allie could respond, he stepped around her and strode toward the front of the store. She considered running after him and . . . And what? Since her body now felt like a lightening rod after taking a powerful hit, she could only stand there, staring in silence as Andrew slapped money on the counter and stormed out through the door.

A tall teenage girl with blue braces and pink hair punched Allie on the arm. "He's toast now. Forget about him."

After a dazed moment of watching her dispersing audience, Allie grabbed the side of her arm and rubbed it, slowly nodding in agreement with the teenage girl's advice.

213

Chapter 17

A Fool's Mouth

Allie did not want to get out of bed the next morning, but she did. She did not want to get dressed for church, but she did. And she did not want to cajole her cousin into going with her to a sermon Allie again lacked the concentration to absorb. With Beth in the house though, Allie had no choice.

Feeling oddly deflated and devoid of emotion after the previous evening's flare-up, Allie floated out of her room on a strange cloud of indifference. She'd baffled poor Joshua when she'd returned to the Bug and insisted they abandon their dinner plans. Instead, at Allie's request, he'd driven the two of them around East Hills, during which time Allie clammed up and fumed. Upon returning home, she'd found Beth on the sofa, thumbing through a thick textbook and already in her PJs. If she had chosen to talk to Beth about what had happened, Allie would have said she'd never get over the anger. But Beth hadn't asked about the double date that never took place; so, on her way upstairs, Allie had simply said, "Everything worked out fine." Pacing her bedroom for more than an hour, she'd mumbled and grumbled to herself, trying to understand what had become of her once-strong friendship with Andrew.

She never did figure it out. And now she was out of time.

"It looks like it might rain." Gretchen stood at the top of the stairs and eyed Allie, who trudged upwards, a steaming mug of tea in each hand. "It might be better if we just stay home," Gretchen suggested. "We could play *Apples to Apples* instead."

"And disappoint all those cute guys going to church today to see you?" Allie offered up the fragrant vanilla honey tea.

"You told them I'd be there?" Gretchen's head twitched in a surprised double-take.

Allie nudged the tea toward her cousin. "They'll be there whether you go or not. You wouldn't want to deprive them of the opportunity to meet you, would you?"

"Oh, heavens no!" Gretchen relieved Allie of the mug and rushed around the corner toward her room, calling out excitedly, "I'll be ready in ten."

Allie shook her head and sipped her tea.

Thirty-five minutes later, Gretchen joined Allie at the dining room table. Beth had prepared and now served them a breakfast of scrambled eggs with cream cheese, apple wood-smoked bacon, and toasted English muffins. The savory scents should have triggered her hunger, but Allie feared she'd left her appetite back in the mini market near Little Debbie and her Cocoa Crèmes.

Beth pulled out her chair and sat down. She gazed with intent across the table, likely trying to puzzle out Allie's mood.

"I wonder if Andrew will be attending church with his *girl-friend, Jen-ni-fer,*" Gretchen said, singing the words in a satirical tune.

Keeping watch on Allie, Beth said, "I suppose it's possible."

Allie picked up half an English muffin and took a bite. She chewed her mouthful slowly then swallowed. "It's unlikely."

"Why is that, Allie?" Beth's eyes narrowed. "Andrew doesn't have any reason to stay away from you, *does he?*"

Gretchen held up a hand. "I know what happened. You two had another fight, didn't you?" She sounded as though she was referring to a couple of disobedient grade school kids.

Coming from Gretchen that was downright insulting.

"No use pretending, Allie," Gretchen continued, "I can see it written all over your face."

"Allie?" Beth pursed her lips. "Is there something you're not telling me?"

Allie straightened her back, casually wiping her mouth with a paper napkin. "He usually goes to the evening service."

"Ha!" Gretchen laughed. "That's the one *you* go to, is it not?"

"Sometimes. *So?*"

"*Sooo,* all the more reason we'll see him this morning. According to *Female in Fashion,* this will probably turn into a textbook case of," Gretchen set down her fork, making finger quotes, "'*avoidance warfare.*' If he thinks you're going to the later service, like you usually do, he'll go to the early service so there's no chance of running into you." She picked up a thick slice of bacon, stopping short of sticking it in her mouth, alongside her foot. "Makes perfect sense to me."

Allie's chin popped up. She wasn't going to let Beth get hold of information that would only be used against Allie—and in Andrew's

215

defense. Nor was she in the mood to be provoked by some hogwash theory about the reverse psychology tactics of men.

Gretchen chomped away on bacon and continued making her pointless point. "The article I read outlines the drastic measures some men take to avoid confrontations with hysterical women, even to the point of changing their daily routines and schedules. And I should know," she grabbed her mug, "men do it to me all the time." After swallowing the last of her tea, she slapped the mug to the table. "The bums."

Keeping her voice measured, Allie faced Gretchen. "I'm not hysterical."

"Not now, you're not, but that one night Andrew came over you were. *Oh!* Carrying on like your clothes were on fire. All the hullabaloo. The screaming, the door slamming . . ."

Allie's strange calm began to evaporate. "I wasn't screaming!"

"Well, *someone* was," Gretchen insisted, before continuing her diatribe of unwelcome words.

Maybe Allie had been trapped in something like a black hole, where a lack of space and time had allowed a temporary numbing of her feelings. Now, she looked at Gretchen's overly made up face and felt her anger begin to bubble up again. Was this because Andrew's name had been mentioned? Or had Gretchen's aggravating yet astute observation been the catalyst? Allie couldn't pinpoint the cause; all she knew was that she was struggling to keep her feelings under control. She decided that for the time being the only reason she would open her mouth would be to put food in it. No talking.

And certainly no screaming.

* * *

In an inexplicable attempt to look more hip, Allie had slipped on her new navy and white-striped waist-length jacket before leaving the house. The scoop neckline and cuffs were detailed with nautical rope, chains, and clear jewels that looked like big diamonds. And even though her base outfit was a plain white tee shirt over khaki pants, she still felt overdressed and out of place.

"It's very flattering," Beth said, when she met up with Allie and Gretchen in the church parking lot. "The dark blue color brings out your eyes." Beth took a closer look at a fancy cuff. "Where did you get it?"

Feeling that it was finally safe to talk, at least about fashion, Allie answered the question. "Self-Expressions."

Her relief, however, was cut short when Gretchen followed up on Beth's compliment with a salute, a crooked smile and a patronizing, "Chips ahoy, matie!"

Blimey. Whose idea was it to bring her along anyway?

"Thanks for inviting me to join you guys, Allie," Gretchen said, demonstrating yet again her eerie knack for echoing Allie's thoughts. "I just hope there's an area inside the church reserved for single, available, attractive men. If so, I want to sit in that section and sort through the pickings, while your clergy man gives his little talk."

Allie pursed her lips. "It doesn't work that way. We're not sectioned off like a herd of . . ."

Beth giggled. "Sheep?"

"Yeah, sheep." Allie shook her head while giving Beth a wry smile and paying closer attention to Gretchen's look du jour: A head full of tight and springy hot-roller curls, a fresh coat of green glitter nail polish, and the application of black liquid eyeliner bold enough to make even Cleopatra envious. Well, at least Gretchen's nails and eyes went well with her outfit, a lime green cowl neck sweater over slim cut black jeans.

As Gretchen pawed at her golden coils, her nails sparkled in the sunlight. "So afterward, does everyone get together in a room to socialize and have cookies and juice. You know, like they do in . . ."

Beth snickered. "Kindergarten?"

"Oh! You two!" Gretchen gave each of them a light smack on the arm. "Don't either of you want a man? You'll have to make an effort to find him, you know. Be assertive, proactive. Take the bull by the horns."

Allie stepped up into the courtyard and walked toward the glass double door entrance to the sanctuary before glancing over at her cousin. "Is that what *Female in Fashion* says to do? A sort of *'Seek and ye shall find'*?"

Gretchen's green eyes twinkled. "Yes, exactly. I'm glad you understand."

Beth leaned down over Gretchen's shoulder, whispered, "Those words are straight out of the Bible, honey," and then waited for the reaction.

Gretchen looked up, wrinkling her bunny nose. "Huh?"

"Never mind that now." Allie held open the door. "Beth can explain it to you later."

* * *

By eleven A.M., Allie and Beth had taken their places in line inside Mo'Joes. Gretchen, however, did not join them. Instead, she stood in defiance in the entrance area. Resting her hands on her hips, she sighed loudly enough to be heard above a dozen voices and the spits, chirrs, pops, and clatter coming from behind the counter. "There's no place to sit in this joint," she called to Allie and Beth. "How 'bout we order our drinks and get on over to the mall. Allrightee?" She grinned long and wide before adding, "Shop 'til you drop."

Allie's exasperation over Gretchen's misconduct during the sermon on Hebrews 13:5 and selected Proverbs had returned. Throughout the service, Gretchen had refused to sit still in the pew. "What does he mean by *'A fool's mouth is his ruin'*?" Gretchen inquired while absently leafing through a church Bible. A few minutes later she whispered to Beth, *"Did he just say what I think he said?"* And finally, she swiveled her head around, scanned the sanctuary and turned to Allie, asking far too loudly, *"Do you know that babe in the back row wearing the blue sweater?"*

Allie and Beth inched closer to the counter while Gretchen continued blocking foot traffic. She repeated her desire to get their drinks to go.

Allie took a deep breath, allowing it to slowly escape through her nostrils. "I don't want to have to juggle driving with drinking my coffee. I just want to relax for a few minutes."

Gretchen blew a raspberry. "Fine." She wormed her way into the line, behind Allie and in front of a teenage couple too in love with each other to realize they'd just been cut off.

When they reached the front, Gretchen looked over the menu board. Beth ordered tea and held up a five. "Pay for my tea, will you Allie? I'll go around the corner and see if there's a spot for us in back."

After Allie convinced Gretchen to try a hot Americano—whispering to Phoebe to make it a decaf—the two visited the cream and sugar counter to sweeten up their drinks. Allie took a second to slip Beth's tea bag into the cup of hot water. She replaced the lid and, with Gretchen following, Allie headed toward the rear section, where she spotted Beth's strawberry blond hair at one of the booths. Weaving her way through the crowd, Allie set the tea on the table. "Here you go, Beth."

The fair-skinned woman looked up at Allie and smiled.

Allie picked up the cup so quickly the hot liquid sloshed through the lid and nearly scalded her hand. "Oh, I'm sorry. I thought you were my friend."

"Hello, Allie."

Puzzled, Allie asked, "Do I know you?"

The woman laughed. "No. Not really."

Gretchen stepped up to the table. "Well, whoever you are, I have a question for you. Did you see another redhead around here somewhere? We've got some serious shopping to do and not a lot of time for chit chat." She tapped her diamond-faced watch with an impatient index finger.

"You mean Beth?"

"Yes, darlin'."

The woman pointed to the back door. "She went that way. To get something from her car. She'll be right back."

Now Allie was even more confused. "Do you know Beth?"

The woman shook her head. "No, but I invited her to take this table. I won't be but a few more minutes, and I see how busy it is in here."

"It's a complete madhouse," moaned Gretchen.

Just then, the back door swept open, bringing in a damp chilly breeze—and Beth. "Oh, good," she said with a smile, "you've already met Jennifer."

* * *

Beth encouraged Allie and Gretchen to take a seat in the booth before she made the introductions. Allie deliberately sat opposite Jennifer, not next to her. And she kept her gaze on her coffee, not on Jennifer's face . . . her far too beautiful face.

"I walked past Jennifer's table and saw her looking over a hand-out from this morning's service," Beth said. "So I stopped to talk to her. Andrew's name came up in the conversation, and Jennifer invited me to sit down. She had a question about a verse in Hebrews, so I went to get my Bible."

Having slid into the booth first, Allie sat next to a window set within the oak-paneled wall. She was positioned directly across from Jennifer. Finally unable to resist studying the woman, Allie raised her gaze.

Jennifer looked so similar to Beth it was uncanny. She had shiny shoulder length hair that was more wavy than curly, an oval face with fair skin, high cheekbones, and a wide, full mouth. The main and obvious difference between the two women was their eyes. Jennifer's were light brown with gold specks, whereas Beth's were deep green with a faint glimmer of aqua—and far prettier in Allie's opinion.

Allie sipped her hot Americano through the plastic lid. So this was the beloved Jennifer, Andrew's sweetheart. Finally they'd met, with no thanks to Andrew, who practically behaved as though she didn't even exist. Typical. It was the same type of behavior she'd gotten from Carl Lansing.

"You know," Gretchen rested a finger above her upper lip to help her think, "according to *Female in Fashion*, this situation is a classic case of—"

219

"You read *Female in Fashion?*" Jennifer asked as she turned to face Gretchen.

"Every month. Every article. Except the dumb ones. I mean who cares about learning how to *downsize* a wardrobe, or recycle old bath towels by cutting them up into washcloths? Seriously."

"Yeah," Jennifer laughed. "I know what you mean."

"How about *Winning Your Man Back Through Texting?*" scoffed Allie.

"Dumb." Gretchen pointed both thumbs down.

"Did you catch this month's story on *Ringing in the New Year*—" Jennifer began.

Gretchen cut her off, nodding with enthusiasm. "*Without a Ring on Your Finger.* Oh, yes, my friend. That one was a dilly."

"You know, the message in church today reminded me of a few things I read in that article."

Gretchen repositioned herself to face Jennifer. "Such as?"

The few minutes Jennifer claimed she'd be staying at the table turned into a tedious hour-long discussion between her and Gretchen on life and love. Each of them revealed more personal information about their past failed relationships than Allie cared to hear about. Especially Jennifer, who became teary-eyed and choked up talking about some poor man named Michael she'd practically abandoned at the altar.

"I couldn't go through with it," she admitted after Gretchen badgered her for an explanation as to why she would do something so utterly senseless. "I just didn't love him enough to spend a lifetime with him. But you know," Jennifer dabbed her drippy eyes with a battered tissue, "I felt a little relieved hearing Pastor John discussing Hebrews 13:5, when he said that the Lord would never leave or forsake His believers. I realized then that only God could make such a promise. If we place expectations like that on another person, we may end up being very disappointed."

"Did he really say that?" Gretchen asked.

"Who," said Jennifer, *"the Lord?"*

"No, the pastor."

"That God would never leave or forsake us?"

"Yeah."

"Yes, but he got it out of the Bible. You didn't hear him say that?"

Gretchen thought for a moment, squinting as though the bright sun was in her eyes. "No, I didn't. It must have been after that bit about not loving money and being happy with what you already have. I pretty much tuned the rest out at that point. That was ruthless."

When the topic of discussion inevitably made its way to Andrew, Jennifer's lashes began flapping like dragonfly wings. "I'm sorry we weren't able to meet for dinner last night," she said to Allie. "Andrew said maybe another time."

Beth gave Allie a sideways glance. "Oh, you didn't make it to dinner? That's too bad. I know you were looking forward to trying their food. And Joshua couldn't wait to get some pita bread into their baba ghanoush."

"He couldn't? *He really said that?*" Jennifer giggled. She moved her green straw up and down through the lid of her icy beverage. It made a loud squeaking sound.

That was annoying.

"Andrew was disappointed as well." Jennifer held the straw still, took a sip then looked directly at Allie. "I think you both should plan to go there soon. Just the two of you."

"What a great idea. Afterward you can come here for coffee," Beth said. She exchanged a look with Jennifer, whose ardent agreement raised a few eyebrows at the table.

Gretchen slurped down the last of her decaf Americano then set the cup on the table. "But Andrew's already dating *you*, is he not?"

Jennifer smiled. "No. We hung out together several times, that's true, and Andrew introduced me to Valley Community Church, which has changed my life. I'm grateful to him for that and for his wonderful friendship. But no, we're not dating." She glanced around the table. "Actually, Andrew's crazy about Allie. He was crazy about her when I first met him, and from what I understand, he's felt that way for a long time."

Allie stiffened, tangled with too many emotions to sort out. *Why was this woman baring Andrew's soul in his absence?* Okay, that was indignation. *And if what she said was true, why couldn't he have told Allie that himself? He'd had plenty of opportunities.* That was aggravation. *Could it be true? Did she want it to be true?* That was confusion.

The feelings-cocktail made her irritable, so she decided to give *that* emotion a voice. "Is that supposed to be funny?" she demanded.

"Not at all," Jennifer answered, half laughing.

That was even more annoying than the squeaky straw.

"Well, well, well." Gretchen tucked her hair behind both ears, exposing twinkling two-carat diamond stud earrings. "Who'd have thought our little Allie would have to make a decision between Andrew and Joshua." Pressing her fingertips to her chest, she slanted her head forward in pretend modesty, saying, "Surely not I," as though the idea of Allie having a man that not even Gretchen could snag was unthinkable.

Beth draped her arm across Allie's shoulder. "Joshua and Allie are just friends." She smiled at Jennifer. "Like Jennifer and Andrew."

"Is that right?" Jennifer asked, first looking at Beth, then Allie. "I mean, well, I know it's none of my business . . ."

"About Allie and Joshua?" Beth's face brightened with amusement.

"Mm hmm."

"Only friends." Beth held up a flat hand. "Brother and sister, if you will."

Jennifer's eyes popped open before she realized the implication. "Oh, of course."

"Huh?" Gretchen didn't get it.

So Beth explained. "They're fellow believers, Gretchen. Brother and sister in the Lord."

After taking a moment to ponder the notion, Gretchen smiled in acknowledgment. "Ah, I understand. Christians." She thought about it some more and nodded. "I kinda like that idea. At first I didn't, I admit, but Andrew and Joshua are super sweet guys. I even tried keeping Allie and Andrew apart, right after he came home. I didn't think he was Allie's type. Or maybe I wanted him for myself." She shrugged. "Then I decided that, for a modern woman like myself, he was just too traditional—which, actually, may not have been such a bad thing after—"

"Gretchen," Beth interrupted, "why don't you go to church with Allie more often? They have Bible studies and other activities for singles."

"They do?" Gretchen's eyes pitched back and forth like a Felix the Cat clock. She nibbled on her lower lip for a moment before saying, "I just might do that!"

"And you may even meet someone special, fall in love, get married, and live happily ever after," Beth said.

"Ha!" Allie shook her head, remembering Beth dishing that same drivel at Caruso's.

Jennifer spoke next. "I meant what I said about Andrew being crazy about you. I think you should give him a call and try to work things out."

Allie's grip on her coffee cup tightened. She wasn't ready to sort through all her emotions yet. She felt more comfortable staying angry. "I've got plans that don't include Andrew. My career has been placed on life support, thanks to him, and I need to focus my attention on reviving it. I planned to receive a huge bonus this year to help my brother and sister pay for college expenses, but instead I may not get an extra dime. Again, thanks to Andrew's uncalled for intervention."

Gretchen's face wrinkled up. "But, Allie, didn't you hear Pastor Jim—"

"John," said Beth and Jennifer together.

"Didn't you hear Pastor John speak about not loving money and being . . ." Gretchen froze midsentence, suddenly leery of finishing the directive.

"Happy with what you have," Beth and Jennifer said, once again in unison.

"I *am* happy with what I have." Allie knew she sounded angry and defensive, which was fine with her because that was exactly how she felt.

"Well, I know one thing for sure." Gretchen stood, raised her arms above her head, and stretched her back. "You may be happy with what you have, but you clearly don't have *Andrew*." She gave the group an expectant look. "Ladies. Enough yakking. How about some shopping?"

Chapter 18

The Decision

On Friday evening at eight-thirty, Andrew and Beth sat across from each other near the front of Mo'Joes. For several minutes, they'd been talking about Allie, but that hadn't been Andrew's planned topic of discussion when he'd called Beth an hour earlier and asked her to meet him.

"I've been home almost two months," Andrew said. "Nothing's changed." Shifting his gaze from Beth, he looked out the window. He saw a Latino man in a black L.A. Lakers jacket slip his arm around the petite woman next to him, pulling her close to his side. The couple continued walking down the sidewalk until they disappeared from Andrew's sight.

"Well . . . maybe now things have changed," Beth said in a soft voice.

"Why now?"

"Last Sunday morning, Gretchen, Allie, and I came here for coffee. We met a friend of yours. Jennifer."

Andrew jerked his gaze from the window.

"Don't worry, there were no confrontations. Everyone got along just fine. Jennifer is sweet, Andrew."

"Yeah, she's great. She's just not for me."

"I know. She told us."

"Told you what?"

Beth cocked her head, giving Andrew a compassionate smile. "Everything."

Andrew narrowed his eyes. "Meaning?" He shook his head and said, "No, never mind," waving her off the way a traffic cop would signal a vehicle. "Spare me the details."

"It wasn't anything I didn't already know." She touched his upheld hand gently. "But Allie needed to hear it."

Aggravated at the idea of a group of women discussing him and his feelings, he moved his hand away and grabbed his iced Americano. He took a forceful swig from the straw. Setting the cup down on the table he drew in a deep breath. "Well, Jennifer shouldn't have said anything, to anyone. But I suppose it doesn't matter now."

Beth sighed. "Talk to Allie. You'll see, things will be different."

"Talking to Allie only leads to conflict. We don't seem to understand each other. I guess we never did." He shook his head again. "No. I've done all I can. I came home. I tried to connect with her. I gave it some time. The results are in."

"And you lost?"

Andrew nodded. "Yep."

"Just call her. *Please.*"

Beth could plead all she wanted. He wasn't going to change his mind. It was too late for that. "It wasn't meant to be, that's all."

"Now you sound like Allie."

Tired of revisiting the lyrics to the same hopeless country western song, Andrew lowered his head, sliding his cup back and forth on the table. "If Allie also says it wasn't meant to be, why would you want to see us together?" He held the cup still while Beth answered.

"Consider me an unbiased, yet well-informed third party. I've known you two long enough to see you were made for each other. Sure, you have your differences, and that's to be expected, but the way your eyes come alive when you're with Allie says everything I need to know about how you feel. And the passionate ways she reacts to you tells me all I need to know about how she feels about you."

"Make that the *angry* ways she reacts to me."

Beth sighed. "Andrew, don't you know Allie is the queen of reserve? She handles her life with coolness, not fire. With regard to you, though, there's fire. Sure, for now, that fire contains some anger; but if she didn't care so much, why would she get so angry?" Beth tapped the tabletop. "Besides, most of her anger doesn't even have to do with you, per se. She's been after a goal that matters to her, a goal to achieve something that will make her stand out . . . but she's being thwarted by circumstances she can't control. Beth leaned in toward Andrew, her hair dangling over the table, her voice calm and reassuring. "Andrew, don't you see it? Apart, each of you is lonely and reserved and maybe a little lost; but together, your chemistry creates dynamism and energy, a lively combustion. It's a powerful force."

"So is an atomic explosion."

"That's your analogy?"

225

Finished with the subject, Andrew, moved on. "I turned the Mustang over to Joshua today. He's a good guy. I can see why he and Allie clicked."

"Oh, Andrew!" Beth looked to the side and laughed. "Allie didn't want me to saying anything to you about this, but now I think you should know. She's not dating Joshua. She never was."

Andrew nodded and did the traffic cop wave again. "I know that now." He snorted a wry laugh. "But Jennifer is."

"Oh?" Beth leaned back in her chair. "She didn't mention that on Sunday."

"She'd only met him for the first time the day before, the day we were supposed to meet Allie and Joshua for dinner." Andrew's stomach roiled at the thought of the convenience store confrontation.

"I heard a *little* about that from Jennifer," Beth prodded.

Andrew rubbed the back of his neck and took a deep breath, exhaling slowly. "Allie and I were in the gas station mini market, exchanging barbs, while Jennifer and Joshua waited outside. At some point they both came looking for us, but apparently, they found each other instead." Andrew gave a half-smile. "Actually, they'd started flirting when Joshua was looking at the Mustang. I thought he was a jerk for doing that while he was dating Allie. Turns out . . . Well, anyway, they're a great pair. I think they can make a go of it."

"So can you and Allie."

He winced. It was time to get down to brass tacks. "That won't be possible. I'm transferring to a research position initially offered to me by JPL. It's still available, so I told them I'd take it, which is why I asked you to meet me here tonight. To say goodbye."

Beth's voice rose. *"Goodbye?"*

Andrew took a sip of his drink and swiped his hand over the moisture left on his mouth. He wished he could just as easily wipe away the gloom that had wrapped around him since his confrontation with Allie. He chuckled over the irony. Here he was in a situation he never thought he'd see himself in again, looking forward to an escape to the dry, hot, miserable desert. Away from all the heartache and confusion. Away from Allie.

"Yes, Beth, goodbye. I'm moving to Phoenix. I leave in the morning."

* * *

When Allie finally heard the 1957 Ford Thunderbird idling outside, she jumped off her sofa and dashed toward her front door. The car

226

pulled away as she crossed the street and bounded up the steps to her sparkly-eyed neighbor's porch.

Removing a bright red scarf from around her head, Gloria led the way inside her unit, then asked Allie, "Too late for a cup of coffee?"

Allie backed up against a stained oak bureau in Gloria's entryway and reached into her hoodie pocket for her cell phone. It wasn't there; she'd left it at home. "What time is it?"

"Must be about ten-thirty."

"Kind of late for coffee, wouldn't you say?"

Gloria folded the scarf with care and set it inside the bureau's top drawer. "Well," she pushed the door closed, "there's always *decaf.*"

"Decaf would be great, thanks."

Decaf or regular, what difference did it make? It was Friday night, after all. And here Allie was with her older neighbor instead of out with Beth or Phoebe or . . . She shook away the thoughts like a dog throwing off rainwater then smiled at Gloria. How could she not smile at Gloria?

Dressed in a striped orange, pink, and red polyester knit pantsuit, Gloria looked flushed from all her happy energy. She'd just returned from a wild night on the town with her new beau, Melvin. It was a night she'd been looking forward to for the past several days.

Allie followed her into the kitchen. While Gloria made coffee, Allie stood next to the rooster clock (it was a cuckoo clock, only the cuckoo was a rooster, and when the clock chimed the hours, the rooster crowed . . . Allie tried not to be in its vicinity at noon or midnight). "How was your date, Glor?"

Gloria's mouth, smudged with red lipstick, broadened in contentment. "How was my date? A romantic dinner at the Elk's Lodge," she said, exhaling with a little whinny. "Poached salmon, green beans almandine, and mashed potatoes as light and fluffy as the chocolate mousse they served for dessert. A little shuffleboard to keep things sporting, and then afterward a hot fudge sundae cake at Bob's Big Boy, split down the middle with my dashing suitor. In a word, *fabulous.*"

Allie's brow creased. "Chocolate mousse *and* a hot fudge sundae cake?"

"No, love," Gloria tucked a paper filter into the coffee basket and looked up, her baby blue eyes still spinning from the overdose of sugar and chocolate, "*half* the cake."

"Okay, got it."

The two retreated to the living room and waited for the coffee to finish brewing. Allie sat down on a gently worn chartreuse green chenille sofa, which looked like a lumbering dinosaur next to the sleeker, midcentury orange reading chair. Gloria claimed she bought both at an estate sale for ten dollars each.

"Beth and Gretchen and I ran into Jennifer at Mo'Joes last Sunday," Allie said, as she began explaining the reason for her late night visit.

"Beth?" Gloria took a seat on a hand-carved wooden Queen Anne chair. She usually chose it for their little chats. Allie had no idea why. It looked uncomfortable.

"My friend. The redhead."

"Oh, sure." Gloria positioned a maroon crushed velvet pillow at her back.

"Anyway, so Beth and Gretchen—"

"Gretchen?"

"My cousin. The blonde. She recently moved into my place."

"Right, right."

"We all ran into Jennifer after church at Mo'Joes." Anticipating Gloria's next question, Allie stopped. "She's the girl we all thought Andrew was dating. Most of us anyway."

"The redhead."

"Yes, but not Beth."

"I know who Beth is, my dear."

"Of course you do."

Gloria got back up and went into the kitchen. "I'm listening," she called out over her shoulder. "Tell me what happened with Jennifer."

So Allie did.

By midnight, after one pot of decaf and several shortbread cookies, Gloria helped Allie reach an illuminated conclusion: Allie was in love with Andrew, and he was in love with her . . . and she'd messed it all up.

She could now see past events in a new light. She saw how her stubborn side interfered with Andrew's ability to communicate with her. She saw how Andrew's orchestration of what turned out to be a fiasco at the conference had been an act of love, not deception. And she saw that convincing herself Andrew was dating Jennifer was Allie's way of avoiding the truth about her own feelings for him.

"It's true that pride comes before a fall," Gloria sniffled. Tears trickled from her eyes. "I remember back when I lived up north. I was young and in love, like you." She nodded absently for a moment but then her lighthearted grin returned. "I met him during my first year of college. He was stunning. Gorgeous, thick, shiny black hair slicked back with just the right amount of pomade, sultry dark eyes, a voice as deep and beautiful as the ocean . . . And oh, could he dance!"

Allie widened her eyes. "You dated Elvis?"

Gloria snapped awake from her mental sojourn. "No, of course not, my dear. His name was Elroy. Elroy Priestly."

Allie started to laugh, but then Gloria's straight face stopped her. Swallowing her mirth, she said, "You're joking, right?"

"*Joking?* This is serious business, kiddo. I broke that boy's heart. Right after he broke mine," she added under her breath.

"Oh, of course. He sounds lovely."

"He was. Oh, he was. He was *so* lovely, and kind, that when a buddy of his, Reginald, told him about Reginald's poor, shy sister, Elroy asked the girl out. I was *furious* with him. *Furious!* How could he take out another girl?! But," Gloria leaned toward Allie, "you see, he was just being nice to her. He thought if he took her out . . . he was quite popular, in the 'in' crowd . . . she'd have the confidence to get to know other boys. It worked too. But I couldn't get over how he was *mine,* and he shouldn't have *done* that. It was my pride, you see. All about my pride. We had a big row, and he got so angry. I played the part of a stubborn mule and refused to see him again. After that, he started taking her out more often, just to spite me. Then she became so confident with herself that when she met someone else she liked better, she threw Elroy over for the other fellow." Gloria waved a hand. "It was a big mess."

Like the one Allie was in.

Gloria sighed. "If I hadn't been such an ninny, we would have spent our lives together. We had a once in a lifetime true romance."

Allie's stomach did a somersault, a back flip, and another move that felt, and even sounded, like a *splat! Oh boy,* she thought, *what have I done?*

Chapter 19

Revelations

G retchen's shrill words blasted through the phone. "He's leaving? *For good?*"

Allie whipped the SUV up the LAX entrance ramp while hands-free communicating with Gretchen. Last night after securing the details of Andrew's flight, Beth had immediately called Allie with the information.

"Yes, he's leaving for good," Allie exclaimed, frantically looking for parking. But finding a spot was not even half of her last-minute battle. She still needed to get inside the airport and through security in time to reach the assigned gate for flight 267 to Phoenix.

Andrew's flight.

And while she attempted to pull off this miracle, she was busy kicking herself for going to Gloria's without her cell phone and staying until after midnight (she didn't even know it was that late until the rooster crowed twelve times) only to come home and go straight to bed, thus missing Beth's late night call alerting her of Andrew's imminent departure . . . but how could she have known Andrew would do something drastic—like leave the state?

"Wow, I can't believe it," Gretchen said with a *tsk tsk*. "That's a bold move. Almost as bold as you bringing that guy Carl to Andrew's welcome home barbecue. Andrew said they used to be best friends but then Carl hooked up with you to get him angry because he knew how much Andrew loved you."

"What are you talking about?"

Gretchen disregarded the question and continued the incoherent babblings of a mad woman. "And at the barbecue, he told Andrew what you had told Beth one night at summer camp. And it wasn't very nice from what I gathered. Very rude and insulting. No wonder the man is leaving you."

Overwhelmed and running out of time, Allie tried to collate her thoughts. Carl had asked her out *only* to make Andrew angry because he knew how much Andrew loved her? And after over-hearing Allie at camp telling Beth something about Andrew, Carl repeated it to Andrew at the barbecue—*ten years later?* What could all this mean? she wondered, knowing she couldn't afford to sort it out now.

"You've got to find him for me, Gretchen. *Please.* I need to talk to him before it's too late. I'm parking now, but if his plane starts boarding in the next few minutes—"

"Didn't you try calling?"

"Yes, of course, but the call went straight to voicemail. He must have turned off his phone, so please don't forget to take yours with you."

Allie heard the rapid-fire tapping on a keyboard. "Flight 267 is leaving out of Gate 20A," Gretchen gasped. "Allie, that's not even kinda close to where I am now, and my flight to Honolulu begins boarding in less than twenty minutes."

"Then I guess you'd better run."

* * *

Andrew stood in front of the glass pane along the back wall of Gate 20A and watched ground crews hustling to load meals and baggage onto the silver and blue McDonnell Douglas DC-10. It reminded him of the active flight deck on the *Nimitz,* and of the V2 Division's choreographed clearing of the field, bringing up the aircraft, and setting the catapult. But with more important things to ponder at the moment, he shook the vision from his head and shifted his focus to the plane on the tarmac. Flight 267 to Phoenix, with continuing service to Chicago, was already running ten minutes behind schedule.

The waiting area at the gate smelled like buttered popcorn, which was an odd thing to smell at that hour of the morning. Taking up more space than was comfortably available were senior citizens, young couples, families, business travelers, and . . . Andrew. With nary an empty seat in which to relax, Andrew remained standing, using the extra time to puzzle over the myriad of thoughts jumbled up in his mind.

His folks were surprised about his last minute decision to move, but they were supportive as always. Younger siblings Mary Anna and Luke had been looking forward to finally having Andrew home for Christmas, and breaking the news to them had been tough; but Andrew told them he'd do everything he could to make up for it the following year.

He had a place to stay lined up when he arrived in Phoenix. JPL arranged a hotel for him for the first two weeks, giving him some time to find more permanent accommodations. At least he'd gotten the chance to talk to Beth before leaving. Other than his family members, she and Joshua were the only people he'd told. And because Jennifer was now officially dating Joshua, Andrew had asked Joshua during the transfer of the Mustang the day before to tell her about his sudden change of plans.

A short, wiry woman with brown hair and restless eyes stood behind the gate counter, managing all boarding-related crises by herself. She handed boarding passes to the last of the undocumented passengers, an elderly couple, whose combined diminished hearing capabilities had forced the agent to speak loud enough to reach the ears of everyone waiting at Gates 19, 20, and 21. Finally, with a heavy sigh, the agent seized the PA handset and cradled it against her shoulder for the first boarding call. Andrew looked down at the pass in his hand. Row ten, seat A, near the front, next to the window. Since a planeload of passengers with boarding privileges would go before him, Andrew settled in to the first vacated seat near the glass wall. The clock on the marquee behind the counter read ten twenty-two.

Anytime now, he told himself, *you'll be on that plane and on your way to a new life.*

* * *

Allie's heart felt like it was ricocheting around her chest. She was having trouble focusing. She kept plowing into people and immovable objects, and somehow, her ponytail had come loose, and half of it was caught up in her mouth.

She'd cleared security in a record twelve minutes and then reconnected by phone with Gretchen, who was off in search of Andrew. Breathing fast, she hurried betwixt and between moving (but not moving fast enough) clusters of passengers while she waited on a muted line, not knowing if the call had been dropped, if Gretchen had been unable to catch Andrew in time, or *what* was going on.

Why had he decided to leave right when Allie had decided she couldn't be without him? It seemed her talk with Gloria had been a blessing *and* a curse. Allie missed Beth's call because of it, but Gloria helped Allie clear the fog from her misguided brain—and heart.

Giving it more thought after she'd left Gloria's, Allie had stumbled upon more than one epiphany. Strangely, it wasn't Jennifer's admission that she and Andrew weren't dating that had impacted Allie. Rather, it was that day's discussion of Hebrews 13:5 and Pastor John's sermon that had combined with Gloria's wisdom and

232

solidified into a couple of huge "aha's." First, Allie had suddenly understood how the second part of the verse, "Never will I leave you or forsake you," applied to her own life. It made her realize that she didn't need the physical presence of her father or grandmother to be strong. And leave it to Gretchen to point out Pastor John's message about not loving money. That was the second big "aha." Allie realized she'd become obsessed with receiving a big bonus check, which she'd believed would not only add to her sense of accomplishment and success, but would also make others love and appreciate her more. Now she understood (and how could she not have seen it before?) that measuring one's worth in that way was not in line with God's word. Nor was it consistent with what was in her heart.

But what did any of that matter if she didn't make it to Andrew in time?

* * *

The agent once again reached for the handset, making the final boarding call. Andrew got to his feet and took his place in line behind the hearing-challenged elderly couple. He'd learned during their boisterous exchange with the agent that they'd been assigned seats 10B and C, the ones next to his. Andrew said a silent prayer. He asked God to bless them with a smooth flight—so smooth, in fact, that the couple might fall asleep—then thanked Him for the flight's short duration.

"It's right here. *Stop!* Stop, you dummy, and let me off this thing."

An electric cart squealed to a sudden and jolting halt right outside the carpeted area of Gates 20A and B. All remaining passengers stared at the short blonde flight attendant-turned action figure, who jumped from the vehicle and looked both ways before dashing toward Andrew like a speeding bullet.

No, not Gretchen, he thought. *Not now.*

"Andrew! Oh, Andrew, I'm so glad I caught you in time!" She reached his side and bounced up and down like a sprung jack-in-the-box.

"Hello, Gretchen," the woman at the counter said with a tight mouth and squinted eyes.

Gretchen slowly rotated her body toward the acidic voice as her Cheshire Cat's naughty smile reappeared. "Oh, hello there, *Daaaph-ne.*"

"Still buzzing around creating traffic jams, I see," the agent said.

"Well, dear Daph, at least I'm on the go and not just standing around letting my engine idle." Gretchen flipped her hair in Daphne's direction, grinning at Andrew and the couple ahead of him.

"Gretchen, what's going on?" Andrew asked, somewhere between embarrassed and irritated.

Leaning in close to Andrew, Gretchen spoke under her breath. "Daphne and I were originally stationed in Dallas. We both interviewed for the same job—the one *I* was chosen for; but because she just *had* to live in L.A., that's the one she ended up with." Gretchen pointed a thumb in Daphne's direction and snorted. "Gatekeeper."

"I heard that," Daphne said.

Andrew shook his head. "No, I mean why are you *here?*"

"Oh! I almost forgot! Allie's somewhere in the airport. She'll be here any minute." Gretchen held up her cell phone. "She wants to speak with you."

As though he'd never seen such a contraption before, Andrew gawked at the phone, hesitating a moment before taking hold of it.

* * *

"Hello?"

When Allie finally heard Andrew's voice, she broke her stride to do a spontaneous happy skipping-dance. "Hello?" she said, hitting her pace again, by then no more than thirty feet from Andrew's gate.

"It's Andrew," he said.

"I know," Allie giggled, ecstatic to be talking to him. She'd been afraid she wouldn't be brave enough to tell him how she felt (and *had been* feeling for so long), but hearing his voice gave her confidence. She sprinted through the nearly empty gate area and ran toward Andrew, who stared at her with his mouth hanging open. Apparently realizing he was gaping, he closed his mouth and gave her a tentative smile before handing the cell phone to Gretchen.

He opened his mouth again, and he might have spoken, but Allie began to laugh and babble. In an avalanche of disjointed words that probably made no sense to Andrew, she launched into a narrative about how she'd forgotten to take her cell phone over to Gloria's the night before and missed Beth's call. She told him about the encounter with Jennifer. She told him about Gloria's lost love. She had never talked so fast in her life. And she could have gone on and on.

But Andrew interrupted. "Allie, they're waiting for my boarding pass. I'm the last passenger."

Taken aback by Andrew's indifference, Allie's verbal motor ground to a halt. She tilted her head. He didn't seem to understand.

He didn't need to leave. She didn't *want* him to leave. She now knew how he felt about her, and she was ready to accept his love. Why didn't he get that?

"But, I, I thought you would . . . I mean, well, can't you postpone your trip?"

"No. It's all been arranged, and I start my new job on Monday."

"This is so sudden. I wish I would have known you were going. You could've called me. You let Beth know and even met her for coffee."

Andrew remained silent with a blank expression on his face. Allie was dimly aware that Gretchen was standing nearby, yammering away at a female agent behind the counter. The four of them were the only people left in the gate area. Then, in three quick moves, the flustered agent grabbed a telephone handset, snapped, *"Oh, go take a hike, Miss Clairol,"* and then announced, "the *absolutely final* boarding call" for Flight 267.

"I have to go." Andrew handed the agent a piece of paper and moved closer to the jet way. Briefly glancing backward toward Allie, he said in a quiet voice, "Take care of yourself."

And then he was gone.

Chapter 20

The Most Wonderful Time of the Year?

F riday, December 21st was Allie's last workday of the year, and she was desperate to see it come to an end. After unloading her samples at the storage unit, she drove to Mo'Joes for a cup of hot tea, thinking it might help ease her into her upcoming and badly needed time off. First, she'd find a nice quiet spot in which to relax; then she'd try to forget about her depressing job and her fouled-up love life.

But Mo'Joes wasn't in the mood to cooperate with her plan. It was crowded and noisy, made worse by four animated middle-aged women dressed in spandex and sweatshirts, blaring above the rest of the discordant clamor. Their overlapping conversations were being projected across the room, and included robust laughing, high-pitched cackling, and one nearly panic-stricken, *"Quick! Someone get a fire hose; I think I'm having a hot flash!"*

Allie placed her order and stood close by the counter to wait. Change of plan. She would get her drink and leave.

"Whoever said, 'It's better to have loved and lost than never to have loved at all,'" said Phoebe, looking uncommonly philosophical while drawing Allie's attention away from the chatty women's group, "is probably the same person who said, 'You can't spend what you don't have.' Hello? Can you say *MasterCard?"*

"Thanks, Scarlett." Allie lifted her cup of chai tea and toasted Phoebe with a nod. "That's very helpful."

"Oh, come on now. Don't go getting all *Roman Holiday* on me. How about grabbing some dinner and catching a movie? I'm off work in a few minutes."

Dinner? A movie? Although it *was* Friday evening, neither sounded appealing. Going home and crawling under the covers made more sense, considering the way Allie had been feeling since Andrew moved away two weeks earlier. How could he have left her forever with nothing more than a cold goodbye in an airport terminal?

"I'll pass, but thanks for the offer."

Maybe it was time for another chat with Gloria. She somehow understood Allie's heartache even better than Beth, though that wasn't exactly Beth's fault. She'd tried communicating her best advice to Allie before Andrew decided to move away, but Allie's obstinate attitude had wanted no part of it.

"I'm worried about you, Rosebud."

"I'll be okay."

"I know you will. They say time heals all wounds."

"You can't believe everything you hear."

Phoebe chuckled. "Oh, I don't. But I did hear on the radio that a big rainstorm was coming, and I do believe that. Should hit us anytime, so be careful driving home, okay?"

Allie laughed, for what felt like the first time in ages. "I'm only two miles away."

"Hey, some people get in accidents backing out of their own driveways."

"Yeah, but is it because of the rain?"

"I'm not sure."

"Okay then. I'll see you later." Allie turned away from the counter with her tea in hand and moved to the front door, pushing it open with an elbow.

Outside, a nippy wind swirled, and the first drops of rain dotted the parking lot. Allie unlocked her SUV and climbed inside, placed her hot tea in the cup holder then sat staring straight ahead. It was a good thing she had kept to herself the details of her unbearable day working with Kevin. Otherwise Phoebe would have really had something to worry about.

It was Kevin's second visit in as many weeks, during a month that should have been winding down in activity. Instead, he monitored every one of Allie's physician calls, each product detail, *and* all her expense items. He said he wanted to get in one last field coaching report before the end of the year, but she knew what he was doing was at Cassandra's request.

While Allie had been caught up in her personal life, her work life had churned along (*churned* being the operative word). Whereas she used to look forward to going to work, she now dreaded it and had for weeks, finding herself mostly just going through the motions.

Yes, she did the best job she could selling to her physicians, but her passion for her work had wilted under the scorching heat of Cassandra's watchful eye.

Commuter traffic crept along Hillcrest Boulevard. As the rain continued its descent, tapping and thudding on the SUV's roof and striking the glass with increasing intensity, Allie kept watch on the endless stream of headlights. After several moments, she backed out of her spot and exited the parking lot through a side driveway. She managed the two miles without incident, arriving home as the deluge began.

She entered her townhouse through the garage and set her purse and tea on the dining room table. After slipping her blazer over a chair, Allie looked up. Gretchen stood at the bottom of the stairs holding two bulging tapestry cloth suitcases by her sides. She glanced across several boxes nearly blocking the entryway before announcing with all the passion and flair of Sarah Bernhardt, *"Allie, I'm leaving you."*

Allie reclaimed the cup of tea and sank onto her sofa. Waiting for a response, Gretchen stayed put, as motionless as a park statue with a ground squirrel on its head. Not at all sure how to react, Allie finally said, "I take it you've made other arrangements."

Gretchen exhaled her relief. Dropping the suitcases on the floor, she took a seat in one of the two matching wicker chairs. "Yes, *of course*, and I'm so glad you understand. I feel terrible about bailing out on you during this catastrophic time of your life, but you probably want your space back anyway so you can think about what went wrong with Andrew and—"

"Where will you go?"

Gretchen folded her hands across her lap and leaned forward a bit. "It turns out Jennifer, or should I say Andrew's ex-girlfriend—"

"According to her, they were never dating."

Gretchen tittered as she straightened her spine. "Right. Okay, Andrew's *whatever* she was . . ."

"I know who Jennifer is, Gretchen."

"Yes, you do. Anyway, this whole thing just happened, unexpectedly. It was a coincidence, like when you and somebody else have the exact same need at the exact same time. The stars must have been perfectly aligned or something." She reached up with both hands, jabbing toward the ceiling at various abstract points. "This is the story. Me and Jennifer started talking after church last Sunday, and I asked her how many bedrooms she has in her house." Gretchen paused, allowing enough time for a recital of the entire Gettysburg Address.

"And?"

"She said two."

Allie kept her eyes on Gretchen and took a sip of tea, waiting for the punch line to arrive. But her cousin just stared back in silence, blinking like an owl. "So, what then?" Allie asked. "She told you she was looking for someone to rent the extra room?"

"No. She said she uses it for stuff like storing her antique dolls and setting up the ironing board and sewing machine . . ."

"Okay, then did she say she needed the additional income from a renter?"

"Er, I don't recall. I don't think so."

"Did she say she wanted, or needed someone to rent the room, for *any* reason at all?"

Gretchen made a monkey face, puckering her lips while she thought about the question. She shook her head. "Nope."

"Then how were your 'stars aligned'?" Allie asked, making finger quotes so Gretchen wouldn't miss the point. "How can you say you were destined to fulfill each other's needs?"

Gretchen flapped a hand. "I don't know. Maybe I didn't word that right. I just asked if I could move in, and she said yes."

"I see."

"But don't worry. Jennifer's new boyfriend, Joshua—they're dating now, you know—is coming by in the morning with one of his big trucks. He'll be moving my furniture over to the house."

Right. Jennifer's new boyfriend. Joshua.

Beth had been wise enough to leave that information out of her voicemail message the night Allie stayed late at Gloria's. Instead, she shared the news in a phone call early the following day. The day Andrew left for good. The day Allie recognized she'd made a huge mistake, and she couldn't wind the clock back to correct it.

"Josh and Jen will be by any minute to pick me up. We'll be dining at The Hummus & Hookah Hut, if you'd like to tag along. But you should probably drive yourself down there because afterward we'll need to get a head start on the moving process and take my suitcases and those boxes over to Glendale in my rental and Joshua's Mustang."

Allie nodded for no particular reason.

"So do you wanna join us?" Gretchen asked.

"Thanks, but I have other plans."

* * *

With the rain pelting her uncovered head, Allie darted across the street, carefully gripping her cup of tea. As she skipped over the second of the three steps leading up to Gloria's front porch, Allie heard the booming sound of a big block engine and looked back. A car pulled into the main driveway. It was a light blue Mustang and, for a split second, she nearly convinced herself it was Andrew coming back to tell her how much he missed her.

Realizing it was instead the Mustang's new owner, Joshua, Allie crouched down. She pressed herself against the side of the unit. A six-foot shrub planted at the bottom of the steps obscured her view of the driveway. Peeking around the tall bush, she watched Joshua park the Mustang in front of her unit. Both doors opened at once. Joshua got out of the driver's side then Jennifer emerged from the passenger's side, giggling, nearly giddy, probably because she'd found a new roommate and friend in glamour girl Gretchen.

The thorn in Allie's side.

She almost laughed out loud. Why was she at all upset that Gretchen was leaving? Why did she still feel so upset about Jennifer? She almost couldn't stand the woman, when in fact she had never done a thing to Allie.

The truth was that Gretchen was a miserable roommate, at least for Allie. Sure, Gretchen was her cousin, so she loved her, but they had nothing in common. Who had Allie been kidding when she thought Gretchen and all her crazy energy would be a good thing? Energy was one thing. Craziness was another. Allie felt overwhelmed by Gretchen's constant chatter and her endless references to that infernal fashion magazine.

In reality, what upset Allie the most was that Jennifer had what Allie wanted . . . the acceptance of her life, just as it was, and a great guy. How could Allie possibly be upset with Jennifer for that? Allie could have had both of those things too. The only reason she didn't was because of her own actions.

Allie stood up slowly. She glanced back at the Mustang while pressing the lighted button on the tan stucco wall. Joshua closed his door and tilted his head back. The area post lights illuminated the rain as it splashed down on his face. He grinned and trotted around the car. Giving Jennifer a playful hug before taking her by the hand, the two nearly skipped as they headed up the short walkway to Allie's front porch.

* * *

"Still no word from Andrew?" Gloria asked.

"No, Glor. Nothing."

Having been out power walking at the onset of the downpour, Gloria's white hair stuck out in all directions. Her head look like a frazzled Q-tip swab. She extricated herself from a drenched hoodless jacket and draped it across the top of a wooden coat rack near her front door. She sighed in commiseration. "What a pity. He's such a handsome rascal."

"Tell me about it."

"Well, here's the deal, Cupcake." Gloria stood still only long enough to make her point. "Men are men. They are not women, and therefore they do not think nor behave like women." She touched a forefinger lightly to her chin. "Personally, I've always found this to be a rather reassuring and comforting fact of nature." She disappeared out of direct sight and began rattling around in the kitchen as she spoke. "Your friend is upset, obviously, because you wounded his pride, which will take some time to heal, but if he really loves you, he'll come back. Give him the space he needs to think things over."

The leaded glass panes on the china cabinet in Gloria's dining room reflected her swift activity. Allie watched her add grounds and water to her coffeemaker. After setting a plate on the counter, Gloria loaded it up with cookies from a pink bakery box.

"Or it's just not God's will that Andrew returns," Allie suggested, tossing out Gloria's words of wisdom like leftover anchovy pizza. "In which case I need to accept it and move on."

Gloria popped her head around the wall. "That's also a possibility. First, though, a man thinks. He always *thinks*. Women, they usually make decisions based on intuition, their emotions, a vision of a white picket fence, and other such irrational things."

The aroma of spiced coffee drifted into the living room. Gloria returned and set the plate of goodies on the oak barrel coffee table, next to a thick stack of *Second Time Around* magazines. Dropping down on the long green sofa, she gave the top of Allie's knee a light smack. "I'd offer you a cup of Joe but it looks like you're already drinking some."

"It's tea."

"*Tea?* Oh, mercy, you need something stronger than that, my dear, and I have just the thing for you to try. My latest Internet find: Handpicked Brazilian beans, roasted to perfection and infused with cinnamon and cloves." Gloria kissed her fingertips, Italian style. "It's got a Christmas feel to it."

Allie groaned. "Don't remind me about Christmas."

"Oh, come on, kiddo, like the song says, *It's The Most Wonderful Time of The Year.*" Gloria began crooning out the tune's first verse using her standard off-key voice. "'With kids jingle bell-ing and everyone tell-ing you be of good cheeeer . . .'"

"Not me."

Gloria combed both hands through her unruly cotton top until it showed signs of behaving. "You know, I didn't realize how much you cared about this fellow."

"I didn't either, until it was too late."

"It's *never* too late." Gloria's face broadened in a smug grin as she stood up again. "And *I* should know."

* * *

Allie inched closer to the cosmetics counter in Rathman's department store. Peering through the glass, she studied its contents, mildly preoccupied by frenzied Christmas shoppers and the predictable jangle of yuletide Muzak. "Have you stopped carrying Providence?" She looked up just as Beth completed a sale to a tall woman in her sixties with blond hair swirled high up on her head. It looked like soft-serve vanilla ice cream. The customer collected her numerous bags off the counter and floor with a heavy sigh. She then grabbed the receipt from Beth and scuttled away, dropping a large, overstuffed bag twice before Allie lost sight of her among countless other shoppers.

"Providence?" Beth asked. "Are you out again? You've bought three bottles from me since Andrew—"

"It's not that I'm *out*; I'm curious, that's all." Allie straightened her back and began rearranging the sample glass fragrance bottles on a mirrored vanity tray. Beth's prior perfume tutorials had taught Allie how to distinguish sweet from flowery, or spicy from peppery, but the scents emanating from the tray created such a potent mixture that it made identifying individual notes impossible. Allie's nose felt accosted. "And besides, I gave what was left in my last bottle to Gretchen before she left." She turned away from the tray to look at a gift-with-purchase display at the counter's end. It was the typical package deal—cosmetics bag, full-size lipstick, mini mascara, and travel size eye cream. "I don't care for that scent any more."

"You don't say?"

"I *do* say."

Beth slid closed the showcase's panel door, locking it with a twist of the key attached to a stretchy coiled bracelet on her wrist. "Look at this asylum," she gestured toward the overloaded escalator outside Rathman's third floor mall entrance. "One and a half shopping days to go and you finally get an idea of the *other* reason for the season." She continued locking up the last of the doors and cabinets. "Where did you park?"

"I didn't. I rode over with Gloria in the Firebird. She needed false eyelashes and a facelift kit from Before and After for her big date with Melvin Tompkins, the man of her dreams. She's meeting his mother tomorrow night. Gloria claims she won Mr. T. over with her prune Danish, which, by the way, she buys from The Sweet Spot next to Mo'Joes, but don't ever tell Melvin that."

Beth smiled. "Who is this Melvin?"

"You know him. Unit twenty-two, distinguished looking, wears the ascot neck scarf and uses a walking stick."

"Oh, *that* guy!" Beth giggled.

Sadly amused, Allie took a peek at her cell phone. Nine fifty-nine P.M. three days before Christmas and still no calls or messages from Andrew.

Why hadn't he tried getting in touch with her? A text or an email—or *anything?* Three weeks and not one word. It was torture for her but, according to Gloria, it was imperative she give Andrew the time and space to decide he wanted to be with her—without her trying to influence the outcome.

"So, when's the wedding?"

Pulling her gaze away from a chattering cluster of girls swirling through the fragrance department like a teenage tornado, Allie's heart leapt inside her chest. "That's not funny, Beth. We're not getting married."

"You and Melvin?"

"What?"

"Allie," Beth leaned across the counter and put a hand on her friend's shoulder. "Are you okay?"

Sure she was, and Beth would not be seeing any evidence to the contrary. Allie stiffened her spine, filling her nose and lungs with perfume-saturated air. "I'm great. Thanks for asking, though."

Beth withdrew her arm and studied Allie's face. "Your voice is convincing, but I believe it hides the truth."

"And what are you going to do about it?"

"For starters," Beth said, opening the cash register, "I'm going to offer you a ride home. Then I'm going to spend the night, so we can get in some chat time, if that's okay. I'm beat, and I know I won't feel like fighting traffic back down to the beach once we get to your place. So, what do you say to that?"

"You think I could use some company. Is that it?"

Beth raised her eyebrows without answering. "Where and when are you supposed to meet up with Gloria?"

Allie reached back across her shoulder, grabbed hold of her long ponytail, and pulled it forward. It made a swishing sound as it slid against her nylon windbreaker. "I'm not." She kept her eyes low for a moment before looking into Beth's. "I told her I'd try to get a ride back with you."

"And see if by chance I'd want to hang out for a while. Was that the idea?"

"Something like that."

Beth smiled. "You're sneaky. And clever. And under the circumstances, I admire you for it. Give me ten minutes to button this place up and we'll be on our way."

Chapter 21

Transformations

C hristmas day arrived with a cloudless blue sky, brilliant sunshine, and no one in town with whom to share the joy, which was okay with Allie because she didn't seem to have much in the first place. Beth was up north for a McKinley family reunion. Gloria spent the night at her son and daughter in law's house in Temecula, while Allie's mom and the twins had returned to Kansas a week earlier, with plans to remain throughout the holiday season. Gretchen, however, was still around. She'd decided she ought to go to her parents' house and had been pestering Allie about joining the festivities. Allie eventually relented, mostly because she was too tired of arguing, and spent the afternoon in Thousand Oaks, a forty-minute drive due west of East Hills.

The day's highlight occurred during dinner. It was a direct result of Gretchen and Jennifer's initial meeting at Mo'Joes and of their subsequent regular attendance together at Valley Community Church. Evidently moved by the Spirit, Gretchen took advantage of the Christmas gathering to profess her newfound faith in Jesus. She stood at the head of the dinner table and explained how she now felt the desire to wait until God sent her a message telling her it was time to settle down. Kind-of like a text message, she explained, but much more profound. She'd seen the light, opened her heart to the Lord, found the road to redemption, and had never felt better—or more hopeful. It was a touching scene, though several guests, including second cousins and a few old family friends, viewed Gretchen's coming out much differently. Mumbling among themselves, they decided that excessive hydrogen peroxide use, prolonged flying at 30,000 feet in a tin can, and Uranus or possibly Pluto squaring her natal Neptune contributed to Gretchen finally taking the plunge—over the edge and headfirst. But Allie knew the truth: That Gretchen had found peace. And in a strange and ironic way, Allie envied her for it. She was also happy for her.

Still, Allie was relieved when the "festivities" had ended. And now, with the holiday season almost over, she prayed that things might start looking up for her.

On Friday, three days after Christmas and just before ten in the morning, Allie received two text messages from Kevin that seemed to confirm this burst of optimism. The first asked if she was in town. The second sounded a bit more pressing: *Have urgent info 2 discuss w/U ASAP. When & where can we meet?*

Did he have promising news about the most current national standings? Maybe Doug had come to his senses and decided to nix Cassandra's harebrained scheme.

That had to be it.

Suddenly, the recent angst she'd been feeling about her job melted away. She felt back in control and ready to have her hard work and efforts acknowledged by Kevin and, ultimately, Cassandra. How sweet it would be to see the look of sheer disappointment on Cassandra's face when Allie walked up on stage to receive the top rep award and a huge bonus check—despite Cassandra's efforts to keep that from happening. Allie's imagination took flight as she contemplated this scenario. She envisioned telling the twins in person about how she'd be able to help them with their schooling expenses. She saw in her mind's eye the three going to Best Buy, where Allie would let Erin and Edward go on an electronics shopping spree and pick out laptop computers, tablets, new cell phones—*whatever they wanted!*

Allie returned Kevin's text message, telling him to meet her at the Corner Café at noon, although she didn't think she could stand the anticipation of waiting even two hours to finally hear some good news.

* * *

When Allie arrived at the restaurant, she saw that Kevin had chosen to sit at a booth in the far corner. He looked like he'd been there awhile already. A tan ceramic mug filled with something steaming hot, probably coffee, sat near his elbow, and his laptop was in front of him, the screen propped open.

"Hey, Kevin," she said, scooting along the bench seat to face him.

"Allie, we need to talk." He looked down the front of his necktie, smoothing it in place with a restless hand.

"Okay, so talk."

After releasing the latches on his camel briefcase and lifting the lid, he removed a few pages of paper from an interior pocket. *Current sales data printouts?* He could have pulled that up on his computer instead.

Holding the papers up by their sides, Kevin tapped them down against the table, bringing them in line. He cleared his throat, setting the pages before Allie. "I need you to read these carefully before signing them."

A quick glance over the top page told Allie all she needed to know. The buzz terms *noncompliance* and *condition of continued employment* flew off the paper, jabbing her in the eyes like two stiff fingers. She laughed. "I won't bother asking if this is supposed to be a joke."

"Nor would I, if I were you."

Allie studied Kevin's face, which showed more lines than usual. His eyes were neither green nor gold, but a murky mix of the two, bleary and lackluster. In less than three months, he'd gone from a respected district manager to Cassandra Hartwell's hand puppet, conforming to her will, blindly following her every order. It appeared, however, that he was no longer an eager puppy, trotting along at Cassandra's heels. He looked more like a whipped hound that now was tired of slinking a few feet behind her.

"This is still only a warning, Allie. You're allowed two. One verbal, which I've already given you, and one in writing."

"I'm *allowed* two? *Allowed?* You make it sound like you're doing me a favor."

Kevin shook his head, his mouth tight. He clicked his ballpoint pen a few times. "It's not my fault you scored poorly on your last review. You should be grateful Cassandra had me wait until after Christmas to show this to you."

"Oh, well since you put it like that," Allie snapped, "please tell Santa *thank you* for the belated gift. Although I'm pretty sure I didn't have this particular one on my wish list."

"The warning is based on—"

"On what?" Allie interrupted, her impatience skyrocketing. "A conversation you had with Cassandra *after* writing the review? *The same one I looked over and signed?* My scores were lower than usual, I admit, but not bad enough to warrant *this.*" She pushed the pages back toward Kevin, sucked in a breath then exhaled sharply. "I'm signing nothing."

"Allie—"

"No! *No more.* I've had it. With *all* of you."

"I know you're upset about the changes in the sales goals. Everyone else is too. This isn't only about *Allie's* territory."

"Speaking of my territory, why hasn't the current list of rankings gone out? I've been tracking my sales numbers through the weekly email reports from the home office. I should at least be back up in the top five. Assuming we keep the PM docs and your evil boss loses the war." Allie's heart began thumping with such force it felt like an elephant's. Kevin stayed quiet, which meant he had something unpleasant on his mind.

"Kevin?"

With an edgy look in his eyes, Kevin raked a hand through his hair.

The life-changing talk with Gloria echoed through Allie's mind like an internal bullhorn announcement. Hadn't Gloria's insight helped reveal that Allie's selfish and stubborn attitude had created all the tension between her and Andrew? And shouldn't accepting that truth have paved the way to a fail-safe resolution with him? She'd thought so, but then look what happened. He left anyway.

To make matters worse, it seemed the same issues she faced back then were being repeated now, with Kevin and Cassandra. If Allie hadn't been able to make things right in her personal life, how could she hope for a different result in matters related to her job? She'd always believed if she created the order and discipline necessary for a successful career, she'd find happiness—the kind she lacked during those trying times in her youth. But the main and still unresolved problem stemmed from issues rooted deep in her past, which caused her to live in denial about her fears and insecurities and her obstinate and willful ways. Mostly though, it made her deny her profound love for Andrew.

So, despite all the soul-searching, she realized, in effect, nothing had changed. And nothing *would* change until she first found the courage to face Andrew and be completely honest with him.

Kevin laid his ballpoint pen atop the three pages, pushing them gently back toward Allie. "Please don't make this difficult, for either of us. It's only a warning, a formality, really. Your signature simply shows you've read the documents and understand that some changes in your performance are expected in the future."

Focusing her attention on the pen, Allie slowly nodded. It was all starting to make sense.

"I need to get these in the mail and postmarked by December thirty-first," Kevin said. "Initial the first page and sign the second two. I'll stop by the post office on my way back home."

Allie didn't move. "What happens if I don't sign them?"

"Are you saying you *won't* sign them?"

"I'm asking if I have a choice. What happens if I refuse?"

Kevin dropped his head down slightly and rubbed his left thumb and middle finger across his eyelids. Clearly the man was frustrated.

He moved his hand away from his face and looked up, shaking his head. "I'll have to report that to Cassandra. I'm sure she'll want me to terminate your employment."

Allie collected her cell phone and keys off the table. "That's what I thought, but don't bother. I wouldn't give her the satisfaction." She slid along the booth and stood. "I quit."

* * *

In the days following Christmas, the atmosphere inside Mo'Joes had become more tempered and peaceful. It almost felt like a library, but without the familiar musty book smell. Allie sat at a booth, sipping hot chocolate and mulling over her latest dilemma. Before leaving a speechless and thunderstruck Kevin at the restaurant thirty minutes earlier, she assured him she'd put her resignation in writing, remove any personal items from the storage unit, and drop off the SUV as soon as her paid time off had ended.

Now, taking a pen from her handbag, she pulled a napkin from the dispenser on the table and jotted down a list of her assets. She tallied the amount of her final paycheck, the money in her savings account, and an estimate of her fourth quarter bonus without pain management numbers. This figure gave her enough money to live comfortably for about three months. After that, she'd have to find another job.

All right, then. First things first.

Allie phoned the airline to buy a ticket for the following day then called Beth. "I'm flying to Phoenix tomorrow to talk to Andrew, and I need his address. I knew if anyone had it, you would."

"You're flying all the way to Phoenix to talk to him?"

"It's an hour flight, Beth. No big deal."

"Couldn't you call him instead?"

"How do you know I haven't tried already?"

"Have you?"

"No, but that's not the point."

"Well, you brought it up."

"Look, I need to see him face to face—to tell him what I want to say, what I've *wanted* to say for a long time."

After a tense fifteen-minute conversation, Allie convinced Beth that flying to Phoenix to talk to Andrew *and* leaving her job at Horizon Pharmaceuticals was for the best.

"Do you want me to come with you?" Beth asked.

"That's sweet of you, but I think I should handle this by myself."

"How about a ride to the airport?"

"I'm good, Beth, but thanks anyway. Just say a prayer for me, will you? My flight leaves at nine A.M."

* * *

The following morning, just after eleven-thirty Mountain Standard Time, Allie stood on the sidewalk of a quiet residential street lined with Spanish-style apartments, duplexes, and small houses. She stared at the main entrance of a stucco box-like structure with a red tile roof. Andrew's building. Her plane flight had been uneventful. Her cabby had been silent and efficient. Her stomach had managed to contain her butterflies. And now here she was.

She took a deep breath and entered the multistory building through glass double doors.

The saltillo-tiled lobby was empty, except for a lingering scent, clean and refreshing. Was it perfume? Cologne? Air freshener? It was hard to categorize, but it smelled nice, adding a calming touch to the Saturday morning stillness. The wall next to the elevator contained a red "house" phone and several rows of putty-colored metal mailboxes. A cork bulletin board hung near the elevator. It was covered with paper scraps, a few bright pink and green index cards, and a flyer with a black and white photo of Jerome, someone's pet iguana, who, as of yesterday, was on the loose. Allie pressed the elevator button and focused on her plan of action for the day.

Kevin would be proud—he had been hounding her lately to have an action plan and a prepared script.

Alone inside the elevator, Allie practiced what she wanted to say to Andrew: "I'm sorry we misunderstood each other. I know I have trouble communicating my feelings, which may be due to painful events from my past. I think we should sit down and talk about what happened on the beach."

The elevator glided to a stop. A faint lightheadedness struck Allie as the doors opened up before her. She knew her carefully calculated message included all the necessary components. The words contained the truth, and they were in the right order; they made sense as she spoke them, but they sounded stilted. There didn't seem to be any feelings *at all* in them. No emotions in her words meant she wasn't connecting to the emotions she knew were in her heart. Was she never going to be able to get this right?

She walked down the long white, faux-stucco-walled hallway, stopping outside unit number 776, Andrew's unit. Confused, she sighed. *This may not have been such a great idea after all.* If she couldn't deliver her message with emotion, wouldn't she only worsen the situation by coming across as impersonal and superficial? Like *A Space Odyssey's* monotonic HAL, or that diabolical ankh-obsessed mainframe in *Logan's Run*.

A tall, hefty male tenant wearing a Phoenix Suns jacket exited a nearby unit, flipping a baseball cap onto his head. Allie pressed the small rectangular button on Andrew's door and greeted the man as he passed by.

"Morning," he muttered as he lumbered down the hall toward the elevator.

Moments passed with no answer. Maybe the bell didn't work. Unlikely, Allie thought, the building looked brand new.

* * *

Allie sat quietly at the gate waiting to board her plane, wondering if she'd just made, or was about to make, a huge mistake. Was she giving up on Phoenix too quickly? Should she have waited at Andrew's building or tried to find out where he worked? Should she have checked into a motel and kept returning to his place until she found him?

Or should she just move on?

She stood. Her confusion was driving her nuts. She'd been sure she should just let it go when she'd taken a cab back to the airport, but now she was conflicted.

She needed an answer. So she left the gate area to look for it.

Striding a hundred feet down the buffed beige concourse, Allie walked past a candy store, a bookstand, a souvenir shop and a pizzeria. The warm and familiar aroma of baking bread drew numerous passersby into the small Italian restaurant, but not Allie. Her failure to find Andrew had filled her with a dull ache that left no room for food.

A gift shop abutted the pizza place. Allie stopped out front, feeling drawn to go inside, but also feeling a little silly. What exactly was she doing? Did she actually believe she'd find guidance wandering around an airport terminal?

She paused in the doorway of the little store and prayed that she'd receive a sign, some sign, telling her what she should do.

The place was empty except for one employee, an African American woman about forty with an austere face and arresting honey-colored eyes. From behind the counter, the woman watched Allie inspect shelves stuffed with books, pottery, Native American blankets, and an array of Arizona-themed souvenirs. Allie looked at everything, eager for the clue she hoped to unearth. It wouldn't be easy finding the answer in a store like this, but she remained on the alert.

Eventually, she came to a section of the store that had mirrored walls lined with glass shelves. The shelves displayed countless different boxes of perfume, making Rathman's own notable scent collection seem lacking in comparison.

"Are you looking for something special?" the woman asked as Allie neared the counter.

Yes, she thought. Something special, but she didn't know what. "You could say that."

"A gift?"

Sort of. "No."

The woman smiled, her light gold eyes coming alive. "We have a large selection of some lovely scents. Do you wear perfume?"

Not anymore, so the answer was no, but the woman's eyes seemed to be encouraging Allie to talk. "I used to wear a certain scent."

Was the clue in Providence?

"You got tired of it, did you? That happens."

Allie thought for a moment. "I'm not sure what happened, exactly. It's still my favorite, I just don't wear it anymore."

The woman chuckled, amused by Allie's indecision. "Would you like to start wearing it again?"

Allie's brow creased. She glanced over the sample bottles on the glass counter. How would her buying more Providence be a sign regarding her relationship with Andrew? Was giving up on Providence the equivalent of giving up on Andrew?

That didn't make sense.

Allie lifted from the counter the distinct sapphire blue bottle, now more than half empty from testing. She removed the lid, and sprayed a light mist on her forearm. Images flooded her memory as she inhaled the soft floral fragrance. She pictured Andrew's face the day he'd given her the first bottle as a birthday gift, recalling both the excitement and the sadness in his eyes. It was the same sadness she'd seen when he stood before her trying to explain what had happened on the beach.

"Yes, I would like to start wearing it again." Allie set the bottle back on the tray with a little smile.

The woman winced slightly and tapped the counter. "I don't suppose I could interest you in trying something different."

Allie shook her head. "No, I don't think so." Wearing Providence again was the answer she'd been looking for, as odd as that sounded. And getting a bottle before leaving Phoenix had become vitally important. "I don't have much time, anyway." She glanced at the time on her cell phone. Her flight had probably already begun boarding.

252

"Of course, I understand, but I feel like I convinced you to go back to your favorite scent." She glanced at the shelves behind her. "I guess I should have asked the name beforehand."

Allie's eyes dropped down to the countertop full of perfume bottles. She again lifted the blue bottle. "It's Providence. I see you carry it."

The woman made a clicking sound with her tongue. "Yes, we do carry it. And as of this morning I still had it in stock. Unfortunately, though, I just sold the last bottle."

Allie suppressed a sigh and set down the perfume. *Now what? Go to the mall when I get back home?* She thought the point was to buy it here, in this shop, *before* leaving Phoenix. That seemed important. "Oh. I see."

"May I show you another fragrance with similar notes?" The woman arched her neatly penciled-in eyebrows. "Maybe being out of Providence is a sign. To try something new."

Yes, it was a sign all right—just not the one Allie was hoping for. "Maybe so." She shifted the strap on her shoulder bag. "But right now I have a plane to catch."

Chapter 22

Providence

It may have started out like any other day, but New Year's Eve was not. Setting it apart from three hundred and sixty-four others—by tradition at least—were the seeds of hope for a brighter tomorrow, a new beginning or, at the very least, a different approach to the same unresolved problems. And Allie was ready for any of it.

Beth's offer of a sales position at Rathman's fragrance counter gave Allie a sense of security about her immediate future. Obviously, it wouldn't pay what her last job had, but it would be enough. Her life had, without warning, shifted its shape from safe and familiar to unstable, from systematic and planned to chaotic. That was okay, for the time being. Like the saying went, "What doesn't kill you makes you stronger."

After parallel parking across from Jennifer and Gretchen's house, Allie set her SUV's alarm and glanced around the unfamiliar neighborhood. She saw Sue Gallagher's champagne Toyota Camry with the bumper sticker, *Jesus Is Coming, Look Busy.* Having seen it before on other cars, Allie always found the saying ironic. With omniscient and omnipresent Jesus, simply trying to "look" busy was a silly concept. Other vehicles parked along the curb near the Camry included Beth's white Ford Focus; Gloria's red Firebird; Gretchen's metallic green rental and Joshua's blue classic Mustang, the sight of which made Allie's stomach feel like a dryer chamber tumbling a full load of laundry. Despite the multitude of Christmas decorations, wreaths, nativity scenes and colored lights adorning the homes up and down Maple Street, the celebratory night seemed cold and lifeless.

Allie swung open a creaky white gate off the sidewalk and took a breath, inhaling the crisp night air. Strings of bright twinkling lights framed the small house before her; they were strung along the eaves and down the sides. A large wooden star studded with clear lights and placed on the lawn at an angle lit up the yard. She walked toward the front door then rang the bell.

"There you are!" Joshua greeted Allie like an expectant host, wrapping his arms around her with a snug embrace. A dual pang in her head and heart produced a vision of Andrew, spending the evening away from home, possibly all alone, but whose fault was that?

Joshua took her coat and rattled off a list of appetizers he claimed to have prepared. "The food's in the dining room." He pointed, saying, "It's that way. Go join the fun. Whoever's not inside is in the backyard keeping warm near the fire pit. I'll be right out." Still holding her coat, he disappeared down a hallway. Allie lingered in the entry for a moment, taking in the sights, sounds, and rich aromas surrounding her. From where she stood, she heard Gretchen and Phoebe chattering elsewhere in the house. They sounded like two high society women, engaging in droll banter and exchanging recipes, while making use of less than impressive Scandinavian accents.

Allie looked down the front of her dark gray slacks. The small entryway beneath her feet had been tiled using ivory squares embossed with a pretty fleur-de-lis motif. She rubbed the soles of her black suede slip-on shoes across an oval mat then took a couple steps onto the speckled cream carpet. The living room wasn't as spacious as Allie's, but at least it wasn't overcrowded. There was a three-person sofa in a brown suede fabric, accented with icy blue toss pillows that matched a recliner chair in the corner; an entertainment center; a flat screen television and, stirring up Allie's memory of an unfortunate incident on the beach, Jennifer's vast collection of dvds. A pale blue wall with arched openings on either end separated the living room from the kitchen and dining room. Allie stared at an old regulator clock hanging on the wall near the kitchen entrance. Watching the pendulum swing back and forth, she waited for the last of nine chimes before moving toward the dining room.

The food was beautifully laid out, and Joshua returned in time to give Allie a guided tour of the table: Pastry-wrapped baked brie with toasted pecans and brown sugar, garlic and rosemary shrimp, Mediterranean pasta salad, and stuffed broiled mushrooms.

She picked up a red and gold paper plate and skewered a mushroom with a frilly toothpick. "I'm impressed. I had no idea you were a chef."

Joshua's blue eyes sparkled along with his shy smile. "I'm no chef, Allie, I just know how to read a recipe and follow directions."

Jennifer crept up from behind Joshua and placed her hands along his broad shoulders. "Plus he did have a little help."

"Oh, yeah." He laughed, turning the same color as the punch that filled a large bowl at the table's end. "Did I leave that part out?"

Watching the two giggling like carefree teenagers reminded Allie of the many special moments she and Andrew had shared over the years, from the humorous to the heartbreaking—all now sadly treasured.

"I made the brownies!" Gretchen sidled up to Allie and reached across the table to grab a shrimp. She stuck it in her mouth, suctioning it out of its tail with a slurp.

Joshua turned away from Jennifer and winked at Allie. "That's right. You don't want to pass up Gretchen's famous brownies."

Gretchen beamed a proud smile then tossed the tail on a plate reserved for discards. "Yep," she pointed to a pyramid of chocolatey squares on a separate, smaller table. "Those puppies are *homemade*."

Although not hungry, Allie politely dotted her plate with samples of each dish. She carefully removed the smallest brownie she could get to without dismantling the ancient Egyptian architecture then set off to make the most of the evening. She figured she'd wear her public happy-face for awhile, then, just after midnight, discreetly slip away from the crowd and return home.

Alone.

* * *

By close to eleven o'clock, with all guests present, it occurred to Allie that the house was filled with couples—some newly formed, others already established: Joshua and Jennifer, perfectly matched and at ease in each other's presence, looked like they belonged atop a wedding cake; Rob and Sue Gallagher, married almost thirty years and still the best of friends; Gloria and Melvin, making a striking duo with Gloria's snow white hair accented with sparkling barrettes, which complemented the glittering and gleaming sequins on her hot pink pant suit, and Melvin, looking dapper in his vintage black tuxedo with its distinct film noir flair; Phoebe and her date, Daniel, an old neighbor she reconnected with one evening at Mo'Joes, who'd moved away after high school but had come back in hopes of finding a wife and raising a family; Beth and Joshua's brother, Steven, meeting for the first time and enjoying a remarkable chemistry everyone at the party noticed. Even Bobbie Brennan found a promising friendship with Melvin's thirty-two-year-old grandson, Robert, who shared with Bobbie a passion for scuba diving and riding motorcycles and, by coincidence, also shared the same nickname—though his was spelled with a Y.

256

Like Allie, Gretchen remained unpaired; but unlike Allie, Gretchen seemed okay with it. Actually, she claimed she rather enjoyed the freedom she felt by not being concerned with finding, as she called him, *"Mr. Right Here, Right Now."* Four weeks of listening to Pastor John's sermons had given her the confidence to stay single for however long it took to find a man who respected her and cared about her as a person, and not just because she had a pretty face. It was a concept she admitted to having entertained once before but then dismissed as impossible.

Allie dutifully mingled for two hours, and now she could hardly wait for the day's final hour to pass. Nearly everyone had gone outside to await the arrival of the New Year. Allie finally joined them. As she stepped through the kitchen door, she passed Sue, who said she was going back inside to nibble on more desserts. The mood in the backyard was upbeat with music, laughter, and lighthearted conversation. Allie's mood, however, was the same as it had been the whole day, evening and, in truth, month: Somber. What did she want? More half-hearted socializing out here, or would it be best to hide in a corner somewhere until it was time to go?

She'd drifted full circle around the yard when Rob noticed her, standing in contemplation, on the tile patio. He waved her over to the firepit then got up out of his chair and removed a kindling stick from a nearby woodpile. Allie joined him as he poked at the burning logs. The fire flared up, spewing sharp smelling smoke, while bright orange embers danced around the flames. "These chairs are pretty comfy, Allie. Just what the doctor ordered," Rob said.

Allie chuckled and eased down into one of four padded wooden armchairs.

Rob tossed the stick into the pit and sat in the chair next to Allie. "Beth says you left Horizon."

Allie nodded. "Mm hmm. My boss Kevin is being kind enough to let me submit my resignation after my vacation, which means I have use of the company vehicle for two more days, but if Cassandra Hartwell finds out, she'll probably have Kevin tarred and feathered for it."

"I heard about her from Joe. Is she the reason you quit?"

"One of the reasons." Allie inhaled the smell of spitting sap sparked by the fire's heat. She leaned back in her chair, gazing up at the clear, star-splattered sky. Cool night air mixed with the warm air radiating from the fire. It made the temperature comfortable, even without a coat. "I discovered a few things about myself recently. Some involving Andrew."

"Hmm." Rob nodded gently in thought. "Care to share?"

A shooting star caught Allie's eye as she gathered her thoughts. Wasn't that a sign that a wish was about to come true? The white streak faded into oblivion with a reflective glimmer.

"For one thing, I learned a tough lesson about what happens when I'm too concerned with the details of my own life to notice anyone else's."

The fire crackled and snapped as the wood continued to release its moisture. Allie relaxed deeper into the chair, an unexpected sense of calm settling into her bones and making her feel almost weightless. She glanced over at Rob.

He leaned toward her. "You're a career gal, Allie. And you're single. Without family concerns, young people tend to focus more on themselves. It's not a crime, you know."

"Thank you for saying that, Rob, but there's more. I'd become so obsessed with work and with trying to make a name for myself through success and status that I couldn't see what mattered most, even though it was right in front of me. I was afraid of becoming distracted by the very thing I longed for."

She exhaled, rubbing her palm against her forehead, not sure if revealing her feelings for Andrew was the right thing to do. Or did Rob already know?

"This is where Andrew comes into the picture." Her voice softened. "It wasn't until after he left for Phoenix that I understood how much I cared about him." She faced Rob. "How much I *love* him."

Rob touched her shoulder, showing more concern and sympathy than Allie felt comfortable with. Her face began to flush, but she shook off the sensation, knowing she had nothing to hide or be ashamed of; she was finally being honest with herself, and with others.

"But I drove him away. I pushed him too far and he left. I can't blame him. I *don't* blame him."

"Maybe he just needs some time to sort things out."

Allie shook her head. "I don't know. I don't think so. It's been almost a month now." A disquieting thought crossed her mind. "He's okay, isn't he? Have you talked to him?"

Rob removed his hand from Allie's shoulder, giving her upper arm a light squeeze. "Andrew's just fine, and yes, I've talked to him recently; today, as a matter of fact. He's spending New Year's Eve at a new friend's house. A small gathering, from what I understand."

She exhaled, relieved but feeling self-conscious. "Oh, that's good to hear."

And it was. However, Allie knew better than to ask any more questions about Andrew's new life away from East Hills. Hearing the details would only reopen the wound she'd been trying to let heal.

Just then, the back door off the kitchen swung open. Beth came outside, carrying a large bag of marshmallows and some long metal skewers with wooden handles. She crossed the yard, set the items on a white resin table and took a seat in the other chair next to Allie. Joshua and Jennifer appeared next, smiling and holding hands. They stopped for a moment on the patio to nuzzle and stare at each other. Beth leaned toward Allie, speaking quietly and keeping watch on the happy couple. "It's nice to be with the one you love on New Year's Eve, isn't it. No one should have to be alone."

Allie's muscles contracted. She shot Beth a look. Was she testing Allie's endurance? "I don't feel like I'm alone," she answered in a hoarse whisper. Her eyes panned across the patio and lawn. "I'm *not* alone, there are people everywhere. Look around!"

Beth laughed, tossing her head backward the way people do when they think they're being cute.

"What's with the marshmallows?" Allie asked. "Are we back at camp?"

"No, silly. Those days are over, past tense. It's time for all things new. A new year. A new job. A new attitude." She poked her finger at Allie's shoulder. "A new *you*."

"Yeah, yeah. I know what I have to do, Beth. I quit my job. Remember? And here I am at a New Year's Eve party having a ball."

Gloria and Melvin joined the group while Rob and Beth chuckled at Allie's sardonic reply.

"What's so funny, Dr. Gallagher?" Gloria asked. "Did I miss a good joke?"

Rob collected himself with a thoughtful sigh and a small grin. "No, Gloria. No joke." He looked at Allie. "We were admiring Allie's resolve to move forward with her life, leave the past behind and start off on a new path."

"Atta girl," said Gloria, leaning down to touch Allie's knee, adding a quiet, "You did your best, kiddo," meant for Allie's ears only. She and Melvin then moved off to the side, becoming engrossed in a conversation with the Bobbies.

After that, Allie relaxed and listened to the chatter around her, contributing little, but not feeling left out. She hadn't realized how much time had passed until Gretchen shouted, "It's almost midnight everyone!" She waved her arms and flailed around like a double-jointed, parka-wearing cheerleader.

Steven approached the firepit trio with a paper bag full of party paraphernalia. He handed Rob a noisemaker, Beth a horn, and Allie one of those crinkly curly mouthpiece things. She blew into it and it unfurled like a snake's tongue. Silently. What good was that?

259

"It was warm a minute ago, but now it's freezing out here," said Beth. "Are you getting cold?"

Allie shrugged. "Yeah, I guess I am. I hadn't noticed until you mentioned it."

"The fire's low. I can fix that." Rob stood and returned to the woodpile.

"Brrr." Beth intertwined her arms across her chest. "Do you know where Joshua put our coats?"

"Not exactly." Allie looked over at Joshua and Jennifer, still all lovey dovey and in their own little dream world. "He took mine and walked down a hallway near the front door."

Overhearing the conversation, Gretchen answered. "They're in my bedroom. It's the first door on the right."

"Okay then." Allie got to her feet, thankful for an opportunity to take a break from all the cozy couples. She placed her mouthpiece thing on the marshmallow table. "I'll get our coats."

"Thanks, you're a doll," Beth said. "I brought the teal short coat. I don't think I'll need the pink scarf. You can leave it by my purse."

Allie passed through the group, now lively in anticipation of the midnight hour just moments away. Joshua momentarily separated from Jennifer to offer Allie a champagne glass half full of something bubbly and sparkling. "I'll get it on my way back," Allie said then entered the house.

It was dark inside except for a dim light above the stove and a floor lamp in the living room. Several lit candles saturated the home's interior with a spicy fragrance. The house was warm and quiet, a pleasant contrast to the backyard's cold and commotion. Allie wished she could stay indoors for the remainder of the evening, but Beth needed her coat. So Allie went down the hall to the first door on the right.

Gretchen's bedroom furniture was arranged the same way it had been at the townhouse, except in reverse. The large armoire she'd fussed over during her move from Dallas was straight ahead in the right-hand corner, and the bed was centered against the back wall. Just inside the door and next to the armoire sat the faded pink armchair; above it on the wall, hung a matching rectangular mirror. Beth's teal coat lay on the chair. Allie drew closer, noticing a box wrapped in white paper perched on the little ledge at the base of the mirror. A small lavender note card attached to the front read, "For Allie."

She removed the box and examined it. Was it an undelivered Christmas gift from someone at the party?

Before she could decide whether to open the box then or wait, a sudden banging noise startled her. It sounded like the back door being slammed shut. Or was it fireworks? No, she was sure the sound had come from inside the house. She waited a moment, heard nothing more, then reached down for Beth's coat. When she straightened back up, she glimpsed a startling image in the mirror and dropped the coat, spinning around with a gasp.

"Hello, Allie," Andrew said softly.

Overwhelming feelings pulsed through her body. Fear, joy, shock, relief—so many sensations hit her all at once that she couldn't move. She certainly couldn't speak. She began trembling, and her knees went weak. She stumbled. Andrew reached out, catching her in his arms and holding her up.

"I, I . . ." she stammered. She gazed into his eyes, knowing she had to tell him how she felt. She swallowed then said, "I have to say this to you now, Andrew, before it's too late."

He relaxed his arms and took a step back. The expression on his face was, what? It was blank, as if he couldn't decide what to feel.

Allie drew in a shaky breath, fighting back the tears she so badly needed to shed. Unable to maintain eye contact, she focused instead on the box in her hands. "I feel like we've known each other forever and that our souls were meant to be connected. There are times I'm sure I can read your mind, see into your heart, and feel your emotions. I dream about being close to you and having your arms around me, holding me against you. My heart aches to be near you, to see your face, and hear your voice." She stopped and looked up, stunned at the words that had flowed out of her mouth. She'd just revealed to him thoughts and feelings she'd never before realized she had. How long had they been buried inside her? Months? Years? And how could she have known, yet not known about them at the same time?

Andrew chose an emotion, and his face reflected it. His beautiful brown eyes lit up and crinkled in the corners as he smiled. He smiled broadly. His face looked relaxed; the bunched muscles at his jawline and the slight furrow between his brow that she was used to seeing were gone. Allie once again almost collapsed in her relief.

"Did you know I flew to Phoenix last Saturday to see you?" she asked. "Maybe Beth mentioned it? Sometimes she talks."

Andrew shook his head. "No, Allie."

"I did."

"Why?"

"To tell you what I told you just now, but it had to be done in person. Face to face. You weren't home, and I didn't want to leave a note, so I went back to the airport."

Andrew half-smiled and opened his mouth. Before he could say a word she continued. "I began having second thoughts about my plan once I got to the airport. I decided I needed to see a sign, something undeniable that would prove I should either continue trying to contact you or let you go. So I went into a gift shop near my gate. They sold perfume, and the saleswoman convinced me to start wearing Providence again."

Andrew's eyes narrowed, and he tilted his head. "Again?"

"I stopped wearing it right after you left. It reminded me of you," Allie looked away, suddenly feeling foolish for what she was about to admit, "and of what I thought I'd lost forever."

He smiled wider and pressed a smooth, strong hand to her face, gently caressing her cheek.

Cheering, hollering, and horn blowing erupted from the back yard as one year ended and a new one began.

"Happy New Year, Allie." Andrew placed his other hand on her face, and, drawing her so close she could smell the clean, soapy scent of his skin, he pressed his lips against the corner of her mouth. The contact sent shivers up her spine. She almost let out a whimper.

Too soon, he pulled back to look at her. He smiled again and stroked her hair. Warm tears slipped quietly down Allie's cheeks as Andrew took her into his arms and held her tight, the way that she'd wanted.

He moved his hand to the back of her head and, with a light touch, he pulled the side of her face to his chest. The steady, soft rhythm of his beating heart soothed and comforted Allie, steadying her breathing and connecting her to Andrew in a way more powerful than she could have ever imagined. She thanked God for answering her prayers, though, as always, in His own timing.

"I left the gift shop, believing I needed to let you go," she said.

Andrew squeezed Allie once then separated from her. He took hold of her chin, tilting her head back a little and making sure their eyes locked together. "Why would you think that way, Allie?"

"Because I went in there looking for a sign, remember?"

He nodded, raising his eyebrows and biting his lower lip, which Allie couldn't stop admiring. Andrew grinned and dropped his hands to hers. Their fingers entwined.

"Anyway," Allie said, feeling a little embarrassed, "the saleslady asked me some questions about perfume, and I decided that Providence was the sign and that wearing it again would be my way of not giving up hope."

Andrew leaned forward and rubbed his face against her neck; she could sense him inhaling her scent. The slightest hint of razor stubble against her skin felt electrifying.

"I don't smell Providence on you," he said playfully.

She sighed, savoring the warm tingling sensations. "I didn't buy it. The woman said she sold her last bottle right before I got there." Allie widened her eyes, a wry smile on her face. "A pretty clear sign, wouldn't you say?"

"That . . .?"

"That I needed to give you up, like I gave up Providence."

Andrew nodded slowly in agreement then said, "No."

"No?"

"Allie, do you know why I wasn't home on Saturday?"

She shook her head.

"Because I was at the airport. We probably just missed each other. I left Phoenix on a one o'clock flight."

"My flight was at one o'clock."

"Flight 23, gate thirty-something?"

"Yeah, I think so. That's sounds right."

"Then we were on the same flight."

"That can't be, Andrew. I would've seen you."

He gave her a sideways glance. "Were you late getting on the plane?"

"Uh," Allie's eyes flitted around before settling on Andrew, "yes, I was."

"They held the plane for you, you know." He stifled a laugh. "One of the attendants made an announcement about it. I was way in the back so I couldn't see much, but I do know the tardy traveler took a seat in one of the first few rows in coach."

"But I was in that gift shop. If I had known they were out of Providence before the saleslady spent all that time convincing me to wear it again, I wouldn't have been late." She met Andrew's gaze, saying with determination, "I didn't want to get on the plane without another bottle of Providence."

He lifted her hand, which still clutched the box. "You didn't."

Allie tugged on the paper at the top of the box, tearing it enough to reveal the perfume's trademark symbol, a billowy white cloud lined in silver, with rays of sunshine peeking out from behind. "Andrew," she whispered, "what made you buy this?"

He laughed. "Remember that girl, Beth, the one who sometimes tells me things?"

Allie clucked her tongue. "She told you I stopped wearing it."

"She did."

"Then I guess I have *her* to thank, don't I."

Andrew stepped closer and brushed the hair away from her face. "Yes, you do." The feather-light pressure he used to outline her lips with the tips of his fingers made her mouth water and her toes tingle.

* * *

A flash of movement in the mirror caught Andrew's attention.

Beth stood in Gretchen's doorway, beaming. "Ahem."

"Oh!" Allie jumped back with a start. "We were just . . ." She looked at Andrew then at Beth.

"I know what you were *just*," Beth teased.

Andrew chuckled then tapped a finger on the end of Allie's nose, marveling at how amazing she looked with her silky brown hair down around her shoulders. The softness of the flowing shine of mocha and chestnut enhanced the already mesmerizing heart shape of her face.

"It sure is extra warm and cozy in here . . . unlike in the backyard." Beth grabbed the sides of her arms. "Brrr, shiver, icicles, freezing."

"Ah! Your coat!" Allie whirled around and picked up the teal coat; she handed it to Beth.

"Thanks. Sorry for the disturbance. It looks like you two were in the middle of getting seriously reacquainted." Beth gave them both a sassy wink while slipping her arms through the sleeves of her coat. "I think you two ought to come outside with me and show everyone what a cute couple you make. We're toasting marshmallows and singing songs, à la summer camp."

Andrew gave Beth a quick look. *"What?"*

"Okay," she laughed, "I'm kidding about the singing, but we *are* toasting marshmallows. Jennifer bought graham crackers and a handful of chocolate bars for the special occasion. How does a messy, gooey s'more sound?"

Andrew grinned. If he'd been alone, where neither Beth nor Allie could see him, he would have pinched himself. Allie was looking at him exactly the way he'd dreamed that one day she would. Could this really be happening? The woman at his side was Allie, but not an Allie he'd ever experienced before. She was everything great about Allie—and then some. He felt as though she was a priceless treasure that for years had been preserved and protected behind a wall of glass. He could see her and talk to her but he couldn't reach out and touch her—not emotionally, physically or, most of all, spiritually. Now, though, the glass had been shattered, setting Allie free to be the person she was always meant to become.

"Andrew?" Beth said.

He blinked. "Sorry. I was thinking about . . ." He grinned wider and extended his hand to Allie, palm side up. "Shall we?"

She gently placed her hand on top of his then clasped it firmly before swinging it down to her side. "Sure, let's do it."

* * *

Allie couldn't believe what she was experiencing. Was she actually walking hand in hand with . . . *Andrew Gallagher?* Her cheeks hurt from smiling so broadly.

They stepped through the back door together . . . and froze in unison when they heard rousing applause. Allie felt Andrew squeeze her hand as her heart did a little jig in her chest. She glanced from Andrew's elated grin to her friends' jovial faces and laughed when they added some glass-shattering "woo-hoos" to their enthusiastic clapping. Gretchen cheered the loudest, or rather she shrieked the loudest. And though she sounded like an enraged monkey, Allie knew the sound was intended to be one of overwhelming approval.

The next several minutes felt like a kaleidoscopic blur as everyone clustered around the new couple. Allie couldn't take in everything that was being said, but she did glean that they all had known in advance about Andrew's late-night appearance.

When the clamor and celebration settled down, she and Andrew stood together at the edge of the brick firepit. They watched Steven and Beth twist marshmallow-laden skewers over the flames. Allie looked at Rob, seated near the pit, and said, "You got me."

Rob stood up. He clapped Andrew on the back, took Allie's hand, and clutched it. "I didn't tell you anything that wasn't true."

"I know, I know. The new friend's house, the small gathering—it all makes sense. Now, anyway."

He gave Allie a sweet smile. "You're a good sport, my dear." Rob turned away then swiveled back, saying to Andrew, "Don't let this girl get away from you, son."

"Never." Andrew slipped his arm around Allie's shoulder.

Rob nodded once in affirmation then went to join his wife, who was chatting with Gretchen on the far side of the backyard.

Allie leaned into Andrew and briefly closed her eyes. She couldn't remember ever feeling as safe and protected as she did in that moment, nor did she remember ever feeling so much like she was in the right place as she did right then. She fit perfectly against him as he tucked her close to his body and rested his chin on the top of her head. Most importantly, she'd never been more at peace or contented than at that moment, a moment she didn't want to see end.

"S'mores in less than ten, Allie," Beth said, before she and Steven took the toasted marshmallows inside to assemble the treats.

Phoebe suddenly appeared in front of Allie and Andrew. Wearing a black striped jumpsuit with a red hat and scarf, an outfit that made her look like an unusually happy convict, Phoebe poked a short finger at Andrew's chest. "You bought those first two Americanos for *Allie*, didn't you?" She squinted at Andrew, her lower jaw jutted forward, challenging him to tell the truth.

Andrew didn't hesitate. "Yes." He moved Allie so her back pressed against his chest. Rewrapping his arms around her, he kissed her hair and squeezed her in a gentle embrace.

Allie had to concentrate not to purr.

"I knew it!" Phoebe grinned and punched the air. "Well, not at first. Only after you asked about Allie and then kept coming in ordering Americanos. Since Allie almost always gets them, I figured there was probably a connection." She held clasped hands above her head as if proclaiming herself champion. "I should be a detective," she said, before rejoining Daniel, Gloria, Melvin, and the Bobbies on the opposite side of the firepit.

Allie laughed at her silly friend before rotating to face Andrew. "You've been drinking Americanos?"

He grinned and looked up at the stars. "I may have ordered a couple. It's possible."

"Because . . .?"

Andrew placed a soft, sweet peck on Allie's forehead. "Because they reminded me of you."

She rose up on her toes to look more directly into his eyes. She hoped every bit of the adoration she felt was reflected in her gaze. "I love you, Andrew."

Hesitating as though he couldn't believe what he'd just heard, Andrew tried responding. "I love . . .," but he was too late. Allie was already silencing him with a tender display of her love, nuzzling against his strong yet beautiful face.

In that instant, fireworks went off. With streaks of light flashing through her closed lids, and the pops and whizzes drowning out the rushing in her ears, Allie wondered if it was all in her mind. Didn't they say that when you connected with your soul mate, it would feel like fireworks going off? Did this all have something to do with the falling star she'd seen earlier?

Hmm, but what about the cheering?

When Andrew laughingly but gently pulled back, Allie put a hand to her lips and looked around at the others, who were pointing at white and pink sparkling streaks in the sky. More cracks and whistles made it clear that the fireworks were real, set off from neighboring houses.

The addition of the friendly pyrotechnics energized the party even more. Everyone was either chattering or laughing. Allie couldn't stop smiling as she and Andrew laughed with their friends. And time became irrelevant, so much so that Allie had no idea how late—or early—it was when Andrew led her to a bench at the edge of the lawn. As they sat, Allie said, "I still can't believe you're here."

Like waking from a dream, the fairytale feeling she'd had since she'd found him in Gretchen's bedroom faded. Her stomach clenched; she wondered how long she had before Andrew went back to Phoenix. She opened her mouth to ask him but then pressed her lips together. Did she really want to ruin this perfect evening?

At Jennifer's request, Joshua replaced the classic rock stereo music with a CD by Anita Baker. The song *No One In The World* began playing, and it was perfect for a romantic first dance of the New Year. Rob and Sue partnered up, as did Gloria and Melvin, and Joshua and Jennifer. They all took to the makeshift dance floor, the patio, and swayed back and forth in relaxed slow motion. The fire's flames flicked intermittent glimmers over the couples; the effect was better than any mirrored ball in a dance club.

Allie and Andrew stayed on their bench, and Allie started to smile at Andrew but then flinched from a sudden jolt. An insistent hip had shoved her so forcefully into Andrew's side that he grunted. The two shifted on the bench to make room for another body.

Gretchen giggled then slung a handful of who knew what into her mouth. "It's much better sitting here by a fire with Andrew than with Carl at camp, huh Allie?" she asked, still munching away.

Judging from the orange dusting around her mouth and the tangy smell of her breath, she was eating cheese-flavored popcorn. She wiped at her face then licked bright powdery residue off each finger with a smack.

"Gretchen," Allie exhaled a short puff, "why do you keep bringing up Carl?"

"Well," she leaned forward and looked at Allie and Andrew, "*Female in Fashion* advises new couples to get everything out in the open before things get serious. So, Allie, I think you need to talk about Carl clinging to you like a . . . What did you call it, Andrew? A bear claw?"

Allie turned to face Andrew. "*A bear claw?*"

He shook his head. "A barnacle."

"And while you're at it, Allie," Gretchen said, "I think you should apologize for bringing Carl to the first barbecue just to show him off. That was rude."

"*What?*"

"Is that true, Allie?" Andrew asked.

"No, of course not! Gretchen, would you mind giving us some privacy. *Please?*"

267

"Sure, no problema." Gretchen bounced to her feet, skipped across the patio, and disappeared inside the house through the back door.

Allie started to turn toward Andrew, but then she just pressed her head against his shoulder and took his hand in hers. She didn't want confrontation. She wanted connection. So she relaxed into him. The outside of his jacket felt cool and smooth on her cheek, but underneath, his muscles were tense. She sighed. Gretchen was right—they needed to talk this out.

*   *   *

A few moments later, Andrew watched Gretchen emerge from the house carrying a full plate of s'mores. As she positioned herself in the center of the patio, Andrew marveled at the incongruity of the zany woman. She was like a bumbling court jester, seemingly clueless but always one step ahead; she was the kind of person who would give you answers to questions you didn't ask, provide information on subjects you never heard of, and stun you by offering advice actually worth following. And then, after all of that, she'd cavort away, leaving in her wake a dizzying whirlwind, and "food for thought" you had no appetite to enjoy.

"Hey, everyone," Gretchen shouted to the crowd, "who wants a s'more?"

"Andrew," Allie asked, "what happened at summer camp?"

Andrew took a deep breath. Yes. It was time. His gaze met Allie's. He was going to tell her how painful it had been to witness that evil trespasser, Carl Lansing, flirt with and fall all over her while Andrew watched, feeling powerless and devastated. He needed her to know how years later Carl added insult to injury by revealing a painful secret Andrew wished Carl would've just kept to himself. And, finally, Andrew would confess that afterward, he was forced to mull over the significance of that secret, day after endless day, which nearly drove him mad, being thousands of miles away, unable to make sense of it all or do anything about it.

Nah, that didn't sound right.

So instead, he asked her, "What do you mean?"

"I mean you must have said something to Gretchen about Carl. I know I only mentioned him to her in passing."

What? In passing? Why mention him at all? Andrew felt an ache in his jaw. He reeled in his aggravation and tilted his head at a casual forty-five degree angle. "Oh, yeah," he said in a calm voice, "I also may have mentioned Carl in passing."

268

Allie squinted at him. "Gretchen made it seem like it was, a more, um, serious matter."

Well, Allie, he thought, that's because it *was*. His palms began to sweat, and he pulled his hand out of her grip and rubbed it against his corduroys. He inhaled the wood-scented air and cautiously considered his words. Repeating what Carl claimed Allie told Beth was the equivalent of reliving the moment—yet again. Andrew had done it so often already he thought it would be easy to say aloud the words that went with the experience. But no, it wasn't.

He turned his eyes toward Gretchen. She was doling out sticky, gooey s'mores to each guest, flitting about like a moth near a hundred watt porch light. And even though Allie had tried to make their bench a no-fly zone for the busy little moth, Andrew knew Gretchen would be back before long. He figured he'd better get on with it.

"Carl overheard you telling Beth something at camp one night."

Allie flinched. Her eyes flicked down then up, and her eyelashes seemed to quiver.

Andrew's spine stiffened. Did she already know what he was trying to say?

"Andrew, I have no idea what you're talking about."

Mm, maybe not. "Uh, well, Carl said you said you could . . ."

Several seconds passed. Andrew could almost hear them ticking in his head.

"I could what?" Allie asked.

"Never see yourself . . ."

More seconds plodded by. He had a flashback to a documentary he'd watched the night before called *Houdini: The Master of Escape*. Andrew had been so keyed up about the New Year's Eve party that he hadn't noticed whether they revealed the technique for breaking out of a straight jacket while dangling from rope-tied ankles. He vaguely wondered if having paid better attention would help him free his camp story from its own confining straight jacket.

Allie peeled Andrew's hand off the top of his knee. Turning it palm side up, she pressed it to her cheek, cuddling it like a teddy bear. Thankfully, by then it was dry.

"Andrew, I didn't love him or anything, but I did like him. We dated for a while, but it turns out he was dating another girl while he was with me."

"I know. He bragged about it at the barbecue. I was furious with the little twerp. I knew that when you found out, you'd be upset."

"I was, but what upset me the most was that he told me I was special and that no one could compare to me. When I found out he'd been seeing someone else—and that they were getting pretty serious—I felt disappointed. And betrayed."

"Then why did you get upset when you thought I was dating Jennifer? I didn't mislead you in any way."

"No, you didn't. I'm sorry for that. It's just that I couldn't stand the idea of you being with anyone else."

Now Andrew was confused. "But Carl told me you said you could never see yourself with me."

There! He'd said it! He'd *finally* told Allie the deep, dark secret he'd been carrying around *forever*. Okay, two years. But the words, as simple as they may have been, had cut him so deep that it felt like he'd had the wound for a lifetime.

Allie buried her face in Andrew's hand. He felt warm tears against his palm.

"What's wrong?" he asked.

"It's true," she whispered, "I did say that to Beth."

He remained silent, his mouth suddenly too dry to form words.

"But what I meant was . . ."

He waited, holding his breath.

"That I thought you were too kind, smart, sweet, gentle, wonderful, and perfect to even consider being with me. I didn't," her voice caught, "I didn't think I was good enough for you."

Andrew started breathing again. And he laughed, glad that he *could* laugh, because he realized he'd just learned a valuable life lesson. Actually, he'd learned two lessons. The first was about how everything fell into place when he moved out of the driver's seat and let God do the steering. The second lesson was about what happened when he hinged his emotions and reactions on third-hand information—without first doing some serious fact checking.

Question: How many painful days did Andrew endure because of his own ignorance? Answer: Countless.

"Allie," he said softly, using the thumb of his captured hand to sweep away her tears, "you're the girl of my dreams. I've been praying with all my heart that one day we'd be together."

"You have?"

He pulled her face to within inches of his. "Yes."

Allie exhaled.

"Hey Andrew," Gretchen yelled from the far end of the patio. She lifted the plate of s'mores. "How about a sweet treat?"

Andrew glanced her way and shook his head. "No thanks." He smiled and touched the tip of his nose to Allie's, saying in a quiet voice, "I've already got one."

Chapter 23

The Secret

Allie rolled over in bed. Reluctantly, she opened her eyes and reached for her cell phone to silence its seven-forty A.M. rude awakening. She'd only been in bed four hours.

The second her eyes were open, though, she looked around and noticed the soft, almost ethereal light bathing her bedroom. The New Year's Day morning sun peeked between the window blinds, creating such beautiful slatted shadows on the pale lavender walls that Allie's spirits were immediately lifted. Or maybe what lifted her spirits was remembering how Andrew had followed her home in his parents' Lexus and then told her for the fourth or fifth, or was it sixth, time how much he loved and missed her. And maybe the glow in the room came not from the sun but from Allie, who was radiant with joy at the knowledge that Andrew would be back later that morning to spend the day with her, picnicking in Wildflower Canyon Park.

Grinning, Allie glanced at her cell phone screen. She took in a deep breath, inhaling the sweet lotus and bamboo fragrance coming from a reed diffuser on her nightstand. She was happy to note that even seeing Kevin Rafferty's name on the phone didn't knock her off her idyllic cloud. Nope. Not even he could mess up Allie's euphoria.

She took the call.

"Happy New Year," Kevin said in a jolly tone.

Could he be that glad to see her go, that anxious to confiscate her company vehicle the next day and clear out her storage unit so he could move on to hire a replacement? Her blood surged at the thought. He could have it. Maybe he might even find a rep who would always do as she was told and never fight the system.

"I just got off the phone with Doug Wylie," Kevin said. "We had a long talk about your situation."

Allie laughed. "Kevin, don't you people ever just enjoy the holidays? You know, turn off your cell phones, stay away from your computers, abstain from checking messages, or having conversations about people who you'll never have to deal with again?"

Kevin snorted in her ear. "Allie, this is good news. You should be thrilled about what I'm going to tell you."

"Oh, really? And why is that?"

"Because Doug decided he won't accept your resignation."

Allie swung her legs over the side of the bed and sat upright. "How is that possible, considering I haven't even submitted it yet?"

"Yeah, I know. After we met last week, I called Doug and told him you wanted to resign. I only did it because I didn't want to see you leave the company. You're too valuable to just let go without a fight, Allie."

She tried not to care, but she had to admit hearing that felt pretty good.

"So," Kevin continued, "Doug thought it over and came up with a plan."

Allie looked down at her feet. She wiggled her toes, admiring her toenails, which were polished bright pink. A few days before, Gretchen had suggested a girls' Pedicure Party at her new favorite nail spa, Toes-R-Us. "We could get white polka dots!" she'd said. At the time, Allie wasn't so thrilled with the idea; but now, as she studied her toes, she was glad she'd gone for it. "I'm listening."

"Good." Papers rustled in Allie's ear. Kevin cleared his throat and said, "First off, you don't resign. You can either keep your L.A. territory or you'll be promoted to regional trainer. That means you'll be working with new hires in the field and periodically going to Atlanta for home office training. Lots of travel involved, Allie. You'd be on the road most of the time, so keep that in mind if you're interested. Next, because Cassandra has made so much noise already, Doug is going to let her have her way with Advantol and the PM docs. He'll give it six months to see if the numbers pan out. In the meantime though, he'll adjust the percentage goals of all other products to distribute the weight fairly."

"Without the pain management sales, I won't finish in first place. Probably not even in the top twenty." Allie was surprised her words felt more like the bothersome tickle of a gnat buzzing past her ear than a karate kick in the ribs.

"I understand that. You'll definitely lose out on certain benefits, including the large bonus, but there is one consolation to consider. Doug wants you to have the trip to Hawaii, even if you don't rank in the top twenty."

"What?"

"You and a guest will be his guests for ten days anywhere in the islands. He says he's got a fabulous time-share you're welcome to use. He'll pay all your expenses, and you won't have to take your vacation in June along with the other reps. He says availability isn't an issue. I guess he's got connections."

Allie stood up and started dancing around her bedroom. A trip to Hawaii? She could almost feel the tropical breeze rustling her hair. "That's very generous of him. Why would he do something like that?"

Kevin was quiet.

Allie stopped dancing. "Did you hear my question, Kevin?"

"I did, but I need to make sure you won't repeat what I'm going to tell you. Part of the reason I want you to know this information is because I feel responsible for not stepping in and protecting you from Cassandra."

"Protecting me? So, you *do* believe that she was out to get me!"

"Do I have your word?"

"Yeah, sure, fine. What do you know, Kevin?"

"Well, I won't say how I learned this, but it seems you bear a strong resemblance to a young woman who worked for MarTech Industries. It's a medical device company, and the same one Cassandra and her ex-husband, Jeffrey Gilbert, worked for. The two were already married when he took the position of director of marketing, and Cassandra signed on as regional manager of sales. Technically, no conflict of interest, but he's since become the national director of sales at MarTech, like Cassandra is at Horizon. Anyway, after their marriage crumbled, Cassandra's ex began dating one of the sales reps."

"Let me guess. The one to whom I bear that strong resemblance?" asked Allie.

"The very same. To keep their relationship above board, the woman left MarTech. Gilbert is still there. Apparently they're engaged."

"Is her name Alexis?"

"Yes. It is. How did you know that?"

"Cassandra made a couple offhanded references to her. In one case, she actually called me by the woman's name."

"I'm sorry about all that, Allie."

"Then I guess Doug knows too. Doesn't he?"

Kevin didn't respond to the question. "So, what do you say? Are you willing to forego the resignation and continue working for Horizon?"

Suppressing a laugh, Allie did a less than graceful pirouette. "I'll have to think about it and get back to you."

A few seconds of silence had her picturing Kevin shaking his head in exasperation. "All right, Allie. I get it. You're showing your, shall I say, *independent* side again? But that still doesn't give me an answer about your job."

Allie continued dancing, ignoring Kevin with silence until he finally sighed into the phone. "Okay. I'll just take that as a yes."

* * *

At 11:30, Andrew parked his parents' Lexus in front of Allie's garage. The satisfaction he felt over claiming that spot was ridiculously huge. Parking spots shouldn't have that kind of impact on people. But it wasn't just a place in Allie's driveway he was claiming; it was a place in her life.

When he got out of the car, she came through her front door to greet him. Her expression was bright and fresh, her eyes alert. The brilliant, late-morning sunshine highlighted both the cinnamon freckles sprinkled across her face and the natural golden streaks in her gorgeous hair. He smiled, remembering how soft both her skin and her hair had felt to his touch.

How was it possible she looked more beautiful each time he saw her?

Andrew trotted toward Allie, scooped her off the front porch, and lifted her into his arms. He carried her to the car, holding her against him while grinning at her childlike giggle.

He set her down by the passenger door and waited until she was in the car before he leaned over and whispered in her ear, "I have something to ask you."

Before she could react, he shut the door and hurried around the car, sliding in beside her and taking her hand in his. She looked at him with a charming crease between her brows.

"You know I fly back to Phoenix tomorrow afternoon," he said.

Allie nodded. The crease expanded across her forehead. "Yes, I know." She dropped her head and looked at their clasped hands.

"Would you like to go shopping with me in the morning?"

Her brow twitched, but she didn't look up. "Shopping?"

"Mm hmm. I need to buy something before I go. It's kind of a big ticket item, and I want your input on it." Andrew felt his heart quiver with anticipation as he watched Allie. In the past, he'd always been the one feeling unsure about *her* feelings for *him*. Now he saw that dynamic at work in reverse. It gave him no feeling of triumph, just perhaps a sense of security. It grounded him, he thought, helping him feel more in sync with her.

"Okay. Sure."

"Great! That means I get to spend almost two whole days in a row with you." Andrew gave her chin a gentle tug upward, taking note of the vivid steel-colored streaks in her light gray irises. He'd never seen those before. He wondered how many more fascinating discoveries about her he would make over time. With unpredictable Allie, the number was likely infinite, and Andrew couldn't wait to experience as many as their time together allowed.

They drove down to Wildflower Canyon Park in silence, but Andrew felt the kinetic energy in the air. It wasn't just the love and devotion they had admitted to each other. He was pretty sure he was sensing Allie's curiosity. How amusing that she wouldn't ask what it was he wanted to shop for. Instead, she played it cool.

Once inside the park, they passed some kids playing on a swing set and a man in jeans and a white sweatshirt tossing a ball to his dog. Andrew led the way to a secluded spot at the top of a grassy knoll. He set out a thick green fleece blanket near a grouping of tall California oak trees. After placing the blue Igloo food cooler off to the side, he tugged Allie down onto the blanket. They lay back and gazed up at the cloudless sky. The light breeze smelled of fresh cut grass and the fiery hot smoke from a charcoal grill. It was a moment of pure peace . . . until Allie sat up.

"So, Kevin called me this morning," she said.

Andrew propped himself up on one elbow. "Oh, right." He smacked his free palm to his forehead, recalling that Allie told him the night before about meeting Kevin at her storage facility to turn in her vehicle. "You can't go with me tomorrow; you already have plans."

Allie shook her head. "No. No, I don't. Kevin called to give me back my job, the one I haven't officially resigned from. He also offered me a promotion to regional trainer."

Andrew sat up beside her. "That's terrific!" He squeezed her hand. *"Congratulations!"*

"Thanks."

"What are you going to do?"

"I told him I'd have to think about it and get back to him."

Andrew rubbed his chin. "So, he thinks you may resign?"

"No. He knows I won't. I just don't want to make myself look too eager to accept his proposition. You understand, don't you?"

He snickered. That was his Allie, all right. She never wanted to look too eager about anything, and was still, at heart, a rebel. Oh, yes, he understood *perfectly.*

"Doug's going to allow Cassandra's fourth-quarter changes, which means no high ranking or big bonus for me this year."

"How do you feel about that?" Andrew leaned toward her.

275

Allie brought her knees up and hugged them. "I'm okay with it. More than okay, actually. I think it was what was meant to be."

"Really? Why?"

She creased her brow. "It's hard to explain. The best I can do is tell you it was a misguided goal. It wasn't what I wanted deep down." She turned her head to face him. "I had it in my mind that a high ranking would bring me peoples' respect, and that using the bonus money on the twins' education would earn me their admiration," she shrugged, "I don't know, make up for not always being there for them. I'll still help out, of course, but not by making a big show of it. I think I may have wanted to rescue them in a way," Allie laughed. "You know, like a white knight or something." She toyed with her hair and looked down. "That sounds silly, doesn't it? Can a girl even *be* a knight?"

"Technically, no," Andrew said, leaving out his own recent thoughts on the matter.

"*Oh! I almost forgot.* There is *some* good news in all this. It turns out I get the Hawaiian vacation regardless of how I place." Her smile turned humble. "It's a gift from Doug, and I can take a guest and go anytime this year."

Andrew dropped back down on his back. "Anytime, huh?"

Chapter 24

The Beginning and the End

Allie held her cell phone to her ear and checked her makeup in the entryway mirror on the wall above the table. She glanced down and smiled at the vase full of beautiful red roses centered on the glass top. The bouquet had arrived a couple hours earlier and was the best start to a Valentine's Day that she'd ever had.

"*The Hummus & Hookah Hut?*" Gretchen scoffed in Allie's ear. "That doesn't seem very romantic, considering the occasion. Even if it *is* just for lunch."

"Trust me," Allie said, "*anyplace* with Andrew Gallagher is romantic." Hearing him drive up, she slipped her arm through her purse strap, opened the front door, and rushed outside. It felt like every nerve ending in her body was dancing in anticipation. Although she talked with or texted Andrew daily, this would be the first time she'd seen him since early January. "I've got to go; he's here now. Happy Valentine's Day."

Gretchen sighed. "Yeah, same to you."

Allie dropped her phone in her purse and nearly skipped toward the brand new, sterling blue Mustang sitting in her driveway. It wasn't like she hadn't seen the car before. She'd taken a test drive with Andrew the day he bought it, but she hadn't yet seen him, from this distance, in the driver's seat. He looked amazing sitting behind the wheel, like the car had been designed just for him. He could have been in one of Ford's car ads, and women would have lined up around the block to buy a Mustang.

Knowing how much he missed the car he'd sold to Joshua, her input regarding his "big-ticket item" purchase had steered him away from the truck section over to the Mustangs. He didn't argue with her much, and after he chose a few custom extras, the car salesman trotted off to locate the exact car Andrew wanted. It turned out no dealer west of the Mississippi had a vehicle with the exact color and option package Andrew chose, but he assured the salesman that he was fine with waiting. The six-week delay for the car's delivery would conveniently coincide with Andrew's next trip to the Valley, on February 14th.

As he got out of the car that was almost as gorgeous as he was, Gloria popped through her front door and galloped down her front steps like a thoroughbred at Santa Anita Racetrack.

"She's a beauty," she beamed when she reached the car. "Just lovely." She winked, "Although, she'd look even better in red. Especially today." Gloria chuckled and nudged Allie's arm.

Andrew rounded the front end of the car. "Yes, she is a beauty," he said, tenderly stroking Allie's cheek before pressing his lips close to her ear and whispering, "Happy Valentine's Day. I missed you, Babe." He then looked at Gloria and grinned. "The car's pretty great-looking, too, and I think it looks just fine in blue."

Gloria laughed.

Allie inhaled the fresh scent of Andrew's cool aftershave and felt her face warm up with a flush. "I missed you, too," she told him. He looked into her eyes, the way he had on the beach.

"Big plans tonight, Gloria?" asked Andrew, still staring at Allie.

"You better believe it, Sport."

Allie and Andrew turned to watch Gloria open the passenger's door of the Mustang and make herself comfortable inside.

Allie giggled softly. "Elk's Lodge again?"

Gloria ran her hands along the dashboard. "Not sure what Mel's got planned. He's very spontaneous. Sometimes he tells me one thing and then changes his mind by the time he picks me up. You never know with that cookie."

Allie's eyes returned to Andrew's. "Aw! I think that'd be kind of fun myself."

Andrew tilted his head back to give her a serious look. "Do you now?"

"Absolutely. Suspense, anticipation. Surprises keep things interesting."

She laughed when she realized how much she meant what she was saying. Apparently, the Allie who had needed so much control was gone.

"That's good, because we're not going to The Hummus & Hookah Hut."

* * *

Allie blinked and dropped her head to the side, revealing, she knew, *her surprise.*

She couldn't say she was sorry they weren't going to the restaurant they'd planned on. She'd finally made it there one night with Beth and although she liked the place, it still reminded her of that evening she and Andrew had fought in the gas station convenience store. She preferred to put memories like that to rest.

Gloria exited the Mustang and joined Andrew and Allie under the barren Crepe Myrtle tree.

Andrew laughed. "You look surprised, Allie."

"Oh, well, I, I just wasn't expecting . . ."

"Touché." Gloria leaned in, lifting a hand to her face in a mock whisper, "*That's* the idea, kiddo."

Andrew checked his watch. "It's almost noon. We should probably get going."

"I'm ready."

"Not quite." He motioned toward the front door. "You'll need a coat. Your warmest."

"A coat? No, I'll be fine in this." Allie tugged on the lapel of the denim-trimmed pink tweed jacket she'd gotten for Christmas—a generous hand-me-down from Gretchen.

"Have fun, you two," Gloria said. Then, before turning toward her unit, she looked at Allie. "Go get that coat, will ya?"

* * *

Without another word Allie retrieved her flannel lined wool coat from the house. She placed it in the back seat of the Mustang next to the same blue Igloo cooler Andrew had packed for their picnic at Wildflower Canyon Park. They caught the 210 East at the top of Ridgeview. It was a route that could have led them up into the Angeles National Forest, but Andrew didn't take the Angeles Crest Highway turnoff, which made Allie wonder just where they would end up. She remained still and quiet, relaxing in the Mustang's warm and cozy bucket seat and listening to Michael W. Smith singing, *Love Me Good* on the stereo.

The warmth from the heater, along with having Andrew comfortably close by, made Allie drowsy in a pleasant way. She reclined her seat a bit and closed her eyes, tempted to let herself drift off, yet knowing that the time she had with Andrew would be limited to today and tomorrow, which he'd taken off to celebrate Valentine's Day together. They wouldn't see each other again before early April. For the first three months of the year, his schedule had him working every Saturday. This left no time on weekends to travel to and from the Valley. Allie's own new position as regional trainer kept her busy and on the road most days. This helped divert her attention away from missing Andrew, even though it still left her longing for more time with him.

The Mustang eased to a stop, and Allie's eyes shot open. Remaining in her relaxed position, she focused on the dashboard clock, which read 1:32. She *had* drifted off. She blinked and rubbed her eyes. That's when she spotted a signpost to the right of the car that read, "SNOW CHAINS REQUIRED BEYOND THIS POINT."

Snow Chains?

Frowning in puzzlement, Allie watched Andrew from the side view mirror while he tended to the tires. They were up in the San Bernardino Mountains, that much she knew. But why? She was tempted to roll down her window and ask, but whatever Andrew had planned was supposed to be a surprise; she didn't want to revert back to Allie-who-needs-to-manage-everything and spoil that for him. So she kept her head tilted in snooze mode and closed her eyes when he opened the driver's door to get back in his seat.

Gravel and ice crunched beneath the tires as Andrew pulled out onto the pavement. Allie felt the car wind up an incline and slow. She opened her eyes in time to see they were at a fork in the road, and she glimpsed a sign she recalled seeing once before, a long time ago.

Her heart began to rev. They took the road on the left and moments later passed through a snow-dusted village. Charming old buildings lined the main street. Allie spotted a small bistro, an antique store, and several houses with cobblestone chimneys. Turning her head to look past Andrew, she saw a familiar grouping of redwood cabins huddled together along the shore of a lake.

Big Bear Lake.

She sat up and looked at Andrew.

He smiled at her. "I take it you know where we are."

"Of course, but why?"

Andrew directed the Mustang toward the cabins, pulling it to a stop in front of one at the far edge of the cluster. He turned toward her.

"I thought we might want to rewind the clock back to where we got a little off track. That way, we can be sure to get it right from this point on."

Allie threw her arms around him. It was perfect.

Pulling back a little, she took his face in her hands, almost painfully aware of just how much she'd longed for this moment. As she once again slipped into the captivating depths of Andrew's dark and dreamy eyes, she knew that if Beth were to ask her about him now, the way she had when they were at summer camp, Allie would say that she could definitely see herself with Andrew. She could see herself being with him for the rest of her life.

CPSIA information can be obtained at www.ICGtesting.com
Printed in the USA
BVOW04s1135150114

341993BV00001B/4/P